THE WISE MAN

PRAISE FOR THE WISE MAN

A riveting, ripped-from-the-headlines suspense that goes behind the scenes of the Supreme Court, *The Wise Man* reveals the magnitude of making a decision on one of the most important issues of our lifetime.
—**Kirk Cameron**, actor (*Growing Pains, Left Behind, Fireproof*), Christian activist, author of *Still Growing, an Autobiography*

Michele Chynoweth takes another familiar Bible story and reimagines it into a modern-day suspense set in the halls of power, luxury, and influence that is especially timely for today. An intriguing and highly relevant read—you won't be disappointed!
—**Nancy Stafford**, actress (*Matlock, First Lady*), speaker, and author of *The Wonder of His Love: A Journey into the Heart of God* and *Beauty by the Book: Seeing Yourself as God Sees You*

PRAISE FOR MICHELE CHYNOWETH'S OTHER NOVELS

THE FAITHFUL ONE

... an exploration of what a contemporary Job might look like, Chynoweth's tale should more than satisfy.
—Kirkus Reviews

Understanding faith can be perplexing for some of us but the story Michele tells in this profound book is worth reading by all of us. She lets us know that faith is not only a mystery, it is a progression of our lives and a product of God Almighty for us to live by day after day.
—Dr. Thelma Wells, (aka "Mama T" of Women of Faith conferences), founder of a Woman of God Ministries and Generation Love-Divine Explosion, speaker, author, television host, and professor

It often seems that the great characters of the Bible are so far removed from us. We sanitize them and dehumanize them. *The Faithful One* puts the character of Job into a whole new contemporary light. The story makes his struggles so much more tangible and relatable to today's audience. Kudos to

Michele Chynoweth for helping us get a better handle on what Job may have gone through. It certainly makes my struggles seem much smaller!

—**Gus Lloyd**, author of *Magnetic Christianity* and *A Minute in the Church* and host of "Seize the Day" on The Catholic Channel, Sirius XM 129

THE PEACE MAKER

In this contemporary retelling of the Bible's First Book of Samuel, the story of David and Abigail stands the test of time.

—*Kentucky Monthly* **Magazine**

The Peace Maker by Michele Chynoweth is the type of story that many young women have lived in one way or another. Many of us have been like Chessa, caught between the one we love and doing what's right ...

—**Samantha Rivera**, 5-Star Review, Readers' Favorite International Book Awards

THE RUNAWAY PROPHET

With another novel that will put you on the edge of your seat, author Michele Chynoweth delights again with *The Runaway Prophet*. Prepare to be swept up inside this page-turner...through one heart-stopping event after another, Rory and a team of investigators battle against the clock to remove the mafia and the dangerous bomb they've planted somewhere underground. *The Runaway Prophet* will keep you riveted.

—**Alexandra Karlessas**, *Delaware Today* Magazine

The Runaway Prophet was hard to put down. The author has done a great job of taking the Book of Jonah

and making it come to life in the modern era. It's a great book—now it needs to be made into a movie!
—**Pastor Chris Whaley**, author of *The Masked Saint*, a memoir and major motion picture (winner of Best Picture, International Christian Film Festival)

THE JEALOUS SON

A family saga that draws on the biblical tale of Cain and Abel ... Chynoweth manages to make the story feel incredibly visceral. She shows a talent for taking small details from the original Bible story and turning them into valuable plot developments; along the way, her characters learn from one another. The key to the novel's success is the author's ability to provide deep insights into her characters' tumultuous mental states. A bold, tragic, and emotionally exploratory drama
—**Kirkus Reviews**

This is edgy inspirational fiction at its best ... entertaining, heart-wrenching and packed with a powerful message.
—**Cindy Bond**, Mission Films, Producer of the movie, *I Can Only Imagine*

THE WISE MAN

MICHELE CHYNOWETH

ELK LAKE PUBLISHING INC

PUBLISHING THE POSITIVE
Plymouth, Massachusetts

COPYRIGHT NOTICE

The Wise Man

Cover and Interior Design: Kelly Artieri, Derinda Babcock, Deb Haggerty

Editor(s): Cristel Phelps, Deb Haggerty

PUBLISHED BY: Elk Lake Publishing, Inc., 35 Dogwood Drive, Plymouth, MA 02360, 2022

Library Cataloging Data

Names: Chynoweth, Michele (Michele Chynoweth)

The Wise Man / Michele Chynoweth

408 p. 13.97cm ×21.59cm (5.5 in. × 8.5 in.)

ISBN-13: 978-1-64949-581-5 (paperback) | 978-1-64949-582-2 (trade paperback) | 978-1-64949-583-9 (e-book)

Key Words: Biblical adaptation or retelling; modern-day parable, Solomon, Old Testament story, Wealth and Power, Corruption, Salvation

Library of Congress Control Number: 2022939536 Fiction

ACKNOWLEDGMENTS

Thank you to the following folks who helped authenticate my story so not only is God's message in the Bible revealed but has plausibility in today's world—and to those who helped polish my writing into the novel you hold in your hands:

Rev. Michael Carrier, Pastor of the Church of the Holy Child, Wilmington, Delaware, for his insight into the story of Solomon;

Barbara (Schuchert) Clouser, MD, a neonatal doctor and fellow college graduate for her medical expertise;

Dwight Thomey, an attorney with Baker, Thomey & Emrey, PA, for his legal knowledge and guidance;

Megan Braunstein and K. A. Kaneshiro for their help as cultural and sensitivity readers authenticating the Chinese characters, setting and culture;

Becca Small, owner of The Bookcycle bookstore, and English teacher Mary Amann for their eagle eyes as my "beta" readers;

Bill Chynoweth, my husband, for his encouragement and support;

And last, but not least, to Cristel Phelps, editor, Kelly Artieri, cover designer, and Deb Haggerty, publisher &

editor in chief, of Elk Lake Publishing for their wisdom in making my words shine their brightest.

Every book truly takes a team, and I'm grateful to be blessed by the best!

AUTHOR'S NOTE

The Wise Man is based on the story of King Solomon as primarily revealed in Kings I in the Holy Bible. This is the latest of my contemporary suspense novels that reimagine Old Testament stories, written so people today can better relate to the Bible story and understand God's message. While certain elements of the original book have obviously been changed to modernize the story for today's readers, I have, through research and consultation with religious leaders and clergy, made every attempt to stay as true to the original storyline as possible.

All my novels are standalone books that modernize an individual Bible story and are not written as a series; however, since Solomon's story dovetails with that of his father, King David, *The Wise Man* is also somewhat of a sequel to one of my former novels, *The Peace Maker*. Readers will see some of the same characters in both novels. Although they don't need to be read in order, I hope fans of *The Peace Maker* will love *The Wise Man* as well. Most of all I hope this latest novel inspires you to recommit yourself to your faith in God and His commands.

—Michele Chynoweth

BIBLE CHARACTERS:

Solomon ....Finn Mitchell

Solomon's wife............................. Lei Mitchell

Queen of Sheba .... Callista Alexander

David (Solomon's father) .... Leif Mitchell

Bathsheba (Solomon's mother)..... Linda Mitchell

Adonijah (Solomon's half-brother)....Tony Sorrell

Haggith (Adonijah's mother)........... Jackie Sorrell

Abishag (David's maid) .... Alisa Tomas

Chileab (Solomon's oldest half-brother)......Harry Mitchell

Abigail (Chileab's mother) .... Chessa Mitchell

Nathan (David's and Solomon's counselor/ prophet) .... Peter Baldwin

Joab (David's nephew and military commander, Adonijah's counselor) .... Ralston Warren

PROLOGUE

This is all my fault. Finn Mitchell stared in shock as he approached the devastation all around him.

Palm trees that once stood regally below his mansion windows were burned down into black stumps.

Finn could hear the sirens in the distance as firefighters, rescue teams, and police continued to multiply. Those who'd arrived first on the scene had been fighting the fire for hours and had managed to turn it into a smoldering flame. But the damage was done. *It's like they're putting a tiny bandage on a gaping, hemorrhaging wound.*

He looked out over the once lush landscape of the island. Now the area looked like a war zone. He gazed out over the smoking ruins of the once towering white marble church which he'd named the Sanctuary—the largest and most magnificent church in the world. *His* church, the one he had commissioned to have built and had himself dedicated one year ago today, now lay in charred ruins—the roof caved, the marble columns singed with soot, the stained-glass windows shattered, the golden statues inside melted.

He had stepped out onto his balcony hundreds, maybe even thousands of times to see the steeple, his eyes always on the lookout for it with each new dawn.

But then he'd replaced the steeple with the huge, glaring copper sun that represented Surya, the Hindu sun god, one of hundreds of gods worshipped by his wife.

Now, even the temple and the gods they had worshipped were all ironically destroyed. *Gone, like all the rest. And it's all my fault.*

He'd run up to the horrific scene with Sheriff John Dunne, who drove him from one end of the island to the other.

The arsonist was clearly after him, and he just hoped and prayed his wife Lei had gotten out of the house in time. *Dear God, let her be okay*, he prayed, dropping to his knees and sobbing in the smoky, soot-covered dark night.

The thirty-minute ride in John's patrol car from the north end of the island had been like an eternity.

His whole life had flashed before him. He'd had and become everything he'd ever wanted ... he was the favored son of a past president of the United States, had a seat on the highest court in the land as a US Supreme Court justice, was one of the wealthiest men in the world, and was now the ruler and owner of the mega-billion-dollar tourist island where he stood. *And none of it means a thing.* He sadly realized that truth. *People have died because of me.*

Ironically, it had all started as a spiritual venture.

Finn had met and married the Chinese president's daughter, Wu Lei, and, while visiting China, had ventured into business with his wife's long-time friend.

They'd developed the latest virtual reality program, which included a VR church, and they'd asked him to be the main speaker.

Finn had readily volunteered and was hooked but insisted they also build a brick-and-mortar church grand enough to one day hold the hundreds of thousands of people who attended virtually across the world.

With an investment of his own huge inheritance and a deal struck with a private major investor as well, Epitome, the greatest virtual reality tourist attraction on the planet, was born. Epitome became a multi-billion-dollar enterprise that lured wealthy tourists from all over the world to Eden, the remote island off of Australia's Gold Coast, which he also owned.

Finn had masterminded the venture, flying back and forth in his private jet from his lofty position on the US Supreme Court in Washington, DC, to his home on the island. He'd worked with dozens of computer geeks, scientists, attorneys, financial consultants, construction crews, and a crackerjack marketing team to put the plan in place that would revolutionize tourism forever.

The ad agents had promoted Eden well with headlines like, "Two Tickets to Paradise," "Visit the Garden of Eden," and "Now You Really Can Have It All."

He had purchased the thirty-five-hundred-acre, uninhabited, unnamed island off the coast of

Queensland for a publicly undisclosed sum, although rumors were he had gotten it in an off-market deal for the lucky sum of less than fifty million dollars.

The island was naturally beautiful with lush vegetation including palm trees, grasses, and a variety of flora and fauna akin to those found in nearby Bali, Thailand, and Malaysia. The landscape designers had actually cultivated the cream of the crops grown on those tropical paradises and carefully transplanted them, along with native varieties of birds, butterflies, insects, and other small but friendly wildlife like koala bears, wallabies, and kangaroos.

Just as God had created the original garden of the same name and on the sixth day made man, Eden was eventually home to Finn, its patron and founder, and then eventually, his wife, employees, and visitors who decided to stay and take up residence there. They in and of themselves soon constituted their own village. Hundreds, and then thousands, of people lived on the island, working as busboys, wait staff, cleaning crews, day care providers, event coordinators, diving and snorkeling instructors, pilots, drivers, tour directors, boat captains, and more. Then, as restaurants and shops opened, a host of proprietors moved to Eden as well.

Finn had his own private staff—five young ladies who attended to his needs and Lei's, as well as many guests who stayed with them when they visited the island. He had picked each based on their intelligence, charm, spunk, and, yes, he had to admit, their beauty. Now they were gone, and the house lay caked in soot and ashes.

He had had it all ... and now it had all vanished ... *because of my lust, my greed, my pride.*

THE WISE MAN

Finn was sure the virtual reality tour the island boasted as its main draw had to have been the cause. The software was inherently evil, he now realized.

Inhaling the acrid smell of thick, black smoke and watching the last of the flames climb around the church's spires, Finn's head clouded for a minute. His memories suddenly drifted back to when he was in fifth grade and he had gone camping for the first time with the Boy Scouts from his hometown of Potomac, Maryland, a posh residential town near Washington, DC, known as one of the richest neighborhoods in the world.

He had enjoyed everything about camping outdoors—hiking in the woods, swimming in the river, pitching tents, making homemade beef stew, telling scary ghost stories. Most of all, he had loved sitting around the campfire at night where they roasted marshmallows and sang songs along with his dad, who played the guitar.

For all his fame and glory, Finn's dad, former United States President Leif Mitchell, was at heart a country boy who loved to write music and sing. Before he became president, he had been a rising country rock music star, and some of his original songs had been made into records. Once he'd retired from the presidency, Leif had performed on big stages at several campaign rallies for political friends and a few good causes.

So, Finn felt lucky when his dad became a scout leader and would go on a camping trip here and there when his schedule allowed. Finn had always been proud of his father, who would make the other scouts laugh with his silly jokes or bolster their confidence working for their different merit badges in fishing, whittling, campfire building, cooking, and the like. Sometimes he was jealous, though, and wanted to keep his father to himself. But his mother often reminded Finn that even in retirement, his dad was still very popular as a speaker and leader, so Finn had to get used to sharing him not only with the Boy Scouts but with the world.

At the end of the day—after the campfires died and everyone fell asleep, only to awaken to the dawn of a new morning and pack up the tents and supplies to head back home—Finn knew he had the best dad ever, even if he did have to share him.

Just like Finn, the American people had put his dad on a pedestal—and then him too as he soared further and higher in his career, in his wealth, in his popularity and fame. Finn had it all, but, of course, he always wanted more.

And one day, even the pedestal became too high—the air so thin he couldn't breathe.

Finn felt like he was suffocating as he was brought back to the present reality. He held a handkerchief over his nose and mouth to mask the dirty air that swirled around him, choking him.

Part of him just wanted to give up and die. But deep down in his soul, he knew that wasn't an option. This was all his fault, and only he could try to make things right—if it wasn't too late.

CHAPTER ONE

He had to tell her. He never could lie to his mom.

"It was this kid at school," Finn said softly. "He hit me."

Before he could resist, Linda Mitchell sat her son gently but firmly in a kitchen chair in their southern Maryland home. She fetched an ice pack from the freezer to hand him along with a plate full of his favorite Oreo cookies and a glass of cold milk. Finn scarfed down three cookies and gulped the milk with one hand, holding the ice pack to his bruised face and bloody lip with the other.

Linda sat at the table across from him, patiently waiting for him to finish.

He took a deep breath. "It was Georgie MacPherson."

His mother nodded. She made it her business to get to know most of the kids who attended the small private school in nearby Rockville.

"It was after the bell rang, and I was headed for the door. Big Joe was waiting out front." Even though it hurt his lip, Finn couldn't help but smile at the memory of his bodyguard's face through the passenger window of the Cadillac as he pulled up to the school's front circle to find his charge decking another schoolboy.

"Why would you possibly hit Georgie?" His mother looked at him with her big hazel eyes framed with long, black eyelashes. She really didn't need to wear makeup. Linda Mitchell had always been a natural beauty with her flawless skin, her thick honey-colored wavy hair now simply pulled back in a ponytail—and her beautiful eyes. They were like the sea, changing colors with her mood or the outfit she was wearing, which today was a pair of jeans and a jade-colored light sweater for the Indian summer weather that graced Maryland. People had often compared her to Bo Derek, the famous super model from the 1979 movie, "Ten."

"He insulted you," Finn simply said and finished his milk and cookies, wiping his mouth with a cloth napkin she'd set out.

"What did he say?" His mother seemed to control her voice, keeping it stoically even, but her eyes darkened and widened ... in curiosity, surprise or ... *maybe she knew something* ... he couldn't tell. Finn looked away, stood to escape before he had to relay anything further, but her strong hand clamped down on his arm. "Sit down, young man, and tell me what happened. All of it."

Finn recounted how Georgie had accosted him in the school hallway after math class. The bigger, stouter boy had stood against Finn's locker, barring him from putting away his books, and mouthed off something about his mother being a ... he couldn't say the word.

"Just say it," his mother's eyes seemed to cloud over, veiled by her long lashes as she looked down and blushed.

8

"Whore." Finn whispered in a choked voice. "And he said that made me *illegitimate*, a *bastard* son. So, I punched him. And he punched me back. Which started a whole fight until the principal, Mr. Peterson, broke us up. You should have seen all the kids who were circled around us. I think most of them were cheering for me. Anyway, Mr. Peterson brought us both to his office, and I guess he tried to call you, he didn't want to bug dad ... and then Joe picked me up. Didn't Mr. Peterson tell you anything?"

"He told me there was a fight, but he didn't know who or what started it." Suddenly, Linda Mitchell released her grip on her son's forearm and stood up, turning away from him, leaning against the kitchen's large granite countertop.

"Mom, what is it?" Finn was worried now about what his mom was thinking. It was bad enough to be in trouble with the school—suspended for a week for fighting. But it would be worse to upset his mom. He hated the thought of ever disappointing her. *After all, I was only defending her honor.* "Mom, I know I shouldn't have punched Georgie, but he was *lying*."

His mother swirled around to face him again, mascara smudged beneath her eye where a tear fell. She quickly wiped it away but then another fell in its place.

"Mom, I'm sorry."

"No, honey, it's okay."

"No, it's not, Mom. Georgie was a jerk. I only wish I'd hit him harder, busted some of his teeth ..."

"George was telling the truth, Finn."

She gazed at him, and he could see guilt and shame reflected in her tear-streaked face. Suddenly, he knew what he had suspected since he had turned

9

seven years old but had denied up until now. He had caught glimpses of the news on the internet but figured it was all fake news—all just made-up stories.

"You know how the media just tells all those lies," his dad had once told him. "Just ignore it all," and so he had. Now, here was his own mother confirming everything to be true. There was no going back to his blissful ignorance. He grew up that day as his mother told him her story at the kitchen table.

Former US President Leif Mitchell couldn't go back to Kentucky once his wife and First Lady Chessa Mitchell had died. There were just too many memories. So, he'd bought a gorgeous home on a few acres on the Potomac to move closer to the political action in DC. There he continued, after his eight-year tenure as Commander-in-Chief, to work as a consultant to the current president as well as the Cabinet and the Department of Defense. The house also served as a convenient homebase for him when he traveled representing the US as an ambassador and speaker around the world.

He and Chessa had a son, Harry Mitchell, whom Leif sent off to a boarding school in London right before she died. Harry was named after his grandfather but looked just like his mother, with his wavy chestnut hair and green eyes, and was a constant reminder to Leif of the pain of losing his beloved First Lady.

Leif had served two four-year terms as the President of the United States and had largely been absent in Harry's life when he was a young boy, never really getting to know him. Harry had been a quiet, intelligent, well-behaved child, but Leif and Chessa had decided never to have another with their hectic schedule and constant exposure in the media as the former President and First Lady.

When Chessa was diagnosed at the age of forty with ovarian cancer during his last year in the White House, Leif had turned all his attention to caring for his wife on top of wrapping up the affairs of the nation and helping as best he could his friends in his party to get reelected. He had felt he had little choice but to send the boy away.

Once out of the White House, Chessa's disease progressed rapidly, and under hospice care in their well-appointed and well-staffed home, she mercifully passed away in peace at the end the week before Christmas. Leif had brought Harry back home for the Christmas holidays and to be with his mother in her final days. He allowed Harry to stay a few days past his holiday break for the services and to properly mourn. But the boy was just as happy to get back to his boarding school with his friends and academia as his father was to see him go.

With his presidency and being on the go so much with his career in public service, Leif had gifted his Derby-winning racehorse back to Little River, his dad's horse ranch in Lexington, Kentucky, to put him out to stud since he couldn't spend any time with him. He had also hung up his guitar once Chessa was gone.

When his mother and father both passed away shortly after Chessa died, his three brothers and he sold the entire horse ranch and split the profits equally, Leif putting his into investments and savings he figured would ultimately go to Harry.

Leif welcomed his travels since the Maryland mansion was much too big and cold with just him in it, save for the staff of three that helped keep it clean and well-landscaped.

One of the staff members, Jackie Sorrell, cooked and cleaned for Leif and eventually became his confidante and best friend, comforting him in his loneliness following the death of his wife and parents.

Still, they were never seen together outside the home, so the American public was stunned when the former president announced he was engaged again to none other than his maid.

Of course, she was young and very pretty, a smart and sassy Latino immigrant from Honduras with sultry dark brown eyes and long black curls that dangled down to her tiny waistline.

But the two were only married a year when they found they were better off as friends than living together as husband and wife. The press covered the divorce for a time, but it was amicable—Jackie received a large sum of money and never had to work another day in her life. Then there were other pressing world matters, like a brewing cold war between the US and China that quickly overshadowed everything. Besides, it wasn't an election year, and Leif wasn't a political factor any longer.

So the fact Jackie was pregnant and had a son, Anthony, shortly after the divorce was largely unnoticed by the press or the public.

Jackie ended up taking her large cash payout, her son, and moving to a remote village in New Hampshire, where they remained hidden away from Leif, politics, the media, and the world. Leif saw Anthony when he was born, and after that, only one more time for a very short visit. He did set up a healthy trust fund to support the child, who went on to graduate from the nation's highest-ranking boarding school, Phillips Exeter Academy, and then attend Northwestern University.

Leif Mitchell was in mourning for the loss of two wives for a time. But with his public persona, distinguished good looks—the tabloids often likened him to actor Matthew McConaughey—and a ton of money and charm as a former country rock star and popular President of the United States, he became known as America's most eligible bachelor.

Leif kept busy in his role as a public speaker and foreign diplomat. Occasionally, he tried to get away from it all, escaping to a remote spa here and there.

He was vacationing for a few days at a new golf resort and spa just off the coast of Hilton Head, South Carolina, when he met her.

Leif had gone to the little-known and highly exclusive Gullah Grove Plantation resort on Dafauskie Island to get some much-needed rest and recovery. He had just returned from shooting one of his best golf games ever at the Grove championship course and just wanted to be alone, so he had booked a massage and soak at the posh Lotus bathhouse.

The former President had exited the private chamber where he had received a hot stone massage and was cooling off standing alone at the balcony overlooking the rooftop pool below when he saw her ... the most beautiful creature he had ever laid eyes upon.

She was unaware of his presence since he was on the penthouse level of the bathhouse reserved for elite VIP members of the exclusive club. His secret security agent also remained incognito, stationed behind the spa's high stone privacy wall.

Leif watched, hidden behind the palm ferns that lined the balcony, as she slowly stepped out of her plush white terrycloth robe, revealing her exquisite body. He felt his gaze trail down her back, noticing how her skin was the color of caramel and how her long, honey-colored hair fell in waves to the small of it, then his eyes fell down her long, lean legs. When she turned to face his direction, he felt his breath catch, and his heart start pounding.

The sun had just set, and the magenta sky was turning violet, but he could clearly see her curves as they pulsed through the moonlit pool, rippling the water. Leif felt the warmth of desire erupt within, a heat he had not felt in years.

At the same time, all rational thought left him as he made his way from the top deck veranda down a winding stairwell, nearly running into his secret security guard, Karl. Leif told Karl, in no uncertain terms, to stand down, or at least to chill out. He had someone important to meet poolside. Karl, a giant German, frowned in dismay but knew better than to argue with his boss, and helplessly watched the former president pursue his heart's desire.

Leif approached the woman as she exited the pool, dripping, and donned a fresh robe and wrapped a towel around her hair. She was no less gorgeous up close. In fact, he considered her even more so, her cheeks flushed with the night air, her wide hazel eyes sparkling with curiosity at his presence, her lips pouty and full until they broke into a beguiling smile.

She seemed young, in her late twenties he guessed, and innocent with her doe-eyed gaze veiled by thick lashes. He approached her, dressed in casual khaki slacks and a white polo shirt revealing his tanned, muscular arms.

"Hi, the water looks wonderful," he said, extending his hand. "I'm Leif Mitchell." He could tell by her look of surprise she had no idea who he was, which was all the more enticing to him. "President Leif Mitchell."

Recognition dawned on her, and she introduced herself as Linda Holland.

After exchanging a few brief pleasantries, Leif asked her to have a private dinner with him in his room, but she objected, saying she was married.

Her eyes followed Leif's as he looked down questioningly at her right hand.

"Oh, I took my rings off to swim," she explained bashfully. "I lost some weight recently and they were a little loose. I was afraid I'd lose them in the pool."

Leif apologized, then cleared his throat. "Where is your husband? Maybe you both could join me for dinner?"

Linda told him her husband was US Army Captain Stephen Holland, currently serving in Afghanistan. She had come down to visit her parents in Florida.

"They gave me this spa retreat in Hilton Head for my birthday." She flashed him her dazzling smile, again taking his breath away.

Leif could feel Karl's eyes on him now, as well as those of an older couple who had appeared to take a swim. Then out of his peripheral vision, he noticed a few more onlookers gathering, staring at them. He looked intently into her eyes and lowered his voice into a whisper. "I know you didn't recognize me, but there are many who do. Once enough people find out I'm here, I'm going to be barraged by the media," he said. "I can't eat in the dining room because I'll be interrupted so much I'll starve. Is there any way I can talk you into joining me in my suite for room service? If it helps, we'll be chaperoned by my secret service agent, Karl, over there." Leif nodded his head in Karl's direction. The big suit was standing off in the distance, pretending to be on his cell phone.

"Well, I'm always hungry after I swim."

It was settled, and Linda joined him in his suite for room service. They dined on lobster tails and drank champagne until they were both more than tipsy. They made love that night under an enormous starlit sky roof on a king-sized bed covered with silken sheets and the finest down. Leif had basically told Karl to get lost, although he remained remotely on standby.

Linda left the next morning without a word, leaving a note on Leif's pillow telling him how forlorn and heartsick she was that she had betrayed her husband.

But as hard as he tried, Leif could not forget her. Later in the day, he made a phone call that would change everything.

Leif had discovered when he was younger that he had a long-lost older half-sister by the last name of Warren. He found out she'd died of "unknown causes" shortly after having a son named Ralston, who was sent off by his father into the Army and had risen through the military ranks to become a general.

When Leif became president, he appointed Ralston Warren to be on his Cabinet. Leif had always respected Ralston's sharp mind and military prowess, although his slightly younger nephew was often hard to read when it came to his emotions or trustworthiness. Still, Leif was always loyal to his family and knew Ralston had a rough upbringing by his abusive father.

Leif forced his voice to remain calm as he now phoned his nephew, who currently served as the Secretary of the Department of Defense.

"Sir," the crisp, no-nonsense voice of Commander Ralston crackled. "Is everything all right?" Leif knew Ralston answered the phone formally most likely because he wasn't alone.

"We need to talk privately," Leif said and waited while his nephew got rid of whoever was in his office. "Okay, I'm alone, what's up?"

"I need you to do me a favor, Ralls," Leif said, calling his nephew by his less formal nickname.

A week later, the incident was just a blip on the national news—the anchor reported another skirmish in Afghanistan. Although the US troops had withdrawn in the summer of 2021, they occasionally were deployed to fight small bands of terrorists who rose to power. Among the three American casualties in the battle was US Captain Stephen Holland. News anchors reported Captain Holland, a decorated war hero, had led his troops to defend a native Afghan village against a rogue terrorist attack when gunfire erupted. Ironically, one news reporter said, Holland had been scheduled to come home two days earlier but he had received a phone call from the Army brass requiring him to stay another week in the war-torn country—the reasons were undisclosed.

CHAPTER TWO

"Dad's phone call ... got him killed?" Young Finn shook his head as he sat at the kitchen table, suddenly feeling sick to his stomach, and not because he had eaten too many cookies.

"I don't know," Linda Mitchell told her son, standing with her back up against the kitchen counter, fidgeting with a strand of her highlighted blonde hair. "Your father and I never discussed it further."

"It seems awfully coincidental." For the first time in his fourteen years, Finn felt an anger rise against his father, whom he had previously adored, worshipped even. "Did you even grieve your former husband?" He knew his tone was biting but he couldn't help it.

"Of course I did."

Finn didn't say a word as he watched his mother's cheeks blush with shame. "But you still married Dad—"

"Yes, your father and I fell in love and got married three months later." He watched his mother's eyes lower to the polished hardwood floor, then raise to meet his again. "There's more ..."

Finn looked away from her, and his eyes landed on the framed photos that sat on a bookshelf in the adjoining family room, zeroing in on one in particular—he had seen it a hundred times before but now saw the picture through new eyes. The photo was of his mother and father smiling into the camera. Behind them the sun along the ocean's horizon cast a rosy glow across waves crashing onto the broad beach at low tide. The man and the woman were both tanned and beautiful in their bathing suits— he with golden wavy hair and laugh lines fanning from his sea-blue eyes, she with caramel-colored curls cascading around her bare shoulders, her bewitching eyes, filled with joy, framed by demure thick eyelashes peering from beneath a floppy white sun hat. They looked supremely happy. Now Finn wanted to smash the photo because it seemed to capture the lie his life was founded upon.

"I don't want to really hear any more, Mother."

"Better you hear it from me than down the line from someone else."

Finn didn't know if he could take anymore, but he remained glued to his seat unable to move. From an early age, curiosity had always been one of his character traits—or flaws depending on how you looked at it. "Okay, tell me."

"Your father and I ... had a baby ... before you." Linda took a deep breath, stood up straight and crossed her arms as if to fortify herself. "He died, though. He was only a year old." She wiped a stray tear that fell.

Finn couldn't summon up the ability to feel sorry for her or his father right now. He just wanted to run to his room and tell his mother to shut up. But he couldn't do that either, so he sat and listened, ignoring the increasing throb in his temple and fist.

"His name was Patrick, we called him Pat. He was born with a heart defect. We tried everything to save him, flew in the best surgeons, but in the end, there was nothing more anyone could have done. God took our poor baby. Your father and I were heartbroken. We thought we were being punished ..."

Finn left his mother's words dangle in awkward silence. He was still just a kid, but at fourteen years old, he knew how babies were conceived.

"... but then you came along." Linda smiled through her tears. "You looked a lot like him, you know." His mother opened her purse that lay on the counter and fished a small photo out of her wallet and handed it to him. The photo was of a blond-haired toddler who looked so much like Finn he thought he was looking at a baby picture of himself at first.

"A brother named Pat, huh?" Suddenly Finn felt an ache inside for the brother he would never know.

"Yes, and we will always miss him ... but then you were the answer to our prayers." His mother put away the photo and walked over to hug him, and he put his arms around her and sobbed.

Finn returned to school after his suspension, no longer worried about what the other kids thought of him. While he was still disappointed in his father's actions, he realized there was nothing he could do to change the past, and he was ready to brave whatever words would be hurled his way, true or not.

Instead, he was met with a silent respect from Georgie and the other students. He was still the son of a United States President, but everyone knew his life, his family, were far from perfect, which gave them common ground.

Weeks and months passed, and it was fall of his sophomore year at North Hampton Prep. Finn felt like he fit in now more than ever, and he became more popular, especially when he came off the bench and actually played in his first football game that November.

One of his teammates, a wide receiver, was injured in the game and Coach Michael Barry was calling Finn to take the field.

It was third down, and the quarterback looked at him and told him to be open. It all seemed to happen in a blur, fast yet slow … he was running down the right sideline, the cornerback a few feet away in his peripheral vision, the ball sailing in the air getting closer, jumping up and reaching out his arms, his hands suddenly enclosed around the hard leather, bringing the ball down to his chest and dropping his toe down, he hoped, in-bounds … and making the touchdown right before the cornerback plowed hard into his side.

Finn took a second to recover and catch his wind before realizing the fans were cheering for him. A teammate grabbed his hand and pulled him to his feet and then slapped him on the back. Soon, all his fellow players were high fiving him, tapping his helmet, congratulating him. He looked up into the stands where his parents were sitting—now standing, clapping, crying—well at least his mom, his dad pumped his fist in the air and grinned, and

Finn could see the pride twinkling in his father's eyes. He waved before being rushed off the field for the extra point kick.

As he removed his helmet to grab a drink of water, another person caught his eye, one of the girls on the cheerleading squad. He had seen her in class before but never really noticed her until now. Her name was Valerie, she was a year ahead of him, a junior. Any other day she probably wouldn't have noticed him, but right now she was glancing his way, looking straight into his eyes with her big chocolate brown ones. Once he met her gaze, she gave him a demure smile and shook her pom poms in front of her, then twirled to face the field with the rest of her team, her glittery mini skirt and blonde curls swirling behind her.

"... Mitchell, did you hear what I said?" Coach Barry's voice boomed through his fog, his big frame looming over Finn. "Don't take too long a break there. You're going back out for the fourth quarter."

"Uh ... sure coach, I'm ready." Finn put his helmet and mouth guard back on. *Don't look her way, she's out of your league.* Still, he was pretty sure she had been flirting with him. *Get your head in the game, man.*

The North Hampton Hawks held the opposing team, keeping them from scoring in the fourth and beating them twenty-four to seventeen, which meant they would be entering the playoffs.

After a rousing locker room talk by Coach Barry, who kept it short since he had been doused on the field with Gatorade, Finn changed out of his uniform into a fresh pair of jeans, button-down shirt and blazer. He was walking past the bleachers toward his parents' waiting car when he saw Valerie, still dressed in her cheerleader uniform. She also donned a big letter jacket to ward off the chilly night air and was talking to another cheerleader next to the stands.

She looked his way, hugged the other girl goodbye, and started walking in his direction.

Finn stopped and waited for her to catch up to him.

She was even prettier up close. "Hey, Finn," she said breathlessly, batting her eyelashes over her dark shimmering eyes. "Congratulations, you were great tonight."

"Um, thanks." Finn felt tongue-tied.

"I always meant to tell you how proud of you I was last semester when you let that bully Georgie have it." A night breeze picked up, blowing her hair, and she playfully pulled a strand behind her ear, her cheeks blushing pink to match her lip gloss.

"Uh, Georgie's all right, I guess," he answered shyly, shifting his weight from one foot to another.

"He is now you whipped him into shape. He stopped bullying the other freshmen. You were a hero that day ... and tonight."

"Finn!" He looked across the school parking lot and could see his mother waving next to their big black Lincoln, the ever-present secret service agent standing nearby. His father was waiting in the driver's seat of the sedan, which was running with the lights on.

He waved back. "Coming in a minute!" Finn turned back to face her. "Do you need a ride or something?"

"No, I drove." Finn felt his face flush hot. *Of course she did, she's sixteen, stupid.*

"Hey, Finn, would it be okay if I ... if we ... see each other again?" She gave him her best cheerleader smile, and he felt his heart pound.

"Sure." He had to think fast on his feet, embarrassed now that his mother was still waving at him. "How about we meet here Monday after football practice and take a walk?"

"Sounds perfect."

That Monday night was Finn's first time. They had met under the bleachers and taken a walk on campus as the sun set, the autumn leaves crunching under their feet. When the cold November wind whipped up, they snuck into school by a secret passageway Valerie knew and made love on the floor in a corner of the dimly lit senior lounge, covered by a blanket, quick and clumsy, the cheerleader leading the inexperienced football star along the way.

Finn and Valerie had just a few dates during that school year before they both discovered they had absolutely nothing in common. He was more serious, studious, and disciplined, while she was happy-go-lucky and skated by in her classes, grades, and life in general on her good looks and charm. She was constantly seeking fun, and her bubbly laugh, which at first seemed so attractive, began to grate on his nerves.

They broke up before summer. Valerie was entering her senior year and had to start concentrating on which university she would attend, and Finn had to focus on football, hoping to catch the eyes of the various college team recruiters. After one last fling, they decided to free each other and part ways.

Finn hooked up with a few girls over the next two years of his high school career, always being able to score partners for dances and dates when needed.

Because of Finn's tan from his beach vacations with his parents, muscles from daily football workouts, his dad's sea-blue eyes and golden streaked wavy hair, and his mom's dazzling smile, he was voted "best-looking guy" and "most likely to be a success" in his senior class.

And he was given a full-ride scholarship to the University of Delaware, where he'd be one of the starting wide receivers.

CHAPTER THREE

Peter Baldwin adjusted the glasses on the bridge of his nose as Finn sat before him, squirming in his chair. The young man's fate rested in the University dean's hands.

The tall, wise, older man, handsome in his younger days but now balding a bit, still had a commanding presence in his tweed jacket, holding his well-worn pipe in mid-air. Pete had long ago given up smoking, but the pipe was still an appendage, an extension of his right hand. He now waved it around with authority as he paced in front of his large mahogany desk and floor-to-ceiling shelves of books. Some of the historic academic tomes dated back to the Revolutionary War and were probably worth a small fortune.

Finn knew Pete Baldwin was a good friend of his father's. A former attorney and legal scholar as well as a very learned philosophy professor, he was consulted by many leaders and heads of state including President Mitchell, both when he was in office and then personally at times. Pete had cautioned Leif after he had an affair back in South Carolina with Linda, warning him not to pursue the relationship with another man's wife. But Leif had obviously allowed his lust to outweigh his common sense and his moral compass.

Oh, well ... I was the result, so it wasn't all bad, Finn smiled.

"Tell me again, Mr. Mitchell, exactly what happened last Saturday night—don't leave out any details." Professor Baldwin sat down in his overstuffed chair behind his ancient desk, leaned back, and put his pipe in his mouth, waiting.

Finn stared straight ahead at the library shelves, the titles before him blurring as he felt a headache starting in his right temple. He closed his eyes and chose his words carefully, recounting the awful night of the frat party and the devastating chain of events that had ensued. The sights and sounds of that fateful fall evening came back to him—the Indian summer sun cast its golden rays across the campus, setting the trees ablaze in golds and reds. It was warm, so dorm windows were open, and music blared across the quad—the siren call for another big party weekend.

Finn found it hard to concentrate as his math professor droned on about the square root of such and such. He tried hard not to gaze out of the classroom window, but he couldn't help himself. Then he saw her—Lisa Frazier. He had met her his first day during orientation and hadn't seen her since, but he'd recognize her from a mile away. He knew it was her, the way she strode purposefully in her pink sweater and tight jeans with the holes, her blonde head bent slightly, her arms wrapped tightly around her books.

"Mister Mitchell?" Dean Baldwin snapped him to attention, standing up and peering over his glasses.

"Sir?"

"The night of the frat party?"

"Oh, right. Tommy Sentry and I went together to Kappa Alpha that night." Finn took a deep breath and slowly exhaled. Mr. Baldwin sat back down in his chair, chewing on his pipe now and staring at him behind his horn-rimmed glasses in consternation.

"We were invited as freshmen for the welcome party, but we knew there would be hazing involved if we were going to be inducted into the fraternity."

"The University banned all hazing years ago," the dean said in a disgruntled tone.

Finn swallowed hard and sat up straighter in his seat. "Yes, sir, but unfortunately it still goes on behind the scenes."

"Behind my back, illegally. Which is why you and I are facing all of this trouble now."

"Yes, sir."

"Go on." Dean Baldwin waved his pipe for Finn to keep talking.

"They had pizza and a keg of beer. A bunch of kids were already there when we arrived." Finn had managed to make it to the end of math class and then ran to the library, tracking Lisa Frazier down to ask her to the party.

"How many kids are we talking about?"

"Eventually, I think there were at least about seventy, maybe eighty ..."

"Girls?"

"Yes, sir. That number included about thirty-some girls from our sister sorority, Alpha Delta Pi."

"Hmmpf. I will speak to their headmistress. Go on."

"I had asked a girl, Lisa Frazier, to go with me. I met her at orientation, thought she was pretty, saw her on campus that day."

Dean Baldwin cleared his throat. "Okay, back to the main event."

"So, after a couple hours, the fraternity president announced the rush ... um, the induction ceremony was going to begin. The executive board guys lined up in the living room, then the rest of the house members and five of us freshman started down the walk of shame as everyone else watched. We, um, had to pass under bottles they were holding up and catch the liquor they poured out in our mouths. If we let any spill, we were sent to the back of the line to start over."

Finn watched as the dean's face grew red with irritation, but he remained silent, intently listening now, his teeth clenched around the pipe.

"For some reason, I guess because he was short and a little clumsy, Tommy couldn't quite catch the alcohol in his mouth. He kept being sent to the back of the line."

Finn could still feel the vodka splashing in his face as he closed his eyes and tried to gulp the stinging liquid down his throat without gagging it back up. He could still hear the thudding rap music in the background and the chants echo in his head. "You loser! You miserable excuse for a pledge. Back of the line soldier ..." and then "Drink! Drink! Drink!"

He remembered foggily watching Tommy's last walk, the way he staggered blindly, his bleary eyes unable to focus, his face a grayish color. "Watch out, he's gonna blow," one kid had yelled, and the rest stepped back and laughed.

"He made it through one last time, and then, Tommy's eyes rolled back, his head flopped forward, and he passed out on the floor," Finn continued.

"And what did they do then?"

"Nothing." Finn sat back in his chair and looked down at his hands in his lap, ashamed.

"What do you mean nothing?" Mr. Baldwin stood up, his frame towering over his desk, glaring at Finn.

"I mean they kept partying. Someone threw a blanket over Tommy, and they rolled him out of the way. That's all I saw, because they started to push us into another room so we could get our paddles and induction pins and make things official."

The dean removed his glasses wearily and rubbed his bald head in his hands. "That is terrible. Inexcusable."

"I agree, sir."

"So tell me, Mr. Mitchell, what did *you* do?" Pete Baldwin re-inserted his glasses on the bridge of his nose and peered at Finn over them, as if he were a judge. "Nothing I suppose, since your crowning, or pinning, was imminent? And I guess you were on a date of some sort?"

"Well ... actually, sir, I ... I did."

"And what was that?"

"I can't tell you, sir. I've probably already said too much."

"Need I remind you, Mr. Mitchell, that Tommy Sentry is currently lying in a coma at Christiana Hospital fighting for his life because of these actions, and you and your fellow housemates are facing possible felony charges as a result?" Mr. Baldwin cleared his throat for emphasis.

Finn closed his eyes to hold back the sting of tears that threatened to fall. He knew full well

31

that Tommy had nearly died of alcohol poisoning that night. Tommy was somewhat of a nerd, a red-headed, freckle-faced boy, who desperately wanted to fit in and just so happened to be Finn's roommate that freshman year. Tommy had begged Finn to tag along when the two of them had first applied to be in the fraternity. The frat students manning the Kappa Alpha booth at the welcome week events had initially frowned at Tommy's application. But they'd let it slide when they realized Finn was a top Blue Hens football team recruit and was vouching for his roommate.

Finn recalled how he had been focused on Lisa while the committee prepared the other room for the final pinning ceremony. He asked her to dance to a slow song, and she felt soft as he had put his arms around her and smelled the seductive scent of her hair, then noticed the top two buttons of her pink sweater were undone, revealing her creamy skin. But just as he bent down to kiss her bubblegum pink lips, his conscience had taken hold, and he pictured Tommy lying there under a blanket, half dead and gagging on his own vomit.

"I'll be right back," Finn had told Lisa, who pouted and rolled her eyes, exasperated.

Suddenly, for some inexplicable crazy reason, the thought of Patrick, his own brother who had died, flashed through his girl-crazed, alcohol-addled brain. Finn ran from the ceremony in the parlor back into the living room where a dozen students milled around or danced in a drunken stupor to the loud rap music playing. One couple was making out on the sofa at the foot of which a mummy-like body lay. The only thing that gave away Tommy's identity was his shock of ginger hair, poking out of the gray wool blanket.

After checking to see that Tommy did, in fact, still have a pulse, Finn had run back into the parlor, interrupting the ceremony much to the chagrin of the Kappa Alpha executive board, and begged for help for his roommate.

He told Lisa to go home at that point, but she refused, tipsy on the beer she had consumed. "You're not ruining this party for me, Finn Mitchell," she'd told him, and then flirtatiously found another young man to take his place dancing to the loud throbbing music.

"So, what happened next?" the dean asked.

"Basically, they all yelled at me for the interruption, then warned me not to contact anyone and just let Tommy sleep it off. But I snuck off to secretly call 911 anyway, then waited with Tommy, trying to administer CPR and keep him breathing until the ambulance arrived."

Unable to safely drive since he had consumed a large amount of booze himself, he had gone home and faced a sleepless night. He couldn't care less at that point whether or not he saw Lisa Frazier for a second date or ever set foot in the fraternity again. Or even if he was arrested and prosecuted.

He was worried sick that night and for the following week that Tommy wouldn't make it.

And he was still worried sitting in front of Mr. Baldwin now.

"All I want is for Tommy to pull through," Finn said, wiping away tears on his shirt sleeve.

Dean Baldwin stood, walked around his desk to where Finn sat, and patted him on the shoulder. "I know, son. I figured you were a good kid because I know your father. I just had to make sure. Most kids in this situation would have stayed in hiding. I know it can't be easy being a president's son. All that pressure. You want to lay low. But when my secretary called you to come in for questioning, you didn't hesitate. And now, I can see you're more concerned about Tommy than you are about yourself. You may have even saved his life. So we will keep this discussion between us, and I'll let you know once I hear from the hospital if ... when Tommy pulls through."

"Can you also tell his parents I'm really sorry about all of this?" Finn sniffed and stood, looking squarely at the dean.

Mr. Baldwin firmly shook his hand. "I'm sure they'd appreciate that."

Tommy did come out of the coma two days later, according to the newspaper article that reported the entire incident, including the fact that the president and entire executive board of the Kappa Alpha fraternity were being indicted on charges of attempted manslaughter and reckless endangerment.

Finn had ignored dozens of threatening calls and texts from the frat house members, who saw him as a snitch when the article was released.

Once the students were arrested and released on bail, however, they lawyered up and refrained from making any more contact on advice from their attorneys.

They eventually all struck plea bargains, which involved expulsion from the university, two years of probation, and community service. The fraternity was suspended for a time and then reopened with stricter rules banning hazing and other alcohol-related events.

Finn continued on at the University of Delaware but dropped off the football team, not wanting to face the scrutiny of some of his teammates who continued to threaten him. He also didn't want to demoralize the team or some of his fellow players who weren't involved and just wanted to play ball and win games.

He did stay in touch with Dean Baldwin, visiting him occasionally for advice, and sought his counsel when it came time to apply for law school. Finn had decided, after the hazing incident, to become a state's attorney.

CHAPTER FOUR

After graduating with honors from the University of Delaware, Finn was accepted into the University of Notre Dame Law School in South Bend, Indiana.

There were no fraternities or sororities at Notre Dame, a fact that wasn't lost on Finn. He knew that wasn't to say there wasn't a lot of drinking on campus, especially on football weekends at tailgaters. But most of the partying revolved around the undergrad student halls, which still weren't coed at the Catholic college, or at a few of the bars in the city. The law school students pretty much stuck to themselves.

There wasn't a whole lot of time for extracurricular activities anyway. Finn spent most of his time holed up in the university's Theodore Hesburgh Library, famous for its mosaic of "Touchdown Jesus" on its massive front, named for the university's president of thirty-five years who was legendary around the world for his works of social activism and humanitarianism.

Being Catholic, Finn loved going to mass on campus at the Basilica of the Sacred Heart or praying at the Grotto of Our Lady of Lourdes hidden behind the cathedral where millions knelt each year to say prayers after lighting one of the thousands of candles that lit up the night.

But his stagnant social life changed when he started dating Trinity Foster, a senior at St. Mary's College.

He met her in one of his classes at Notre Dame. Some students from St. Mary's attended classes at Notre Dame, which was literally across the road, and vice versa as part of a co-exchange program.

Finn had been called upon by the legal ethics professor, James Dobbins, to answer a question, and he was stumped. The girl who sat next to him scribbled the answer on a piece of paper and held it out in front of her for Finn to see in his peripheral vision. He quickly glanced down, then up, and answered correctly.

Satisfied, Professor Dobbins moved on to question the next student across the room. Finn took the opportunity to smile at the girl and whisper, "Thanks ... uh—"

"Trinity ... Trinity Foster," she whispered back, answering his unasked question. "My pleasure. And you are?"

"Finn Mitchell."

She flashed a dazzling smile at him and turned back to hide the paper with the answer back in her notebook. Was that mischief he'd seen in her eyes? Finn started to whisper to ask for her number when he realized the professor had stealthily crossed back over again to their side of the room.

"Mr. Mitchell, certainly you're not talking in class?" Finn could feel Mr. Dobbins standing directly in front of his desk without having to look. He slowly turned around and saw the short, stocky, middle-aged law professor bent over, glaring back and forth between him and Trinity Foster.

"Sorry, Mr. Dobbins." He looked at the clock on the classroom wall. Thankfully the class was ending in a minute.

"I would suggest you keep your eyes on me from now on," Dobbins said, stroking his graying beard and adjusting his glasses. Finn disliked the haughty professor, who bragged he had once single-handedly defeated a corporate behemoth in court in a major civil case and therefore seemed to think he was one of the greatest lawyers of all time.

So why is he teaching then? Finn had wondered. But he knew he had to pass this course in order to become an attorney himself. "Yes, sir." Finn said softly now, forcing himself to sound humble.

After class, he rushed to catch up to Trinity, who was walking down the hallway ahead of him with a friend. "Hey, I just wanted to thank you, um, properly." He interrupted the two girls chattering, and they turned to look at him.

"You're welcome," Trinity said, flashing him her brilliant smile.

An awkward moment of silence apparently gave her friend the hint, and the other girl said, "Gotta run," and dashed off down the hall.

"Sorry, didn't mean to interrupt."

"That's okay, I see her every day. Did you get your paper done that's due tomorrow?" Trinity's eyes sparkled.

"I did—let's just hope it passes. I'd hate to have to take that class twice."

"You don't like ethics?" Trinity teased.

"No, I just don't like the professor who teaches it."

"So, what do you like?" Trinity gave him that mischievous smile again as she leaned her back against the beige hallway wall, hugging her books.

Finn appraised her outfit—a pair of jeans with a few strategic rips over one shapely knee, a cream-colored sweater that hugged her curves, and a thin gold chain with a cross that lay at the little indentation at the base of her dainty neck. She took his breath away, and he fought to keep thinking rationally and forced himself to make words come out of his mouth. He wanted to say "you" but knew that would be one of the corniest answers he could utter.

"Well, a lot of things." *That buys me a few seconds.* She gazed up at him quizzically, waiting. "I like my law classes, although I don't like studying. I like cheeseburgers, French fries, and milkshakes, not salad so much. I like hiking and fishing and boating and traveling and doing just about anything outdoors. Oh—and I like pretty girls, especially those who are mature enough to take their faith seriously."

She blushed and her hand went to her necklace, her fingers touching the gold cross.

"So what do you say to grabbing a cheeseburger and then visiting the grotto and hiking around the lake tonight?

"I'd say that all sounds good."

"Okay, meet you at the Huddle, let's say seven?"

She nodded, her ponytail bobbing and her eyes twinkling.

They met that night at Smashburger in the Huddle student center and were lucky to find a small vacant table with two empty chairs in the crowded fast-food venue. Finn ordered a double bacon burger and she, a black bean burger with avocado.

"Vegetarian," she explained.

"Meat lover," he countered, grinning.

The two talked over hand-spun chocolate shakes, a love they did have in common.

After they ate, they walked hand in hand to the grotto, where they both lit a candle and knelt to say a prayer, then they strolled down and walked around St. Joseph's Lake in the moonlight.

"What did you pray for?" Finn gently asked as they stood looking at the full golden hunter's moon casting a glow onto the lake.

She looked at him with her liquid brown eyes. "You to pass Ethics," she said, and they both burst out laughing. "How about you?" Trinity asked after their laughter subsided.

"For a second date with you," Finn said in a sincere tone, then bent down and tenderly kissed her.

Finn had dated a bunch of girls at the University of Delaware, but they had always seemed immature. None captivated him the way Trinity Foster did.

It was the end of Notre Dame's football season, but Finn and Trinity still found plenty to do that winter and spring. They dated through the rest of the school year, taking lots of walks around the lakes when it was warm enough, dining out, going to hear live bands or to the movies in South Bend, attending a handful of Notre Dame basketball games, and most of the time just hanging out in Finn's little off-campus apartment.

He was lucky to still get financial help from his parents as well as a set of wheels. Finn had been given a Nissan sports car for his birthday he had driven out to Notre Dame, so he would often pick up Trinity after school and bring her home later that night—or sometimes, the next morning.

Finn had introduced his parents to Trinity via FaceTime on his iPhone and looked forward to when they could finally meet her in person that coming summer. Trinity would then be heading off to Harvard where she had received an assistant teaching position on the law school faculty. He was really proud of her—until the unthinkable occurred.

One Friday evening, Finn realized he had forgotten a textbook he'd left in the classroom. He needed to finish a homework assignment over the weekend to hand in Monday. He wasn't supposed to see Trinity that night since she had told him she was getting together with some girlfriends at St. Mary's for one of their birthdays.

He decided to take his chances and walk across campus to Eck Hall and see if the classroom was still open so he could dash in and grab his book. It was a warm spring evening, and Finn whistled as he walked along the north quad. A stray Frisbee landed near his feet, and he stopped to toss it back to its owner. Footballs flew through the air, and rock music drifted out from an open dorm window. The whole campus seemed to be in a good mood ... summer break was just three weeks away.

Finn would be headed home to Maryland, and he and Trinity had talked about how she would fly out from her home in Houston to meet his parents for the Fourth of July holiday. They planned to go to Washington, DC, since she'd never seen the nation's capital, and stay to watch the fireworks.

All was quiet as Finn climbed the steps of the tan brick building with its landmark arched window walkway. The shadowed hallway was dim, and Finn felt a bit creeped out, so he hurried his steps, praying the classroom door was unlocked.

As he approached, he was surprised to hear muffled sounds coming from inside the classroom.

The door wasn't locked, so Finn opened it and stopped short.

It all happened so fast, he didn't have time to react, and yet ... it all seemed to happen simultaneously in slow motion.

He adjusted his eyes to the waning daylight in the classroom, blinking, following the sounds of a soft female voice and a guttural male's, rising and falling ... and then he saw it, saw them ... the back of his professor, still dressed in a light blue Oxford shirt, sweat stains in the arm pits. Looking closer, he knew it was Dobbins from the back of his greasy shoulder-length brown hair with a bald spot at his crown. He didn't have to see the man's face. Finn didn't have to see the face of the girl either to know from the sounds she made that it was *her* ... his girl, his Trinity. That's all he needed to see, to hear. He ran from the room as fast as he could down the hall and out into the warm night and vomited into the nearby bushes, heaving big gulps of air, his eyesight blurred with tears of rage.

Finn inhaled and exhaled until he could breathe normally. Once his vision cleared, he ran the entire mile to the student parking lot. He reached his car, out of breath, his lungs and his face burning hot.

Mercifully, it would be the last time he would ever set eyes on Trinity Foster or Professor James Dobbins again.

He headed straight that night to Corby's Irish pub in South Bend, pulled up a stool and drank as much Guinness as he could stomach before he puked again in the men's restroom. He had left his car on the parking lot and gotten an Uber ride home, returning with a terrific headache and hangover the next morning to fetch his car, retching once again behind the dumpster behind the bar in broad daylight, hoping no one could see him but not really caring after all.

When his mother called him that Sunday as was her weekly custom to see how he was doing away at school, Finn told her very little, just that he and Trinity had broken up.

But his mother could always read him, even if he wasn't face to face with her. Like most mothers, she could hear the pain in her son's voice.

"What did she do?" Linda Mitchell fumed through the phone.

"Nothing," Finn lied unsuccessfully.

"She did something, and it must have been pretty bad because I know you really liked this girl ... loved her even. Finn, you can tell me, I'm your mother."

"Okay, Mom, if you must know, she cheated on me." Finn sighed, wishing he hadn't told her. *Too late now.*

"Why, of all the low-down ... well this just goes to show she didn't deserve you," Linda said, her voice seething with anger.

"I know, Mom, can we just drop it now? I shouldn't have told you. Now you'll just be upset." *I should have known better*, he chastised himself. Luckily he heard loud, boisterous voices coming through the front door of his apartment. His two roommates were arriving home after a trip to the grocery store. The three of them had planned to have one last end-of-year backyard barbeque bash that coming weekend to celebrate finals being over.

"Mom, listen, I gotta run, my roomies are home, and I have to help unpack groceries."

"Okay. But if you need to talk more, I'll be here for you."

"I know, Mom, thanks, I'll be okay."

The barbeque the following Friday night helped lift Finn's spirits a bit, and he actually met a pretty girl at the party and asked for her number, although he was sure he would never ask her out.

But he no longer cared much about hurting women's feelings.

He now felt like members of the opposite sex were all lying and manipulative—except for his mother, of course.

Finn looked at women now as fleeting distractions, a necessary evil or a guilty pleasure, one that should be indulged sparingly. *A guy needed to protect himself at all costs from falling in love.*

Finn never reported the incident he saw between his supposed girlfriend and their professor, nor did he return to the ethics class again, not wanting to face complete humiliation. He knew he'd have to accept the possibility he might fail the course since he'd missed the last two classes, although he did manage to email in his final homework assignments.

Fortunately, Finn received a passing grade of C, which meant there was a possibility he could still graduate with honors. *Dobbins probably didn't want to fail me and risk me reporting him. He knows who I am, who my parents are.* Finn hoped he would never have to face Mr. Dobbins again.

As for Trinity, he ignored her calls and finally answered one of her texts asking where he'd been by typing the words, "I saw what you did with Dobbins."

She had messaged back, "Please talk to me," but he ignored her plea. Then came a long text: "I'm so sorry. It only happened once. I did it because he helped get me the position at Harvard. Please forgive me. I love you."

Finn thought for a moment, then typed back, "We are done," and he proceeded to block her number and all social media connections from his phone and laptop.

CHAPTER FIVE

Finn graduated in the top ten percent of his law school class, not an easy feat, but he had remained determined the next two years to not let anything stand in his way of academic triumph—including and especially any girls.

The graduation took place on a glorious spring day. The sun gleamed on the golden dome under a brilliant cloudless blue sky.

Leif and Linda Mitchell attended, and TV cameras, of course, caught the former US President and First Lady as they stood in the wings of the stage along with their Secret Service aides in the Notre Dame stadium where the final commencement ceremony was being held.

When Leif Mitchell had initially been asked by the University Provost to give the law school commencement address, he had sat down with Finn and told him he had decided to decline, not wanting to take the spotlight from his son.

After all, President Mitchell had already given the commencement address to the University of Notre Dame's undergraduate class thirty-four years ago. Notre Dame's tradition was to invite the newly elected President of the United States to deliver the address and receive an honorary doctorate degree during their first year in office. Mitchell had joined a long line of former presidents including Eisenhower, Carter, Reagan, George H.W. Bush, George W. Bush and Obama, all of whom had drawn protestors from the right or left.

Leif had a high popularity rating and was the youngest president to ever be elected, in addition to being Catholic and upholding the church's teachings in his politics and platform. He hadn't incurred nearly as many protests the first time he spoke as some of the other presidents had. Although the media still proclaimed his first wife, Wendy Greene Mitchell, had a much-publicized abortion, raising the issue from the ashes once again, Leif had still been glorified back then—First Lady Chessa Mitchell had been beyond reproach in her integrity, her duties as a wife and mother, and in her worldwide efforts to champion the rights of underprivileged women.

But this time might be different, Leif knew. The scandal buried long ago involving Leif's marriage to his maid and servant, Jackie, would probably not come up. And although there were rumors revolving around the suspicious timing of Leif's marriage to Finn's mother, Linda, following her husband's military slaughter in Afghanistan, they had never been confirmed nor reported.

If he accepted, Leif would become the first president ever to speak at a Notre Dame graduation ceremony twice. Still, he hesitated to accept based on the chance of garnering unfavorable press that would hurt his family.

Finn vehemently objected when his father wearily told him he had decided not to cast a potential pall over his son's graduation. "Dad, I'd be proud if you spoke to my graduating class," he'd told his father over the phone when Leif had called him to discuss it. "I'd be disappointed if you didn't."

"I just don't want to overshadow you and your accomplishments," Leif said. "Plus, I'm getting up there in age and don't want to embarrass you." He had chuckled, but Finn saw right through his father's humble façade. Leif had a lucrative career in public speaking after his presidency, and while he was now retired, Finn was sure his father would not disappoint as a commencement speaker. "Listen, I have a few days to make the decision and get back to them, so think about it and let me know."

"I don't have to think about it," Finn said, smiling through the phone. "I'm going to tell my roommates now." He shouted to the back of his apartment where his buddies were making sandwiches in the kitchen. "Guess who our commencement speaker is, guys? My dad!"

They came around the corner of the hallway where Finn was in the small living room, cell phone in hand, cheering and shouting, "No way!" and "That's awesome, dude!" and clapping him on the back. Finn spoke into the phone again. "See, Dad, now you have to do it."

"Okay, if you're sure—"

"I'm positive."

The former president had just celebrated his seventieth birthday and looked healthy and dapper in a navy suit, starched white shirt, and red tie. Linda Mitchell looked elegantly beautiful in a robin's-egg blue dress with a smart matching jacket and pumps, her tawny tresses framing her flawless face.

They were both tan, having just come back from a vacation in Hilton Head, still a favorite hideaway where they tried to go each year to get away and relax, he to golf, her to swim and get pampered at the spa.

Finn sat in the rows of chairs on the green turf football field with his fellow students arranged in alphabetical order. He took a deep breath as his parents walked up onto the dais. His father then proceeded to the lectern after stopping to smile for the cameras and shake hands with the University President and other dignitaries.

This is it. Finn hoped he had made a wise choice in not discouraging his father from delivering the address.

"Second chances." The start to the speech would be heralded as one of the most unconventional ever. "My fellow Americans, everyone deserves second chances—in grace, in love, in life. I'm here today to talk about how I have been given a second, and in some cases, third, fourth, fiftieth chance, and how you will go out there today and need to not only get but give second chances—how everyone deserves them because that's what God is all about."

After thanking the University, the president, and the students, President Mitchell continued. "Law school is, in itself, a second chance to excel in academia and your purpose in life, your calling.

Your graduation today marks an ending—to the long nights of studying, mulling over all those tomes of this versus that and that versus this—" Leif smiled as laughter erupted from the stadium. "—and it also marks a beginning. Some of you can't look around the bend, around the perimeters of South Bend for that matter, and see what's in store for you in your careers, in your love life, in your families. I'm sure there will be heartache and tragedy, but I hope there will be triumphs too, victories the likes of which have never been seen before ... because as John says in his Gospel, Jesus told us, 'whoever believes in me will do the works I have been doing, and they will do even greater things than these ... You may ask me for anything in my name, and I will do it.' What strength, what power we all have at our beckoning if we just tap into it. You, graduates of Notre Dame Law School, are called to do greater works than ever before. Don't let anything or anyone hold you back when you hear that higher calling."

Leif concluded his speech to thunderous applause and a standing ovation.

Finn blinked back tears of pride as he stood shoulder to shoulder with his classmates to clap for his dad.

After the ceremony was over, Finn sat with his parents, guarded as always by the Secret Service agents who hung in the background, for brunch at Tippecanoe Place, a historic and legendary mansion turned restaurant overlooking the St. Joseph River in South Bend. The proprietor had managed to find an alcove for the three to dine privately.

"That was an awesome speech, Dad," Finn said softly as he glanced over his menu.

"Yes, I agree, dear," his mother said, smiling. "And we are so very proud of you, Finley Daniel." Linda rarely used his proper name but said it now with adoration glimmering in her eyes.

"Mother, did I mention you looked stunning today?" Finn grinned at her as she blushed.

"Hey, what about me?" Leif feigned a hurt look, and the three of them shared a laugh.

"You look good too, Dad."

The waiter delivered plates of Belgian waffles covered in strawberries and whipped cream, shrimp and grits, and biscuits covered in sausage gravy to their table. The men ate every bite, while Linda had a seafood salad and fruit cup, always watching her weight.

As they were sipping on a second round of mimosas and coffee, Leif pulled out a tiny box wrapped in royal blue paper with a gold bow. It was the size of maybe a pen knife—*or car key*, Finn noticed, hoping.

"We are really proud of you, son." His father handed him the gift, beaming.

Finn carefully unwrapped it and opened the lid to find a single business card bearing his name, Finley Daniel Mitchell, with the initials, "J.D." following. Under it was the title, "Law Clerk" and the firm name, "Vance, Clay & Reed, PA," with the customary phone number and address—124 LaSalle Street, Chicago, IL.

He looked up to see his father gazing at him with misty eyes full of love.

"I ... I don't know what to say," Finn stammered, at a loss for words. "Does this mean ...?"

"Yes, a position at the largest law firm in Chicago, one of the top five in the country," Leif smiled proudly. Finn looked at his mother, and she nodded, tears in her eyes too.

"Thank you," Finn said, swallowing hard. *I can't very well tell them I had my heart set on the south where it's warm, now can I?* Finn had always disliked the harsh and gloomy northern Midwest winters and knew the Windy City could be worse than South Bend, Indiana, when it came to the bitter cold and snow.

"Of course, it's just a law clerk position until you pass the bar, which I'm sure won't be a problem, and then my friend Larry Reed will see to it that you become a full-fledged attorney."

In a private practice. Representing who knows who. Finn had always wanted to try his hand at being a prosecutor in small courtrooms trying cases to put criminals behind bars, defending the victims ... not the criminals themselves. *But how can I possibly say no to this opportunity?* He couldn't.

"Cheers to your new career!" Linda Mitchell raised her half-empty champagne glass, and Finn clinked his glass to hers, gulped down the orange juice blend and held it up for the waiter on standby to fill, then drank down another. But the drinks did nothing to ease his sudden anxiety. The party called college was over. Seven years of blissful schooling, even though tedious at times, would now end. *Life got real now.*

Finn entered the marble and glass lobby with its new LED chandelier sparkling in the vaulted ceiling like a beacon to those in trouble, needing a way out. Those with money to afford it, of course.

He boarded the elevator and hit the button for the twenty-fourth floor. He would be meeting his father's long-time friend and the current senior partner of the firm, Larry Reed. Vance had died many years back, but the legendary law firms never changed names that spelled success.

Finn stepped out of the elevator into a spacious, modern office foyer flanked all around by floor to ceiling windows that overlooked the Chicago skyline. It took his breath away, and he blinked to focus on his mission, turning to face the huge granite receptionist counter with a pretty, diminutive blonde giving him a pink-lipstick smile. "You must be Finley Mitchell?" she smiled politely, revealing perfect white teeth.

"You can call me Finn."

"You can have a seat. Mr. Reed will be with you shortly. Can I get you some water or coffee?"

Finn had already had three cups of coffee so his heart was practically racing. "I'll have some water, please," he said, heading toward the waiting room with its plush, burgundy microfiber-upholstered seating. The thin young blonde in her gray pinstriped suit and starched white collared shirt introduced herself and handed him a bottle of Fiji water, then swiftly and efficiently returned to her post.

Finn gazed out onto the skyscrapers that jutted up into the blue sky. This would be the vista he would see each day. *Not too shabby*, he mused. He felt comfortable in his brand new, fitted dark gray suit, another gift from his parents, but his new black Italian leather shoes they gave him to match would take some breaking in and getting used to.

"Mr. Mitchell, Mr. Reed is ready to see you now."

Finn realized he'd been so nervous he couldn't recall the young blonde's name and felt bad. "Thanks, uh—"

"Rebecca," she answered with the same smile, standing to shake his hand again and lead him down a hallway to a remote corner of the building, then through massive double doors. "Good luck," she said softly, almost in a whisper, and winked at him flirtatiously before exiting, shutting the doors behind her.

Finn saw the panorama of the Chicago skyline once again, although it was veiled by blinds that softened the room's lighting so it wouldn't be blinding. A large burgundy leather chair swiveled around, and his host stood to greet him. Lawrence Reed was an imposing figure, tall and well-built with a ruddy, tanned complexion and piercing dark brown eyes. His perfectly trimmed gray hair framed his clean-shaven handsome face. Many years of swimming, golf, and living well had clearly paid off.

He rounded the desk and firmly shook Finn's hand. "Nice to finally meet you. Congratulations on your graduation, Finn. We are looking forward to having you here at VCR."

Finn noticed he wore a gold wedding band on his left hand, and a matching gold Rolex peeked out from the starched cuff of his white shirtsleeve.

Larry motioned for Finn to have a seat in one of the leather wingback chairs in front of the large wooden desk. The office was tastefully decorated with a full-size globe in one corner, bookshelves full of law books and classics lining the walls, a Persian rug covering most of the hardwood floor, and some interesting sculpture pieces accenting dark wooden tables here and there. Finn glanced at the framed diplomas that hung on the left wall—Northwestern, Harvard, Yale.

"Have you heard of the 'loop elite'?" Larry sat back down in his chair and leaned forward, resting his elbows on some files which were arranged neatly across his desk.

"Yes, sir, I have." Finn sat up as straight as he could in his chair, although it seemed he was sitting lower than his superior, which was strategic he supposed. Of course he had heard of the term given Chicago's top law firms. He had done his homework before coming here and knew Vance, Clay, and Reed was ranked second amid all the city's law firms according to wealth and prestige, constantly vying for the number one spot with the top dog, Wade and Wade, PA. "And I am honored to be sitting here for this interview."

"Okay, we can cut to the chase," Larry Reed said abruptly, although still sounding friendly enough. "Your father is a close friend of mine. I've actually been to your grandfather's ranch and am one of the co-owners of a fine little filly sired by one of the studs at Little River. She won a few races back in the day."

Finn guarded his surprise. He hadn't followed the ponies closely like his father had, realizing over the years he had a light gambler's streak in him that could lead to dark places if he allowed it to take hold. He had never had a chance to ride since his dad and uncles had sold Little River before he was born. Plus, he had been busy with school and football—and girls.

Larry cleared his throat, bringing Finn's attention back into the room. "So, I know your father has spoken highly of you and thinks you would be a good fit here. And he also thinks highly of us and feels like we would be a good place for you to eventually hang your shingle. But what do you think?"

"I would be proud to work for you, sir, if you'll have me."

"Hmmm," Reed stroked his chin with his hand thoughtfully, then looked up, his eyes boring into Finn's. "I don't want any bull, son. I know you were wanting to be a prosecutor. And you know our mission is to eat prosecutors for lunch every single day." He looked at Finn seriously and then laughed at his own remark.

Finn forced a small laugh. *How could he possibly know I wanted to be a prosecutor?* He didn't think his dad even knew.

"You're correct, Mr. Reed, I did," Finn acknowledged. "And one day, maybe I still will. But in the meantime, I believe it might just pay off to work for the other side, to learn what I'll be up against."

"Good answer—smart man." Larry stood, his bulk casting a shadow across the room. "We can start you out in pro bono work, helping Marvin Fitch, chief of that department. What do you say to that?"

"I'd say sign me up. I'm ready to get started." Finn smiled, stood, and shook the senior attorney's strong hand across the desk as the nearby grandfather clock chimed and the bells of St. Peter's Catholic Church rang in the distance.

Marvin Fitch was a no-nonsense whip of a man—thin, balding with glasses, the typical nerd-like attorney Finn expected might head up the pro bono department. Today, he was wearing a white, button-down shirt and black suspenders. Finn wondered, suppressing a laugh, whether his pants would actually fall down without them.

Unlike the upper echelon of fee-paying attorneys who occupied the top twenty floors, the pro bono department was located in the building's basement. *So much for seeing the skyline every day,* Finn ruminated as he followed a harried overweight secretary to a desk behind a cubicle wall.

The offices smelled vaguely of sweat and cheesesteaks with fried onions, and Finn's stomach growled. He had only had time to scarf down a small yogurt in order to catch the subway downtown for his appointment with Mr. Reed.

All the filling out of paperwork and drug testing and touring the offices had taken hours, and it was now past lunchtime.

Finn longingly looked at a snack machine on the wall.

"No lunch, huh, dear?" Lois Dunlevy, the middle-aged plump secretary caught his gaze, peering at him over her purple spectacles that matched her grape-colored dress.

"Don't you worry, I'll get you a sandwich from the café in a bit. Go make yourself comfortable."

"Thanks, I am a bit hungry but—" She bustled away before he had a chance to let her know he could just do with a snack from the vending machine.

Finn knew he was going to like Mrs. Dunlevy way better than Rebecca the cheerful blonde, even though the top floor receptionist was easier on the eyes. Looks weren't everything, he knew after all his dating experiences. Lois seemed genuine from the minute he'd met her.

Five minutes later, as Finn poured over his first case Marvin Fitch had unceremoniously dumped on his desk, he looked up to find a corned beef on rye sitting there and his mouth watered gratefully.

"Make sure you eat a bigger breakfast tomorrow before you come in, okey doke?" Lois said with her midwestern twang, which Finn figured some might find annoying, but he found charming.

"Will do, Mrs. D."

Her face creased into a big smile, and she wagged a finger at him. "You're going to be trouble, I just know it. Welcome aboard."

CHAPTER SIX

Finn straightened his navy tie with the small gold ND emblem in his tiny medicine cabinet mirror. He appraised his newly cropped, golden-brown, wavy hair, sighing at the slight gray circles under his blue-green eyes that stared back at him now with a mix of nervousness and excitement. His white shirt made his complexion look somewhat tan even though it was still winter. He hadn't really seen the sun in weeks, holed up in his office by day and at night in his cheap second-floor Lower West Side flat. His apartment building wasn't located in a stellar part of town by any means, but it was close enough to work that he could walk most days and was affordable on his meager salary. His parents had offered to help him with the rent, but he had firmly declined. He wanted to pay his own way and be independent, even if it meant listening to the upstairs racket of occasional late-night brawls and the heat clanking through faulty pipes and a leaky faucet now and then.

Today was going to be a big day. He would be meeting his first client.

Finn had studied at night for three months straight that summer while working as a law clerk.

He passed the bar on his first try, moving up the ladder to become an associate attorney with Vance, Clay, and Reed's pro bono department within his first nine months, which had flown by.

They were deluged with cases due to the recent Coronavirus pandemic that had plagued the world, and which hit the United States particularly hard. While Covid cases had eventually subsided, and the virus was no longer as threatening due to a plethora of vaccinations becoming as readily available as flu shots, the fallout over the years was undeniable. Crimes were still way up, especially violent crimes, including alcohol-related homicides, domestic violence, and political protests resulting in crime.

Marvin was aided from time to time as needed by attorneys at VCR, but he mainly handled most of the cases himself, with the aid of his associate attorneys and law clerks.

Besides Finn, there were two other associate attorneys, several law clerks, and a small secretarial pool run by Lois.

While he was still stuck in the basement, Finn's workspace moved from a cubicle in the middle of the room to an actual office like Marvin's once he became a lawyer after passing the bar.

His job as an associate, at first, didn't seem too different from clerking. Finn helped Marvin handle the mounds of paperwork that piled up each day from the never-ending stream of cases, most of which were handled out of the courtroom through plea bargain arrangements.

Even though it was a far cry from being a prosecutor, which he still aspired to, Finn felt like he was learning a lot in helping the city's indigent population in need of defense attorneys and maybe even doing some good. He believed in the American right to be proclaimed innocent until proven guilty and to a proper defense in court, even when you couldn't afford one.

Nonetheless, Finn had objected to taking on Jay Walker's case, telling Marvin he'd rather one of the other associates handle it—that he was too inexperienced. He had done his homework and had seen pictures of Walker, a huge and scary looking Black gang member convicted of brutally murdering a liquor store owner in Chinatown. But being the lowest lawyer on the totem pole, so to speak, Finn lost that battle.

"Besides, it will be open and shut, most likely," Marvin had assured him. "This Walker dude is definitely guilty, there's no two ways about it. Still, we've taken on his case because we need to reach our pro bono quota, and it's a "JAB" issue, so if there's any chance at all we win, we'll be heroes. But no pressure, it would take a miracle for that to happen. I just need you to handle it."

Finn knew Marvin was referring to the "Justice for All Blacks" protest movement sweeping America over the past few years. *You'd have to be living in a cave not to know about it.*

He drank down his last cold swig of coffee and steeled himself, then headed out the door of the VCR building and into the icy winds coming straight into the coast from Lake Michigan. He hailed a cab to take him to the Cook County Department of Corrections.

Finn waited to be buzzed in by the security guard after showing his ID. Even though he was bundled in the thick wool overcoat, leather gloves, and

Shetland scarf he'd received from his parents that past Christmas, he shifted from one foot to another to try to keep warm, watching his breath escape in puffs of smoke.

He looked out into the distance where the razor-wired fence and gates surrounded the eight city blocks in downtown Chicago. Cook County was one of the largest jails in the country, a city in itself with its own health services facility, classrooms, food services, dayrooms, four sheriff's departments, and of course, thousands of jail cells. The group of monstrous brick and concrete box-like buildings on ninety-six acres that made up the facility was home to more than seven thousand inmates, with roughly one hundred thousand circulating through a year, although that number had decreased during the pandemic.

Jay Walker was Black as night, and his eyes had a vacant look in them, as if there were no light or soul within. Sleeves of tattoos covered his arms, a small lightning bolt was inked across his right cheek and another on his shaved head. Finn also noticed he bore the brand of the Vice Lords gang on his inside right wrist.

Even though it was cold inside the jail as well as outside, Walker wore no long-sleeved shirt under his short-sleeved orange uniform like some of his fellow inmates, revealing his dark bulging muscles and broad hairless chest.

If looks could kill, I'd be a dead man right now, Finn thought, sitting across from his client. He looked down at the rap sheet before him. The liquor store hold-up and murder was the latest in a list of crimes this man had allegedly committed, although this would be his first conviction if he were found guilty. Apparently, Jay Walker had managed to skate free on his prior arrests on theft, assault, and drug possession charges.

Large, sleepy brown and yellow eyes stared into his through the plastic window that protected him. He spoke through a microphone.

"Good morning, Mr. Walker, I've been assigned as the attorney in your case, and I'm here today to discuss it with you," Finn said, trying his best to keep his breathing normal and the sound of his voice as low and unemotional as possible.

Jay Walker grinned, revealing a gold filling on one front tooth while the other was broken and jagged.

Finn had to try hard to keep from cringing in his chair.

"Nah, I can't believe they assigned a rookie like you." The hulking inmate shook his head. "Just my luck. Look at that tie. They'd eat you alive in here."

Finn chastised himself for wearing the Notre Dame tie today of all days. He ignored Walker's comments and commenced to outline the case.

"While the evidence they have so far seems ironclad despite the missing weapon—your fingerprints on several store items, a spot of blood on the shoes they confiscated from your apartment, and the lack of an alibi—you, like everyone in this country, deserve a solid defense, and we at Vance, Clay, and Reed will—"

"This is a joke." Jay Walker was frowning now, clearly perturbed. He leaned back in the metal chair, crossing his muscular arms across his broad chest. "First, I'm framed by the police, then I get a shoddy lawyer like you. I ain't laughing, Mister ... what'd you say your name is again?"

65

"Finley Mitchell."

"Hah, Finley. Of course. Let me tell you something, *Finley*." The big man's voice was dark and mean like his visage. "Listen good 'cause I'm only gonna say it once. I didn't do it. I didn't kill that Asian store owner, and I don't know who did, although I 'spect I know who it was, but the cops have no interest in going after anybody else now that they got me behind bars. So either I need to know you believe me, or we're both just wastin' our time."

Finn loosened his tie and sighed, waiting a few moments before answering. "Why should I believe you, Mister Walker? And you can call me Finn."

"Because it's the truth, Finley."

Finn smiled despite his whereabouts and circumstances, hearing his proper name again. He felt a little punchy. Maybe he had had too much coffee. Suddenly he felt wired, and a thought crept through the fear-exacerbated fog that had clogged his morning brain. *Let's suppose, for just a minute, this guy is telling the truth.* "So maybe you can help me out here by telling me who you think *did* do the crime?"

"Yeah, right, if I want to be dead tomorrow."

Finn stood to go. "Well, Mister Walker, there's not much I can do with no new evidence, so I can just ask for a plea deal and call it a day."

He was nearly to the exit door to the visitor's hall when he heard his client say softly, "Wait a minute."

Finn turned and looked at Jay Walker sitting there. Was that humility he saw in those big brown eyes, veiled now with lids that looked weary? He sat back down in the hard-backed steel chair. "I'm listening ..."

"John Brown." It came out in a whisper.

"What?"

"Who. And that's all I'm gonna say. You'll have to figure it out."

And now it was Jay Walker's turn to stand and go. But he never looked back.

CHAPTER SEVEN

Finn knew he had his work cut out for him taking on Jay Walker's case, and he only had a few weeks to find out the truth, if that was even possible.

Of course. It would have to be a name like John Brown, Finn thought miserably as he combed through internet searches each night, getting two or three hours of sleep before waking up to start again. *Might as well have been John Doe or John Smith.*

But finally, something useful hit his radar screen when he found a John Brown who graduated from Notre Dame. He hadn't known John, but once he came up in the search, Finn explored his background and found he was an ROTC recruit who had gone on to obtain his degree from Notre Dame and sign up for the US Army. John was currently stationed in Washington, DC, working for the US Department of Defense.

Finn figured it was probably a fluke that *this* John Brown could possibly be the same man that Jay Walker told him to investigate, but he spent days searching anyway and was ready to give up when he finally hit what he thought just might be his golden ticket.

He stared now at the image on his computer screen—the face of John Brown, dressed in full camo, his head shaved. Even though it was just a photo, Finn could feel malice blazing out of those brown eyes, evil in the small, crooked smile that played across his face.

Put a black hood on the guy and it was the image of the man Finn saw on the playback video footage taken from the Chinatown liquor store—whose owner was robbed, shot point blank, and murdered—supposedly by Jay Walker, who was also seen browsing the aisles in the same footage.

Finn had watched the security video over a hundred times, had seen the partially hooded mug of the man—one of a handful of customers—but now he recognized that face. He had seen him on campus, and now here he was before him in muted color on his giant computer screen. Brown had been questioned by Chicago police detectives in the murder but was never a suspect once they had Jay Walker in custody. Finn scribbled some notes on a legal pad, made a phone call, and added John Brown's name to the list of witnesses to be subpoenaed.

Anthony Sorrell went into the bathroom of his luxury condo in Springfield, Illinois, to take a quick shower before work and caught his reflection in the huge, gold-gilded, brightly lit mirror. Many would call him strikingly handsome. He had his father, Leif's, chiseled features and blue eyes and his mother, Jackie's, dark complexion and jet-black hair.

He worked out each morning before court at a private gym, lifting weights and running on a treadmill, ate a healthy, low-carb, high-protein diet, and didn't drink or smoke. His one vice was coffee, which he preferred strong, hot, and black.

Tony leaned over the Italian marble vanity, which matched the walls and floor of the spa-like Roman bath with its sunken tub, walk-in shower, and roomy interior. His private interior designer had outfitted the entire condo according to his neo-classical tastes.

He picked up his razor and nearly nicked himself shaving, his hand slightly trembling. Today was the day. And he, Judge Anthony P. Sorrell, would be hearing the opening statements in the case of The State of Illinois vs. Jay Walker.

Ralston Warren had assured him everything was going exactly according to plan, but Tony wasn't so sure now that he knew his half-brother Finley would be representing the defendant.

Tony would be serving as the presiding judge in the Walker jury trial in the Supreme Court of Sagamon County, Illinois, where he had heard an array of civil and criminal cases almost daily for the past year—but none as important as this.

He had been elected to the position after working as a defense attorney at Wade and Wade, PA for several years following his graduation from Northwestern's Pritzker School of Law.

The Wade brothers who owned and operated Chicago's top law firm had hand-selected Anthony Sorrell from the incoming batch of attorneys as their most likely candidate to be groomed for the Illinois Supreme Court vacancy after interviewing each extensively. He was good-looking, well-spoken, highly intelligent, ambitious, and driven. Most importantly, he seemed to have the proper lack of scruples when it came to getting ahead.

The top partners that comprised the Wade law firm elite unilaterally decided to fast track the young attorney. Then they prepared him for the seat on the bench they knew would be opening due to a retiring judge, raising the money needed to fund Tony's campaign. It helped to have a sitting judge in as many Illinois counties as possible whenever changes of venue were granted.

And now they were cashing in with the trial of Jay Walker.

Tony had welcomed the judgeship, even though he despised the thought of staying in the Midwest with its cold temperatures and bleak landscape outside of Chicago. Still, it was easier for him to keep tabs on his younger brother, whom he hated with a passion.

All his life, Tony had yearned for the father-son relationship Finn had with Leif, one that he had never been able to enjoy since he'd been raised by his single mom, Jackie Sorrell, in New Hampshire, after she and his father had amicably divorced.

As part of a sealed divorce settlement with her ex-husband, Jackie agreed to forfeit her last name of Mitchell. She also agreed to Leif's request to never let her son—or anyone else—know of his true heritage.

So his father had never visited them in their ritzy suburban cottage in Bedford when he was a child, although Leif made sure he and his mother wanted for nothing and kept tabs on his son by phone.

Still, Leif wasn't there when Tony learned to ride a bike, to watch his Little League games, attend his performance on the cello in his high school orchestra, or for his graduations from Phillips Exeter, Dartmouth, or Northwestern. He never got to go on vacation with his dad, or even enjoy a Sunday dinner.

Then one day, Tony learned the truth about his father's identity when he took an at-home DNA test with a high school friend for laughs. He confronted his mother, and Jackie ended up telling him the test was accurate—that his father was none other than former US President Leif Mitchell. But she swore her son to secrecy, telling him if he wanted to keep his high school and college scholarships and his inheritance, he'd keep his mouth shut.

Tony had agreed, but from that day forward, he grew into a young man with a bitter resentment. Since it was hard to be angry with a father he never knew, he directed his jealous rage toward the one who received all the love, time, and attention that should have been his—his half-brother, Finn.

He had occasionally kept tabs on his half-brother. As far as Finn knew, it was purely coincidental they were both working in the state of Illinois now, both practicing law. Tony knew Finn had no clue they were related, since his last name was Sorrell. And in fact, he'd never actually met Finn, who was several years younger than he. But today would be the day when all that changed. The showdown.

While Tony had traced Finn's whereabouts through his fellow bar members, he had still been stunned several months ago when he saw his half-brother's name on the docket as Jay Walker's defense attorney.

No sooner had the docket hit his desk with Finn's name staring up at him than his intercom buzzed, his assistant's voice announcing he had a call from Ralston Warren.

Theirs was a strange relationship, his and Ralston's.

The retired US Department of Defense commander had served as a general under both his father and the next President of the United States before being honorably dismissed by the following Democratic President.

Tony had met Ralston at a huge Bar Association function in Chicago held by a mutual friend. Tony and Ralston hit it off, discovering they were kindred spirits as well as cousins, both being proverbial black sheep in the family. Tony saw the older Ralston as a man of great stature and a tough, stern, yet quiet composure who commanded—or rather, demanded—respect, even though some of his actions were reputed to be more than questionable in hushed, behind-the-scenes conversations. No one dared utter such accusations aloud, however.

Ralston Warren was known among the US people as having been one of the most capable and powerful Secretary Generals of all time. Even now at age sixty-seven, he had great influence on US politics and public affairs, which was often exerted for good. But he was also known as imperious, revengeful, and unscrupulous in his punishment of those who crossed him.

Although he'd retired from his military and political offices, Ralston Warren retained his power in a different way now. He was hired as a consultant by several former presidents and politicians as well as various power brokers. He played both sides of the aisle politically but was most loyal to whoever lined his pockets with the most cash, and many owed him for their political offices and fortunes.

Lately, it was rumored that those he was covertly "employed" by included a mafia boss and terrorist group leader, the powerful head of the anarchist, anti-fascist group, Antifa. The terrorist group had spurred many past and some present uprisings of radical protest organizations that were anti-fascist and anti-racist, turning some into violent bloodbaths. The current leader was known only as a billionaire terrorist, rumored to be Russian, who had never appeared in public but worked underground, mostly in the Eastern hemisphere. He went by the code name Lucifer.

It had been reported in the news that Lucifer protected his financial interests by controlling various people in high-ranking positions of political influence. He did this by paying them large sums of money or contributing to their campaigns to make sure they won or stayed in office to do his bidding. Lucifer's agenda reportedly was to cause chaos and anarchy to represent America as more divided than ever ... so that terrorists could once again gain a stronghold.

Ralston Warren had at first been reluctant to accept the undisclosed huge sum of money offered by a middleman to carry out his first JAB project. But after the first bribe, working for Lucifer had become quite easy. It wasn't like he ever had to interface in person with the mafia king—just make a few phone calls or use his connections.

This latest item on the agenda was a relatively easy one. Ralston had been told Chicago was the perfect city to carry out his boss's orders. And, of course, he had a relative in the perfect place and position.

Ralston Warren was first asked to choose a military officer who would be willing to take a risk and carry out a shooting in the name of Justice for All Blacks and to possibly take the fall if he was found out and arrested. Then, he had to select the right judge who could be bought to hear the case so this officer would get off easy—without doing time. John Brown and Tony Sorrell were the men Ralston chose. John because he had nothing to lose. Tony because he had everything to gain, plus he was family.

John was in ROTC to get through college, then was serving his first year of a four-year term in the Army when he was dishonorably discharged for striking a superior officer in a drunken brawl. Alcoholism ran like sap through the branches of John's family tree and hadn't escaped his DNA, so he never knew when to quit. The night he was on leave at the bar in Portsmouth, Virginia, he was in a total blackout. He would later be told the argument with his sergeant was over a billiards match he had lost, claiming his opponent had cheated. They were playing for ten bucks at the time. John was sent home and was facing a court-martial, which Ralston promised him would go away if the dishonored ex-officer helped him out. The former Department of Defense Commander was intimidating, to say the least. You just didn't say no to Ralston Warren after all. He was at the top of the food chain on which you survived.

John Brown was told the consequences of his actions—shooting the Asian liquor store owner—

would be minor if he was ever found out, but that this would be highly unlikely. The ex-Army officer wasn't told to shoot to kill. Unfortunately, he had been drinking that night too and misaimed his gun. He was a sharpshooter, so even though he knew he'd had a few highballs at happy hour and dinner, he still didn't know how this was possible.

John would later learn he had drugs in his system as well—that one of his drinks had been spiked with LSD, which not only made his eyesight blurry but made him hallucinate and cause him to miss the mark, causing the death of Bo Kim.

Someone on the Lucifer/JAB team had been planted in the restaurant where John dined, and while he was using the restroom, secretly spiked his drink. The team had decided long ago it would be easier to argue in court, if and when the time came, that John didn't know completely what he was doing when he shot Bo Kim. With the judge on John's side, even if he was discovered to be the shooter, his arrest would hopefully result in a conviction for aggravated assault, which would only carry a sentence of six months to twenty years in Illinois depending on whether the crime was classified as a misdemeanor or felony.

Ralston promised John he would get him off on the minimum sentence, or maybe even less, since they would know the judge and get him a crackerjack attorney, and he would also receive one million dollars in cash.

The former defense secretary had done his homework and knew John was hard up for money.

He was divorced with a small son for whom he was paying full child support. On top of that, the ex-ROTC officer didn't even receive veteran benefits because of his dishonorable discharge. And his drinking habit sucked up every dollar he put on his credit card until it was maxed out. John Brown was flat broke, so it was easy for him to quickly decide a million dollars waiting for him—plus pleasing someone like General Warren, who might help him get a position back in his beloved Army again—was well worth taking a chance that he might have to spend a few years behind bars.

"But it certainly will never come to that," the former DOD Secretary had said soothingly over the phone as they sealed the deal. "The whole point is to frame this Black guy, Jay Walker, who will be in the liquor store that night. He's the real sacrificial lamb. If all goes well, you'll walk out of this scot-free. Oh, and a million bucks richer of course."

Meanwhile, Ralston knew Tony was a man just like he was—shrewd, ambitious, who would do anything to get to the top ... and the top for Tony meant eventually landing a spot on the US Supreme Court.

If anyone could make that happen, good old cousin Ralston could.

Tony clicked on his large computer screen, and Ralston's face filled it. He noticed his cousin, fifteen years his senior, had aged quickly with time and stress. His marine-cut black hair had turned gray, then white over time, and had slid back with a receding hairline to make his big ruddy leather face even larger and paunchier, only now lined with deep wrinkles.

"We have a problem." Ralston scowled into the screen. The words you never wanted to hear come out of his mouth, in person or even over the phone—ever. No pleasantries, no "hello." This was serious.

"Ralls ... what's up?" Tony tried his best to sound nonchalant, although his heart was thudding.

"Have you seen the latest name added to the list of defense witnesses in the Jay Walker case?" Ralston growled. Tony was glad there was a distance of several states between them. His older cousin looked like a tornado ready to rip apart whatever lay in its path, his face looming like a black thundercloud across the sun.

"Uh, no ... but let me take a look." Seconds ticked loudly on the grandfather clock in his office while he scrambled to find the paper in the docket. The name stood out in fresh blue ink. *John Brown.*

Tony didn't have to say a word. Ralston yelled into the phone. "How did this happen?"

"I have no idea," Tony answered in a whisper, fighting not to be sick all over the paperwork on his desk.

"Well, you better find out. And fix it. *Now.*" The phone line went dead.

CHAPTER EIGHT

Today was the first day of the jury trial of the State of Illinois vs. Jay Walker in the Sagamon County Courthouse, Judge Anthony Sorrell presiding.

The few trees that lined the front of the mammoth brick courthouse building were budding green, sprouting hope the warmth of spring would finally arrive.

Finn didn't feel too hopeful, though, as he waited for the trial to start. He had discovered to his dismay that John Brown had been readmitted into the military, had been called out of the country on a top-secret assignment to an undisclosed location, and had been excused from his order to appear in court. *How convenient.*

Through the past two days of *voir dire*, Finn also noticed most of the jurors darting fearful glances in the direction of his client. Even though he was dressed in a suit and tie, Jay Walker still managed to look menacing. Finn had warned him not to cross his bulky arms so he wouldn't look defiant or to slouch back in his chair so he didn't appear uncaring or slovenly.

Finn had done his best to select the most jurors who might be sympathetic during the voir dire process. Still, he could tell most of the men and women seated in the jury box, whether White, Black, Hispanic, Asian, or otherwise, felt nothing but disdain toward the man who had shot the little, old store owner just trying to make a living in Chicago's Chinatown.

Prosecuting Attorney Ron Fletcher stood to give his opening statement. Finn's opponent looked a lot like a younger version of director Ron Howard, after whom he was appropriately named, his freckled young face crimson to match his red hair. Fletch, as he was known to his fellow bar members, stood six-feet-six-inches tall, was lanky, and had been a fairly decent basketball player in his high school and college days. Fletch had had high hopes to play professionally before a bout with diabetes in his twenties took him out of the game. He had become popular enough locally, though, and Tony and the Wade brothers had secretly asked him to handle the Walker case in hopes he'd sway some of the jury.

Finn stated he would defer giving his opening statement, which caused Judge Sorrell, Mr. Fletcher, the jurors, and even his client, Jay Walker, to stare at him in disbelief. He just needed a little more time to come up with something. *Something.*

The prosecuting attorney painted the cold-blooded murder as a tragedy. Bo Kim had left behind a wife, two grown children, and three small grandchildren.

Finn's opponent went on to efficiently question the police on the stand, who outlined their case against Jay Walker. All the evidence, minus a smoking gun which had apparently been somehow discarded, pointed to Walker. The case couldn't be more open and shut, the prosecutor had said in his opening arguments.

Now it was the defense's turn to present their case, and Finn called a few character witnesses to testify.

And then, the night before his closing arguments, he got the miracle he'd been praying for. Finn had received a phone call from the detention center warden letting him know an inmate by the name of Maxwell Simms had pertinent information in the Jay Walker case.

The next day, Finn called his surprise witness, Mr. Simms, to the stand. As he was calling him, the bailiff and a guard walked a prisoner in the side door. "Max" was a lanky, rough-looking older man with a five o-clock shadow, sunken eyes, and a comb-over. He was outfitted in full prison garb, the orange making his sallow skin look gray. His chains were gone, and now, the guard unlocked the handcuffs around his wrists and removed those as well. Max had received a twenty-five-year sentence for dealing drugs and was about to come up for parole in six months. If he testified, Finn told him he could hopefully arrange his hearing to be bumped up so that he'd only have to wait six weeks. No guarantees, but Finn did have some connections, he'd told Max.

The tattoo-covered prisoner nodded and smiled at Finn and Jay Walker as he walked into the courtroom, revealing half of his teeth were missing. *Here goes nothing*, Finn thought, whispering instructions to his client to keep his eyes focused forward and ignore his fellow inmate.

"Wait a minute, Your Honor, objection!" Ron Fletcher shouted his protest, his face as red as his hair. "Objection!" The prosecutor screeched the word again, flailing both of his long arms in the air. "We were not given advance notice of this witness, Your Honor."

"We just discovered this witness and his testimony last night, Your Honor," Finn said loudly, keeping his eyes on the judge. "I apologize to the court, but his testimony is vital to our case."

Finn gazed pleadingly at the jury, making eye contact with several of the jurors who looked at him suspiciously.

The courtroom filled with murmurs and rumblings that rose to the point where Tony Sorrell had to bang his gavel to maintain order. Finn could see the jurors now nodding in approval and knew Judge Sorrell could see them too. *They want to hear what this witness has to say.*

The judge wearily overruled Mr. Fletcher's objection but warned Finn to keep his line of questioning brief and to the point.

Max took the stand, looking almost amused that he was sitting up there in the limelight.

After questioning Max on his background and asserting that he had not been paid, bribed, or otherwise coerced to testify, Finn asked the prisoner if he knew Jay Walker. Max answered that he did know Jay as a fellow inmate. Then Finn asked his main question, not wanting to waste any of the court's precious time. "Do you know anything about Jay Walker that would be relevant to his defense?"

"I heard he was being set up to be the fall guy in a shooting to be carried out by this military guy, some sharpshooter dude who got away with it and pegged poor Jay here for the killing."

"Objection!" Ron Fletcher stood up and angrily shouted, pounding the table in front of him with both fists, his face scarlet now. "Judge, this is inadmissible hearsay! The jury has been prejudiced by hearing this witness's statements. I move for an immediate mistrial!"

"Judge, I would like to continue my line of questioning, and—"

"Mister Mitchell, that is enough!" Tony bellowed into his microphone, glaring at Finn now.

"But, Judge, I have the right to question the witness."

"Enough! One more word out of you, Mister Mitchell, and I will find you in contempt of court! Mister Mitchell, Mister Fletcher, I would like you to both approach the bench." Tony yelled in a raised voice above the din. "Quiet in the court!"

Guards appeared seemingly out of the courtroom woodwork, holding their hands threateningly on their gun holsters, and everyone else settled a bit while Finn and his opponent stepped forward.

Max just sat on the witness stand grinning at the circus-like atmosphere of it all.

Finn barely arrived at the bench before he spoke in a hushed tone. "Judge, I would like to either question the witness, or I'm going to call for a dismissal of all charges against my client and ask for his immediate release from prison."

Tony leaned over to whisper to the two attorneys so no one else could hear, covering the microphone in front of him with both hands. "Is that a threat, Mr. Mitchell? I don't take kindly to threats. If it is, trust me, I will send you out of this courtroom so fast your head will spin." The judge was seething now. He turned to the prosecutor. "Mister Fletcher? What do you have to say for yourself?"

Finn remained quiet as Ronald Fletcher stammered out an answer. "This is the first I'm hearing about this witness." He looked at his opponent. "I'm thinking this guy is pulling a fast one."

"Is that true, Mister Mitchell? Because if it is—"

"Of course not, Your Honor."

Finn looked at the judge, incredulous at his venomous demeanor. *What have I ever done to him?* Still, he knew it was wise not to cross him since he believed he would still be gaining a small victory with the declaration of a mistrial.

"Clearly, Your Honor, we can't continue this mockery of a trial now." Mr. Fletcher spat out the words.

"Take your seats, gentlemen," the judge ordered the two attorneys.

Judge Sorrell's gavel cracked loudly, hushing the din in the courtroom. Finn couldn't believe it was all over so quickly after it started.

"Ladies and gentlemen of the jury and those gathered here today, I am declaring a mistrial in the case of the State of Illinois vs. Jay Walker. Mister Walker ..." Finn had retreated back to his station behind the defendant's table and motioned for his client to stand up next to him. Jay nodded, at attention. "You will be free on your own recognizance until further notice. You have not been declared guilty nor have you been found not guilty. The state has the right to try you again at a future appointed date. Do you understand, Mister Walker?"

Jay Walker looked confused, and Finn put his hand on his client's shoulder. "I'll explain it to him, Your Honor," he stated to the judge, who turned his attention next to the jurors. "I'd like to thank you for your service, you are free to go." He stood tiredly, his black robes looking a bit worn and gray in the afternoon's light filtering through the courtroom windows. "Court is dismissed."

"All rise!" The bailiff bellowed as Tony quickly made his escape.

"Wow, I can't believe Jay Walker was innocent, and it was all a set up." Marvin congratulated Finn once again the next evening, toasting him with a plastic glass full of champagne in the pro bono offices of Vance, Clay, and Reed. "Tell us again how you think Brown was ordered to murder this liquor store owner ... and how that inmate Max found out."

"It's pretty complicated," Finn answered, weary from the past two weeks of the trial, during which he'd gotten very little sleep or exercise and hadn't eaten regularly, binging on junk food now and then. The champagne was already going to his head. "Basically, Max overheard another inmate talking, who knew John Brown when they were both in the Army together and involved in some drunken brawl. The inmate had stayed friends with Brown, who was drunk again and bragging about his sharpshooting capabilities and how he'd killed this Chinese liquor store owner for a million bucks. It turns out Brown was apparently ordered to shoot Bo Kim and make it look like Jay did it. Those orders came down a long command chain, but apparently it was all to rouse the Antifa protest movement once Jay was eventually freed after being jailed for several years. I'm still putting the pieces together, but it all seems to fit. Once I put my report together, I'm going to give it to the FBI to investigate."

"If that was the end game, I think it was successful, look at this …" Lois Dunlevy had turned on the small television on the wall of their offices and placed her half-empty champagne flute down on the desk to motion the handful of attorneys and clerks over to see the news.

"… As you can see behind me, people are already protesting en masse against the unjust incarceration of Jay Walker for a crime a White man committed," the young female Chicago news reporter said breathlessly, standing next to the defendant-turned-overnight-sensation and hero. Behind them, the city's dark night was lit up by fires and explosive flashes, a mob of protestors yelling in the background, carrying signs that read, "Justice for All Blacks," which had become the latest national and international catch phrase tweeted and posted on social media with the hashtag, #JAB. The reporter turned around as the sound of smashing glass was heard. "I'm on the Loop, and it's beginning to get violent as cars are being overturned, businesses are being looted, and police are under assault—" the Latino reporter suddenly ducked, then turned into the camera. "We are going to head for safety, back to you, Laura."

The phone started ringing, and Lois looked at the two attorneys with questioning eyes. Marvin nodded at her to pick it up, his eyes warning, *be careful.*

"Hello? Fox News, you say? Uh … yes, it is … yes, he is …" Lois held out the receiver toward Finn, her brown eyes large, mouthing to Finn, "It's for you."

The next morning, both Jay and Finn were dressed in suits, being interviewed on various national TV news shows by local correspondents in Chicago.

A few months after the trial, John Brown pled guilty to charges of manslaughter, claiming his weapon had "accidentally" gone off, killing Bo Kim, and Judge Sorrell sentenced him to five years in the county jail. Brown never revealed his marching orders.

As part of Brown's plea deal, a gag order was put in place by his attorneys at Wade and Wade, where the case would not be discussed further. Judge Sorrell approved the order and sealed the case from further scrutiny. Meanwhile, the JAB movement continued to gain momentum, although the violent outbursts quieted down after a time.

Jay Walker was declared not guilty, and all charges and the case against him were permanently dropped by the State of Illinois.

Maxwell Simms, meanwhile, received an early parole hearing, but his parole was denied.

After his success in getting Jay Walker off, Finn was promoted to a full-fledged defense attorney at VCR, where he worked for two years taking on some of the firm's most highly publicized cases and winning each one.

He became a rainmaker and was able to move out of his tiny apartment into a luxury condo in downtown Chicago.

Shortly after settling into his new home, Finn received even more good news—he was offered an appointment to become an associate judge of the Circuit Court of Chicago. He accepted. His upcoming placement on the bench was swiftly approved.

Several years had passed when the news hit that US Supreme Court Justice Robert Geller, who was suffering from Alzheimer's at the age of eighty-six, was declining in health. All of the news channels were predicting Judge Anthony Sorrell would be the top pick to take his place.

Judge Sorrell had received his own positive fanfare following the Walker trial in the years that followed. People were elated that the judge had set their hero free and had sentenced the real killer.

Video footage from the original Walker trial replayed on the news showing a confident Judge Sorrell walking out of the county courthouse building after declaring the mistrial. Political pundits and attorneys giving their perspectives said the judge had ruled correctly and that he would be a natural to fill Geller's shoes.

The September sun cast a fiery glow that flamed between the skyscrapers through the large picture windows of the law firm's boardroom. Ten members of the firm were gathered around the sprawling conference table, plus one judge.

Finn sat quietly at the table across from his former bosses, senior partners Larry Reed and Norman Clay, as well as pro bono division chief Marvin Fitch, and a handful of other top-ranking lawyers at Vance, Clay, and Reed. Mrs. Dunlevy had already served them all coffee and exited quietly. Tension filled the room. It had been a long day, and Larry had called them all together at five o'clock in the evening for an impromptu meeting with their former colleague Circuit Court Judge Finley Mitchell.

They had all heard the news that Justice Geller had passed away two weeks ago from Alzheimer's. The attorneys at VCR knew Judge Geller's death would most likely affect the outlook of many of their appeals cases, most not in a good way. Justice Geller had been more on the conservative side of the nine-member Supreme Court bench, who usually ruled in their law firm clients' favor. United States President Robert Newman, a Democrat, would most likely select a more politically liberal justice. Anthony Sorrell fit the bill perfectly.

"I just hung up the phone with Judge Sorrell," Larry said frowning. "I was calling to congratulate him on his news."

Finn heard the rumors but had no idea why he'd been called to this impromptu meeting.

"He apparently is officially being considered for the vacant Supreme Court seat left open with Judge Geller's death." Larry continued. "President Newman will, of course, have to declare a nominee for the vacant seat, which will then have to be approved by the US Senate through a simple majority vote. Apparently, I interrupted Tony during a big party they're holding in his honor." He looked at Finn. "I'm surprised you weren't invited, being a judge now."

"Well, I'm not. I'm probably the last person he'd want to invite." Finn cleared his throat, his impatience mounting. What was Larry getting at? He could feel all the eyes in the room on him now.

"Well, I certainly thought I would have been invited since every other top law firm in Chicago—and in the country—received an invitation," Larry said.

"Hmmm, I wonder if perhaps I wasn't invited due to a certain judge in the room?" He said it jokingly, but the smile on his face didn't reach his eyes.

"I'm sorry, Larry—there's nothing I can do about the fact that, for some inexplicable reason, Judge Sorrell does not like me—"

"I know Finn, I wouldn't have gone anyway. Or maybe I would have just to be a fly on the wall. It doesn't matter, it's a moot point now. It was clearly by invitation only. Sounds like quite the party. They rented the entire rooftop spa at The Peninsula hotel and spared no expense.

"I'm sure the champagne and caviar are flowing as we speak." Finn knew he sounded jealous but couldn't help himself.

The board room in which they sat was a stark contrast to the extravagant party under bright lights going on a few hotels away, the room filled with cameras and Hollywood stars. The attorneys sat glumly finishing their coffee. Larry stood and retrieved a decanter of whiskey from a nearby credenza. Lois had gone home, so he passed out highball glasses. "Here, at least we can switch to something stronger." Larry poured the liquor into his glass then handed the decanter to his right.

"I'm surprised your father wasn't invited either, since he is, after all, a former president," Larry said to Finn. "I'm sure he could have flown out here for it, right?"

"I guess Judge Sorrell knew he was too sick to make it. He's not doing well lately, according to Mom."

"How is your mother?" Larry asked, feigning interest.

"She's fine." *What's your point?* Finn wondered again, knowing Larry was always thinking ten steps ahead.

"I wonder how she would feel about you and your father not being invited?" Larry was instigating now. Finn was sure of it.

"I wouldn't know. What are you trying to get at, Larry?" Finn bluntly asked, noticing Marvin's eyes open wide in shock. Even though Finn was a judge now, Larry still held more power and sway as the senior partner of the biggest law firm in Chicago.

Larry sat up straight in his chair, downed the last of his whiskey, and leaned forward. "I'm also sure all it would take is a word from your father to President Newman and someone else could be appointed instead. I don't trust Anthony Sorrell, and I know you don't either. Your father is probably just too sick right now to care much. But I know someone who could, as they say, put a bug in his ear to make him care."

"Are you saying my mother could suggest someone else to my father, who would then suggest this person to the President?" Finn was putting the pieces together and beginning to realize the bigger picture of the puzzle forming.

"Exactly."

"But who?" Finn asked curiously. "Certainly, you're not suggesting ...?" He let his question dangle like a light bulb hanging from a wire.

"You, of course." Larry smiled at Finn.

"But how in the world ... I don't have the qualifications ... and the president already selected Judge Sorrell. Isn't it too late?"

"You do, and no, it isn't," Larry said, standing triumphantly to grab the whiskey and refill his glass. "But we have to act fast." Larry pulled out his cell phone. "And I know just the person who can facilitate it all."

CHAPTER NINE

Linda Mitchell had cut a few fresh flowers growing in the garden next to the gazebo in the back yard of her sprawling Potomac home and was arranging them in a crystal vase on the kitchen table when the doorbell rang.

"I'll get it!" Alisa Tomas called, peering around the kitchen door frame, a stack of freshly laundered towels in her arms.

"Thank you, Alisa," Linda smiled politely at the young woman, being careful not to prick herself on the thorns of the roses in the vase.

The beautiful young Latino woman cheerfully returned her smile, setting the towels down in a nearby laundry basket on the floor and smoothing the skirt of the black uniform dress she wore each day to work for the former president and First Lady. "You're welcome, Mrs. Mitchell." Thick, black eyelashes framed large, dark brown eyes in a face that could have easily belonged to a model or actress. But young Alisa was never given the opportunity. She and her three younger brothers and sisters had been raised in poverty, and Alisa had been made to work as a teenager cleaning homes after school to help her single mother afford the rent in the dilapidated two-bedroom apartment that housed their family of five.

Her black ponytail bobbed as she hastened to answer the door.

Linda looked jealously after her, painfully aware of the thirty-five-year gap in their ages. *I was that beautiful once*, she ruminated, mourning the loss of flawless tight skin, high cheekbones, and girlish figure. *Youth is definitely wasted on the young.* Sometimes she would let her imagination run wild and wonder if Leif looked at Alisa as anything more than a nursemaid, like he once had gazed at her all those years ago in South Carolina when they'd first met in the spa ... lustful, desirous, his eyes tracing her curves.

But Leif had not only grown older—in fact, he was a full twelve years older than she—but sickly too, suffering the past few years through chemo treatments for lung cancer. Still ... as Alisa leaned over to puff the pillows under his head, did he smell the lemony soap scent of her hair? Did he gaze into her eyes or long to touch her like he had Jackie Sorrell all those years ago?

Don't be silly, she often told herself. If she ever found any signs of impropriety, Linda would fire Alisa on the spot and make sure she never worked again, plus she'd have her deported back to her native Mexico along with her mother and four siblings and any other relatives they may be harboring here in the US. She was a pretty smart cookie, Linda knew. She wouldn't dare lose everything over a sickly old man, even if he had been a very handsome and powerful former president not too long ago. Plus, Linda believed her husband still loved her with all his heart, even though his body was incapable of showing it anymore.

Linda could hear a conversation, a man's amused deep voice mingling with the young girl's familiar one, and she grew annoyed. She laid down the scissors and patted her shoulder-length blonde hair into place. Then she dabbed on some lip gloss from an always-handy tube in a drawer under the kitchen island and walked out to see who her visitor might be.

A tall, attractive White man who appeared to be about her husband's age, in his early seventies, dressed in a tweed jacket, striped Oxford shirt, and jeans stood in the open doorway. He looked at her now with blue eyes that seemed to sparkle with mischief or mirth, she wasn't sure which, and gave her a charming smile. "Mrs. Mitchell, how very nice to meet you, I'm Peter Baldwin, dean of the University of Delaware and an old friend of your husband's ... and son's."

"Ah, Professor Baldwin! Won't you come in? I've heard a lot about you, how nice to finally meet you. I'm sorry our maid Alisa didn't invite you in right away. I guess I've instructed her to be careful with strangers, but as it turns out, you're an old friend."

Alisa held the front door open for the tall gentleman to enter, casting her eyes downward as he passed by her into the expansive marbled foyer and into the formal living room, where Linda motioned for him to sit in one of the winged-back chairs.

"Alisa dear, could you please get us some tea and cookies?" Linda smiled sweetly and sat across from Peter Baldwin on the leather couch, crossing her long, tan legs. She was dressed comfortably for the Indian summer weather in beige Bermuda shorts and a pink collared shirt, although even her casual clothes spoke of wealth.

"That's okay, Mrs. Mitchell, I can't stay too long, though I appreciate the offer." He nodded and smiled at Alisa, who gave a small curtsy and quickly left the room so they could talk in private.

"I'll get right to the point," he said, leaning forward, resting his elbows on his knees and folding his hands. "I have known your son for many years, and am quite aware of his integrity, intelligence, and potential."

Linda couldn't help but smile. She missed her son, so talking about him was a welcome subject, and she warmed to the formidable dean, who seemed quite sincere. "Why thank you Professor Baldwin, we are quite proud of our son."

"Please, call me Peter."

"Okay, Peter, if you'll call me Linda."

He smiled. "How is Leif doing? We go way back to our college days at Thomas More University in Kentucky."

Linda recalled Leif mentioning many years ago he was going to talk to his friend the dean confidentially about helping get Finn out of some trouble he had innocently gotten into at a frat party at the University of Delaware. She hadn't talked to her son in months, figuring he'd been busy. Suddenly she felt a rush of panic. "You came all this way to talk to Leif? Is something wrong? Is everything okay with Finn—"

"Everything is fine," Peter said quickly, reassuring her. "It was just a short drive. Actually, I came to see you. It's important, and, I hope, it's good news."

Linda relaxed, relieved her son was all right, but sat up straighter, curious.

"As you know, Finn made quite a name for himself in the Jay Walker case. I've followed the headlines and am quite proud of him, just like you and Leif are. In fact, I recently received a call from Larry Reed, a partner at Vance, Clay, and Reed, the law firm where your son was employed before he became a judge. Larry and I are also old friends. He called to tell me that Judge Anthony Sorrell held a big party last weekend to celebrate what appears to be his imminent nomination to the Supreme Court by President Newman."

Linda nearly dropped the teacup she was holding and sat it carefully down on the coffee table in front of her. She clasped both her hands together to keep them from shaking and pasted on a smile.

Linda knew, of course, that Anthony was her husband's son. But Leif had told her long ago they needed to protect Finn from finding out at all costs. As far as they knew, Jackie had never breathed a word to anyone.

This can't possibly be good, she thought now, feeling a slight sense of dread. *Did Peter ... or Larry ... know that Anthony Sorrell was her husband's son? No ... they couldn't possibly. So why was this man telling her about Anthony and his party?* She couldn't fathom the reason, so she remained silent and nodded for him to go on.

"I know this comes as a surprise, but I came to ask you to talk to your husband and persuade him to suggest President Newman change his mind on the Supreme Court nomination—from Anthony to your son, Finn."

Linda was stunned. "But I still don't understand. Why wouldn't Finn just ask me himself? Why are you proposing this? And does Finn even know?"

Peter Baldwin sat back in the damask chair. His brows knit together in a frown. He tented his fingers under his chin in thought before trying to explain. "Yes, Finn does know, and he didn't want to approach you or his father. Too humble, I guess. He's not even sure he would want the nomination if he were to get it. But Larry told me that all the attorneys in the firm, in fact, most lawyers in Chicago, would probably agree he's the better man for the job. And, of course, I believe this as well.

"Which is the 'why,' actually." Peter leaned forward and lowered his voice. "Even though he's qualified, Larry has inside information that Anthony ... Tony ... has been involved in some ... shall I say, shady dealings, and would be a bad choice for the position. I can't really get into specifics. Larry told me everything and would have come himself to talk to you, but he's wrapped up in a huge civil case with one of his big clients in Chicago. Since it was a relatively short drive from Delaware to your home here in Maryland, I figured I'd come down and talk to you personally. I'm sorry to drag you into this, but I realized Leif is going through so much with his cancer right now, and I didn't want to bother him with it all. I knew you were the closest person to him to discuss it—and could handle everything delicately and discreetly."

Linda told the professor she'd try her best as she saw him out the door. *He has no idea what he's asking me to do.*

Leif had been sleeping peacefully upstairs, taking his afternoon nap during her conversation with Peter Baldwin, and was just waking up as his wife walked into their master bedroom. Alisa had been puffing up pillows under the aging president's graying head and hurriedly bent to gather some worn socks from the floor into the laundry basket at her feet as she saw Linda appear in the bedroom doorway.

"Hey there, sleepyhead," Linda said, dismissively nodding at Alisa.

"I'll just be going, I have laundry to do," the young Latino woman said, taking the cue and picking up the basket.

"Thank you, Alisa," Leif said in a gravelly voice, reaching out his frail hand in her direction. The nursemaid smiled at him but kept her distance, then nodded again at Linda as she scooted past her out of the room.

"She's such a gem." Leif looked at his wife and smiled weakly. "But nowhere near as beautiful as you, my love."

Linda rolled her eyes and closed the space between the doorway and the bed, sitting on the edge and taking her husband's outstretched hand. It felt cold to her, and she tried to warm it between both of her own. "You're lying, but that's okay," she smiled, basking in the attention.

She bent down and kissed his cheek, his skin paper thin and cool to her lips.

He smiled and gazed up at her, his sea-blue eyes filled with love, even though the sparkle in them had faded.

"There's something I need to talk to you about," she said, propping him up further to a seated position against the pillows. "Actually, it's a favor I have to ask. It's about Finn ... and Tony."

"My sons," Leif said fondly. "How are they doing?"

"I guess both are doing well, although both seem to want the same thing, which is why I'm here. I've been told by very good sources that Finn and Tony both want to be nominated for the open Supreme Court seat vacated by Justice Robert Geller."

"Justice Geller ... where did he go?" Leif looked at her, his eyes glazed with confusion. Linda knew her husband was starting to slip. He had always been so sharp, but his age, his illness, and the treatments were starting to affect his mental acuity.

She inhaled, then exhaled patiently. "Remember, my love, he died several weeks ago? We saw it on the news."

"Ah ... yes, so sad. I will miss that man." Leif nodded in remembrance. "So, both of my sons want to fill the seat? Hmm ... only one can be nominated."

"Exactly. Which is where the favor I have to ask comes in. I was hoping you could recommend our son, Finn, to President Newman."

Leif looked at her, perplexed. "I realize Finn is our son ... but so is Tony."

Linda took a deep breath and exhaled. She wanted to say, '*Finn is my son, not Tony,*' but couldn't bring herself to do it. "Yes, but a very good friend of yours, Finn's employer Larry Reed, said Tony has been involved in some—he used the word 'shady'—dealings that would make him unfit for the job. Meanwhile, as we've seen on TV and in the papers, Finn's reputation is stellar."

"Did you talk to Larry about this?"

"Well, no, but I did talk to someone who did speak to Larry directly. Your old friend Peter Baldwin stopped by."

Linda proceeded to tell Leif the short version of everything Peter had imparted to her. "And to add insult to injury, Tony didn't even invite Finn or Larry, or you for that matter, to his big party to celebrate what he is calling his "imminent nomination"—even though it took place just blocks away from Vance, Clay, and Reed's office building."

Leif started to cough spasmodically, and Linda rushed to get him a glass of water from the adjacent master bathroom. His face was red when he finally regained his composure.

"Linda, come here," he commanded, and she sat on the edge of the bed. "You know what you're asking me to do, right? Choose between my sons?"

"I'm sorry you have to deal with this, but you are the only one who can make a call to President Newman and try to resolve this," she said. "And based on what two of your best friends are saying, there really isn't a choice."

"Why didn't Finn come to me directly?" Leif asked, weariness setting into his tone.

"I asked the same thing," Linda said. "Apparently, he didn't want to ask this of you. He was too humble, I guess, so he refused. But I think we all know Finn is by far the better man for the job, for the country."

Leif was quiet for a few moments, contemplating all he'd heard. Then he nodded and reached out his arms to embrace his wife.

Linda fell into her husband's arms. "Thank you," she whispered.

CHAPTER TEN

Tony and Ralston ordered another round of Bloody Marys as they watched the Senate hearings on the big screen TV. The large flatscreen hung over the bar just a few feet away from the maroon-cushioned booth where they sat in Rosebud's, a classic Chicago Italian restaurant, recessed below street level creating a dark, clubby feel.

Tony's eyesight blurred as he looked over the Italian menu. He was hung over with a pounding headache from the night before, and his stomach lurched at the thought of eating anything, especially the rich Italian fare the restaurant was famous for, but Ralston went ahead and ordered their usual—eggplant stacks and veal scallopine. A young and chipper waitress, who cheerfully introduced herself as Sally, smiled as she jotted down their order.

C'mon man, get it together, Tony told himself. *It's just a matter of time now before the last nail goes in Finn's coffin.*

Tony still reeled from receiving the nomination—and then having it snatched away like a Christmas gift from a kid.

Ralls had told him just a few weeks following Justice Geller's funeral that he was a shoo-in for the vacant seat. Ralston and the Wade brothers had made all the necessary connections—had talked in person to President Newman himself, in fact—to position Tony for the nomination. He'd even held a party for a few hundred guests in the penthouse suite of The Peninsula Hotel to celebrate.

And then Tony had received the President's call a few months later. President Newman had even apologized, saying another leading candidate had surfaced. "I know you are qualified for this, and you *were* my first choice for the nomination, but—" President Newman had begun over the phone that late fall evening. Tony had held his breath on this last word, fear overcoming his original anticipation. "—another candidate was presented to me since, and I'm afraid I have no choice but to consider nominating him instead. But don't give up hope, Anthony, there will eventually be another opening ..."

Before he'd had a chance to ask who and how and why, the president excused himself saying he had to run, and the conversation ended with an administrative aide coming on the line, thanking him politely for his service.

Outraged, Tony had called Ralston, and when Warren didn't pick up his phone, Tony called Stephen Wade.

"Huh," the middle-aged Wade partner said softly, seemingly not surprised at all at Tony's relay of the president's call. "I guess the rumors I heard were true."

Tony saw red. "*What* rumors?" he shouted into the phone.

"That former president Leif Mitchell called President Newman and asked for his son Finn to get the nomination over you."

Tony was shocked, as if someone had thrown ice water into his face. "Finn Mitchell is now going to get the nomination?" He'd practically shouted, not caring how undignified he sounded. *My brother Finn?*

"It looks that way." Before Tony had a chance to ask, Stephen Wade filled him in on the details.

The two presidents, although from different parties, had been tight over the years, even friends, and President Newman had often relied on Leif for his advice on a vast array of matters. And while Tony was in line with President Newman's party affiliation as a Democrat, the president knew he had to get the nomination approved by a Republican-majority Senate.

Unlike his right-wing father or left-wing brother, Finn was a known Independent, which would appeal to both parties, had vast popularity and notoriety with the electorate as his father had before him, and had a good chance of being quickly approved.

Tony was speechless as Stephen finished his explanation. He knew his father had always favored his half brother over him and that Finn's mother, of course, held sway over her husband, who'd been smitten with her from the day he met her. But to deliberately campaign for one son over another— would his father do that?

Tony realized he would, and he was so infuriated he had been on a drinking spree ever since.

Today at Rosebud's, however, he was ironically celebrating. The Senate had been conducting the televised hearings over the past two weeks to determine whether to accept President Newman's nomination of Judge Finley Mitchell. But as fate would have it, according to the media coverage, it wasn't looking good for the former president's son.

Tony now pushed the remnants of his second Bloody Mary and half-eaten balsamic glaze-drizzled stack of crispy eggplant and mozzarella slices aside, his stomach roiling.

"Get them to turn the sound up," he barked at Sally, who had come by to check on them. "And get us a double Scotch neat." She scurried to the bar, where the young bartender grabbed a remote and raised the volume before filling two highball glasses with their top-shelf malted liquor, glaring in their direction, apparently protective of her.

Tony downed his drink in one gulp, then watched as an elderly senator grilled Finn Mitchell, who sat cool and collected in his tailored navy suit and red tie next to his attorney, Larry Reed.

Republican Senator George Hodges, who looked to be a hundred years old, rasped into the microphone. "Why didn't you question your witness, Maxwell Simms, further during the Jay Walker trial? It seems you gave up a little too easily when you had him up there on the stand."

Finn hesitated a full minute before leaning over to whisper something in Larry's ear.

"Well, Mister Mitchell, I'm waiting," the old senator growled, his face puckering into a nasty scowl.

Finn spoke clearly into the microphone in front of him, enunciating his words. "It was out of my control once the prosecutor moved for a mistrial. I was prohibited from doing so."

"By whom?" the senator raised a white, bushy eyebrow.

"By the judge in the case."

"And who was that, pray tell?" The senator clearly did not think much of the young nominee being questioned.

"Judge Anthony Sorrell."

"Do you think it would have made a difference?" the senator asked gruffly.

Finn didn't hesitate before answering this time. "Absolutely. But it's a moot point now. All's well that ends well."

The senator's wrinkled face turned beet red, and he huffed and shuffled some papers in front of him, but he seemed at a loss of what to ask next.

"Is that all, Senator Hodges?" Larry Reed asked coolly into his microphone.

"Yes. For now. But I want to state for the record that Mr. Mitchell seems to be quite defensive in this line of questioning, and I want to retain the right to question him further on the trial as we get new information."

Score one for the home team, Tony thought, smiling into his Scotch.

Just then Larry Reed's son Hamilton Reed walked into the bar, nervously searching for someone ... until his eyes landed on the booth where Ralston and Tony sat. The young attorney strode over to them, looking distressed, running his hand through his unruly, sandy-brown hair.

"Hamm, what's up?" Ralston wiggled out of the booth and pulled a chair up from a nearby table, clapping the young man on the back and practically shoving him down to have a seat with them.

The waitress appeared, and Hamilton ordered. "I'll have what they're having ... not the food but the drinks," he said. "Let's start with two, I need to catch up to these guys," he said, winking at her. The bartender frowned in the distance, glowering at them.

Once she walked off, the young man's expression turned worried and serious again. "I'm afraid I have some bad news. Really bad," he whispered.

Hamilton was Larry's oldest son and had just passed the bar after several failed attempts. He was street smart but not academically intelligent, and he was determined to climb the ladder at his father's law firm, no matter what it took. His end game was to become richer than his father—heck, his dad and all of the partners combined for that matter—even if it meant working with the enemy and double crossing his father, who always seemed to put him down anyway.

Hamm often hung out behind closed doors at Vance, Clay, and Reed, PA, and as a result, ended up with very valuable inside information he could sell at a premium price to the Wades. He worked as a double agent, a snitch for the Wade brothers, and had gained inside intelligence by hanging out in the Capitol building in DC. Young, good-looking, charming, and well-known, Hamm became everyone's friend and confidante in the halls of Congress.

Hamilton Reed was also backed by the deep pockets of Lucifer and Ralston Warren. As the Senate hearings on the Supreme Court nomination for the open seat vacated by the deceased Justice Geller were conducted, Hamm had paid informants and lobbyists to glean any information he could. He then started paying for the senators' votes against Finley Mitchell to pave the way for Tony's subsequent nomination.

And the reports had looked good so far. Until now.

"It looks like a few votes have turned in the past twenty-four hours," Hamilton whispered. "Finn Mitchell's nomination is going to go through, I'm sorry to say."

"Sorry to say?" Tony's voice raised an octave. "Sorry to *say*?" He nearly squealed the word, and a few nearby diners turned their heads to peer in the direction of their booth.

Hamilton's face turned a shade of pink, and Ralston glared at Tony, imparting with his stare that Tony needed to hush up.

"That's a lie," Tony said under his breath, lowering his voice. "If you're playing us, Hamm, so help me I'll—"

"No, I swear it's true."

"How do you know? How is that even *possible*?" Fear choked his words out into a high-pitched, strangled question. "Surely they had enough evidence provided to them that they'd vote against the appointment?"

Tony did a mental calculation of the "facts" mounted by the secret team of researchers hired by Ralston and the Wades against Finley Mitchell. Those facts were then provided to the senators ahead of the hearings along with bribes to those who accepted them.

There was the proof Finn had participated in the University of Delaware hazing that was responsible for the near death of that college boy, Tommy Sentry. There was the allegation he'd slept with Trinity Foster Dobbins behind his law professor's back—the same professor she'd married and had two kids with.

And then there was the ultimate trump card they'd played—the fact that Finn Mitchell had gotten his client, Jay Walker, off by playing dirty, putting a shady prisoner on the stand, and thereby forcing a mistrial in the murder trial of Bo Kim. They flipped the script and claimed John Brown had been framed, then persuaded some reporters to air this latest piece of information, stirring the proverbial pots of every white supremacist and radical right-wing group they could find throughout the country. They'd started in their fair city of Chicago, secretly sparking protests of thousands. The mobs were mainly made up of people sick of the JAB movement who urged their senators not to accept the president's irresponsible nomination of an attorney who'd championed the freeing of a Black man who'd been charged with gunning down an innocent Asian store owner in cold blood.

Tony knew they'd had enough votes against the nomination as of just yesterday. *So ... how?* Tony was livid and incredulous at this latest news, trying to wrap his head around it.

"I have a source high up in the cabinet who confirmed the nomination is going to be passed tomorrow morning," Hamilton said quietly. "It's going to be close, a 51-49 split, but all he needs is a simple majority."

Ralston was eerily silent. Tony couldn't even look at him now, because he knew the ex-military colonel's cold gray stare would be filled with disappointment—no, disdain.

"I've got to get some fresh air," Tony said, climbing out of the booth and heading up the stairs and out the door into the bright midday sunlight of the city.

He gulped a few breaths of air, laden with car smoke from the thick traffic that crammed the city streets and started walking briskly toward Lake Michigan.

As he marched on, his head bent into the collar of his overcoat to hide his face from the winter wind, a dark cloud grew on the horizon, it started to thunder, and then, the sky opened up in a downpour.

Tony cursed the sky, the thunder, the rain, and the God who made them. Hate seethed in him like black, burning tar, and he put on sunglasses to hide the tears that stung his eyes. No one could see them, though, since they mixed with the rain that pelted his cheeks.

His own father had rejected him, his brother had betrayed him, and God himself had turned on him. He knew that even his cousin Ralston, his champion before now, held contempt for him. He was a complete and utter failure.

Walking for nearly a half hour, Tony approached the edge of the cement wall that bordered the lake's icy water below. The driving rain had stopped, and he shivered, but not because of the cold, and put one foot up on the ledge. *No one would even care if I jumped.*

CHAPTER ELEVEN

The South Lawn of the White House was swarming with professionally clad guests including dozens of select reporters, members of Congress, the eight other Supreme Court justices, Larry Reed and his law partners, Peter Baldwin, and former First Lady Linda Mitchell, who was seated in the front row of folding chairs. Unfortunately, President Leif Mitchell was too sick to make the trip.

Linda was smartly dressed in an emerald-green short jacket and skirt which perfectly matched her eyes, a cream-colored silk blouse underneath. The blonde highlights in her hair, blown by a gentle breeze, were accentuated in the midday sun, and her smile radiated to all those gathered. She sat next to First Lady Joyce Newman, who was also stunning in her royal blue suit and matching heels.

After a brief version of Hail to the Chief, the announcement sounded over a speaker. "Ladies and gentlemen, the President of the United States accompanied by Justice Richard Blackwell and Justice Finley Mitchell."

President Robert Newman walked out of the White House doors and up to the lectern set up at the front of the lawn, followed by Finn, who stood to the president's right facing the audience, an American flag behind him, and the Chief Justice of the Supreme Court, who stood to his left holding a Bible.

"I'd like to thank everyone gathered here on this momentous occasion," President Newman said as the cameras clicked loudly. He was short and somewhat overweight, but a tailor had designed a slimming navy suit that made him look trim. He had a new haircut and sported a fashionable blue and white striped tie, both making him look distinguished and younger than his seventy-two years of age.

Yet people would comment the new justice being sworn in was who turned most heads that day. Finn was dressed in an impressive dark gray-blue suit and signature red tie, his light brown hair blowing in the wind. His smile lit up his face, which was tanned from the few days he'd spent golfing with friends in Kentucky to celebrate after receiving the nomination.

"I'd like to welcome all of the friends and family gathered today including Justice Mitchell's mother, First Lady Linda Mitchell," the president smiled and then introduced the other eight Supreme Court justices, including Chief Justice Blackwell, whose robes swirled around him in the breeze. "I'm sorry President Leif Mitchell could not be here to join us," he added after the introductions. "I know he is quite proud of his son, Finley.

"Today is a joyful occasion for me, as it is my honor to appoint such a qualified young man to the seat vacated by the late Honorable Justice Robert Geller, may he rest in peace." After thanking the late justice's wife, the president went on to list

Finn's credentials. "Justice Mitchell is wise beyond his years, and I am sure he'll impart his gift of wisdom to rule on the bench along with the other eight justices fairly, impartially, and with respect to the Constitution which he upholds—and will serve this great nation and the American people with the dignity and integrity he has shown thus far in his practice of law.

"I'd like to apologize to Justice Mitchell and to his parents, President Leif Mitchell and First Lady Linda Mitchell, for the indecent scrutiny and witchhunt the Senate inquiry became in the name of politics," President Newman concluded, harkening back to memories among the media and guests of Justice Brett Cavanaugh's swearing in ceremony by President Donald Trump years ago. "Thankfully, all's well that ends well, and justice was served."

He waited for the subsequent round of applause to quiet down again before continuing. "With that, I would like to ask Chief Justice Richard Blackwell to come forward to conduct the swearing-in ceremony. And, ladies and gentlemen, this is an especially significant moment because the Bible Justice Blackwell is going to use is none other than the same used to swear in Justice Mitchell's father as President of the United States many years ago. Today we witness history ... a father and his son serving two of the three branches of our government within their mutual lifetimes, both dedicated to uphold and defend our Constitution and the freedom of all Americans."

Linda Mitchell stood and stepped forward onto the stage to join her son. Finn raised his right hand, holding his left upon the cherished Bible, held by his mother now, upon which his father had laid his hand so many years ago. Justice Blackwell then asked him to repeat the words of the judicial oath.

"I, Finley Mitchell, do solemnly affirm that I will administer justice without respect to persons, do equal right to the poor and to the rich, and that I will faithfully and impartially discharge and perform all the duties incumbent upon me as a Supreme Court Justice under the Constitution and laws of the United States. So help me God."

Finn hugged his mom, warmly shook Justice Blackwell's and President Newman's hands, then took the lectern to deliver a brief address.

He thanked all three, then recognized the other eight justices, as well as First Lady Joyce Newman, Peter Baldwin, the partners of Vance, Clay, and Reed, and his fellow justices.

"Thank you, Mister President, for appointing me to the nation's highest court," Finn began in a humble tone. "I am grateful to you and Mrs. Newman both for all of your support through this process. I am honored to serve with my colleagues gathered here today. I am grateful to my mother who is here by my side, and to my father who sadly could not join us, but I know is here with me in spirit."

Finn still held the worn leather Bible in his hands and held it up with a proud smile as the crowd cheered. "I have been inspired by both of my parents who have so honorably and fearlessly served this country we all love. I hope I can also bring justice and honor to the Supreme Court in the years to come. I pray that God grants me the wisdom to serve well. I intend to work hard to fulfill my duties to which I've been appointed, to be a faithful servant to the

Constitution and laws of this great country, to humbly serve this one nation under God, and to follow these words out of the Book of Wisdom—" Finn opened the brown leather Bible to the page he'd bookmarked and read the first line. 'Love righteousness, you who judge the earth; think of the Lord in goodness, and seek him in integrity of heart.' I will seek to do this to the best of my ability, with all my heart, mind, and soul, so help me God. Thank you."

Finn followed his mother, Justice Blackwell, and President Newman, joined by the First Lady, into the White House accompanied by "God Bless America" blaring over the speakers as the audience gave them a standing ovation.

Give me a break. Tony watched the proceedings on his big-screen TV at home.

He hadn't had the courage to jump into the freezing cold lake, although he'd wanted to the day the Senate voted to pass the nomination.

So instead, he'd gone home and drunk himself into a stupor.

He was halfway there again as he sat on the couch in his fancy condo, viewing his pompous half-brother prattle on at the lectern after his swearing-in ceremony.

It should have been me. He swore, chugging down a tumbler full of Scotch and pouring a second refill, and then a third. *I should have taken old Judge Geller's place. I deserved it far more than my dumb brother. Just because my mother wasn't as pretty or as controlling or as conniving as Finn's tramp of a mother was ... just because she was a lowly maid Leif Mitchell could marry then toss aside, and his mom was a woman he lusted after ...* He threw his glass at the marble fireplace on the far end of the living room, smashing it into bits. *Well, what goes around comes around. That brother of mine will get his comeuppance. He'll fall off that high and mighty throne of his. It's just a matter of time ...* and then his anger dissipated as fear started to grow deep down in Tony's core. What if Finn learned the truth of all he and Ralston had done—conspiring against him both in the Jay Walker trial and the senate vote for the Supreme Court nomination?

He swallowed the lump in this throat.

Maybe Finn would never find out the details or about his involvement.

Tony refilled another glass with Scotch, but his hand trembled so badly holding the glass that he set it down again on the end table and then sat back down on his living room sofa, holding his head in his hands.

He didn't know what to do when a thought hit him. The local Catholic church was open just a few blocks away. *That's it, I'll just go in and say some prayers,* he thought, heading to the bathroom to brush his teeth and throw on some cologne to freshen up so no one could smell the liquor on his breath or the fearful sweat oozing out of his pores.

Leif watched the swearing-in ceremony from his bedroom television set with Alisa by his side, she placing a warm cloth on his forehead and giving him sips from an Ensure milkshake every now and then.

After the ceremony, Linda came home to find her husband cold even though Alisa had covered him with several quilts and blankets. Finn arrived shortly after his mother, who was talking quietly to Alisa upstairs in the hallway.

They motioned for him to go into the master bedroom.

"Hi, Dad," Finn said, mustering a cheerful countenance. "Did you see us on TV?" He walked up to the side of the bed and took his father's cold, waxy hand in his own. *He's so thin and frail*, Finn realized. Still, he forced a smile.

"I did son, and I was very proud," Leif said, then rattled out a cough, trying to catch his breath before continuing. "Finn, you know I don't have much longer on this earth. You'll have to be strong for your mother once I'm gone."

Finn protested, fighting tears. "Sure you do, Dad." He pulled up a nearby chair to better hear his father's words, which were coming out in short, winded rasps.

"None of us have forever. So just listen to me while I still have a few breaths left in this tired old body. First, you need to be wary of a few people, including Judge Anthony Sorrell. In fact, Finn, there's something I need to tell you, something you need to know." Finn sat patiently as his father coughed again and then settled back down. "Before you were born ... before I married your mother ... I was married to a woman named Jackie. We had a son, and he is living today. We got divorced, and they moved out of state. I haven't seen either one for many years. That just seemed to work out best for everyone."

"I have another brother?" Finn asked with complete surprise. "Where does he live? What does he do? What's his name?"

"Well, son, you're going to find this hard to believe, but Jackie's last name is Sorrell. Your brother's name is Anthony—or Tony."

Finn inhaled slowly, making the connection and almost forgetting to breathe out, suddenly feeling light-headed. "Wait! Are you saying that Tony Sorrell ... Judge Anthony Sorrell ... is my brother? That can't be!"

"I'm afraid so. Finn. I don't have enough time to tell you too much. Just know that you have to be very careful around Tony. I believe he is very resentful toward you."

"What did I ever do to him? I didn't even know he existed until just now!"

"I know, but I think he took all of his anger with me out on you. I believe he is jealous of you, and now that you have become a Supreme Court judge instead of him ... well, there's no telling what he'll do."

Finn sat silently, processing it all. Suddenly he had flashbacks of the trial, Tony's hateful glare, not being invited to the party—

"Another thing. I think Tony has been involved with Ralston Warren."

Finn vaguely remembered Ralston, whom he'd only met on two occasions at family gatherings. Although they were distant cousins, Finn didn't really think of him as family. He'd always sensed a cool reserve between his father and Ralston, so he'd stayed away from the military commander, who was aloof anyway.

"I'm pretty sure Ralston and Anthony have been up to no good." Leif paused, waiting until his next coughing spasm quieted down before talking again. "Ralston was the head of the Department of Defense and one of my chief advisors. But something I confided in him ... how I met your mother and what I did to eventually end up marrying her ..." Leif's face turned red and he started coughing again uncontrollably, his body shaking.

Finn ran to the adjoining bathroom and brought his father another cup of water, helping him sit up to drink a few sips. As his father finally regained his breath, Finn said quietly, "Dad, I know all about what happened with you and Mom. How you had mom's husband ..." he let his words trail off, watching as his dad's eyes became downcast, and he lay his head back on the pillow again wearily.

"I have a lot of sins I've committed over my seventy-seven years of life for which I need to atone," Leif whispered. "I am most ashamed of what I did back then, but if I never married your mother, I would have never had you as a son, so I guess God did have a plan. The reason I'm even bringing it up now is that I want you to know Ralston ended up using what I told him in confidence against me. I don't trust him, and I believe your brother Tony is tangled up in his web, so you shouldn't trust either of them."

"What did Ralston do?"

"What he did isn't important, and my connections were stronger than his, so his betrayal didn't get him very far. And since I've been so sick and weak, I didn't pursue it further. What's important is you now know to be wary of anyone that's tied in with him. And that includes your half-brother, Tony." Leif lay back exhausted and pointed to his nearby nightstand. "Open the drawer."

Finn opened the top drawer to the nightstand. In it were a few items his father used regularly—lip balm, reading glasses, a magnifying glass, and a large print Bible, on top of which lay a single business card. Finn picked up the card and looked questioningly at his father, who nodded, saying "read it." The plain white card had the name Richard Layton on it and underneath that, the title Private Investigator with a DC phone number. "That's it. Call him after ..." Leif went into another coughing spell, and Finn held the glass of water to his lips again. "Just call him. He knows what is happening, it's too much to explain now ... not enough time."

Finn's eyes filled with tears, but he held back his emotions and patiently sat, holding his father's hand as he listened to his heavy, ragged breaths. Finally, his dad spoke again. "I know you'll do a fine job on the Supreme Court, Finn. When you were swearing-in on the Bible—the same one I was sworn-in on—I thought, this son of mine will be a great leader, better than I, and I said a prayer of thanks to God that I could be here to see it. Just always make sure you do God's will and walk in his ways. Always keep his commandments and you'll succeed in all that you do."

Even though it felt like a sauna in the bedroom— the heat was turned on high and his father was covered in multiple quilts and blankets—Leif shivered with cold, and his hands felt like ice. Finn was sweating in his polo shirt and shorts. Suddenly, he noticed his father grow silent, saw his father's eyes flutter, watched as he took one last wheezing breath, then lay there lifeless.

"Mom ... Mom!" Finn yelled.

CHAPTER TWELVE

The national funeral was held on a cold, gray DC morning, the first day of winter. Snowflakes flew through the thick, raw air, and people moved quickly down the city streets seeking warmth.

Still, over two hundred thousand people flocked to Washington to pay their respects to their beloved president over the course of the week, to get a chance to enter the US Capitol building where President Leif Mitchell's body lay in state in the rotunda, his closed casket guarded by members of the armed forces. The public stood in long lines waiting up to seven hours for a turn to say goodbye. About five thousand people per hour passed the casket.

After three days of lying in state, the doors of the Capitol were closed to the public, and Finn escorted his mother in, where she had a moment alone with her husband. A military honor guard entered and carried the bronze casket down the west steps of the Capitol to a twenty-one-gun salute, where Linda met it, holding her hand over her heart. The casket was placed in a hearse, then proceeded behind a multitude of police escorts and limousines that snaked along several blocks past the US Capitol building and then to the Basilica of the National Shrine of the Immaculate Conception. Crowds lined the route as the parade made its way.

President Newman declared the day of the funeral a National Day of Mourning. Washington had all but shut down as the roads were snarled with government and business traffic. Most of the people in DC either crammed onto the mall to watch on jumbotrons erected for the occasion or stayed home to view the historic event on their TV screens. It was the biggest gathering of people, VIPs, and statesmen across the world—and of television viewers—ever recorded in history for a funeral. The numbers were even larger than those attending and viewing the funerals of Presidents Bush, Reagan, and Kennedy.

Finn's other half-brother Harry, the late Chessa Mitchell's son, sat in the first pew to the right facing the altar next to he and Linda. They were all that was left of the family along with Tony, Jackie, and Ralston who sat together in the far back of the church. Leif had outlived his parents, three brothers, and a half-sister.

Three living presidents and their wives sat in the front pew across from them including Robert and Joyce Newman. Many other dignitaries packed into the church behind them—leaders from two hundred countries across the globe including the King of England, several former vice presidents, all fifty governors, several cabinet members past and present, the Supreme Court justices, a host of senators and congressmen, cardinals and archbishops, and many more dignitaries—the largest gathering of world leaders for a funeral ever. Altogether six thousand people packed the church.

Finn delivered the final eulogy, following many other remarks given by several presidents, kings, and heads of state. "On behalf of our family ..." Finn began, smiling at his mother, "I want to share a bit of what life was like growing up—not in the shadow but in the light—of President Phillip, or as many of you know him, Leif Mitchell." Finn shared some childhood memories of life with his father—fishing on the Potomac, apple picking at the local orchard, Thanksgivings and Christmases spent volunteering at the local food pantry or with the Salvation Army. "I missed a few holidays with Dad when he had to fly halfway across the world to bolster morale with the troops overseas, speak at a charitable fundraiser, visit a sick friend ... but now I realize he was always looking out for others, which made me appreciate when he was around even more.

"I loved when Dad would pick up his guitar and play a song he'd written," Leif recalled fondly. "Sometimes he'd make one up on the spot. There's one I'd like to share with you now.

He knew he was no Leif Mitchell, who had actually been a recording artist, but Finn did have a fairly decent singing voice, and although it cracked with emotion at times, he was able to sing the words to one of his favorite tunes his dad had written and sung to him when he was a boy called "Inherently Good." The song had comforted him all his life when he was filled with doubt or fear, and he sang it now a cappella to comfort himself and the people in the pews.

> When times get rough, and you want to give in,
> And it's hard to do the things you should,
> Remember, my boy, that God is watching,
> And he made you inherently good.

When it's tempting to settle for the middle road,
And to do less than you normally would,
Remember, my boy, that God made you for more,
That he made you inherently good.
When you've come to the end of your days on earth,
And you feel you've done all that you could,
Even though it may seem like it's not enough,
Rest assured you were inherently good.

Finn's eulogy and song was followed by the Washington Performing Arts Gospel Choir singing "Amazing Grace" and "How Great Thou Art," and then the Christian band MercyMe singing their hit song, "I Can Only Imagine."

Later that day, after the service, Leif Mitchell's casket was transported on Air Force One to Louisville, Kentucky, near where the president had grown up on his family's horse farm and where he'd resided as governor.

Leif's casket was then driven in a motorcade to Zachary Taylor National Cemetery, named for the twelfth president of the United States who was interred there along with Leif's parents and brothers.

Thousands again gathered on the cemetery grounds around the tent reserved for immediate family and a few friends.

Finn sat next to his mother facing the coffin draped in the American flag, hugging her as she wept the tears she'd held in throughout the day as a single military bugler played "Taps."

A twenty-one-gun salute followed in the field next to the cemetery, then Father Michael Finnegan, who'd presided over the Mass, delivered a final benediction and prayer. A representative from each branch of the military stood at the four corners of the casket, then slowly and reverently folded the flag into a tight triangle. An Army officer knelt before Linda Mitchell and presented the folded flag to her, then they all stood, saluted, and crisply turned and walked off.

Finn held his mother's hand, and together they walked up to the now bare casket. He watched, letting his tears finally flow, as Linda Mitchell bent over and hugged the casket, saying her final goodbye.

US flags across the country and around the world were ordered to be flown at half-mast for thirty days in a presidential proclamation by President Newman.

Linda Mitchell invited about two hundred family members and friends back to the mansion and its now-tented grounds for a catered dinner following the interment, including her stepson, Tony, and his mother Jackie Sorrell, Chessa and Leif's son, Harry, Peter Baldwin, Finn's partners from his law firm, her bridge and tennis club friends, and several close former friends and colleagues of her husband's. Ralston Warren was not invited. No one dared question the former First Lady about her nephew's no show—nor the strange appearance of Judge Tony Sorrell. Most didn't notice, the rooms were so crowded. Alisa Tomas was a guest, not a servant, at the catered affair hosted by a locally sourced farm-to-table outfit that brought in dozens of wait staff and servers.

Finn was at the indoor bar set up in the mansion's expansive banquet room getting a glass of wine for his mother when he noticed, in his peripheral vision, Tony approach Alisa and pull her into a far corner, whispering in her ear, causing her to smile up at him.

She was outfitted in a flowered black and pink print dress that flattered her slim yet curvy figure, flouncing out above her knees, revealing her long tanned legs. Her black wavy hair was pulled up on one side, held by a hot pink flower which matched her lipstick and shoes. She was stunning and captured glances from all the men in the room, over and above those drawn by Linda Mitchell, who was also beautifully but much more somberly dressed in a black tea-length dress and matching jacket.

"You're not jealous, are you?" Linda asked her son.

Finn turned to see his mother gazing at him with concern as he handed her the glass of chardonnay he'd brought her.

"Of course not." Finn questioned himself for a moment, his ire at his half-brother rising. He wasn't jealous. *But* ... "I just don't trust him." Finn gazed again at Tony, who bent conspiratorially toward his father's former maidservant, the two of them breaking out in laughter together.

Neither Linda, Finn, Tony, nor Jackie had ever told another soul about the fact that they were linked together through Leif. None of them wanted the truth to come out, so it stayed buried. Ralston was the only other family member who knew that Tony and Finn were half-brothers, and he certainly didn't want anyone else to know, much less the media.

Finn's attention was suddenly diverted by Larry Reed, who stepped through the crowded room to engage his mother in conversation. Five minutes later, Finn turned to peer toward the far corner again, but Tony and Alisa were gone. Linda stepped away to talk to a group of ladies who pulled her into their circle to give their condolences, and Finn was again engaged in conversation by his other half-brother Harry, who shook his hand and gave him a hug.

"Hey, brother, it's good to see you although, of course, not under these circumstances." Harry stood taller than he by about two inches and was handsome, with his mother Chessa's chestnut-colored wavy hair and her big green eyes.

"Harry, good to see you too." Finn liked this half-brother, who'd never asked for much and, unlike Tony, never had an agenda and always seemed content with his lot. "What have you been up to?"

"Ahh, keeping the city of London on its toes," Harry said good-naturedly in a slightly British brogue that seemed to stand out more when he was in American company.

"Good of you to fly all this way for the services." Finn said. "So—where is your girlfriend? Marisa, right?"

"Correction, fiancée," Harry grinned, his eyes twinkling.

"Congratulations!" Finn was truly happy for his oldest brother and clapped him on the back. "This calls for a toast. Let me get you a drink."

The two migrated through the throng of people and found their way to the bar to get two whiskeys to toast Harry's engagement. "Why didn't Marisa come with you?"

"She's actually over in Africa right now on a mission trip from our church. She asked me to pass on her regrets and condolences. I'm going to be joining her after this. Taking a red eye to Kenya. I have business over there." Harry had been at the top of his class in boarding school and had graduated with honors from Oxford, studying agriculture and environmental engineering. He now owned the world's top organic coffee production company.

"You two are definitely the world travelers, I'm jealous." Finn did feel a pang of envy over that. His schedule would keep him tied down to Washington now, and travel seemed all but impossible, at least for the near future.

"Yes, but congratulations to you too, being appointed to the Supreme Court!" Harry clinked his glass to Finn's again, a genuine smile on his face. "I'm sorry to eat and run as they say here in America, but I best be off if I'm going to catch my flight. Look for a wedding invitation in the mail. If you can't make it, we'll understand—but maybe it will give you an excuse to take a break."

"You know I'll try." Finn hugged his brother again, wishing him a safe trip, and headed to the bar for another drink.

Finn tiredly surveyed the damage. Everyone had finally departed from the dinner. A young waiter and waitress, dressed in matching uniforms of white, long-sleeved shirts, black slacks, and black bowties, picked up stray wine and cocktail glasses and plates of half-eaten appetizers, sandwiches, and cake from around the banquet room and adjoining living room and terrace, where most of the guests had gathered to pay their respects.

THE WISE MAN

He sat on the deep blue-gray velvet living room sofa, polishing off his fourth Jack Daniels on the rocks, when his mother walked in and wearily slumped down next to him. The sun had set, and it was dark outside the floor to ceiling windows.

"How are ya doin', Mom?" Finn asked, his words slurring a bit.

"I'm fine—exhausted—but you seem a bit tipsy. I guess I can't blame you."

For the first time, Finn noticed the haggard lines around his mom's mouth and the dark circles under her eyes, and his heart went out to her. "I'm sorry, Mom, I know this has been really hard."

She looked at him with mournful eyes, and a tear slipped down her cheek. "I really miss him."

"I know. I do too. Is there anything I can get you or do?" His mother's grief-stricken expression sobered him up.

"No, just sit with me. I have a few things to talk to you about."

"Now?"

"I guess now is as good a time as any. Maybe you can get me a drink after all. Bourbon and soda, please."

Finn walked up to the bar and emptied the remaining contents of a bourbon bottle into a tall tumbler of ice and splashed some soda on top. He handed his mom the drink with a cocktail napkin and sat back down against the velvet cushions, suddenly exhausted himself. "Okay, shoot."

"I wanted to let you know about your father's will now that he's gone." Linda sipped on her drink slowly.

Oh no, do we have to do this now? Finn thought, but as always, allowed his mother latitude and was quiet.

135

"It's simple really. He left everything to me, and I in turn will leave everything to you." Linda smiled, lines fanning out from her tired eyes. She uncrossed her legs, removed her pumps, and rubbed her feet before taking another sip of her drink. "I just wanted you to know."

"*Everything?*" Finn rubbed his eyes, shocked. He thought that his brothers would get something. "What about Harry and Tony?"

"Your father said to me a while back that he'd already provided for them through their mothers, although I believe Harry and his mother Chessa, God rest her soul, did get the lion's share. We talked about giving them more, but your father did not trust Tony nor want to give him any of your inheritance."

"Surely there was plenty ...?" Finn didn't finish his statement, leaving his question dangling. He had no idea what his mother and father were worth, but he could guess the figure was in the millions. *Tens if not hundreds of millions.* He couldn't really wrap his alcohol-fogged head around it right now if he tried.

"I'm sure Harry won't care one bit. He and his fiancée seem so happy with their careers and with each other. Now Tony on the other hand ..." Linda massaged her temples and took a gulp of her drink this time.

Finn chugged the remnants of his whiskey and sat his glass hard down on the carved wooden coffee table.

"Finn, a coaster please," his mother said tiredly.

"Mother, really, I don't care what Tony wants or doesn't want or how he feels. I know I don't have any proof, but I still think he sabotaged the Walker case. And I wouldn't be surprised if he and Cousin

Ralls were somehow campaigning for the Senate not to approve my Supreme Court nomination."

"I don't know about all that, honey, but I do know Tony is extremely upset he didn't get a dime of your dad's money in the will."

"How do you know that?"

Linda frowned and took a deep breath. "That's the other thing I need to talk to you about. Tony pulled me aside at the dinner and—"

"I can't believe he bothered you today with that!" Finn was livid, always feeling very protective of his mother. "He's got a lot of nerve."

"Finn, calm down. There's more." She sat back, taking another gulp of her drink. "He told me how he felt it was really unfair your father sided with you on the nomination, and then to add insult to injury, left him nothing in his will. I guess he had an attorney look into it for him. Anyway, he asked me if I could talk to you about something ... about his feelings for Alisa, and whether you or I would mind if he asks her to move in with him. He said it would soften the blow about how he'd been shortchanged, that they've already been seeing each other a few times and—"

"No way!" Finn stood and balled his hands into fists of rage. "Is he crazy? Does he know what the press would do with that juicy piece of information? I can see the headlines now ... President Leif Mitchell's servant girl has an affair with his son ... and the sheets aren't even cold yet." The thought suddenly made Finn sick to his stomach.

"As far as we know, neither the press nor the public are aware Tony is your father's son."

"But they'll start digging, they always do, and when they find out—"

"I told him you'd probably react this way, but he caught me at a weak moment." Linda looked sideways at her son. "I guess I shouldn't have brought it up."

"No, I'm glad you did. He probably just wanted to get a rise out of me. Well, guess what? He did. But he's going to be sorry he did."

CHAPTER THIRTEEN

His first call the next morning after his third cup of coffee was to Richard Layton. Finn had spent the night in his old room but hadn't slept much, his anger making sleep hard to come by. He stared for what seemed like hours at the University of Delaware and Notre Dame pennants on his walls, the "Play Like a Champion" gold sign that was a replica of the one that the Notre Dame football players all touched as they headed through the tunnel onto the football field, his high school plaques and trophies. His mother had kept the room just as he'd left it when he went away to college and then off to law school and his career in Chicago.

He had a townhome now in DC he'd recently purchased, but it had been after midnight when his mom and he were finally finished talking, and he'd decided it best not to drive.

His tenure at the Supreme Court would not begin for two months, as the court would be in recess soon for the winter holidays, and he was still on bereavement leave.

Enough time to find out what really happened in the Walker case—and with my Senate nomination process, Finn said to himself, dialing the private investigator's number on his cell phone. His mother was home but busied herself making phone calls to friends who couldn't attend the funeral but had left her messages and sent fruit baskets and flowers.

He kept the bedroom door closed and his voice down just in case, realizing he felt a little creepy making a call from his boyhood bedroom as a grown adult, a Supreme Court judge no less. Oh well, no time to worry about little things. "Hello, Mister Layton? It's Finley Mitchell, President Leif Mitchell's son. My father told me he began an investigation involving former Department of Defense Secretary Ralston Warren. Now that my father is deceased, I'd like to continue ... and, um, broaden your investigation." Finn agreed to meet Richard later that afternoon in his offices in downtown Washington, a half-hour drive away from his parents' house in Potomac.

Layton Investigations LLC was located on the first floor of a concrete and glass office building on Massachusetts Avenue, just a few blocks away from the Supreme Court building. *At least it will be convenient going forward.* Finn's stomach still felt a bit queasy after the whiskeys he'd downed the night before, and he also had a case of jittery nerves. *No one likes this spy stuff,* he reminded himself, wearing a black fedora hat, a long black raincoat, and a light gray scarf pulled up over his face despite the unusually warm, rainy weather, trying to stay incognito.

Finn opened the double glass doors of the ten-story building into an expansive lobby with a large placard on the wall indicating various names of companies and in which rooms they were located.

THE WISE MAN

He found Layton Investigation and saw a "B" next to it for Basement.

He took the elevator down a floor, which opened into a hallway with several doors. The first one he came to said Richard Layton, PI. Finn had already been instructed to knock a certain way on the door ... a "code" knock. Otherwise, the door would not be opened, Richard had said. He knocked four times, then waited a beat, then knocked once again.

A middle-aged, slight, brunette-haired woman wearing a suit and heels opened the door. "Hello. You must be Finley Mitchell?" she asked cheerfully.

"Yes, that's me," Finn answered.

"Well, come in," she said and opened the door wider into a rather plain foyer, decorated only with a gray upholstered couch, a tall plastic plant, an oak coffee table and a few padded chairs. Finn noticed there were three doors off the foyer—one to a conference room, one to a small office, and the other one was closed. "Mr. Layton is on the phone right now, but he'll be with you shortly. Please have a seat. Can I get you anything, water, coffee—?"

"No, thank you," Finn answered politely and took a seat in one of the chairs.

There were a few magazines strewn on the table— *TIME, Golf Digest, People, Good Housekeeping, GQ, Vogue*—he must have both men and women as clients, Finn surmised.

Finn pulled out his phone and checked his emails and messages ... good, nothing important. He was about to ask for a cup of coffee when a stocky middle-aged man with greasy, graying brown hair and a beard, wearing a frayed Nationals baseball cap and glasses came out. The man was absentmindedly smoking a pipe with one hand and reading a newspaper with the other. He was dressed in a tweed blazer, khakis, and loafers. He looked up as if distracted by Finn's presence, his bushy gray eyebrows knitting together in mild annoyance. "Mr. Mitchell?" he asked gruffly.

"Uh, yes, I'm Finn Mitchell, you can call me Finn, you must be—"

The man turned, cutting Finn off, and started walking back into the room he'd exited, apparently expecting Finn to follow.

Finn looked over at the receptionist, who'd reappeared as the man stepped out. She smiled, looking like she was about to burst into laughter, and shrugged. "You can go in now, Mr. Mitchell." She stifled a giggle.

Richard Layton, assuming that's who he was since he hadn't even introduced himself, had already sat down at his desk and pulled his pipe out of his mouth. He pointed it to the two chairs in front of his desk, which was littered with stacks of papers, folders, coffee cups, soda cans, water bottles, books, pens, two laptops, two lamps—in fact, Finn didn't really see the desk at all—every inch of it was covered with stuff.

Then Finn watched in amazement as the man began to—he guessed the best word for it was "shed"—what, apparently, was a costume. He lay down the pipe on top of a stack of papers, took off the glasses, and removed the baseball cap, randomly tossing them into a corner chair. Then he pulled off the beard, and what turned out to be a wig of hair, piling them on top, then finally peeled off his eyebrows and removed the jacket.

He grinned at Finn now, who sat with his mouth open, staring.

"Good to see you, Finn. I'm Richard." He held out his hand, and it took Finn a few seconds to recover before shaking it. "I was trying out a new outfit—I guess it was a success."

The good-looking man who now stood before him appeared to be much younger, in his forties Finn guessed. He was dressed in a white Oxford shirt and was clean shaven with trimmed, sandy-brown hair and mischievous blue eyes. Except those changed too as the investigator removed a set of contact lenses into a nearby container of solution, revealing he really had hazel eyes.

"I'd say," Finn agreed, taking a breath and exhaling. "I can see why they call you the chameleon." Finn had read up on Richard Layton the same night his father had given him Layton's business card.

"Some people can still see through the charade, though, which is why I have a team of investigators who work for me," he explained, sitting in his big leather office chair. "Some of them are only known by me and their immediate families. And some only by me. So how can I help you?"

Finn went on to explain what he needed Layton to do—find out if his half-brother Tony and his father's half-nephew Ralston Warren had ulterior motives in the Jay Walker case, and if they were behind any of the slander that was spewed before the Senate in the Supreme Court nomination hearings.

"That's it?" Richard asked, leaning forward on his elbows.

"Isn't that a lot?" Finn asked, also leaning forward in his chair.

"Well, I've had much worse ... but yes, that should keep me busy for a few weeks." Richard and Finn both stood and shook hands. "Very nice to meet you, and congratulations, Judge. Personally, I'm very glad you finally made it on the bench. And I'm very sorry to hear about your father's death. He was a good man."

"Thank you, Richard. I'll be taking a break since I have two months before the Supreme Court goes in session. I'm planning to go out of town for two weeks on vacation—is that a problem?"

"No, in fact, it's perfect, we can meet when you get back, I should have something by then. Enjoy your trip."

Finn was sitting in first class aboard a 737 jet the next day headed for San Francisco where he'd board a connecting flight to Sydney, Australia, and then hop aboard a private plane to his ultimate vacation destination, Hamilton Island.

He'd pulled thirty thousand dollars out of his bank account, which held ten million in it—only a small part of his inheritance which was still being collected, sorted, and invested by his parents' attorneys and financial advisors back home. Finn wanted none of the details. *That's what we pay these guys for,* he thought. Right now, he just needed a getaway where all he had to do was think about what he wanted to eat or drink or do for fun each day.

Stepping off the small charter plane, Finn was met by a concierge who put his single suitcase into the trunk of a gleaming Mercedes, then held open the back door. After he was seated on the plush leather, the driver handed him a cold towel and glass flute of fine champagne for the short ride to his luxury suite in "qualia." The hotel, spelled with a small "q," was known as one of the world's best resorts where A-list stars such as Oprah, Taylor Swift, Johnny Depp, and Leonardo DiCaprio had stayed.

Finn could already feel his cares evaporating as he sipped the champagne, gazing out the Benz's window as they cruised past a variety of palm trees and flowers, yacht club marinas, and a myriad of sailboats, charter boats, and huge private yachts dotting the serene turquoise water of the Coral Sea.

The car meandered on the one-lane roads and made its way beyond the huge iron gates onto the north end of the island into the exclusive, expensive, waterfront resort.

Finn refilled his glass in Long Pavilion, the resort reception area surrounded by the aqua water and a view of the Whitsunday Islands. *Like a scene from a movie*, he thought, the champagne giving him a happy buzz.

Another concierge showed him to his private suite which had its own infinity pool that seemed to extend into the clear aqua water of the sea with a phenomenal view of the islands in the distance.

He stretched onto the huge bed in the elegantly simple, yet spacious, room. It was warmly surrounded with cedar wood walls and flooring that extended into a deck that led to the outdoor pool and hot tub. Tomorrow, he would explore walking from his bed into his pool into the ocean, but for now all he wanted was to take a nap to shake off the jet lag.

A few hours later, Finn showered and shaved and headed down in his private golf cart, the island's primary mode of transportation, to one of qualia's premier restaurants, Pebble Beach, saving the welcome fruit and cheese plate in his room for a later snack. From his table sitting right on the water, he ordered saki, sushi, and sashimi for starters and then the tasting menu—a half dozen raw oysters and a plate of prawns and porcini risotto, both with wine pairings, then a fresh fruit cup over a dulce de leche for dessert.

Glancing over his menu, he could see several tables were occupied by other guests, but his eye was caught by one in particular. She was sitting with another young lady. They were both of Asian descent, seemingly two sisters enjoying dinner with one another. Finn inconspicuously watched as she smiled and then laughed at something the younger woman said, flashing brilliant white teeth in a flawless face framed by jet-black hair that blew in the breeze and caught the rays of the fiery golden-red sun as it set on the horizon. But what caught Finn's attention in particular were her eyes. They were sparkling, dark, enchanting, and he had to force himself to remove his gaze and look back down at his plate to finish his food.

Still her image was burned into his brain, and he couldn't forget her as he finally drifted off to sleep that night.

CHAPTER FOURTEEN

The next day Finn was ready for adventure on the sea and decided to take a private snorkeling excursion on the Great Barrier Reef. He rode in the back of the charter boat expertly driven by a seasoned captain. As he enjoyed the sun on his face, sparkling off the deep teal water, he listened to his female guide explain how the reef was finally coming back to life after half of the coral and sea life had died due to El Nina. Soon, he was following her in the water wearing flippers and snorkeling gear. He saw all kinds and sizes of fish in a rainbow of brilliant colors, sea turtles, a stingray that magically floated past, and even a baby shark amid the coral gently waving in purple, green, and yellow fans along the ocean floor.

On the ride back, his guide respected Finn's need for a little quiet as he soaked in the sun in his swim trunks, laying on the cushioned seats as the boat made its way over the smooth sea and into the resort's harbor.

After thanking and generously tipping the captain and guide, even though tipping was frowned upon in Australia, Finn reapplied sunscreen, put on his sunglasses and straw hat and ventured onto qualia's private beach. Most of the guests must have been out on their own adventures, but Finn appreciated the solitude.

Still, he looked for the girl from the night before. He was disappointed to see that neither she nor her family showed up on the beach or at the pool. They also weren't at dinner that night as Finn dined at his same table in Pebble Beach, once again hoping to catch her. Ah well, at least he was able to enjoy a different tasting menu of local seafood the chef had prepared.

The next day, rested and ready for more sightseeing, Finn took another charter boat out to Whitehaven beach, the local favorite of Australian holiday visitors. It was known as one of the world's finest beaches for its pristine white sand and clear, warm aqua-blue water, a few hammocks in the nearby trees, and really little else.

This must be what paradise is like. Finn spread a blanket down, taking off his backpack. The bag was filled with the lunch the resort had packed for him, a Fiji water bottle, his sunscreen, and a Lee Child paperback novel he'd bought at the airport he'd yet to crack open. *Maybe today.* He closed his eyes, but soon he felt the afternoon sun burning his arm, and he realized he'd fallen asleep.

He yawned and sat up, hearing the sounds of laughter. Strange, they sounded familiar. Finn looked down the beach. He squinted to see only a handful of people were visible—a couple walking along the water's edge snapping photos, a family with three small children picnicking on a blanket about twenty yards away, and—yes, there she was, splashing in the water with the other young woman just ten yards away.

Finn's breath caught in his throat, and he pulled the brim of his hat down over his eyes, hoping no one would see him staring.

He watched as she playfully kicked up sprays of water, a look of pure joy on her sun-kissed face, her wet, black hair flying in the sea breeze. He looked down to see she was in a red, one-piece suit which hugged her curves above long shapely legs. *Stunning.*

Her companion was equally pretty but there was something about *her* that captured Finn's attention. There it was again, a look of wildness in her eyes ... he could see it from where he sat. And suddenly he ached to see those eyes up close, to peer into her soul, to touch her beautiful, white skin, to hold her.

But that would be impossible unless ... Finn jumped to his feet and walked to the water's edge, feeling the warm saltwater lap onto his ankles. *Go for it,* he told himself, and soon was swimming out into the blue and then parallel to the beach. He walked out of the water, dripping wet, and found himself only about four yards from where she now sat with the other girl, who upon closer inspection, almost looked identical, although she was in a two-piece blue suit. They sat in matching beach chairs on the sand, both donning white, floppy hats. They could be twins, he thought, mesmerized.

Shoot, now I have no towel. He suddenly realized he had not thought his plan through. He began his trek back to his blanket, past where they sat, and heard giggles erupt.

"Hello, ladies." He slowed his walk and casually nodded and waved.

149

"Hello," the blue two-piece said, which was all the invitation he needed to stop and smile at them. He tried not to stare but couldn't help it. Her eyes really were that entrancing up close—dark, inky pools where you could get lost easily in their depths. She must be half Chinese and half ... *something else*, he realized.

"Sorry, I'm here by myself, from America ... my name is Finn, Finn Mitchell. Nice to meet you both." He felt awkward, placing his hands on his hips. "I guess I got a little lost at sea out there and was a bit off the mark from where my stuff is over there." He pointed at the blanket and backpack in the distance.

He hesitated for a moment, not sure what to do next, when the two-piece stood up and shook his hand. "Hi, I'm Wu Alana, and this is my older sister, Wu Lei," she said, introducing them by their formal Chinese names with their surname first. "But you can call us Alana and Lei." Finn couldn't see Alana's eyes since they were hidden behind mirrored Aviator sunglasses, but her smile was similarly bright. "Why don't you bring your stuff over and join us?"

Lei looked up at her younger sister, shielding eyes that screamed "what are you doing?" but she simply smiled politely, nodded, and stood to shake the stranger's hand since it was too late to do otherwise. "Pleased to meet you," she said a little stiffly.

"If you're sure it's okay?" He asked, looking into her dark, sepia-brown eyes, holding his breath.

"Sure, I guess," she said, turning to frown at her sister, who was enjoying every moment of the bashful exchange.

So much for cracking open my book, Finn thought with a mix of fear and delight.

After about an hour of sitting on their blanket making small talk, Finn learned a lot about Wu Lei. She was the oldest daughter of China's reigning paramount leader, President Wu Shin Hai, and his wife Wu Kai, who was originally from Hawaii. Lei, as she was called less formally, was an up-and-coming fashion designer and had just had a showing at Fashion Week Australia in Sydney. At their mother's insistence, their father had begrudgingly allowed Lei and Alana, who accompanied her, to stay over for a weekend in Hamilton Island on their way home.

Just my luck. Finn gulped down his water, almost choking on it as he found out the news the girl he found attractive was the daughter of the supreme ruler of Communist China.

Alana did most of the talking. "... our mother is from Hawaii, she met my father when he was vacationing over there, and he flew her back to China where they married ... and had us," she said. This one wasn't shy at all, Finn realized, sharing a plate of hummus, crackers, and grapes the girls offered, ignoring the chicken salad sandwich and chips he had packed in his backpack.

Lei mostly stayed quiet, and Finn felt awkward again. It had been nearly an hour since he'd lumbered out of the water, so he decided it was time to leave them alone again. He told them it was great to meet them, but he had to get back.

"You *are* going to the mix and mingle tonight on the island, right?" Alana asked him, sparks in her eyes.

"I didn't know about it," Finn responded. "But if you two are going, I guess ..." he gazed down and

151

tried to catch Lei's eyes, but she glanced away and sighed.

"We're definitely going, right, Sis?" Alana poked at her sister's shoulder, Lei pushed back, and in a second, the two were playfully wrestling.

"Okay, my cue to go. I'll see you ladies soon."

"Tonight, right?" Alana stood and handed him a small flyer she'd fished out of her knapsack which had the details of the event.

Finn looked at Lei again, and this time her eyes bored right into his heart, which skipped a beat. "Right."

A steel drum band played reggae music as trays of hors d'oeuvres were passed along with glasses of champagne at the Hamilton Island "Mix and Mingle" party on One Tree Hill, a summit with a café and sweeping, magnificent views, known as the best place to catch a sunset.

But only some of the partygoers paid attention to the main attraction as the sky put on its nightly show, casting red and orange beams of light that faded behind wispy pink clouds into purple and indigo hues.

Some had ordered dinner and were lucky to get one of the few tables, but most were busy mixing and mingling, drinks in hand they'd ordered at the café bar.

Finn had debated whether to attend, since Lei had never committed to going. But he finally decided it wouldn't hurt for him to get out here in Australia, since most probably didn't know him like they did in America.

He parked his golf cart and walked up the hill just in time to see the sun dip below the horizon. He stood alone along the rock wall at the edge of the cliff to watch the sun set over the sea and surrounding islands. It really was a breathtaking view.

He turned and looked over the crowd of partygoers—mostly young people dressed in casual island clothes. He'd worn a simple, white, short-sleeved polo shirt and pair of khaki shorts, since he'd gotten sunburned, and it was the most comfortable outfit he owned. He scanned the crowded deck and patio for the two sisters but was disappointed when he didn't see them.

Suddenly, a familiar voice called his name.

"Finn, you made it!" Alana was dressed in a flowery, multi-colored sundress. A yellow flower adorned her sleek, black, shoulder-length hair. She was holding a fruity pink cocktail and gave him a friendly smile.

He gave her a hug. "Yes, thanks for inviting me ... did, um, Lei come with you tonight?"

Alana sighed. "My sister is over there." She pointed to a small table in the distance where Lei was seated alone with her back toward them, sipping on a drink. "She's never much of a partier, unlike me. And how about you?" She batted her eyelashes flirtatiously and gave him a mischievous grin.

Finn swallowed. She was pretty, but he couldn't help but still feel drawn to her older sister, despite her aloofness. "I guess I'm more like Lei nowadays, sorry. Why don't we go over and cheer her up?"

"You can go, I want to meet some new people and have fun." She danced off and headed to a group of guys who whistled appreciatively at her, basking in their attention.

Finn walked over to where Lei sat and tapped her on the shoulder. "Is that chair taken?"

She turned and again, her eyes melted through him. *What was it about those eyes ...* "Suit yourself," she said, pointing to the empty chair across the table for two.

He sat across from her. "Can I buy you a drink?" he asked.

"No, I'm okay." She held up what looked to be a Shirley Temple, nearly full with the cherry still on top. She looked down, not smiling.

"Why the sad look?"

Lei peered up at him and was quiet for a moment. "Well, if you must know, I'm really just tired of all of this. My parents want me to meet someone or else they're threatening to marry me off to a man of their choosing, just like they did in the old days."

"Wow, that's so ... old school." Finn sat down across from her, surprised at her revelation.

"That's China for you. And, of course, my dad is really conservative. He would die if he knew how Alana is flirting tonight."

"I guess he'd be proud of you then."

"Not really." She looked sadly down again, and Finn noticed how beautiful she was. Compared to most of the other girls at the party, who were in fashionably short, tight cocktail dresses, Lei wore a more modest, long, loose-fitting navy sundress with spaghetti straps. But her soft-looking dark hair and even softer eyes, her full lips ... "did you hear what I said?" she asked in annoyance.

"You were saying how your parents are more demanding of you, you being the eldest, and how your father is never satisfied." *Phew, I'm glad I was*

154

listening, Finn thought. *Snap out of it. She's not interested.* "I'm sorry to bother you. Clearly you'd rather be alone, so I'll just get going. This isn't really my scene either." Finn stood to go, but Lei suddenly took his hand in hers.

"I'm sorry too … you're not bothering me. I guess I was just venting. It seems I've been feeling so lonely for so long I forgot what it's like to have a guy my age like you to talk to. And then I was so rude … can we start again, please?" She still held his hand and gave him a smile that lit up her whole face, like a dark cloud had suddenly passed by and the sun shone through, warming him.

"Of course." He gladly lowered himself into his chair again, trying to contain his big grin of delight.

They talked for an hour, shutting out the rest of the party around them. Lei told him about her dream of becoming a fashion designer, how she'd sketched and sewn several gowns that had fetched thousands of dollars but how none of that really mattered to her parents, who seemed to just want her to get married and have their grandchildren. Finn told her about his life back home in the states, his rise to the Supreme Court, and how he could relate to her since his parents had pushed him to become an over-achiever as well. Lei took his hand in sympathy when he told her about his dad's recent passing, which gave him the opportunity to take both of her hands in his across the table.

"Will you join me for dinner tomorrow night, just the two of us?" he asked.

Before she had a chance to answer, Alana walked up. "Hey, you two, didn't you notice the party's over?" Finn looked up to see only about a dozen young people left, walking to their cars and golf carts. "I'm freezing, plus Lei, we told Mom and Dad we'd be calling them from our hotel a half hour ago. Our driver's waiting over there giving us dirty looks." Finn saw a black Mercedes parked a few blocks away, a big hulking driver behind the steering wheel, his eyes squinting and staring straight at them.

Lei let go of his hands looking embarrassed and stood to go. But as she walked away, her arm linked in her sister's, she glanced back over her shoulder and with a smile, nodded, and winked at him, and his heart skipped a beat.

Finn had spent hours carefully going over the arrangements with the maître d' and the menu with the head chef at qualia. He wanted everything to be perfect ... and it almost was.

They were in the middle of their lobster dinner under a full moon and a sky full of stars at their private candlelit table on the beach, the ocean lapping gently on the shore, when a quick island storm whipped up and started spitting rain.

Lei had looked like a princess as she sat before him at dinner, the moonlight glowing on her white silk dress, which complemented her complexion. She was gifted with good looks from both sides of her heritage. Her makeup, a touch of gray eyeshadow and kohl-black liner, intensified her big dark brown eyes, and a rosy blush and lip gloss accentuated her smooth, creamy skin.

All of that washed away as the rain pelted them now. Finn grabbed Lei's hand and they ran to the overhang of his suite deck but not before they were soaked.

Finn frowned, his hair matted down and his shirt clinging to him. *Of all the luck* ... Then a giggle bubbled up from Lei, and soon they were both laughing so hard their tears mixed with the rain on their faces. When their laugher subsided, they realized they were huddled close together, and Finn took Lei's face in his hand and kissed her gently. Her full lips tasted sweet and salty, and a desire rose in him. *Slow down*, he told himself.

But she looked at him with the same hunger in those liquid-brown pools, and he kissed her again hungrily this time. Her body pressed close to his, and he could feel the warmth of her skin through the rain-drenched dress, which had become almost see through. He averted his eyes, trying not to stare. *Stop*, he willed himself, fighting an urge to invite her into his bed which was just ten feet away.

"Let me get us some towels." He parted from her, breathing hard.

"Good idea," she agreed breathlessly.

He retrieved a few towels from his bathroom and was back in a minute, and they dried off the best they could.

"How about some dessert?" he asked and saw her give him a wary look. "No, I meant that innocently. I can order some from room service. I promise I'll behave ... if that's what you want."

"I really should get home," she said, biting her lip, which drove him crazier still. "We are leaving early tomorrow morning, and I still need to pack."

157

"But … when will I see you again? Will I see you again?"

She suddenly took his face in her hands and kissed him long and hard, then just as fast, said goodbye, grabbed her purse, and fled out the door without a word, glancing back only once, giving him a sad yet hopeful little smile.

CHAPTER FIFTEEN

His trip back home was uneventful. Feeling refreshed but sad to leave the new paradise—and the woman he realized he'd fallen in love with—behind, Finn reluctantly returned to Richard Layton's office to hear the private investigator's findings. As he sat back down in the chair he'd left before his vacation, he felt like he'd lost his original enthusiasm to dig up dirt on his half-brother and cousin. But he'd gone this far and, of course, had to listen to Richard's findings. He took a deep breath and sighed.

This time, Richard sat behind his desk all business-like, dressed in a gray Armani suit, starched white shirt, and navy tie, his hair neatly combed, his face cleanly shaved. He pushed a plain manilla folder across the desktop toward Finn, who tiredly opened it to see several papers inside.

"Why don't you just summarize it for me?" Finn asked wearily.

"Jet lag?" Richard asked. "Or is it something else?"

"I don't know ... I guess it was just hard to come back with all I have ahead of me."

"I'll bet. Well, I'm not sure if what I have to report is good or bad news then. It may add to your already full plate."

"Just give it to me straight."

"Your hunches were correct." Richard pulled the folder back in front of him and took out the papers. "We followed the money trail. It's true what they say, money is usually the root of all evil. And from what we discovered, Anthony Sorrell and Ralston Warren are going to be put behind bars for a very long time—if that's what you want."

The PI proceeded to tell him everything he and his team had found.

It turned out the son of Senator George Hodges— one of the senators who had brutally questioned Finn during his nomination hearing and not only voted against him but was vocal in persuading others to do the same—had gone to school with Tony at Phillip Exeter Academy. The Layton investigation team had discovered the Connecticut senator's granddaughter was in the hospital with a rare lymphoma, and Tony had donated nearly a quarter-million dollars to the fund for her cure in return for his testimony and vote, along with his arm twisting of a few other senators.

A large sum of money was also found in an offshore account under the name of Thomas Sentry, the kid whose life Finn had actually saved. A deposit of another quarter-million was found deposited shortly before the senate hearings. Tommy, who was a stockbroker, had been scheduled to testify on Finn's behalf but then refused and had instead left the country to fly to Haiti on an alleged three-week "business" trip.

A third deposit appeared in the account of another man who had been a witness to the hazing but was never charged. The man had testified before the Senate he saw Finn not only taking part in the drinking but watched him "kick" Tommy's body to the side to go to the frat's pinning ceremony and party some more with the blonde girl, Lisa Frazier.

Then there was Trinity Foster Dobbins, who'd provided written testimony that Finn had had an affair with her behind Professor Dobbins's back at Notre Dame *after* she was pregnant with the professor's child and was engaged to be married. Her timeline was questioned by Finn's defense attorney during the hearings—Finn knew they'd been intimate well before Trinity had even thought about getting engaged to the professor or was pregnant with his child—but basically was waved aside by Senator Hodges as irrelevant. No money trail was found in any of Trinity's bank accounts. She had probably lied on her statement to save face in her marriage.

But one of Richard's crackerjack investigators had hacked Trinity's laptop and uncovered a string of emails between the pretty law student grad and Ralston dating back to just before the hearings. The emails were more than suggestive that Trinity cooperate or else the possessive professor would receive several unflattering photos of his wife in various compromising positions with a few other young men.

Finally, and the pièce de résistance that had nearly sealed Finn's fate until the truth finally set him free, was a check that somehow escaped the hands of one of JAB's leaders. The man had unwittingly signed it, not thinking of the repercussions his signature might incur should it ever be discovered.

Florence or "Flo" Howard worked for the Baltimore headquarters of Stormfront, the White pride supremacist group. She was a single mom in her sixties whose adult son was in jail and whose live-at-home daughter was pregnant out of wedlock with her third child. Flo worked as a maid during the day and at the headquarters most nights answering the phone to add to her just-get-by income.

She was a squat, angry, gray-haired White woman whose husband had cheated and left her for a younger girl. Flo was full of resentment on how life had treated her unfairly compared to her friends who were all retiring, playing bridge, traveling, having fun.

Flo was approached by her superior one night in the tiny basement Stormfront office and offered five-thousand dollars if she'd write a letter to her senator protesting the Supreme Court nomination of Finley Mitchell, then make hundreds of copies and distribute them for her friends and family and anyone else she knew to sign and send in. She'd not hesitated to comply. After all, her boss explained, she would be "killing two birds with one stone"—doing something good for her community, the White minority, and for herself.

But little did she know, or anyone else until it was tracked down by one of Richard's team members, that the check was signed by one of the leaders of the Justice for All Blacks organization.

"I had to report our findings on this to the FBI, and they're investigating as we speak," Richard said matter-of-factly. "They've suspected for some time that JAB was being run by a terrorist out for money who is manipulating Americans who sympathize with Blacks who truly have been oppressed or wronged ... and who is capitalizing on that sympathy by stirring up more hate crimes and oppression to keep their anger and the movement fueled and donations pouring in.

"Who signed the check?" Finn asked, trying to wrap his head around it all.

"Ahhh, well, you won't believe our fortune on this, but it was actually your cousin Ralston."

Finn couldn't believe it and let out a loud string of epithets. He didn't care at this point who heard him, he was so enraged.

"And there's more—" Richard said, waiting for it all to sink in.

"Go ahead." Finn clenched his teeth and his fists, taking short shallow breaths, trying not to hyperventilate or totally lose it.

"We found out, again through a money trail, that Tony and John Brown were both on Ralston's payroll. Which means Ralston was behind the shooting and framed Jay Walker to rile up the JAB movement. And it means Judge Tony was somehow biased in the court case involving Mr. Walker. We traced calls made by Ralston to Tony before, during, and after the case. You were lucky it ended up the way it did, actually. Tony took on the case even though he should have recused himself, knowing you were his half-brother. Of course we can't prove that last part, at least without giving him a lie detector test. But there's enough to put him behind bars anyway. And we have proof he bribed a few legislators to vote against your Supreme Court nomination too."

Finn was seething now and couldn't speak.

"The FBI believes there is a kingpin behind even Ralston—the guy at the top of JAB and probably other movements designed to take down this country as we know it, and in the process make billions of dollars. It's a mob boss who goes by the code name of Lucifer. Sadly, he is out of my scope and even out of the FBI's reach for now. But at least we've nailed the two you're after."

Finn inhaled a deep, ragged breath, held it, then exhaled, feeling light-headed.

Richard noticed Finn growing pale. "Let me get you some water." He buzzed his secretary.

Finn was dazed by all this information, and his anger ebbed, hurt replacing it. Why would his cousin and half-brother betray him? Why did they hate him so much? He didn't know this Lucifer guy, and he supposed money and power were enough to drive people, but still, they were family. He had done absolutely nothing to harm them in the past.

Sally brought them two glasses of cold water and quietly left them again. Finn took a long drink but couldn't quench his anger and hurt. "Richard ... I just have one question left. *Why?*"

"Why did they do all of this? Money and power, I suppose."

"No ... why do they hate me so much?"

Richard averted his eyes, and the chameleon turned a shade of red for a moment as he clearly pondered how much to divulge to his client.

"Richard, please tell me why."

"It wasn't you so much as your father, rest his soul." Richard loosened his tie. "Ralston was always jealous of your dad, of his relationship with his father, your grandfather Henry, of the Little River horse ranch, all the fame it brought when your father's horse won the Derby. He is jealous of all of it. He'd tried his hand at buying and raising prize-winning horses, always picked wrong and failed miserably. Guess he had bad luck. He carried that grudge with him as he grew in military and political power within the Department of Defense and the White House, a position he could control.

"When your father asked him to help get rid of your mother's former husband in Afghanistan, Ralston was easily able to do so. But later, he took his festering jealousy out against his Uncle Leif by leaking that secret out to the press and public. You were probably unaware, since you weren't born yet, but it did great political damage, nearly turning the tide in the next election. And Ralston knew it would do personal damage too when you and others Leif loved found out. It would forever tarnish his otherwise stellar presidential career.

Finn sat putting the pieces all together. "And Ralston knew Tony felt the same jealousy toward me?"

"Yes, they were kindred spirits, so it made sense they work together to bring your father and you down."

It all made sense to him now. "What happens next?" Finn managed to choke out in a whisper.

"Once the FBI investigation is wrapped up, and they're brought before a Grand Jury, Tony and Ralston could each be looking at up to fifteen years in prison or more." Richard closed the file folder. "I am now compelled to report my findings, I hope that's okay with you?"

"Absolutely, go get 'em." Finn stood and shook the investigator's hand. "Thank you, Richard, great work."

"Thank you, Judge." Richard bowed with respect.
"My pleasure."

Finn watched on his living room TV as his cousin and half-brother were led in handcuffs from their federal court sentence hearing at the Everett McKinley Dirksen US Courthouse into a security van to be transported two blocks down the road to the Metropolitan Correctional Center, the federal prison skyscraper located on the Loop in downtown Chicago.

"Judge Anthony Sorrell, who has served as a Circuit Court judge here in Chicago for ten years and his cousin, Ralston Warren, who has served as Director of Defense for two presidents of the United States and as Chief of Staff to a third, were both sentenced today to the maximum fifteen years in prison," the male reporter spoke into his handheld microphone on the front steps of the courthouse as his cameraman captured Tony and Ralston being led down in handcuffs by several security officers into the waiting police van. "The two high-profile government officials were charged with multiple counts of bribery, both in the murder case of Jay Walker and in the Senate hearings that confirmed the recent Supreme Court nomination of Judge Finley Mitchell. Justice Mitchell, who is the son of the former president, was recently seated on the Supreme Court after failed attempts by Sorrell and Warren to bar his nomination."

The reporter had apparently done his homework. "Both appeared to be acts of vengeance against

Justice Finley Mitchell, who was actually related to Judge Sorrell, his half-brother, and Ralston Warren, who was former US President Leif Mitchell's half-nephew and DOD Secretary and both Judge Mitchell's and Judge Sorrell's cousin."

The news had eventually leaked out, first in the prison, then in the press, and finally, was becoming public.

Finn's phone had been ringing non-stop from people asking if it was true that he was actually related to Judge Sorrell and Ralston Warren. He fielded a few but ignored most.

I hope they rot in prison for a long time, Finn thought, clicking off the TV.

While the Loop's triangular tan tower, constructed by "brutalist" concrete architecture standards, looked like any other skyscraper office building from the outside, inside it was the prison it was meant to be.

Tony sat and stared from the bottom cot of the steel bunk bed in his ten-by-ten cramped concrete jail cell that otherwise had a steel toilet and sink, a tiny steel desk and nothing more. The tiny enclosure did have a five-inch-thick window, but it had been frosted and barred after the last several escape attempts occurred. There was no view and no way to escape.

He looked down at his bright orange jumpsuit and wanted to vomit. *This is where I've sent hundreds of people who will now all be out to get me,* Tony thought miserably, trying not to panic. He was informed by his sentencing judge that he would be transferred within the week to the Metropolitan Detention Center in Brooklyn, New York, where he'd be less of a target. He hoped he'd make it through the week.

Since the twenty-seven-story prison was understaffed and overcrowded at its capacity of six-hundred eighty-three prisoners, he'd been temporarily assigned into a cell with a roommate who would not be a threat, at least not for now.

Tony was informed that his roommate, "Big D" as he was aptly nicknamed due to his huge size, was visiting the medical treatment facility within the prison for a sore throat. Danny Duke, who many knew just as Big D, was big in brawn but not in brains, and many at first were intimidated by his brute size, but then realized he was like a very large child or teddy bear. He reportedly had only a fifth-grade education and the IQ of a ten-year-old trapped in the very large body of a man. Big D was incarcerated after he was found guilty of grand larceny—a few members of a street gang in Chicago had conned him into breaking into a street corner mom-and-pop grocery store telling him one of them needed emergency baby supplies for his infant. When the cops showed up, only Big Danny was left staring into the police car lights glaring into the broken storefront window.

Tony hadn't seen his cellmate since arriving at the prison the day before and hoped he'd have the luxury of a single room for his stay.

Three uneventful days passed in solitary confinement for Tony, who hadn't seen his roommate or Ralston, who was also temporarily housed on a different floor in the prison facility awaiting transfer.

But then a guard informed Tony he wouldn't be so fortunate. Big D was headed back after getting some meds—the huge inmate's fever had dissipated, and he was on an antibiotic so he could return to the cell block that evening.

Well, I'll have to make friends and hope for the best, Tony thought, sitting on his bottom bunk reading a worn Stephen King paperback from the jail's small library. *Maybe it will be a good thing to have him on my side, for protection around here.*

Tony stood as the two guards approached, one on either side of the six-foot-six, hefty yet soft looking bald man who had sad sunken brown eyes with circles underneath. Tony guessed he was only in his thirties or forties, although his size, along with his five o'clock shadow, made him look like an older, seasoned con. His bright orange outfit made his skin look pasty and sallow. *Dead man walking.* Tony told himself, *be nice.* He waited until his roommate made eye contact.

"Hello Big D, I'm Tony and ..."

"Shut up in there," one of the guards barked gruffly, standing watch, his hand on his revolver as the other guard quickly removed Big D's handcuffs, gently pushed him into the cell and then shut the steel door with the barred window, which automatically locked.

Now it's just the two of us. Now what? Tony felt fear prick his skin as Big D stood silently staring at him just inside the door.

But then Big D broke the ice. "They're so nasty. Why do they have to be so mean?"

"I know, right?" Tony grinned which elicited a small smile on the giant's puffy face. "We're not that bad in here." He held out his hand and it was engulfed by a leathery mitt that seemed the size of a boxing glove.

"I'm Big Danny, but you can call me Big D." Danny smiled revealing two missing front teeth that made him look a bit goofy ... or more dangerous, depending on a person's point of view.

"Wanna play cards?" Tony asked.

"You got cards? Sure!"

And the two sat on Tony's lower bunk for the next two hours playing Crazy Eights, Go Fish, War, and Gin Rummy. *"Misery acquaints a man with strange bedfellows."* The Shakespeare quote came to mind, and Tony smiled to himself. *How true.*

Tony barely heard the creaking sound as he lay on his bottom cot, Big D fast asleep and snoring above him.

I probably wore him out with all those card games. Tony triumphantly lay on his bunk staring into the blackness of the room. *I've got the big lug on my side now.*

He heard the creak again. *Great, now I'm going to be hearing this all night. I'll never get to sleep.* At first Tony thought with annoyance that the sound was just Big D rolling around up there. But then he realized while the noise was coming from above, his cellmate didn't seem to be moving much. Tony was now on full alert, and his heart started to thud in his ears.

The creaking grew louder and became a groaning, like metal gears grinding or a bed spring bearing a heavy load or the corners of a steel bed frame slowly coming loose and then ...

CRASH!

Silence.

CHAPTER SIXTEEN

No one ever discovered how the bolts on the corners of the iron clad bed frame came loose, causing the entire top bunk to come crashing down on the lower bunk, how the three-hundred-pound inmate lying on top a sturdy steel bunk came suddenly catapulting down, smashing former Judge Anthony Sorrell beneath, crushing him to death.

Big D was devastated, so beside himself it took a team of guards and a horse-sized shot of tranquilizers to get him to calm down. His bawling could be heard through the entire cell block. The other inmates were soon talking, then shouting, until the warden ordered an announcement to be made over the loudspeaker that an accident had occurred and an inmate, Anthony Sorrell, was dead. Loud cheers erupted and an extra half dozen prison guards were summoned on deck to restore order.

The news hit the media early that next morning, and although there was "wide speculation" that the judge's death was orchestrated somehow, it was being called an "unfortunate accident."

Only five people knew for certain the speculation was the truth. They included the unknown inmate who loosened the bolts when Big D was still in the infirmary and Tony was out in the yard, the guard who had handed him the money and looked the other way, the mysterious man who had called in a favor from the assistant warden, the assistant warden of course, and then Ralston Warren, who just knew in his bones he was next on the hit list.

Ralston was shaking with fear as he sat on his bunk after hearing the news.

He only ate a few bites of the plate of cold, congealed scrambled eggs and piece of hard brown toast one of the guards had brought him, and then threw it all up in the steel toilet.

He was incarcerated in a single-cot cell up on the twentieth floor of the tower and tried desperately to ignore the catcalls. News, gossip, and judgement sped like a race car on ice down the cell block, and Ralston had heard about Tony's death within minutes of it actually occurring. Ralston couldn't see who was saying what, he could only hear the threatening voices filled with hatred.

"You're next, lover boy," an inmate next door hissed.

"What happened to the judge is nothing compared to what we're gonna do to you, Warren," another called.

Ralston's heart started beating so fast he felt his chest begin to hurt, and he could imagine having a thousand pounds crashing down, crushing him like it had his cousin.

He lay down on the bunk, closing his eyes and trying to slow his breathing, but the panic in his brain wouldn't let him, and he started hyperventilating and had to sit up again. He broke out in a sweat, his shaved, white fuzzy head now red and pounding, a painful buzzing feeling like electric volts running down his left arm. Suddenly, Ralston felt a vise-like grip tightening his chest.

He felt his mouth water, and then foam mixed with bile started to rise and drip out, and he felt an acid-like burning in his abdomen and esophagus, then a constricting, choking in his throat.

The "heart attack" lasted only a few minutes, caused by the combination of rat poisoning in his eggs and trembling fear in his soul. No one was there to see it, though.

The same guard who'd delivered breakfast was bringing lunch at noon when he discovered Ralston Warren dead, face down on the cold cement cell floor. He disposed of the breakfast remains down the toilet, cleaned the spittle mix of blood and foam from the former army general's mouth, then called in the inmate death to his command center.

Ralston was removed in a body bag and taken to the Cook County coroner who was also paid to report that he'd suffered a heart attack as the cause of death.

Finn listened with mild surprise but not shock to the news about the death of his two family members who'd been locked up thanks to his investigation.

"... notorious inmates Anthony Sorrell, a former Cook County judge, and Ralston Warren, former Director of the US Department of Defense and chief counsel to the past two presidents of the United States, were found dead in their cells in the Metropolitan Correctional Center in Chicago. Both were found guilty of tampering with evidence in the case of the State of Illinois versus Jay Walker, which caused the Justice for All Blacks movement to rally and riot in the city streets when the case was suddenly dismissed by Judge Sorrell for a lack of evidence."

Finn sighed, grateful his name wasn't mentioned. He straightened his tie, then ran a hand through his hair in the hallway mirror, sad blue eyes staring back at him. *They did have it coming to them.* But then he felt a tinge of guilt and remorse at thinking this. After all, his investigation with Richard Layton had caused his half-brother and cousin to be locked up, which had resulted in their deaths. So indirectly, he supposed, he'd played a part in it all, although he knew there were probably more than a handful of people who wanted them both dead and actually plotted to kill them.

He took a deep breath and sighed. He needed to move on, the Supreme Court was starting its deliberations on a big new case in just a week, and he wanted to be prepared.

Not to mention Wu Lei was flying halfway across the world to meet him here in Washington. Of course, she would be with her family, since her father was visiting as Head of State with President Newman on a few political matters. He realized his luck with the timing of the Chinese-American foreign diplomatic exchange planned months ago.

The young couple had stayed in touch via their computer screens, but this would be the first time they would physically meet again since Hamilton Island. Finn spritzed on some cologne and appraised himself one more time in the mirror. His starched white collar gleamed against his fading summer tan. He noticed a few gray hairs. *Comes with the territory.* His cheeks flushed. *I hope she still sees me as handsome.*

No time to worry about that, he reminded himself. Her plane would be arriving at five o'clock, and he had a full day in front of him.

Lei had already updated Finn on life back home in Beijing, where she and her younger sister lived with her parents in Zhongnanhai next to the Forbidden City. She was studying to earn a Master of Fine Arts degree, and while she didn't have to work to make a living, she still loved to design fashion, especially dresses and gowns. Her creations had been shown on the runways in Japan as well as Australia, and she had recently made a name for herself outside of her family fiefdom, her label known as "Lovely by Lei."

She stayed with her family in Blair House in Washington while they visited the President, First Lady, and other dignitaries over the next five days.

Finn made sure the Supreme Court was a must-stop site on the tour for the heads of state, and he forced himself not to stare at Lei as she and her parents and sister greeted each Supreme Court justice. But when their eyes met, it was like an electric jolt coursed through his veins.

Lei bowed then shook his hand. "Judge Mitchell," she said formally.

"Ms. Wu Lei," he said, calling her by her proper Chinese name. He thought she looked lovely, dressed in a smart aqua-blue jacket and skirt.

Alana flirted with him of course. "Finley Mitchell, why, how nice to see you again!"

She curtsied in her red suit and matching beret, which flamed brightly against her jet-black tresses. The family spoke perfect English but their words were still translated by an interpreter which was customary in America. Finn watched out of the corner of his eye as Lei's father, Wu Shin Hai, shot him a wary glance from beady black eyes. His wife, Wu Kai, stood next to him, and Finn realized the girls got their beauty from their mother, who was elegantly gorgeous, her slightly graying black hair swept up in a fashionable chignon. Kai's perfect skin was unmarred by wrinkles, and a dash of dark pink lipstick set off her lighter pink jacket and skirt. Finn noticed she was gazing straight at him, appraising him with her glimmering dark brown eyes.

Finn ceremoniously bowed to Alana, giving her a small smile, but he dared a look ahead at Lei, who darted a quick glance back at him, hiding her smile behind her aqua fan which matched her smart suit and pumps. His heart beat wildly. *This will be my family one day,* he mused.

CHAPTER SEVENTEEN

Taking advantage of the Christmas holiday, Finn chartered a flight to Beijing that following December to visit Lei and ask for her hand in marriage. They had seen each other two more times, again in Hamilton Island on her family vacation, which he'd managed to work around his busy schedule, and on a similar weekend jaunt in Fiji. He'd only gotten to see her two nights each trip, but it was enough for him to know she was the one.

And he knew Lei loved him, and her mother and sister approved. It was the Chinese president who was the problem. He would just have to get through the stony wall of her father's heart.

To facilitate that, he brought along his mother on the private Cessna jet he'd chartered. The flight from DC to Beijing Capital International Airport was approximately fifteen hours, and they were scheduled to arrive two days before Christmas.

Chinese custom called for the groom's parents to literally propose to the bride's parents, bearing gifts. Linda and Finn had shopped together, first to pick out a beautiful necklace for Lei since engagement rings—either giving or wearing one—were not part of the Chinese culture. Then they selected a hand-plated gold vase with an American bald eagle emblem on one side and a Chinese phoenix on the other to signify the joining of their two families. Finn worried now, hoping they'd like it as he sat on the plane gazing out over the carpet of clouds stretching as far as he could see. The sun's rays suddenly burst through the gray, and Finn smiled. Good omen. He pushed his fears aside and began to imagine his life with Lei as his mother dozed, reclined in the seat across from him.

He had already had a construction company start building a house in Bethesda on the outskirts of DC, where he'd been living in the Supreme Court building along with his fellow eight justices, shuttered away from the world so they could debate the highest law cases in a fair and unbiased arena.

Linda stirred, blinking her eyes open and sitting up yawning. "Wow, I must have dozed off," she said. "How long was I asleep?"

"Just a couple of hours. You're lucky, I wish I could sleep. I'm too worried about everything."

Linda smiled sleepily. "Relax, I'm sure Lei's parents will love you the way I do."

"You didn't see how they were looking at me when they visited the Supreme Court. I got the evil eye from Lei's father."

"Well, he would have told you not to come to China at all if he really disliked you."

"Let him try." Finn grinned, relaxing a bit. His mother had a knack for making him feel at ease, even during the tensest moments. She was his biggest ally and fan, and he was grateful she was accompanying him.

"You really love her, don't you?" Linda touched her son's cheek fondly.

"I really do, Mom."

Although their visit was considered a private one versus an official and ceremonious 'head of state' reception, a few of the media were gathered as Finn and Linda stepped off the plane and were greeted by President Wu Shin Hai's chief representative and the US Ambassador to China.

They were whisked away by a waiting limousine to the Diaoyutai State Guesthouse, a historic hotel complex in Beijing.

Finn marveled at the vast array of Chinese architecture—buildings, houses, gardens all designed in typical fashion using symmetrical layers, the ancient pagoda-style structures with pointed corners bearing symbols in red, black, and gold. All were blanketed under fresh snow that made the scenery look like a Christmas card ... including the traditional decorations, even though it wasn't a religious holiday.

Some Christians practiced in China, but they were few and far between and still came under attack at times by the Chinese government under the People's Republic, which called for religious unification. The official religion that had swept over much of the country was a combination of atheism and Chinese folk religion that was more of a cultural society versus anything spiritual. Up until this point in their relationship, Finn and Lei hadn't discussed religion much, agreeing not to let it interfere with their love.

Linda and Finn Mitchell freshened up at the guesthouse and got ready for a private dinner with the Wu family.

Finn wore his best suit, a solid black Armani with a festive white and red striped tie.

"You look dashing," Linda said, appraising her son as the two waited in the hotel lobby.

"Thank you, Mom. And you look gorgeous."

Linda smiled, basking in her son's compliments. She wore an elegant, black velvet, tea-length dress with a red satin sash around her waist. Her blonde hair was cut short and showed off her ruby earrings which Leif had given her a few Christmases ago— selected by Alisa, she was sure.

The limo took them to meet the Wu family for a private dinner at Zhongnanhai, where the Chinese paramount leader, his wife, and two daughters lived in what was China's equivalent of the US White House. They meandered past Tiananmen Square and the Forbidden City, which was adjacent. The limo driver drove them through the fifteen-hundred-acre private compound of Zhongnanhai, a city in itself—past gardens, lakes, and the red-lanterned wall which stopped everyone except the Communist party leaders and reigning family who resided there. Security had been heightened ever since the nearby Tiananmen Square fiasco in the eighties. Zhongnanhai was now considered top secret and off limits to the public.

Finn drew in his breath as they drove up to the red gates, their Chinese writing scrawled left and right. Translated into English, they read, "Long Live the Communist Party of China' and 'Long Live the

Invincible Mao Zedong Thought'. Inside the gate was a screen wall inscribed with the slogan 'Serve the People' penned by Chairman Mao Zedong, former Communist China leader and the founder of the People's Republic of China. Linda and Finn gazed for a few moments at the intricate colorfully painted pagoda building that towered above them. Then their limo doors were opened. They stepped out and walked up the red carpet leading to the massive red and gold front doors, which were opened for them by flanking guards.

Inside, the two marveled at the golden interior with chandeliers overhanging marble floors and sparse yet plush upholstered furniture.

"Wow," Linda said, expressing Finn's sentiments exactly. "And we thought the White House was impressive."

A suited young gentleman greeted them, introducing himself as President Wu's representative, and showed them into the formal dining room where the Wu family stood and welcomed them.

All three women looked ravishing in traditional Chinese silk robes, one more colorful than the next— Lei was in a royal blue dress, her sister in a red one, and her mother in yellow.

They were served tea and then dined on Peking duck, chicken, and fish.

Retiring to the sitting area, a fire crackling in the huge marble fireplace, Finn and Linda sat in ornate upholstered chairs facing their hosts.

They enjoyed more tea and a dessert of almond and sesame cookies and chocolate five-spice cake. But Finn could barely eat anything, he was so nervous. He managed to force down a cookie to be polite.

After dessert, they talked about Finn's plans for his new house and a bit about the current Supreme Court case.

Finn then stood, looked at his mom as a signal for her to stand, and the two presented Lei's parents with their gift.

They politely smiled, opened it, and thanked their guests.

Then Finn gulped and humbly bowed before the Chinese president and asked for his daughter's hand in marriage.

He spoke in nearly perfect Mandarin as he'd practiced over and over in his head and out loud during the fifteen-hour flight, and even in the limo ride with his mother. But the Communist leader scowled and gruffly said, "No, we will not allow it," taking Finn aback and causing Linda's mouth to hang open in shocked umbrage.

"We will not allow our daughter to marry any man who is not Chinese and who does not share our belief as nationalists," Wu Shin Han said sternly. He handed the gift back to Linda Mitchell. "We cannot accept this."

Linda looked helplessly at her son at that point.

Lei stood and pleaded, "but Daddy…" A cold hard glare from her father cut her off. Tears in her eyes, she turned and fled the room. Finn balled his fists angrily, but realized saying anything would be futile, and maybe even dangerous if he couldn't control his temper. Without a word, he motioned to his mother and they silently walked out into the winter night. A driver was already waiting to escort them off the premises.

Just as Finn was helping his mother into the black sedan, he heard Lei's voice call out to him.

"Finn, wait!" He couldn't believe his eyes. She ran to him, her face tear-streaked, and threw herself into his arms. "I want to go with you."

"But ... what will your father do if—"

She released him and looked down, shedding more tears. "He has already disowned me. I am now no longer part of the family. But I don't care as long as I'm with you."

"Lei, I can't ask you to do that, to sacrifice your home, your family for me—"

"I have already decided." Her tearful eyes steeled with resolve. "I will not let my father rule my life anymore."

He held her face in his hands and looked into her eyes, which once again softened. "If you're sure—"

"Yes. I want to marry you. I love you."

"I love you too, Wu Lei." Finn grinned, hugging and kissing her as snowflakes fell around them.

Lei explained her mother had talked her father into letting her stay long enough to pack her belongings and then would fly her to a temporary private residence in Washington, DC, until they could get married.

Finn reluctantly parted with his betrothed, joining his mother, who had watched everything from the back seat, a wary expression plastered on her face.

The plane ride back to the US with his mother was long and arduous. Linda now felt free to let her feelings out.

"Finn, are you sure you know what you're getting into here?" Linda leaned forward in the leather recliner seat in the private charter plane, her brow furrowed with concern for her only child who sat across from her staring out of the plane window, thinking of all the plans that lay ahead. "Do you hear me, Son?"

He forced himself to turn and face her piercing eyes that glittered now with worry. "I do, Mom. But I love her, and it will all work out. Our love will be enough to see us through anything."

Linda sighed. "Sometimes, love is not enough," she said. "The heart can have the best of intentions but if it bends the will against God ..."

"Mom, don't you think you're being a little judgmental and self-righteous?"

"Finley Daniel Mitchell! I'm your mother, and I'm only looking out for your best interests, not to mention your heart and soul." Linda Mitchell's indignity turned into a hurtful pout, an expression that always moved him.

"I'm sorry, Mother. It's just that, maybe your generation ... and Lei's parents too ... are more devout when it comes to religion than ours. I know Lei will honor whatever God I believe in even if she doesn't believe it, and vice versa."

"And what God is that, Finn?"

"Mom, you know." Finn was growing exasperated with their conversation. All he wanted to do was daydream about his bride to be, the wedding night, their future in the new home he was having built—not talk about God and religion.

"I want to hear you say it, Finn. It's been a long time since you and I have talked about any of this or even went to church together, so maybe I'm not sure anymore—or maybe you're not either. I just want to know."

Finn settled back into his seat, gripping the armchair rests with his hands, taking a deep breath in and out. "Okay ... I believe in God the Father, God the Son, and God the Holy Spirit."

"And that's not just lip service, right?"

"No, I really do. I realize I don't go to church as often as I should. I will try to do better at that, Mom. In fact, I'll even go with you this coming Sunday before the Court goes back in session again. We'll make a day of it, okay?"

His mother smiled, seemingly appeased—at least for the moment.

But Finn himself was worried now. What if Lei tried to talk him out of his belief in God? What kind of Higher Power did she believe in, if any? Her father? The Communist Party? He closed his eyes, but his mind churned, ruminating on the possible turmoil their vast difference in religious outlooks could cause. Luckily the Dramamine kicked in, and he started to fall asleep but not before a final foggy thought drifted through his head ... *will love really be enough?*

CHAPTER EIGHTEEN

Finn and Linda had thought long and hard on where the perfect wedding venue would be, and with Lei's approval, settled on the exclusive and historic Engineers Club of Baltimore for its privacy and elegance.

The day finally came, dawning warm and bright, although thankfully not as hot and humid as some Baltimore summer days could be.

Finn had chosen his older half brother, Harry, to stand up for him as his best man. Although they hadn't been close over the years, they had become reacquainted somewhat at their father's funeral, and Harry had warmly accepted. He flew in with his new wife, Marisa, from London to DC a few days before the wedding to get together with Finn for a celebratory dinner. The couple stayed along with Lei at Blair House.

All the guests were shuttled by limousines to the Garrett Jacobs Mansion in Mount Vernon Place where the Engineers Club was located. Lei had invited her best friend, Mei, who had flown over with her husband for the wedding and would be standing up for her as maid of honor. Peter Baldwin, a few of

Linda's and Finn's family and close friends, and the other supreme court justices and their families were also invited, but Finn and Lei had kept the guest list relatively small with only fifty people in attendance.

It was perfect, Finn thought as he waited for his bride to walk down the aisle of the magnificent historic blue ballroom where guests were seated in white lawn chairs lined on either side of the parquet wood aisle.

Mei glided down first sheathed in a stunning, plum satin, tea-length dress, her hair falling to her shoulders.

But Finn only had eyes for his bride. She looked radiant in a traditional elegant red satin gown she'd designed, a white lotus flower in her ebony hair, which was swept up to the side with a few stray curls falling softly around her flawless face. Chinese tradition did not call for wedding rings to signify if a woman was single or married—their status was signified by how their hair was styled—up for married, down or free-flowing for single.

Linda was seated in the front row, smiling through her tear-filled eyes.

Finn glanced at his mom and smiled but wondered if her tears were of happiness in gaining a daughter, or sadness in losing him, her son, then told himself it didn't matter. His heart was filled with joy, love, and anticipation.

The couple had chosen a fellow judicial friend licensed to marry to conduct the non-religious ceremony. Lei had acquiesced when Finn insisted they exchange wedding rings and gasped when she saw the exquisite band of gold inlaid with tiny diamonds he put on her finger when the time came, looking up at him with love glimmering in her dark brown eyes.

They wrote their own vows.

"Wu Lei, my beloved, I take you to be my wife, to honor you and be faithful to you, in good times and bad ... to laugh and cry with you, to support you and believe in you, to love and cherish you all the days of my life." Finn meant every word with his whole heart and soul.

"Finley Daniel Mitchell, my beloved, I take you to be my husband ..." Lei repeated the vow, her eyes glistening.

At the reception, they feasted on a Chinese banquet of roasted suckling pig, Peking duck, dumplings, and a variety of rice and noodle dishes, and then cut and shared their tiered wedding cake, a bow to the American tradition. They had a deejay playing music and danced their first dance as husband and wife to the song "A One in a Million You" by Larry Graham.

The reception ended with tea and fortune cookies stuffed with various messages of love bearing "Finn and Lei" in cursive on the other side.

They'd hired a private photographer and managed to keep the media hounds at bay for the small private gathering but knew they'd be waiting just outside the mansion to snap pictures when it was over. While he didn't mind basking in the limelight, Finn knew his future wife and her friends did, so he gave specific instructions to the Secret Service agents and security guards stationed around the perimeter of the building and asked them to make sure they would get by as unscathed as possible by publicity. The couple would dash into a waiting limo while the rest of the guests would exit a back door into black vehicles with dark tinted windows that would take some straight to the airport for their flight back to China.

Their first argument was over decorating their new house, which happened a few days after they returned from their honeymoon on Hamilton Island. They'd spent two glorious weeks revisiting the same hotel and beaches they had been to before, only this time together, experiencing everything as a couple.

Unfortunately, Finn had to keep in contact with the construction crew nearly every day during his honeymoon trip to make sure the final details were carried out to his specifications.

The new house was completed upon Finn and Lei's return. Finn had had an interior decorator fully furnish it so his bride would not have to bother.

Finn carried her over the threshold of the entrance door to their massive new home and breathlessly awaited her reaction as they both stood in the foyer surveying the first floor.

He watched his wife's face with anticipation as she walked into the sprawling estate home and surveyed the vast living room with its modern western décor—a tan leather sectional sofa, exposed adobe walls, turquoise and red accents, high ceilings, and an original Matisse painting adorning one wall.

But instead of the surprised smile he expected to spread across his lovely wife's face, Finn watched Lei's expression turn into a frown.

"Don't you like it?" he asked, crestfallen.

"Well, it's big," Lei said. "And I realize all of the time, effort, and money you put into it, but ... this will be my home, and I just don't love ... well, like even, some of these decorations."

"Which ones?" Finn narrowed his eyes toward her warily.

She turned to him, blushing, her eyes downcast. "Any—all of them."

"Why not?" Finn felt a resentment bristling within him, and though he tried to fight it, it crept up and overwhelmed him, turning into anger. "I can't believe you don't like any of this. I had the best interior decorator in the United States fly out here from California." He had given the designer carte blanch—an unlimited budget—and he felt like she had delivered. He loved the simple yet elegant décor with its rich cream, tan, and coffee-colored walls adorned by original paintings by Matisse and Monet which had cost a fortune, along with the modern sectional furniture and dark cherry and mahogany wood pieces. Skylights and recessed, contemporary light fixtures gave the room an airy yet warm and homey feel.

Lei walked through the far arched doorway and turned to face him across the room as he stood in place, waiting for her answer.

"I'm not quite sure—I just want to add my own flair, I guess." She sighed. "I'm sorry, it is lovely." She crossed the room to him and gave him a big hug, but he resisted, still disappointed in her reaction. *She's just pacifying me,* he thought. Still, how important was it to argue over this? Finn wouldn't even be living here while the Supreme Court was in session anyway.

He conceded. "All right, I guess it's only fair to have you add your own flair," he said, smiling down at her upturned, eager face, kissing her forehead.

She smiled. "Just a few touches, I promise. I'll wait until you go off to the court and surprise you when you come home again."

Finn ignored the dim warning signal going off in his head.

CHAPTER NINETEEN

Finn sat at his desk with a cup of hot black coffee to begin reviewing the stacks of paperwork that comprised the court briefs of the monumental case before his fellow justices on the Supreme Court and him. The thick docket held all the original court transcripts, describing in detail after vivid detail the case of *Birch vs. Walters.*

Marianne Birch, aka Mary Smith, had sued former healthcare worker Christine Walters for custody of her son, Jesse Walters. Mary had born the child but had given it up—not for adoption but for abortion.

Christine Walters had been on her shift that day at the small new practice run by Nathaniel Townsend, M.D. in Tallahassee, Florida, and was pulled in by the doctor to help with the procedure when Mary started crying hysterically. The teenage mother had waited to get the abortion procedure until she was five months along. At first, she waited because she couldn't make up her mind if she wanted to have the baby or not. She'd said the father of the child was unavailable, and he'd dropped out of their school and skipped town—so she'd had to wait until she'd saved enough money for the procedure. Then she was faced with having to cross state lines to find a place that would provide a late-term abortion, given the anti-abortion climate in her home state of Alabama.

She was given local anesthesia and a mild sedative and was out of it when the fetus was extricated from her. Mary wasn't expecting her child would come out alive, nor was the doctor, nor Christine. And yet he was, born a little over ten inches long and weighing just a pound, heart beating, all his body parts intact, sucking his thumb.

Doctor Nate Townsend stared at him for a moment, then swooped him up, simultaneously telling Christine to calm the mother. "Get her to be quiet, she's going to scare our other patient out of here," he hissed under his breath. There was one other woman sitting in the tiny waiting room.

As the doctor quickly injected more sedative into the IV drip, Chrissy went from the foot of the gurney where Mary lay, her feet still up in stirrups, up to the head of the bed, and took Mary's hand, squeezing it, shushing her, whispering "it's okay, it's okay," while her own heart thumped wildly in her chest because she knew it was absolutely *not okay*. Mary finally drifted off to sleep, exhausted.

"What are you going to do with ... um, him?" she'd asked the doctor in a shaky voice, feeling her own tears fall, nodding her head toward the infant now wrapped in a small towel.

"You know what to do, take it to the disposal," Doctor Townsend said, handing her the bloody towel with the fetus wrapped inside, and walking out of the room.

She'd saved him and named him Jesse. And although he struggled to breathe, to even stay alive for the first six months of his life, he was two years old now, and Mary, or Marianne Birch, wanted him back, saying he was hers to begin with.

After he'd become strong enough to survive on his own, Christine had brought Jesse back to her tiny apartment in Tallahassee, struggling to make ends meet. Her current job was as a receptionist at an accounting firm, the latest in a string of day jobs she'd performed after she quit working in abortion clinics for good the day Jesse was born. Her mom was a big help, watching Jesse for her during work.

But when she was served the family court papers in which Marianne Birch claimed custody, she'd immediately had to pay to hire a lawyer to fight to keep the little boy she now called her son.

Ms. Birch had pleaded her case to a local district court judge, then a state circuit court judge, who passed it up the ladder to finally land on the docket of the Florida Supreme Court.

Christine had maxed out every credit card, drawn every last dime out of her checking and savings accounts, used her entire small inheritance, then even filed for bankruptcy. She finally moved with her son from her tiny apartment she could no longer afford in with her aging mother in an effort to keep fighting for custody.

Christine reflected on her career at the abortion clinic, remembering how it all started as if it were just yesterday.

It was the first day of her internship at the Pro-Choice Providers women's healthcare facility in Tallahassee, Florida. Christine Walters, freshly graduated from Florida State University, looked up at the nondescript beige box building with the familiar logo, took a deep breath, and headed in the front door.

An older woman named Trish, dressed in a white lab coat over a navy pantsuit, her hair done up in a tight bob, greeted her from behind the lobby's front desk, handing her a badge with "Chrissy" on it, the name her friends called her, a large envelope bearing the words "Welcome Packet," and some paperwork she needed to fill out. When she was finished, Trish gave her a tour of the facility.

They went down a flight of steps to the medical and health care units. "... and here is where the doctors perform the pregnancy termination procedures," Trish had said.

Otherwise known as abortions. Chrissy lingered at the door of one of the rooms and darted a quick glance through the glass pane. Inside she noticed two young women about her age seated in the lobby bent over clipboards filling out paperwork.

Chrissy had majored in social work at Florida State. Her grades were average, and she struggled to get through college, finally making it into her senior year. But there was no time to take any breathers since she still needed to get a working internship under her belt in order to graduate. She'd applied to various healthcare and government organizations as graduation loomed. Pro-Choice Providers was not her first choice for an internship, since she knew she'd face her parents' wrath over it. Still, she needed to work *somewhere* part-time in order to receive her Bachelor of Social Work degree, and her school counselor had recommended she apply everywhere she could.

Her parents were devout Catholics and had frowned upon her announcement over the Thanksgiving dinner table that November. Luckily her brother's antics with having too much wine that night overshadowed her internship news when he spilled his Merlot all over the cream-colored carpeting of their ranch home.

She'd excused herself, saying she had semi-finals to study for, relieved she hadn't had to elaborate on the details.

That was many years ago, and she had worked there for twenty-five years. They'd even celebrated her twenty-fifth anniversary and gotten her a huge sheet cake that said "Congratulations Chrissy" written in big loopy blue letters across the top.

Never in her wildest dreams as an intern, then as a receptionist, and finally as the administrative assistant, did she think she'd remain employed there that long.

They had a high turnover and she was able to move quickly up the ladder. She'd had dreams of one day owning her own private practice as a psychotherapist, getting out of there—but then there was an opening, a need, cajoling from the boss, an advancement, a big raise. She always told herself she should be happy to stay in Tallahassee to be close to her parents. She was an only child and they suffered from various health problems and needed her. And she told herself she should be grateful to work in the women's healthcare field, to "make a difference."

But then the fateful day when she did try to make a difference was the beginning of the end.

Her parents had never really talked to her about her field of employment, preferring not to show their disappointment—until her father finally told her how he felt on his deathbed.

"... Christine," he had always called her by her given name. "I need to give you a last bit of advice."

"Oh, Harold," her mom had chided him. Obviously, she knew what he wanted to talk about.

"I need to warn her," he'd said.

"Dad, it's okay, just rest." Chrissy had tried to keep her voice soothing even though she felt a sense of dread.

That's when her father reached out his knobby, spotted hand and opened it, dropping a blue crystal rosary bead necklace into her hand. "This was mine. My grandmother gave it to me when I was your age, and I want you to have it." He'd choked back a cough. "I've prayed using it every day since, many times for the unborn babies ..."

Chrissy's eyes welled with tears. *I'm sorry I've brought you so much disappointment Dad,* she wanted to say but didn't.

"... and I pray for you, that one day you'll see the truth ..." another phlegm-filled cough rattled from his throat.

Chrissy looked down at the blue crystal beads in her hand with the silver crucifix. It seemed like Jesus was looking down, away from her. *He's probably disappointed just like they are, she'd thought.*

Just then her father had taken one last rattling breath, sighed, closed his eyes and his hands fell limply at his sides.

Chrissy cried softly, her mom came over and they just sat together for a while.

On the day she went back to work, exactly one week after bereavement leave following her father's funeral, the unthinkable happened.

They were short-staffed that particular day and Chrissy was busy at the front desk answering the phone and making appointments. Most were for contraception, STD or STI testing, HIV tests, and 'pregnancy termination' procedures, although a few were for regular health checkups and cancer screenings.

The phone rang constantly, and aside from bathroom breaks and a half-hour lunch, she worked almost nonstop that day. She was counting down the minutes until it was time to go home when she saw the wall clock read three-forty-five. She had just fifteen minutes to go before her shift ended when her last call of the day came in—one that would stick with her into the night and beyond, coming back to haunt her at times.

The very young female voice on the other end timidly asked if she could speak to someone about an abortion. Chrissy introduced herself as the administrative assistant and told her she was there to help direct her after taking her identification and insurance information.

"Can I have your name and birth date?" Chrissy asked politely.

"Jane ... uh ... Jones." Chrissy wondered if that was the girl's real name, and when she figured out Jane was barely eighteen from the birth date she stated, she began to wonder if the girl was telling the truth.

"I ... uh ... don't have insurance," Jane nearly whispered in a soft voice, "but I ... um, my boyfriend ... can pay for the procedure with cash. How much does it cost?"

"That depends on how far along you are." Chrissy had been trained to ask the right questions. "Do you know the date you conceived?" Several seconds ticked by on the clock. "Got pregnant?" Chrissy offered, trying to be helpful.

"Oh, sure ... I'm about uh, well, about four months along and ..."

Chrissy was stunned at first. Most of the women she'd talked to during the day said they were only ten to twelve weeks pregnant. One was thirteen weeks. But none were more than three months pregnant—until now. "Oh, well, in that case, since you're pretty far along, you would be looking at the maximum amount of fifteen hundred dollars." She could hear the sharp intake of air and gulping sound Jane made on the other end. "Are you still there? Does your boyfriend or a close family member have insurance, or are you on any government subsidized programs that might pay for the procedure?" She could hear a sniff and a muffled whimper and could tell Jane was crying now.

"I don't know what to do ..." Jane wailed on the other end. "I can't have this baby, I just can't ..."

Something inside Chrissy broke that day, and her heart went out to Jane as she heard her father's last words—*you'll see the truth.* "Let's talk," she said trying to sound calm and soothing. "It will be okay ..."

Just then her boss had bustled into the clinic. After Chrissy hung up, the administrator grilled her, and she told her the truth. Chrissy had talked the girl out of having the abortion she'd planned. She'd cost the clinic another client and another fifteen hundred dollars. And she was proud of herself and said she'd do it all over again if she had the chance.

Christine was fired the following Monday.

After nearly a year of searching for a job and realizing she'd been blackballed, she stumbled across a brand-new doctor in town who hung an OB-GYN shingle on a tiny clinic in a shopping center and recently opened for business. Doctor Nathaniel Townsend didn't even ask her any questions when she went in for an interview. She was hired on the spot. Just coming out of a bitter divorce, the young doctor had bills and loans to pay and desperately needed to start making money. He needed help, and Christine Walters needed a job.

CHAPTER TWENTY

Finn opened the huge, thick docket titled *Birch v. Walters* that lay on his desk. He could picture the courtroom drama unfolding as he looked at photos and artists' renderings of the people involved and read the transcripts.

Judge Howard McNamara had presided over the court case in Florida. He was a burly, weathered-looking Irishman with a slight brogue and still some red showing in his gray hair and beard, indicating he was probably in his sixties.

"All rise," the bailiff bellowed. Marianne Birch and her attorney stood to the left of the room from the judge's bench view, Christine and her attorney to the right. Behind them sat only a few onlookers, made up of a few members of both the plaintiff's and defendant's families, as well as a local newspaper reporter and an assistant defense attorney taking copious notes.

Miss Birch was dressed in a navy skirt and matching blazer with a white collared shirt and inexpensive black pumps, all of which she'd purchased at a thrift shop for the occasion. Her long, wavy hair was dyed in an ombre style—dark brown at the roots with blonde strands at the tips. Heavily applied makeup couldn't erase the hard lines that time had etched on her face already, nor hide the rage of a lifetime that had deadened her eyes.

Her attorney, Annette Dahlia, an attractive young woman of Middle Eastern descent with perfect teeth and flawless skin, dressed in a dark gray Anne Klein suit, approached her client. "Tell us about how you got pregnant ... and why you decided not to have the baby," she asked softly, her voice just above a whisper.

Marianne's eyes flitted up to the judge, who nodded compassionately, then to Ms. Dahlia. "I was dating Kenny Jackson. He was the lead guitarist in a punk rock band named Skull Island," she started, her high-pitched voice faltering at first, quivering with emotion, then becoming hard and defensive. "I followed him everywhere, to all his gigs. He played in some of the top bars in Alabama. They were great. I kept telling them they needed to do more marketing if they wanted to make it big, but they kept saying they weren't about the money, just all about the music." Marianne sighed.

"Kenny worked a few part-time jobs, but he drank or smoked away most of his paychecks. Still, I loved him, and well, one night I think we forgot to use protection. I missed my next period a few weeks later, so I got a pregnancy test kit, and it was positive. I wanted to have the baby at first ..." Mary brought a tissue up to her eyes and wiped a tear that fell, smearing her mascara. "But Kenny was really upset and said there was no way we could raise a kid with him on the road playing with the band all the time and working in between gigs. So, I started to think about, you know, having an abortion. I was really torn. I was only eighteen and had just graduated from high school with my whole life in front of me. I was studying to be a cosmetologist." She smiled wistfully.

"Anyway, I was also working at a salon in my senior year and had managed to save up a few hundred dollars. I couldn't talk to my parents about the whole thing. I went to the local Pro-Choice Providers clinic in Birmingham where I lived but they said abortions were prohibited in Alabama under a new law that was passed. I had no idea." Marianne dabbed her eyes with the tissue again, her voice cracking.

"I tried to talk Kenny into marrying me and having the baby, but he wouldn't have it. In fact, the night we talked about it after one of his shows, he got furious. Hardly anyone had showed up that night at the venue, which was just a tiny dive bar, a hole in the wall really. Only about a dozen people were standing around, and the band hadn't practiced in a while since one of the guys had a kid the month before, so the audience started booing them. It was awful. Kenny got drunk that night, so my timing wasn't that great. I was already starting to show, and I told him about my visit to Pro-Choice Providers and how I had the money with me but they said no. I started crying which only made him madder ..." Marianne started weeping.

"Would you like a few minutes, Ms. Birch, to collect yourself?" Judge McNamara asked in his kind, Irish brogue, leaning toward the plaintiff to hand her a box of tissues.

Marianne sniffed and shook her head no. "I'd like to finish, if that's okay with you, Your Honor."

Ms. Dahlia tossed her shoulder-length black hair behind her. "Are you sure you don't want a break, Miss Birch?"

"No, I'll continue," Marianne said, taking a deep breath.

"So, what happened next?" Annette Dahlia walked closer to the witness box, nodding her approval.

"I kept at it, yelling at Kenny that he should grow up and be a man and take some responsibility, telling him if he really loved me he'd let me have the baby—" Marianne emitted a small cry, then blurted out, "and that's when he slapped me."

"Your boyfriend slapped you? In the face?"

Mary nodded, her cheeks growing red with shame and her eyes welling with fresh tears. "That's when I knew ..." she whispered.

"Knew what?" Ms. Dahlia paced, her tone deliberate now.

"Knew I could never bring a child into the world with a father like that."

"So, you ended the relationship?"

"I did. I never went to another concert ever again. I was done. I had friends whose boyfriends hit them, and I had promised myself I would never put up with that. No guy was worth it. It was hard, I really did love him and his music, but I realized it was over."

"What happened next?"

"I called a friend who said she knew of this new doctor in Tallahassee who she'd heard was doing, uh, procedures. She said she thought Florida's laws were less strict than Alabama's, but it still might be tough, and she wasn't sure they'd still do one since I was so far along. I called, and the doctor himself answered and said he might do it if I hurried in and got it done right away. So that same day, I packed up my things and left my parents a note telling them I was moving out. I told them not to try to come find me. I drove to Florida, straight to Tallahassee and got a hotel room. And that's when my baby boy was born."

"No further questions, Your Honor." Ms. Dahlia took her seat and the defense attorney, Randy Stone, rose from his seat and approached the witness.

"I'm sorry to hear you went through all of that." Finn could imagine the tall, handsome middle-aged lawyer unbuttoning his tailored suit, crossing his arms, and leaning against the railing of the empty jury box. "Tell me, Ms. Smith ... or Ms. Birch ... which one is it?" Randy Stone paused for effect, then continued. "I know you gave Doctor Townsend's office the name of Mary Smith at the time, correct? Why didn't you give your real name—Marianne?"

"Umm, I was, you know ..." Miss Birch stammered.

"No, we don't know. Please tell the court why you used a false name."

She sighed. "I guess, I was ashamed."

"You were ashamed of being pregnant? Or getting an abortion?"

"Objection!" Ms. Dahlia rose to her feet indignantly. "Mr. Stone is badgering the witness, Your Honor."

"Overruled. Please answer the question, Miss Birch."

"Of, uh, terminating the pregnancy." Obviously she'd been coached, choosing her words carefully, Finn realized.

"So why did you go through with the abortion?"

"Objection, Your Honor," Annette Dahlia said again. "The witness already answered that question."

"Sustained."

"Let me rephrase the question," Mr. Stone said. "If you felt ashamed about getting an abortion, about using your real name, did you have any second thoughts about having the procedure?"

"I guess so."

"And did anyone try to talk you out of it at the time?"

Marianne looked at Christine, seated at the defense table and nodded in her direction. "She did."

"Can you please state the name of the 'she' in question for the record, Miss Birch?"

"I believe she said her name was Chrissy."

"And that would be my client, Miss Christine Walters, seated here?" Mr. Stone waved his hand in the direction of the defendant.

Finn had seen photos of Christine Walters and imagined her in his mind's eye ... Chrissy sat staring, her big brown eyes wide, observant, glittering with expectancy and a hint of fear. Her light brown hair was neatly brushed, parted to the side, and curled slightly at her shoulders. She wore a pinstriped gray suit, a cream-colored silk blouse and a dusting of makeup on her cheeks, with a bit of lip gloss and mascara, and looked a little bit younger than her years.

Marianne's glare and tone toward her belied her disdain toward her adversary. "Yes."

"What did she say?"

"That's hearsay, Your Honor." Ms. Dahlia objected.

"Overruled. Please answer," the judge said.

"She told me I might want to rethink my options, that I was pretty far along."

"But you decided to go through with the abortion anyway?"

"Yes."

"Were you healthy at the time?" Mr. Stone peered over his glasses at the witness, who hesitated long enough for the attorney to get agitated. "Miss Birch?"

Marianne hesitated a few more seconds, unsure how to answer. "Umm, as far as I remember."

"And was the baby—the fetus you were carrying—healthy at the time?"

Again, the plaintiff hesitated, causing the judge to prod her. "Miss Birch, please answer the question."

"I ... I don't know, I'm not sure."

"Let me provide the OB-GYN's statement to the court as Exhibit A." Mr. Stone strode back to the table where Christine sat, picked up a manilla folder, opened it and read from a sheet of paper within. "This is a signed medical record from the offices of Oakington Obstetrics, Gynecology and Nurse-Midwifery stating that an ultrasound was performed at nineteen weeks showing baby Jesse—"

"Objection, Your Honor! The fetus in question had no name at the time."

"Sustained." Judge McNamara tiredly rubbed his eyes. "Be more careful in your line of questioning, Mr. Stone."

"I'm sorry, Your Honor." The handsome attorney suppressed a small smile and cleared his throat. "A matter of semantics."

"Semantics are important in my courtroom, Mr. Stone." The judge cast a warning glare toward one attorney, then the other. "As is time, which is running short, so please wrap up your line of questioning."

"The fetus was healthy, was it not Ms. Birch?"

"I guess so." Marianne fidgeted in the witness stand.

"No signs of abnormalities, a regular heartbeat. In fact, you were told it was a boy?"

"Yes." Marianne glanced wildly at her attorney, looking uncomfortable.

"So, the *only* reason you decided to get an abortion ... was not because you were raped or forced to have sex, not because your life or the child's was at risk, not because of any chance of birth defects or health problems ... it was because you *wanted* one?"

"I had no money, no support, no place to live, no full-time job, no way to take care of—"

Mr. Stone cut her off mid-sentence. "We don't need to hear any more excuses, Ms. Birch. No further questions, Your Honor."

Ms. Dahlia resumed her questioning.

"Marianne, why are you seeking custody of the child, Jesse Walters?"

"Because he's my son," the young woman answered in a direct, defiantly curt tone, which she immediately softened, her eyes shining with tears again. "I had no idea the amount of love I'd feel for him. But I do love him. I am his mother, and nothing can change that. I realize I made a terrible mistake."

CHAPTER TWENTY-ONE

On redirect, Mr. Stone was apparently a lot less laid back in his line of questioning. "Miss Birch, if you didn't want a child two years ago, what would possibly make us think you'd want one now?"

"I've grown up a lot."

"In just two short years?" the attorney asked incredulously.

"Yes, I believe so. I finished cosmetology school, I got a full-time job, and I've reconciled with my parents, who are here today and have agreed to help me raise Jesse in their home." Finn had seen photos of Marianne's parents, the child's grandparents, who looked like they were in their fifties or sixties and appeared to be fine, well-dressed citizens. He'd read that Mr. Birch was a pipefitter, Mrs. Birch a librarian, and both lived near their daughter now in Alabama.

"So, you couldn't raise the child on your own?"

"No, I could, it's just this way, I don't have to pay rent so they're helping me save money toward Jesse's college fund."

Good answer, Finn thought.

Following a break for lunch, it was the defense's turn, and Mr. Stone called Christine Walters to the stand.

After stating her name, the attorney kindly asked his client to tell the court what happened that fateful day in September when Jesse was born.

"I was called in by Doctor Nate Townsend to assist with a late-term abortion," Christine said. "He told me he was a little nervous since he'd never done one after twenty weeks before, and he'd need some help. It wasn't part of my job description, but since I was his only employee, I didn't see any other option."

"There was a tornado watch in the area that day, correct?"

"Yes, the roads were pretty bad. It was windy and raining hard. We were going to close early, but then Mary Smith arrived. Another girl came in a few minutes later, but she must have changed her mind because when we were finished with Mary, she was gone."

"Tell me about your conversation with Mary."

"I saw she was in some distress, her face looked red, and her eyes were puffy—I assumed from crying. She also had a faded bruise on her cheek. I felt really bad for her."

"Go on."

"I asked her if she wanted to talk, and she started to cry, so I sat down next to her in the lobby, and I put my arm around her. She looked like she could use a friend. Then she started to tell me about her boyfriend hitting her, how he didn't want the baby, how she'd broken up with him, and how she didn't have anybody else in the world. I asked her if she was sure she wanted to go through with the abortion procedure. She said yes, she was sure."

"And then what happened?"

"Doctor Townsend took Marianne's ... Mary's blood pressure, and it was pretty high. He also had me help him do an ultrasound, and we found out the fetus was right at twenty-four weeks in gestation. Since the patient's blood pressure continued to climb, the doctor told me it was incumbent upon him under the law to carry out the procedure. He gave Mary—that was the name she'd written on all the paperwork—a mild sedative and a hormone to induce labor. But then it was raining, and the wind suddenly started blowing hard outside. Hurricane Nila, the one they'd been predicting, was hitting sooner and harder than we'd expected. We had to hurry and get done and get out of there. Dr. Townsend said we didn't have time to give the fetus an injection that would stop its heart, and he would just have to get it out ... deliver it. He used forceps and suction to extricate the baby ... I mean the fetus.

"And then what were your instructions from the doctor at that point?"

"He instructed me to dispose of the fetus as usual after it came out."

"And what does that mean, 'as usual'?"

"It means I was supposed to put the baby ... excuse me, the fetus ... in a plastic bag and then dispose of it in the medical waste bin in the custodial room."

"Which is basically a janitor's closet?"

"Yes."

"But what happened instead?"

"He handed me the fetus in a small towel, and I thought I felt something. I unwrapped the cloth and saw it's ... his ... little chest moving—" Christine started weeping on the stand, so the judge allowed for a ten-minute recess.

Chrissy came back on the stand, her eyes puffy and red, but her makeup in place after having refreshed herself in the ladies' room.

"Tell us what you did next."

"By then the doctor was focusing on taking care of Mary, of calling 911, and getting her transported to the hospital so we all could all get out of there. I just couldn't leave that little thing to die. I called a friend of mine who's a nurse, and she instructed me on how to keep the baby alive until I could get him to the NICU which was just a block away."

"At the hospital?"

"Yes."

"And how did you transport the fetus there?"

"I ran."

"You mean you ran on foot? Through hurricane winds and rain? To save the life of the fetus?"

"Yes."

In a dramatic move, Mr. Stone flicked the 'on' button of a hand-held remote and an image of a two-year-old boy flashed up on the television screen that had been wheeled in. A picture appeared of a cherubic little boy dressed in an adorable sailor suit replete with white sailor cap. The cute toddler was holding a small stuffed teddy bear that was as big as he was—widely grinning with dimples in his cheeks, revealing two tiny bottom teeth showing, his dark brown eyes shining with laughter. The photo made everyone in the courtroom gasp, including the judge.

"Is this the same boy you carried in a bloody towel, running to the hospital that day, to save his life?"

Christine couldn't speak, tears falling down her cheeks. She nodded and the judge softly asked her to speak into the microphone so they could record her answer.

"Yes, that's my Jesse."

The attorney flicked the remote switch again and another image appeared on the screen—that of a tiny preemie baby, hooked up to a myriad of tubes in a NICU bassinet, his skin a purplish, bruised color, his eyes shut tight against the light, his blueberry-sized fists clenched, his sunken chest rapidly rising and falling above his miniature diaper. "And this baby?"

"That's him the day they saved his life."

"The day you saved his life, you mean?"

"I guess you could say that."

"No further questions."

Annette Dahlia gently approached the witness stand for her redirect. "Good afternoon, Miss Walters. Thank you for being here today, I know you've been through a lot up until this point, so I won't keep you too long. I can only gather from the circles under your eyes that you're already tired. I have a toddler of my own, and I know you don't get very much sleep."

Finn could imagine the attorney smiling kindly, sympathetically even. *She's getting ready for the kill.*

"Of course, my husband is a big help in raising our two young daughters. So, I can't even imagine how you do it all on your own."

"I manage," the defendant sniffed. "My mother helps when she can."

"How old are you, Miss Walters?

"Forty-seven."

"And the child you're raising—"

"My son, you mean." *She's getting defensive.*

"Okay, your son is two, correct? That means when he turns eighteen, you'll be sixty-three years old, isn't that right? Old enough to be his grandmother."

"What's your point?" Clearly the attorney was getting a rise out of the witness. *Not good*, Finn thought.

"My point is that this child, born prematurely with, I'm sure, plenty of health issues, is going to require someone to raise him who has a whole lot of energy, time, and money. Which by the way, you have none of, wouldn't you say, since you are currently bankrupt and jobless *again*?"

Christine lost it at that point, yelling. "That's not fair! It's all because of this court case. Because of her ..." she pointed to her opponent, who Finn imagined was sitting pretty smugly in her seat at that point.

"Life's not fair, Miss Walters."

Mr. Stone requested a short recess, but the judge denied him, so Ms. Dahlia proceeded.

"Were you forced to take a job at Doctor Townsend's office for any reason?"

"No. But I had been unemployed for a year after I was, um, let go from the Pro-Choice Providers clinic where I'd worked before."

"Isn't it true you were at Pro-Choice Providers for twenty-five years, that you actually liked your job, defended it even to your parents who questioned your line of work? And isn't it true you aided in hundreds or maybe thousands of abortions, never speaking out against any of them along the way?" The attorney didn't give Christine a chance to answer but volleyed questions in rapid-fire secession. "And isn't it true, Miss Walters, you were disobeying direct orders from the doctor in your actions the September day in question? So you were fired once again from your job? Not a fine example of responsibility, Ms. Walters, is it?"

"No, I ... well, yes. I was fired again, but I wanted out and—"

"No further questions, Your Honor."

Finn imagined the two attorneys poised like snakes, standing ready to strike with their closing arguments.

Ms. Dahlia went first.

"Good morning, Your Honor. And it is a fine morning out there, even though we can't see it from the inside of this courtroom ... blue skies, beautiful green trees, flowers blooming. Springtime, a time when some teenagers might try to cut class early and run around, goofing off, experiencing life and all its wonderful adventures. Ah ... to be young again." The attorney paused, letting her words linger for a minute, then resumed. "But not Marianne Birch. She could be out there enjoying this fine spring day with her peers, her friends, not a care in the world. But she can't because she's in here, fighting to keep her baby son, who matters more to her than anything or anyone else in the world.

"Sure, she made a mistake. I would venture to say all of us make mistakes when we're young. It's why I believe God gives us second chances."

"They say we're adults at age eighteen, but really, we all know better than that. We're all still immature, don't know what love really is, aren't ready for real responsibilities. So when we're faced with choices, we're bound to make bad decisions along the way. That's what happened to Marianne. She was faced with the seemingly impossible decision of whether to bear a child into the world who had a drunk, drug addict, lazy, irresponsible, abusive, violent young man for a father. Kenny Jackson just wanted to get high and play music. He didn't want any part of being a dad. He told my client to get an abortion. He hit her for arguing with him. She was scared—terrified of what Kenny might do next. She had no money. And she felt like she couldn't tell anyone about her pregnancy, especially her parents, since they were upstanding Christians in the community, and she knew they wouldn't understand. She was stuck, trapped, and felt like she had no way out but to terminate the pregnancy and try to start her life over the best she could.

"Your Honor, we all deserve a second chance. A springtime to bloom again after the cold hard winter. A do-over. That's all Marianne Birch is asking, Your Honor. For a second chance at being a mom to her son." Finn could picture Ms. Dahlia laying her hand gently on the shoulder of her client who sat silently, her hands folded on the table before her like a schoolgirl listening to her teacher, her sad, tearful eyes looking innocently forward. "Thank you."

Finn imagined Mr. Stone slowly stand, unbutton his suit jacket, stuff his hands into his pockets, then shuffle forward to the stand before the judge's bench.

There were a few moments of uncomfortable silence before Judge McNamara nudged him on. "Mr. Stone? I'm ready whenever you are."

"Sorry, Your Honor. I was thinking about Ms. Dahlia's words just now. Second chances. Wow. You know, I had a whole speech prepared, but I think I'll let her words speak for me. Second chances."

Finn fondly remembered his father's speech at his college graduation with the same theme. His heart started to beat faster as he read on, knowing how the case would end but still captivated by the proceedings.

"I agree with Ms. Dahlia, Your Honor, that we all deserve second chances. Which is exactly what my client, Christine Stone, gave a tiny baby boy born on a rainy day in September two-and-a-half years ago.

"Mary Smith—Marianne Birch as we now know her real name to be—came into Doctor Townsend's that day ready to get an abortion, to terminate the life growing in her womb, knowing she and her child were perfectly healthy, because she didn't want to be a mother, she didn't want a baby, a child, a son.

"Christine Walters acted out of compassion, out of love for this precious life she found in her hands, wrapped in a towel. She ran on foot to the hospital to save him, then once he was ready to be released, she adopted him, fed him, clothed him, took him to numerous doctors to make sure he not only survived but thrived until he became the healthy, and might I add, adorable baby boy you just saw on the screen yesterday.

"She sacrificed everything to raise this baby, who she could have just left to die as instructed by the doctor—who told her to just discard him in a plastic bag and throw him in the trash. But she followed her conscience and chose life ..." the lawyer turned and faced Marianne Birch. "... unlike her opponent, Marianne Birch, who clearly and selfishly chose what *she* wanted that day."

Randy Stone quietly walked back to the defense table and looked down at his client, who was softly crying. "Christine Walters was brave, Your Honor, selfless, and is here to continue to fight for the life of her son. To rip him away from her would be a crime, just like it would have been criminal to take his life that day. Let's not give anyone a second chance at destroying a life, but let's reward the mother who gave this little boy a second chance at living."

Finn read on, picturing Judge McNamara pull his hand through his graying red hair, his tired eyes sunken in his wrinkled face, as he pulled his microphone close to speak into it and deliver his remarks. "I have reached a verdict in the matter of Birch vs. Walters. Will the defendant and the plaintiff and their attorneys please stand."

Christine Walters and Mr. Stone stood on the left of the bench to face the judge, Marianne Birch and her attorney Ms. Dahlia to the right.

Judge McNamara continued. "This was a hard decision to make, as both sides had merit. But the court has come to a conclusion. The child, Jesse Walters, will be put into the custody of his biological mother, Marianne Birch—"

The record stated Christine fell into her seat sobbing.

"Thank you, Your Honor," Marianne said. The transcript ended there.

CHAPTER TWENTY-TWO

Christine Walters was bereft for a time, but then a whole host of Right to Life movements rallied behind her to fight to get Jesse back, hiring a crackerjack legal team to represent her. Pro-abortion rights groups did the same for Marianne Birch. A war had thus morphed out of the women's custody battle that had been waged, once again resurrecting the historic 1973 *Roe v. Wade* case.

It was a war of words evidenced in the piles of paperwork that now sat in front of a very weary Supreme Court Judge Mitchell and his cohorts, titled *Walters vs. Gold et. al.*

After seven straight hours of reading the court briefs until past midnight, Finn finally closed the docket folders, rubbing his tired eyes. *This will be a tough one.*

The US Supreme Court was challenged with reviewing and either upholding or overturning the *Birch v. Walters* case and the Florida judge's decision.

Christine Walters and her team had filed the appeal to the Supreme Court asking that they overturn the decision by the Florida judge to award Marianne Birch custody of little Jesse. The suit was filed against Florida's State Attorney General Albert Gold. The lawsuit argued that Marianne Birch had no rights to Jesse since she had gone in for an abortion and thereby given up her claim to her child.

The Walters team had hired an advocate attorney for Jesse, maintaining he had rights as any child did. It also claimed that every child—both born and unborn—had rights under the law. There was an appendix in the appeal in which Jesse's appointed attorney recommended that Christine Walters obtain full custody of the child.

The 'et. al.' included Doctor Townsend, claiming he had performed an illegal abortion under Florida laws that restricted late-term abortions, stating they could not be performed if there was no danger to the health of the mother and if the fetus was viable.

If the appeal was upheld, it would mean that all "unborn" children would have the right to an attorney. And while Dr. Townsend would not be criminally charged, he would lose his license to practice.

Several court cases had already weakened *Roe v. Wade* in recent years. The fifty states now had the power to decide their own laws and regulations on abortion. Some had no restrictions, while others outlawed abortions for fetuses under "viable" status, or twenty-four weeks, others at less than fifteen weeks or even six weeks of gestation. And in some states, abortion was strictly illegal now, which was why Marianne Birch had to travel from Alabama to Florida to get her procedure.

Pro-choice proponents argued that if the appeal was not overturned by the Supreme Court, it would mean any future abortion could potentially be blocked by any advocate or attorney and that all of this would set women back to the "stone ages." They further said that if upheld, the outcome would hamper or even eliminate abortion providers in the US who would be in constant fear of being sued. Many if not most abortion providers would probably go out of business or be shut down completely if the appeal was granted, effectively overturning *Roe v. Wade* completely and possibly forever.

The media and political pundits predicted eight of the nine justices on the Supreme Court would be split down the middle on the *Walters* case—four on the side of upholding it, four on the side of overturning it. Finn understood his was what they called the "swing" vote. *Not a great place to sit, here on the fence.* Some would say he held all the cards, all the power. At this moment, he felt like he wanted to hop on a plane and fly far away to some deserted island.

Being the son of a Republican President, although he himself was an Independent, Finn had been played up in the media as a justice who would support the pro-life vs. the pro-choice movement. But he wasn't as sure of how he'd ultimately vote.

There was a lot at stake when dealing with such a politically hot button issue as abortion, which always resurrected the Supreme Court's 1973 *Roe v. Wade* landmark decision legalizing abortion in the US. The cries would be deafening, led by many women leaders in the Congress and Senate who were either pro-life or pro-choice.

To rule in favor of Gold and Florida and leave Jesse where he was—in Marianne's care—and maintain the status quo would be the easier, softer, less explosive way to rule, Finn knew. Nearly a year had passed since Marianne Birch won legal custody of the boy. Jesse Walters Birch was already three years old and would probably turn four before the case was decided. To rip him out of his mother's care for a second time didn't seem right, Finn thought. *But neither does endorsing what happened to Christine Walters, nor condoning what Doctor Townsend and others like him did—continued to do on a daily basis—allowing, facilitating, performing these late-term abortions, disposing of these babies like they're garbage.*

Oral arguments were scheduled to start January 22nd, the same day the Roe decision had been announced and ironically, the date of the annual March for Life on Washington, which was still going strong.

Finn watched out of his office window as hordes of people, marked by a rainbow of colored hats and flags, paraded up the hill toward him, their final destination—the front steps of the Supreme Court building, his home. They carried an array of signs that read "Pro Life Is Pro Choice," "Choose Life," and "Pro Life Is Pro Woman." Signs carried by opponents of the March for Life were sprinkled in too with sayings like, "My Body, My Choice," and "Keep Abortion Safe and Legal."

Although a few shouted through megaphones, the march was largely peaceful. He watched as the throngs waited to hear the next keynote speaker appear on the stage set up on the national mall for the occasion.

"We march because we love life," a young woman spoke joyfully into the reporter's microphone as Finn flipped on the TV in his living quarters. Finn guessed the young girl being interviewed was in her early twenties. She had long brunette hair and her cheeks were rosy in the cold winter air. "We want to stop the senseless murder of millions of babies in America," she said. "These are tiny miracles, created by God, being killed every day. They don't have a voice, so we are their voices. We speak for those who can't speak for themselves."

Finn turned off the television, mulling over the girl's statements. One stuck in his head and he replayed it over and over again. "... tiny miracles, created by God ..." *What if my mother had chosen to abort me?* he wondered, knowing the truth of how he came to be in this world.

And yet Finn couldn't fathom a country where girls who were pregnant—through rape, incest, domestic violence, or even as willing participants, who felt they'd made mistakes or who were afraid to be single moms—had no place to go to get legal abortion procedures and were forced into "back allies" with "butchers" to end their pregnancies as the pro-abortion advocates claimed they'd have to do.

Perhaps abortions would stop, he thought, but then realized a cessation of the procedures was most likely an outcome that would never occur. *Women will find a way.*

Still, they'd probably decrease significantly if abortion facilities went out of business and were shut down. And weren't the babies who wouldn't have been born otherwise, but would now possibly live, be tiny miracles, created by God?

Please guide me Lord, Finn prayed quietly, looking out at the late January sky, a shade of innocent light blue, and then down over the sea of humanity, moved by their passion and perseverance. He felt so alone, full of doubts, so young and inexperienced. For a few moments, Finn got caught up in daydreaming of sitting among his fellow justices, red curtains drawn behind them, ready to rule, then he suddenly awoke in a state of panic. *Who am I to make such a big decision? Just a man, who certainly doesn't know of a woman's plight of bearing an unwanted child.* "Lord please give me an understanding heart to discern and judge wisely," he prayed quietly.

To say the debate between the justices had become heated was an understatement. Oral arguments took place, and the attorneys for Christine Walters and Marianne Birch argued very succinctly since each side only had an hour.

Finn had been elected by his peers as Supreme Court Chief Justice, which meant he would run the conference in which the justices convened to debate the case. Their deliberations were scheduled to take place over the course of the next several months, and they'd decided they would release their final decision by the end of June when their current term officially ended.

After they all shook hands as was customary, Finn and the other eight judges took their seats around the conference table to discuss the case.

Justice Theresa Gomez sat across from him, glaring with a pink lipstick smile, her manicured hands folded neatly on the large table. She was the youngest and only Latino on the Supreme Court bench and was seated next to one of her liberal cohorts, Justice Lisa Skalicky, the second Black woman to be voted in, slightly her senior. On his right sat Justice Daniel Hale, a conservative Black man in his fifties, who had been appointed right before him by the current president. And to his left was Justice Mark Obermayer, a White conservative judge who'd been seated on the Supreme Court bench for several years.

The other four justices around the table were White males in their sixties and seventies, two of whom were considered liberal and two conservative. The most senior member, Justice George Hensley, was nearing eighty, and folks predicted he'd retire soon since his health was fading. Judge Hensley had been diagnosed with late-stage prostate cancer which he'd been battling for years.

Finn prayed Judge Hensley made it to the end of their conference on the Walters case so they had balance ... and so that they wouldn't have to suspend the proceedings. *At least he looks healthy today.* Finn smiled at the elderly justice, who was gruff until a person got to know him and realized he was really a kind old soul.

"You're looking well today, George," Finn greeted him.

"Let's get on with it, Finley," George scowled, and Finn suppressed a laugh.

"Sure thing. Why don't we go around the room and see who has any questions left over from the oral arguments?"

"I'd like to go first if I may," the outspoken and energetic Theresa Gomez blurted out.

No surprise there, Finn thought. *She's always got to get her opinion on the record.*

"I don't understand how Christine Walters reportedly isn't working now. How can she support herself much less a baby? It's as if she came into a windfall of money. Do you think she's been paid off somehow for her testimony?"

"Who would be paying her off?" Judge Mark Obermeyer frowned, peering over his wire-rimmed glasses, his white tuft of hair falling over to one side. "I can't imagine the March for Life people have any extra money lying around. I believe they use it all for their speakers and campaign literature and such each year. I think the other side has the deep pockets in this case to protect their interests."

"I've just heard trusted sources say she's been wearing high end clothes, driving a fancy car, and that she isn't presently working." Theresa sat up tall in her leather chair, her hands gripping the armrests.

"You mean rumors?"

"No, I have a reporter friend at the *Washington Post—*"

"Ahhh, well, that's a trusted source," Judge Obermeyer said sarcastically. "You know, Ms. Waters isn't on trial here ..."

"Yes, but she is, in fact, the plaintiff—"

"All right you two, knock it off," Judge Daniel Hale interrupted.

And so the day went by, a few judges dominating the conversation, Judge Hensley nodding off following their catered lunch.

Finn truly was the least biased of all the judges, which is why, he gathered, the rest of them had appointed him as Chief Justice.

That night Finn lay on his bed, the only sound in the night his breath, inhaling and exhaling ... when he felt a huge weight bearing down on him that grew heavier by the second, squeezing the air out of his chest, suffocating him. He knew there was a woman in a bunkbed above him, and she and the bed had fallen and were slowly crushing him. He realized right before his air left his lungs that it was Lady Liberty. In her hands she held scales, which in turn held huge, heavy bars of iron, and she was intentionally pressing down her weight on him.

He awoke sweating, sucking in air, unable at first to catch his breath, his chest heaving.

Then he realized he'd had a bad dream and mercifully dozed back off to sleep.

Suddenly, he was holding a small infant in a tiny mud hut in Afghanistan. Shots ripped through the smoky, grimy, hot, dry atmosphere, and he again felt like he was suffocating.

He looked down at the child in his arms. The boy was dead.

Finn awoke in a panic, his heart thumping so loud he could hear it as it beat in his eardrums.

He knew what he had to do.

CHAPTER TWENTY-THREE

Christine Walters walked through the throngs of people who were shouting and chanting pro and anti-abortion rhetoric, shielded by her attorney, Randy Stone, his team of assistant attorneys, and multiple security guards who strong-armed the mobs on either side with their batons.

Five months had passed since the original oral arguments. Jesse Walters Birch was now four. Still, the pro-life protestors demanded he be switched back into Christine Walter's custody, arguing he should have never been taken away in the first place.

Christine had quit her job again and lived with her mother. Her cause was taken up by several states which had joined her as plaintiffs in the Supreme Court case including Texas, Mississippi, Tennessee, and Alabama. They claimed the State of Florida, the Florida Supreme Court, and Judge McNamara had violated human rights under the constitution by upholding Jesse Walters be given back to Marianne Birch.

Mobs of people crowded the Supreme Courthouse steps, and Christine looked terrified as she was captured on live TV making her way through, her eyes downcast, avoiding the hateful stares of those yelling nasty epithets in her direction. She looked up only once before entering the iconic, Roman temple-like building with its sixteen giant Corinthian pillars, carvings of ancient lawmakers including Moses and Muhammed, and the etched quote that had stood the test of time—"Equal Justice Under Law."

Once she was safely through the bronze front doors and into the Great Hall, nicknamed the "marble palace," she gawked at the vast marble interior which included more columns, marble walls and floors, and a beautiful ornate ceiling. Christine walked up to one of the massive white marble columns and laid a hand gently on its smooth, cold surface, leaning against it to steady her nerves.

Randy Stone tugged her arm gently. "We have to keep moving, Christine," he whispered, and she followed her lawyer down the long hallway through two huge dark oak doors that led into the courtroom itself. Both were professionally dressed as they had been in the original court case, Christine in a tan jacket and black skirt, Randy in a dark navy suit. Across from them sat two attorneys, both older, gray-haired gentlemen in suits representing the state of Florida.

Marianne Birch was also in the courtroom, sitting in the audience section behind them, but since children were not allowed, Jesse Birch was being protectively sheltered in an undisclosed daycare mother's home known only to Marianne and her attorney, Annette Dahlia. Both women were in somber attire, Marianne in a black dress with pearls and her attorney in a gray suit with a black blouse.

It almost looked like a funeral, and the atmosphere in the courtroom was similar too—silent, tense, but more anticipatory. Seconds ticked on the clock above the bench as everyone waited for the Supreme Court justices to appear in threes from behind the famous red curtain backdrops to reveal the results.

No visitors had been allowed, except for a handful of select reporters who furiously scribbled notes, since the Covid global pandemic had shut down many public gatherings. No cameras, video equipment, or cell phones were permitted in the court.

"Oyez, oyez, oyez." the court bailiff intoned the traditional opening of the court in session and announced the case.

It was then Chief Justice Finley Mitchell's turn to deliver the high court's opinion.

"This body, known as the United States Supreme Court, thus announces its decision in the matter of *Walters vs. Gold*—the Court has deliberated and reached a decision in a five-to-four majority vote in favor of the plaintiff, Ms. Christine Walters, that the abortion performed by Doctor Nathaniel Townsend that resulted in the birth of a live baby was illegal and therefore the Florida Supreme Court erred in its judgement in the case of *Birch v. Walters*, and as such its decision in that matter is null and void. Furthermore, we are accepting the recommendation of the advocate attorney for the baby born out of the said abortion, Jesse Walters, that the appeal of Christine Walters be upheld, and that the child be placed back in Ms. Walters's care and custody."

Christine broke down loudly sobbing with relief as Finn read the majority opinion.

Copies of the entire document, which Finn had written, edited, and then polished late the night before and into the early morning hours, were printed by the Clerk of the Court and then handed to interns who stood waiting in the hallway outside the chamber. Then there was the traditional "Running of the Interns." These interns raced down the front steps of the building and across the marbled fountain terrace to their waiting broadcast teams.

Within minutes the decision was being read on national and international television.

"We believe there is a constitutional right to life that belongs to each person at the point of conception when life begins," Finn wrote in the majority opinion. "The states have become a battleground and there is a civil war raging much like the one over slavery, only this one is about the enslaving of human life or the rights of the unborn. This issue of anti- vs. pro-abortion has divided our country long enough and needs to be settled once and for all. I hope this decision will pave the way for laws to be made that will heal our country and cast this division aside, bringing back into federal hands what needs to become a constitutional right to life for those who have no voice other than the laws of this nation, the Constitution, the rights granted by God himself. That day is not here yet, but I pray it's on the horizon." Cheers erupted, both inside and outside the Supreme Court building.

"Miracles happen every day. Jesse Walters Birch is a miracle. He could have been ripped in two ... just like the states were ripped in two, but Christine Walters saved him from that fate. Up until now it seems like we've been playing games with semantics. God, our Creator, alone gives life. Life is life. America was based on the tenets of Christianity. Would Christ, if he came down here on earth today, say killing a fetus is okay? The answer is a resounding 'no.'

"It is the opinion of this court that unborn babies have a constitutional right to life. We encourage Congress and the states to review their laws on abortion, that "viability" be re-examined as science continues to show that life begins at conception. Finally, I would like to quote the Bible in this matter. As King David prayed in Psalm 139, *'For you created my inmost being; you knit me together in my mother's womb. I praise you because I am fearfully and wonderfully made; your works are wonderful.'* We are still 'one nation under God,' as it states in our national Pledge of Allegiance to the Flag. And as our great Declaration of Independence states, 'we hold these truths to be self-evident, that all men are created equal, that they are endowed by their Creator with certain unalienable rights, that among these are life, liberty, and the pursuit of happiness.'" Long live Jesse Walters, and all babies who are saved from the fate of being aborted when they could be born alive. This court has spoken."

People cheered wildly on the steps of the Supreme Court building, waving their signs, while the other side shrieked in despair.

Famous new actress Carly Bay took a microphone from one of the TV crew's sound systems and hopped up onto a makeshift stage, starting a chant, "Women are slaves, women are slaves, women are slaves ..." until she drew the attention of hundreds in the audience gathered.

"This is a dark day for women in our country, who will go back to getting back-alley abortions from butchers," the young actress said into a dozen TV cameras that had rolled over to capture her. She was the latest star to rise to the top of Hollywood. "We've just enslaved women, taking away their rights and freedom—"

"They'll be free of sin," a young mom cried as women booed her. "They will have babies and beautiful families, and if they can't take care of them, we will." She handed out baby bottles full of change.

Another woman with spiked black hair and leather pants spit on the bottle and knocked it out of her hand and to the ground. "You people are out of your minds," the woman said angrily, flexing her muscular arms that were covered in tattoos, looking like she was ready to hit somebody.

Some people were hugging and crying, while a few had started fist fighting right there on the steps of the Supreme Courthouse.

"This isn't over!" Carly cried as a policeman led her off the stage to rallying cries.

Finn watched the protest, unable to hear anything besides muted sounds coming through the thick windows of his room. Thankfully the justices didn't have to exit out into the mob scene but could hide away until the furor died down, or at least became controllable by the police.

After an unusually quiet dinner that night with seven of his fellow justices—Judge Lisa Skalicky had pleaded off with a migraine and had sequestered herself in her chambers—Finn headed to the basketball court on the fifth floor of the Supreme Court building, nicknamed the "highest court in the land."

He tried to get some form of exercise in each day. On sunny, warm days he'd sneak out early in the morning and jog around the block in his sweats, a hoodie drawn up around his face so no one would notice who he was. On rainy or cold days, he'd work with his personal trainer in the upstairs gym next to the court and sometimes shoot some hoops. Occasionally, one of his colleagues would join him in a pickup game.

He really needed to let off some steam tonight and even though it was warm, it had started to rain, so he asked Judge Daniel Hale to meet him at eight to play a game of one-on-one. Daniel had become his best friend, even though they didn't always see eye to eye on legal issues.

Finn pumped the ball, dribbling it down court as Daniel parried back and forth, his arms up in the air protecting the basket. They'd been playing for an hour already. Sweat dripped down his neck and back, and he was breathing heavily but the score was tied, twenty each. They were playing until one of them got twenty-one points.

He shot the ball up with a perfect arch, and it hit the rim and bounced off. Daniel retrieved the rebound, snatching it away from Finn's sweaty hands and ran down to score an easy layup. "Woo-hoo!" he yelled and then collapsed on the court, laying on the hardwood floor for a moment with a huge smile on his face, his arms up in a "V" for victory sign above his head.

Finn put his hands on his hips and bent forward, drawing air into his burning lungs. "Okay, hotdog, you win." He walked down court and helped Daniel to his feet, and the two men shook hands and headed to the nearby bench to towel off and drink some water.

"I'm sorry, can you say that a little louder, I didn't quite hear you?" Daniel gloated. He'd lost five of their past seven matches.

"Well, I should've won but ..."

"Ah, here it comes, the woulda, shoulda, coulda," Daniel smirked. "Give it a rest, old man."

Finn laughed. Daniel was ten years his senior but was in better shape than he was, his muscles well-defined under his Kentucky Wildcats T-shirt, honed by daily rounds of golf during his summer breaks in DC. "Well, you don't have a wife to worry about, so that's why you're able to stay in better shape I guess. Not to mention you played in college. Why didn't you go pro again?" Finn teased his friend, knowing the answer. Daniel had confided in him that he'd tried to make it to the NBA but hadn't been good enough to get selected. His defeat had led him to study law, though, and here he was, a Supreme Court justice. Still, he loved the game of basketball, and the fact his residence had a court above the court was a huge bonus.

"You're not jealous?" Daniel teased back, sitting down on the bench to sip the remains of his water bottle. "Seriously, I'm actually jealous of you and your marriage. I just don't seem to have the time anymore to find the right person. You're lucky you did before all of this craziness."

THE WISE MAN

Finn looked at his friend with admiration. Daniel had movie star good looks like Denzel Washington and could probably be one of the most desired men in DC if he wanted to be, but he was committed to his career ... and staying single.

"How is Lei?" Daniel looked at him, his eyes filled with concern.

"She's okay, I guess, I haven't seen her much with this Walters case in session." Finn wearily slumped down on the bench next to his friend.

"What's wrong? You don't look happy—and I'm guessing it's not about losing to me?"

Daniel was a good friend, but Finn wondered if he could relay the angst in his marriage of late and trust him to keep it confidential. Lei had warned him not to say anything to anyone, that their argument was between the two of them. But Finn knew if he kept it to himself much longer, he might have a stroke or something, and he really didn't have anyone else to talk to. All of the justices worked so hard and long into the days and nights that they became consumed sometimes with a case. *And what good are we if it eats us alive, and we end up returning to our homes as empty shells? Everyone probably thinks we lead a glamorous life, but that couldn't be further from the truth.* It's more like a jail sentence sometimes, he thought, feeling isolated even though he was with his friend.

He'd heard stories of Supreme Court justices who'd ended up divorced, choosing their lifelong legal careers over love. He didn't want to end up like them, his marriage a casualty of his work. He decided to take the risk and confide in Daniel, swearing him to secrecy.

241

"Like the rest of the world, Lei watched the announcement of our decision on television today." Finn fingered the basketball in his hands, feeling its smooth yet rough surface—a paradox, like his marriage. "She knows I cast the swing vote in favor of Christine Walters and to say she isn't happy about it is an understatement."

"She's pro-abortion?"

"She'd say she's pro-choice, and she claims I just can't understand how she thinks and feels as a woman, especially one of child-bearing age."

"Are you and she trying to have kids?" Daniel asked in a hushed voice. "Or are you trying *not* to?"

Finn knew Daniel was asking in a roundabout way if he or his wife were using birth control. The answer was 'no,' Finn and Lei were open to having a child. In fact, he'd hoped his wife would become pregnant over the past two years, but he was also okay with the fact she hadn't since this case had weighed him down for so long.

At least I don't think she's using birth control, Finn now mused, realizing it was possible Lei could be hiding it from him. *Maybe, given how she feels on how women should control their own bodies ... maybe she is.*

Suddenly he felt an anger boil up inside, and he wasn't sure where it came from. *Why shouldn't I have a say, as a man, in whether we, as a couple, use contraceptives or not? Why shouldn't I stand up for the rights of the unborn?*

"Hey, dude, sorry if I broached a touchy subject." Daniel interrupted his thoughts.

"No that's okay. I don't think Lei's using contraceptives but ... well, I'm not sure. I know she does feel strongly that a woman should decide."

"And you don't agree?"

"No, I think we should be a team and decide together on everything, but especially these important things. Don't you?" Finn looked at his friend, suddenly wanting validation.

"Hey, please leave me out of this. I have to see you both at the mock trial." Daniel was referring to the annual Shakespeare Theater's Mock Trial coming up in August. He was one of the key players in the comedic court play which was featuring 'Hamlet vs. Uncle Claudius.' "Plus, it's been a long day and I need a hot shower. C'mon, let's go get a nightcap downstairs and then call it a night."

Finn got up to follow Daniel down to the kitchen and adjoining wet bar. His friend turned around before they turned off the lights to the gym. "You know, if it makes you feel any better, I thought the decision you wrote and handed down today was nothing short of brilliant."

"Thanks, Daniel, that means a lot." Finn gave his fellow justice a small smile. He'd hoped Lei would feel the same—but he knew she wouldn't. He was actually dreading going home this time.

CHAPTER TWENTY-FOUR

Finn was happily surprised that Lei did not want to talk about the Walters case after he returned home for the summer recess. He offered to discuss it as much as he could within the parameters of the court's sworn oath to secrecy about their proceedings, but Lei didn't want to hear any more than she'd already heard on the news. It was over, she said, time to move on.

"So where do you want to go on vacation?" Finn asked the morning after his return over coffee and bagels in their sunroom.

They'd enjoyed a quiet dinner and movie the night before, then fell asleep on either side of their king-sized bed. Finn was almost grateful his wife was distant that night. It was just great to be home in his own bed, and he slept peacefully for eleven blissful hours, making up for lost time.

Lei sat across from him now wearing her red kimono robe he'd bought her last Christmas, her long black waves of hair falling across her shoulders. He wanted to ravish her until she spoke. "I want to go to China." She sat down her coffee cup and looked across the table expectantly.

Finn's heart sank. *Anywhere but there*, he thought dismally. "Why?"

Lei looked at him with her big sad eyes. "I'm really homesick. I have a friend we could stay with—"

"Well, I just thought since this past year has been really rough with the big case we argued, we'd do something low key ... hey, maybe the Florida Keys?" Finn thought quick on his feet, but not fast enough.

Lei's mind was already made up, and apparently she'd done a lot of planning while he'd been gone. "Please Finn, I really miss China. It's a big country so if we somehow go incognito I'm sure we can avoid my family, go for just a short time—" She slid her arms around his waist, hugging him, and gazed up at him blinking her big brown eyes and long black eyelashes flirtatiously.

He couldn't resist those eyes, of course. "I guess a week or so over there will be okay."

"Well, I was thinking more like three." She paused for effect. "But maybe we can compromise at two? It's such a long flight."

Two long weeks in China. *Just shoot me now*, Finn said to himself.

"There may be a reward in it for you," Lei teased, standing, taking his hand, leading him upstairs, playfully untying her robe as she climbed the steps to their bedroom.

Finn slept for most of the privately chartered nineteen-hour flight from DC to Beijing, not even realizing how little sleep he'd gotten over the past few weeks as the Walters case came to a close. He'd taken a double dose of Ambien to aid in helping him fall and stay fast asleep. He awoke to find his wife gazing out of the plane window.

"Hey sleepyhead! Wow, you must have 'napped' for fifteen hours straight," Lei said, using air quotes. She smiled sleepily.

"Did you get any sleep?" he yawned and stretched.

"Not much, maybe a few hours. I finished a whole novel, though."

"Okay, tell me about it after I run to the little boys' room."

After they finished a meal of chicken cordon bleu with baby peas and garlic mashed potatoes they'd ordered from their private chef onboard, they polished off a dessert of carrot cake and espressos. Lei snuggled up next to her husband, who put his arm around her and looked with her out of the window as the plane started its descent.

Millions of tiny lights like a galaxy of stars came into view. They were flying via a private jet into the huge, bustling city of Shanghai, where hopefully they could get lost in the throngs thanks to disguises Richard provided them. Finn had also sworn the pilot and crew to secrecy, paying them handsomely for their silence.

He hoped he and Lei would find some time to break away and explore some of the countryside incognito. He'd already toured some of the famous historic spots such as the Temple of Heaven, Tiananmen Square, and the Summer Palace, in addition to visiting the Forbidden City. Still, he'd never walked along the Great Wall of China, nor experienced typical life in his wife's native country.

She was the boss on this trip, he realized, and let out a long sigh.

Finn knew Lei had a good friend named Zimo who lived in Shanghai. An astute businessman with many connections, Zimo had helped Lei get her start in fashion design. She told Finn that she'd love to see Zimo, and that he could keep their meeting secret.

Lei casually mentioned, as the plane continued its descent, that her friend was wealthy and lived in a gated, secluded estate that was very private. She explained that Zimo now worked for a high-level tech firm that manufactured virtual reality games, and he traveled most of the time to make sales pitches to big investors around the globe.

"I'm sure he'll tell us all about it," she said as the plane touched down.

I can hardly wait, Finn said to himself sarcastically.

Soon their limo arrived at Zimo's estate home. Finn felt anxious, hopped up on caffeine, as he walked in with Lei to greet her friend.

Zimo was there sitting in the sprawling family room, waiting for the couple, and greeted Lei with a hug and a kiss. He wore a white, long-sleeved cashmere sweater with a V-neck that showcased his tan, and his jet-black hair was razored in a high and tight haircut that revealed his square jawline. He was perfectly fit and trim and seemed like a cross between a male model and a fighter pilot for the Marines.

"Hey, how's my angel?"

Lei gave Zimo a radiant smile, and for an instant, Finn felt weirdly jealous, even though he knew they were just friends.

"And who do we have here? Is this the famous Judge Mitchell?" Zimo firmly shook Finn's hand after quickly glancing up and down as if checking him out, then gave him a broad smile that didn't quite seem to reach his eyes. *Maybe I'm too wired from the flight to accurately assess this guy,* Finn thought. Still ... there seemed to be a mischievous, if not downright malevolent gleam in Zimo's glittering black eyes.

"Finley, right?"

"Yes, but you can call me Finn."

Zimo gripped his hand hard and then let go. "Nah, I like Finley." He sat back down on the white leather sofa. *A study in white on white.* Finn felt a bit giddy and tried not to laugh at the Hollywood superficiality of the scene.

They all sat down on the expensive white leather furniture, and tea was served by an older Asian woman in a maid's uniform. A white Persian cat that had slipped into the room unnoticed jumped up onto Zimo's lap.

Well, doesn't that take the cake? Finn sipped his tea, mildly amused.

Finn and Lei slept in one of the many guest rooms in Zimo's mansion. A double dose of the sleeping pill aided him in zonking out once his head hit the pillow. But Finn's head felt full of concrete the next morning, so when his wife offered him a third cup of strong, black tea he accepted, wishing it were an espresso. A hot shower helped.

It was already noon in China by the time they woke up, and Finn's stomach roiled at the smell of fried shrimp. He prayed his stomach would settle down.

They came down the grand spiral staircase that led from the upstairs guest rooms into the parlor area, and Finn saw Zimo and another young Chinese man who was about Zimo's age but of slighter build.

To Finn's surprise, Lei apparently knew the strange man and hugged him. "Mai-Yong, how nice to see you!" He bowed to her formally and then shook Finn's hand.

Zimo rose. "Finley, I'd like you to meet my friend Mai-Yong, he is from Hong Kong and is very successful in the tech industry. I invited him to our meeting to present you with a possible investment opportunity."

Lei cast a sly look at her husband, then excused herself to go freshen up. Finn was left to sit and talk business with the two men, helplessly watching her walk out of the room.

Zimo let Mai-Yong do most of the talking as they told Finn about their new company. "It's a virtual reality experience like no other called Epitome, where anyone can personalize an adventure to suit his or her tastes. It goes beyond VR games out there. We've tested it here in China, and we'd like to consider you as our corporate ambassador in America." Zimo's friend was ultra-enthusiastic as he outlined the scope of the business which he'd conceptualized years ago as a nerdy yet extremely bright and gifted teenage prodigy. Zimo simply watched with pride while his friend described the program.

"If this system takes off, it would be bigger than the internet, bitcoin, or even the metaverse." Zimo put his hands on his hips confidently. "I have overseen international sales, and I couldn't think of anyone more prominent, wise, and respected than you, Finley, to help us promote Epitome in America. What do you say, brother?"

"But I'm just a judge." Finn objected. "A law man really. I don't know a thing about technology. In fact, I'm one of the most technically challenged people I know." He forced a small laugh, but his self-deprecating humor bounced off their armor of resolve.

"Exactly." Zimo's eyes glittered. "You are both every man in America, and yet uphold the law, the people. If you say you like and trust our product, then millions more will too. It's like that old commercial in your country that the cereal company, Life, ran. If that kid Mikey likes it, everyone will like it."

"But I've never even tried it, much less can wrap my head around it."

"And that is about to change."

Zimo's executive chef announced lunch was prepared and ready. The maid on duty had set the room and was on standby to clean up after they were finished dining.

After lunch, Lei asked Finn if he would mind if she joined a girlfriend to go shopping. She promised to stay in disguise and that she'd join him later for a romantic walk, dinner, and drive, just the two of them, that evening.

He felt like he couldn't refuse but was suspicious that somehow his wife must have known Zimo and his friend wanted more time alone with him to discuss 'the project' as they were calling it. Zimo and Mai-Yong led Finn into the mansion's library, a spacious gallery of books that looked like it could have belonged to Galileo or even Confucius. It took Finn's breath away, seeing the many walls lined with ancient writings, some dating back to the Ming Dynasty. The library was as big as the one in the Supreme Court.

They entered the library's large reading room and Zimo motioned for Finn to sit in a padded office chair that was placed in the middle of the room in front of a big flatscreen monitor.

"Welcome to Epitome," he said, handing Finn a headset he'd retrieved from a nearby shelf. It looked like a typical Oculus Quest headset, only a bit bigger and made of a light metallic substance that was opalescent and colorful depending on how the light in the room hit it.

"It is pretty," Finn said, admiring the set in his hands.

"Put it on," Zimo encouraged him, and for a moment, Finn doubted whether he should.

But then I'll be disrespecting them, he realized. *Besides, what could it hurt to try their little game?*

Finn fit the lightweight plastic headset with goggles on and slipped his hands into the controls. He had never tried a virtual reality set before, so he had no idea what to expect. He put it on and was amazed as the voice in the headset changed from Mandarin to the English language, as if it intuitively knew him. *Incredible*. Zimo walked him through the instructions on how to select a game or sporting event, a rock concert, or a tour through any city or land in the world, an experience like a jungle safari,

THE WISE MAN

hike through the Amazon rainforest, or cruise down the Nile. And then Zimo whispered in Finn's left ear, "or you can even have a sexual encounter if you choose."

Finn gulped and shook his head left to right. "Of course not," he replied indignantly. "I'll try a tour through the White House."

"Wow, not too imaginative, but okay, whatever you wish." Suddenly, Finn was standing in the Oval Office. Seated before him against the south wall was the President of the United States, Robert Newman, signing a paper on the large oak Resolute Desk. President Newman looked up at him and smiled, laugh lines fanning out from his blue eyes.

He looks so real. Finn sucked in his breath as the president reached out to shake his hand and he could even *feel* the handshake. The president motioned for him to sit on one of the two cream-colored guest sofas facing each other and then sat across from him.

It was as if Finn were *there* casually talking to the president.

He felt tongue-tied and panicked a little, asking Zimo to change the channel. "What would you like next?" Lei's friend inquired. He didn't think, he just picked one of the examples Zimo had thrown out already.

"I'll take that safari ... can I go to the Serengeti?"

And before he received an answer, Finn was transported in space and time to the plains of Africa riding in a jeep down a dusty, bumpy road. There was nothing except dirt and scrub brush as far as his eye could see, and he felt a little disappointed at first that he'd ended his trip to the White House. He started to think of a few things he could have asked President Newman about when suddenly he heard a distant thundering sound of hooves.

It grew louder and then he saw a dust cloud forming on the horizon and the thunder grew deafening as hundreds of gazelles ran toward him, chased by a lion that bellowed a roar behind them. The lion then pounced on one of the young calves and ripped its sharp teeth into the calf's neck as it screamed. Blood spurted and the calf's terrified eyes grew dim. The rest of the pack of gazelles disappeared and the lion lay down to eat his prey. Two female lions joined him, a few cubs in tow, and it was like a family feast.

Finn felt like he wanted to yank off the headset and avert his eyes but was held spellbound. Suddenly two elephants with a baby elephant in tow lumbered up and passed by, the lions still feasting and unconcerned. Everything was so violent, and then so ... peaceful, and Finn took a deep breath and exhaled. He could feel God's presence.

CHAPTER TWENTY-FIVE

As if the virtual reality system could read his mind, the sun's rays broke through the clouds, streaming down on the plains turning them golden. And then Finn was magically transported to the inside of an enormous, beautiful cathedral the likes of which he'd never seen before. It was more magnificent and glorious than St. Peter's Papal Basilica in Rome or the Duomo in Milan. He could hear organ music playing, soaring and a choir singing like angels and suddenly he felt like he was in heaven, or at least the heaven he'd always imagined.

He wanted to stay longer but reluctantly removed the headset and blinked. Zimo was over in the corner of the library perusing the books on one of the shelves while his friend Mai-Yong was missing, apparently having left the room. "Where's your friend?" Finn asked.

Zimo turned around, laying a book in his hands down on a nearby table. "Oh, he just had to go to the men's room, he'll be right back. How did you like your little experience?" Zimo grinned, nodding at the headset in Finn's hands.

"Not so little ... it was actually huge," Finn said.

"I knew you'd appreciate it."

Mai-Yong casually strode back into the library and closed the door behind him. He smiled, nodded at Zimo, then waved at Finn to follow and the two went over and sat at a table in an alcove in the far corner of the library, motioning for Finn to sit with them.

The two had serious expressions now. *We're getting down to business.*

"Finn, what we have here with Epitome is not only a top-of-the-line, never-before-seen virtual reality system," Mai-Yong said. "It has a built-in fantasy feature that is intuitive. It's as if it can almost read a person's mind through brain waves transmitted into the set while a person is wearing it. It follows voice commands but also *thoughts* and *feelings.*"

"And it can be interactive," Zimo added. "For example, if you and my sister were wearing sets, and you both wanted to travel together, let's just say to Hawaii, and wanted to see a volcano erupt, you could experience it together by selecting each other's avatars as partners on the same adventure. You could even hold her hand while you surf the ocean waves, or climb Mount Everest, or walk up to the pyramids in Egypt. People wait their whole lives, save their whole lives, to travel to far off places or even close by ones, and then in an instant, their dreams vanish when they have health problems or financial strains, or God forbid someone dies. It reminds me of that Disney movie, "Up.""

"Yeah, that movie always did make you cry." Mai-Yong snickered.

"Shut up, wise guy." Zimo elbowed his friend. "But you get my point. Why should people who are confined to their homes be stuck watching life on a flatscreen TV when they could be experiencing it in 4-D reality?"

"Wow. That is incredible guys. But couldn't it be dangerous? What if someone was thinking about being violent? You mentioned that one could have a sexual encounter. What if a man was thinking about rape, for example? And he has a woman on a date in the room with him?"

"We are still working out the bugs in the system. Just like blocks on pornography for children, we are going to install safety measures that prevent those experiences from playing," Mai-Yong asserted.

"And I have another question." Finn rubbed his chin. "How much do these babies cost?"

"Well, they won't be for sale, we don't want our intellectual property rights to be copied or pirated in any way. We plan to have them manufactured in bulk and then make them available for rent in mass quantities to the public in a tourism-like location, so that we can maintain control. That way they can be used repeatedly over time."

Zimo's eyes shone with the possibilities. "Multiply that out and we're talking millions ... or billions."

"It will be like selling ride tickets, with the ride being the virtual reality experience," Mai-Yong added enthusiastically.

The two of these men had obviously thought this through, Finn realized. "But who has the kind of money to buy all of those sets, much less owns a tourist destination like that?"

The two Asian men stared at him and smiled, not saying a word.

Finn could hear a distant grandfather clock ticking. *Tick, tick, tick.* Then it dawned on him.

"You're not talking about me? I don't have that kind of money. Nor the place for it. Nor the time for it. No way. I'm not sure what you two are getting at—I think this is a great idea and all, but I'm not your guy." He stood up, wanting to go, forget all about this whole thing, go be with his wife, get outside, get some fresh air, live life for real.

"You haven't even heard what we're proposing." Zimo frowned, looking hurt and offended, still seated, his eyes downcast.

Mai-Yong just looked sad.

Finn slowly sat back down. "All right, but I don't have all day, so can we wrap this up?"

Zimo and his friend filled Finn in on all the details of how they knew a private investor who was already involved with the manufacturing of virtual reality sets and had agreed to purchase ten thousand sets to loan to whoever would be setting up the tourist attraction.

So the investor would get a cut of the profits, then the tourist attraction owner, and then the Epitome founders—Zimo and Mai Yong.

"All we need is the middle-man, someone to help us set up the tourist attraction," Zimo said. "And then we are going to have a virtual reality adventure island, where people can explore the depths of the ocean, places they've only dreamed about on their bucket lists, even outer space. And also find a real piece of heaven if they'd like, with lush tropical gardens, mountains and waterfalls, cliffs and vistas, beaches along a clear blue sea, anything the heart desires."

"Is there going to be a church?" Finn asked, doubtful.

"Well, as you saw on your Epitome headset, you can attend VR church if you like. But you were in an empty church. And it's interesting to hear you mention that because we are looking for someone to lead it, be our preacher, or pastor. And that's where we are hoping you might come in."

"What? Need I remind you, I'm a Supreme Court *judge*?" Finn emphasized the last word. "A judge, a lawyer, not a tourist guide or pastor for heaven's sake."

"We know. And you've been a wise one, in fact, inspiring millions around the world who have praised you for your recent decision that further upheld the pro-life movement and quashed *Roe v. Wade* for good. Hindus, Buddhists, Muslims as well as Christians all over the world have taken notice of the Supreme Court decision you wrote, praising it as one of the best-written decisions of all time. Which is why, we believe, they will listen to you further, as a speaker, teacher, preacher—and maybe even pastor."

"I'd have to abandon my seat on the Supreme Court bench, vacate my judgeship."

"Not necessarily. We are several years out from making this a reality. You could start by preaching just an hour on weekends from the comfort of your home. And eventually you would be the most powerful preacher in all the world. To any and all religions. You would be the biggest evangelist of all time. Bigger than Billy Graham."

Finn looked Zimo squarely in the eyes and saw that he was earnest, sincere.

"But what if I don't want to do this?"

Zimo sighed. "Do you?"

"I don't know." Finn sighed as well. "Let me give it some thought."

"That's all we ask."

Finn excitedly started telling Lei about his conversation with Zimo and his friend over a quiet, candlelight dinner at Raiku, a local sushi restaurant nestled in the suburban hills off the beaten paths of the city. But before their dinner even arrived, Finn could tell by his wife's quiet demeanor that she already knew about the virtual reality proposal.

"That's why you brought me here to Shanghai in the first place, isn't it?" he fumed, losing his appetite.

"No, honestly, I wanted you to see more of my country—and then, yes, listen to what my friend had to say. He can be a little smug and sarcastic at times, I know, but he's a brilliant creator and tech genius. I didn't know any of the details. I just knew he wanted to tell you about his plans in person. He insisted."

The waitress appeared then with a large tray of colorfully elaborate sushi rolls and fresh salmon and tuna sashimi set off with delicate birds carved out of vegetables and beautiful edible flowers.

"Isn't this wonderful? Look, Finn, the chef even carved our favorite bird from Hamilton Island." Lei pointed to a cockatiel carved out of a white radish.

Finn was not amused. "Don't try to change the subject, Lei. You should have warned me about all of this. I was totally blindsided by it all. Great performance. You should get an Academy Award."

He asked the waitress for a check, not even eating one bite of the sushi, and told Lei he'd wait for her in the car. She had the food boxed to go and met him a few minutes later, tears in her eyes. "Finn, I'm sorry, you're right, please forgive me."

He was surprised she didn't try to defend herself at all. Maybe her Chinese culture, where women were more subservient to men, was rubbing off on her a bit. Still—he didn't want to forgive her, not right away at least.

Finn and Lei walked quietly along the Great Wall of China the next day, taking in the vast views of the surrounding green mountains—lush in their summer splendor.

After the night before, Finn was still angry with his wife and decided to give her the silent treatment.

They hadn't spoken since her apology, leaving the house very early before anyone else was even awake, donning shorts, T-shirts, and hiking boots with light jackets they could remove when the summer sun arose high in the sky.

He'd eaten a few bites of cold sushi as a quick breakfast and downed a cup of strong, black coffee, but it was nearing noon now, and Finn was parched and starving.

Lei was hiking behind him, and he turned around to see how she was doing. Compassion moved his heart as he watched her wearily walk, her eyes downcast and sad, beads of sweat forming on her forehead, her hair limply hanging, fatigue setting in. His ire started easing. They'd walked for hours along the wall and not said a word, which was more tiring than talking for both of them.

"How about if we take a break?" he called to her. "Get some lunch?"

She smiled, joyful gratitude in her eyes, and his heart danced with the love he felt for her.

He waited for her to catch up to him, closing the few yards of distance between them. When she reached him, he looked into her eyes, those big, dark, glimmering pools he'd originally fell into but had stayed away from lately. Instead of being cold they were warm and inviting now. "I love you," she said, and they hugged each other, sweaty yet content.

They went into one of the valleys below the Wall to a little restaurant serving Chinese street food and gobbled down big bowls of fried rice and noodles. Feeling nourished and reenergized, they walked along the Wall for another few hours.

Sunset along the Great Wall of China was truly a sight to behold. They held each other's hands and stood feeling like they were on top of the world as they watched the brilliant blazes of fiery light crisscross the sky, lighting up the hills on the horizon in golden splendor.

Finn suddenly got an idea and was half afraid to vocalize it, but then realized he trusted his wife. "Hey, Lei, what if I were to write a book during the rest of the summer while I'm off ... after we get home of course. Or I could start it on the plane ride home. About how God granted me the wisdom to discern my decision and write it on the Walters case? I know that sounds a little arrogant, but I feel I could help a lot of people figure out how to really know God's will. So many probably struggle with that. And sometimes I feel that I have such a strong connection—and I want to share the power in that. The joy in that."

THE WISE MAN

He saw his wife's eye squint for a second, possibly since the dark was coming on, but maybe out of doubt, he wasn't sure. But then she reassured him. "Finn, that would be a great idea. You're right, thousands—no, millions would want to find out how to get closer to knowing God's will in their lives. I often struggle ..." she looked down at her feet. "I am jealous sometimes of your connection. I would love to read it." She smiled at him, and he remembered once more why he'd fallen in love with her.

Finn wrote on his laptop nearly the entire fifteen hours of the flight, buoyed by coffee and energy drinks. When he got home, it was like he was possessed, and the words flowed from his fingertips. He'd prayed to the Holy Spirit, asking his help to write, and before it was time to start his next Supreme Court term in October, his manuscript was finished. Since he was well known now, his agent easily landed his book with one of the top publishers.

The book was simply titled, "The Pursuit of Wisdom." Finn told his story of being raised as an "only" child in the most prominent home in the most powerful country in the world, the White House, to working his way up to gain a seat on the most prestigious court of the land, the Supreme Court, to rendering the decision in the most politically charged, publicized case in history, *Walters v. Gold*. And along the way, he wrote about his pleading for intercessions from Jesus, the prophets and saints, and all wise people who went before him including

Socrates, Plato, Shakespeare, Buddha, Moses, Muhammed, and even his father, Leif Mitchell, praying for God to give him wisdom each step of the way.

Finn wrote about how he'd been rewarded by finding fulfillment of his purpose, but that he was always in pursuit of wisdom because one could never fully know God's will or get to know him completely. It was a lifetime journey, but more than that, he shared how it was a "forever pursuit" in which one was never really satisfied. And he finished with an open ending ... he admitted he still had not found the full meaning of his life, or his final purpose, that he was still striving for God's will even though he'd caught glimpses of it, and was still trying to see the big picture for his future.

CHAPTER TWENTY-SIX

The Pursuit of Wisdom became an international bestseller over the next year, and Finn found himself fighting off the media which bombarded him with requests nearly every day for author interviews. Mega bookstores wanted him to do book signings, colleges and conferences wanted him to do speaking engagements and keynotes, TV and movie producers wanted him to make a documentary film or series.

Another year passed, and the hubbub did not die down, so after much prayer, Finn finally realized it was time to step down from the Supreme Court because he was casting too much of a spotlight on it, tethering it from doing its job effectively. He was much too popular to be an impartial and sequestered, secluded judge. Finn had grown to love the limelight, the attention, the adoration, and simultaneously dislike the boring, black robe. So, he decided to vacate his seat—and take Zimo up on his offer to pastor the VR church.

After stepping down from the Supreme Court, Finn started pastoring online and wrote another book titled, "The Pursuit of Love," which drew even more fans and had two million readers within a year, double that of his first book.

Every Saturday, he'd spend several hours in his study—in prayer and meditation, then preparing the next day's homily to deliver in his virtual reality church. While Finn had inherited his father's gift of oratory, he still felt it prudent to practice as much as possible. Of course, Sunday was a day set aside for preaching and worship through his new "Epitome Church of God."

Before Finn put on his headset the next Sunday morning, he performed his usual ritual after getting out of bed with the dawn. He showered, shaved, and put on a clean suit, shirt, and tie, even his dress shoes, although no one would ever see them. It was important to him to *feel* like he was dressed for church even though his avatar would appear on screen.

Then he sat in his study, his desk empty except for a lit incense candle, a cup of hot green tea and honey, his laptop, and his Bible.

After a half hour of prayer and meditation, Finn donned the headset and began his welcome, read the Scripture readings, and then went into his sermon.

Today he was preaching about getting in touch with nature. It was November, a season of change, a time for gratitude.

"We read in Ecclesiastes, 'to everything there is a season and a time for every purpose under heaven. A time to be born, a time to die, a time to plant, a time to reap ... a time to embrace, and a time to refrain from embracing ... a time to cast away stones, and a time to gather stones together'." Finn paused and suddenly, inexplicably, he felt an overwhelming sense of isolation.

The Epitome corporate reports, which included church attendance numbers, showed Finn was now preaching to crowds online of well over a half million subscribers. Today would be no different.

And yet, Finn realized in that instant, he sorely missed human physical contact. He missed the repartee he'd enjoyed with his fellow students in college and law school, his fellow attorneys at his law firm, the justices on the Supreme Court. He missed looking into the eyes of real, live people.

He paused for a few seconds, took a deep breath, looked into the camera, and asked, "Do any of you miss being in a real, live church? I know I do. I realize many of you, for whatever reason, can't get to church. Maybe you're sick, handicapped, or otherwise impaired. Perhaps you're even imprisoned or hospitalized. But I'd venture to say most of you are here in this virtual reality church because ... well, because you're like me. It's convenient. Trendy even. And yes, because you're anxious to walk into a real church now. Because you don't like seeing people anymore. You feel like churchgoers are mostly hypocrites. Or it would take way too much time and energy that you don't feel you have.

"Well, friends, I've experienced all those feelings. But I just now realized for the first time in a long time that maybe they've become excuses and I miss real, live people. I miss hugs and looking into your eyes. I even miss the church itself. The inside of a church building, the sanctuary of it all. The feeling I get when I'm *in* God's house. Not my safe little office in my nice, cozy house where, you know what?—I've become totally isolated, removed, far from God.

And I can pretend all I want that I can call up a connection to God any time or place. But the truth is, God did call us to be in community with each other.

"So here's what I'd like to propose to all of you listening, probably in shock right now, to my words. I'm going to build you a place to go, no matter what it takes. A church where we can meet—not hiding behind our avatars, not safely over a computer screen, but in person. I realize this will take a lot of time, years even. Until then we'll keep this conversation going, I'll keep preaching through Epitome. But one day soon, we shall fill this new church—with our words, with our songs, with our hearts, with our souls, and yes, with our bodies.

"Now back to Ecclesiastes ... it has been a season of technological breakthrough, and we can give thanks for the progress this has brought us, the unity over many miles, the globalization of Christianity. Virtual church has been a lifeline for many who otherwise couldn't join us because of religious oppression, or for those who started attending online back when the Covid pandemic hit and never returned in person again. But I believe we soon will enter a new season of togetherness, fellowship, and community like never seen before, live and in person. I feel it, I believe it. Amen."

Finn smiled and then asked all online to join in the Lord's Prayer together—those who were left. He'd seen the number of viewers, out of his peripheral vision glancing down at the bottom number on his screen, drop from over half a million to less than fifty thousand as he talked. He was okay with that.

"What was that all about?" Zimo fumed through Finn's large computer screen after the service was over. "You had no right to go off on a rant like that! What were you thinking? Did you see how many viewers we lost?"

"I did, and I'm sorry. I know I didn't give you advance warning. That's because I didn't have any either. I felt the Holy Spirit move me, and I went with it. Don't worry, we'll get them back, and then some, maybe even double ... people are hurting and want to be healed, and they can't get that over a computer screen. They need friendship, love, human interaction to get closer to God. I know they still want all the thrills of a virtual reality experience too. So why not give them both?"

"What are you talking about? I'm starting to think you've lost your mind."

"Listen to me for a minute, Zimo. The VR Church gets the most viewers of any of the Epitome programs out there. We need to draw people to our tourist attraction on the island once it's built, right? We may have lost some of our viewers temporarily, but when we open up for business, who's going to be first in line? The ones who want to step inside the church they've been seeing online. And guess what will happen when first-time visitors step foot in the church? They'll go back home and want to keep coming back for the experience ... which they'll only be able to get on our Epitome system."

"Hmm ... I don't know ... this sounds far-fetched to me. We were doing just fine up until now with our viewer base."

"Trust me on this."

"But who's going to come up with the capital to build the church? Not to mention develop the island, the tourist attractions, hire the staff—the list goes on. And need I remind you, we haven't even purchased the island yet?"

Finn had agreed to hire a realtor and search along with Zimo for a good location, and then invest his inheritance ... all one hundred million of it, if that's what it took, to purchase it. He wanted to be the sole owner if possible. But he knew he couldn't afford the Epitome system, tourist attractions, facilities, operations, and staffing—much less the magnificent church he had in mind.

"What about your mysterious investor friend?"

"I guess I can ask him. He's not very religious but it won't hurt to talk to him."

"And I thought of something else. To keep the VR folks interested in actually coming to the island, we should feature programs they can only get when they are there. In other words, they have to be there live to get certain virtual reality experiences through the headsets we provide. It will work both ways. We'll appeal to both people who want a new VR experience, and people who want a live experience based on VR adventures they've already had. It will be so advanced it will blow people's minds."

Finn could feel Zimo's tension lessen, hear and see his anger fade over the screen. "Okay, I'll talk to my investor friend and get back to you."

"Thanks, Zimo."

"You're welcome. Tell Lei I said hello."

"Will do."

"The Investor," as Zimo's connection was called henceforth, forked over fifty billion dollars for start-up funding to not only build the church, but landscape the island, construct condos to house thousands of people, construct the main tourist attraction and purchase live animals to populate it, build golf courses, swimming pools and stores, restaurants and spas along the main drag, and finally to purchase ten thousand special Epitome headsets to be rented to visitors during their stay.

But first, they needed to find an island.

Finn and Zimo had many online and phone conversations, searching through real estate sights and talking to a variety of agents until they finally settled on one.

It was an unnamed island off the coast of Australia in the Coral Sea, perfectly situated halfway between Cairns and Sydney—much larger than Hamilton Island but with all of the same beauty and almost totally uninhabited.

Finn flew first-class in a commercial plane to Sydney to meet Zimo the week before Christmas, then the two of them hopped aboard a private charter plane which flew them to the island a little over two hours away.

As he stepped off the plane into the warm Australian summer sunshine, Finn sucked in his breath at the sight before him. Towering palm trees swayed in a light breeze, their fronds flickering against a bright, cloudless sky. The land was lush and green with tall grasses and bright wildflowers. The vegetation had become overgrown in places, but Finn could see beyond to what it could become with a little loving care. He gazed onto the horizon where the makeshift tarmac ended. Finn could see a white sand beach along the coastline of the clear aquamarine waters of the Coral Sea and knew beyond lay the Great Barrier Reef, which had been "seeded" or cultivated over the past few years and was starting to teem with a vast, colorful array of fish and other aquatic wildlife again.

"Wow, it's more amazing than I even imagined." Finn turned to see Zimo looking up toward the trees. "What are you doing?"

"Seeing how high the condos can be built," Zimo said matter-of-factly.

"So there's nothing or no one on this island except us?"

Zimo smiled mischievously. "Yeah, why? You thinking I'm going to get rid of you somehow? Maybe turn you over to the natives so I can take charge?" Finn looked at Zimo and saw his eyes and expression look serious for a few seconds before he burst out laughing.

The thought made Finn a little nervous for a moment, then he chided himself for being silly. *Zimo needed him, right?*

"Nah, just kidding you," Zimo said after his laughter subsided. "There might be some crocs and sharks around, hopefully not a whole bunch of snakes, and who knows how many dangerous spiders and scorpions, you know how crazy Australia is. But I promise I won't feed you to any natives."

Finn laughed at himself. Still, he didn't fully trust Zimo. There was something about him, something ... cold, calculating, and if he weren't his partner now, Finn might even say sinister. *But you're in too deep now to turn back*, he told himself, starting to perspire. "Why don't we go over there in the shade at least?" He'd worn khaki pants and a long-sleeved cotton button-down shirt, but the temperature was starting to creep into the high eighties, which would have been perfect if he'd worn the right attire. He wished he could just peel off his clothes and jump into the gorgeous waters.

Zimo was more appropriately dressed in shorts and a lightweight polo shirt.

They walked across the tarmac, the pilot staying in the cooler nose of the plane to wait for them. They hadn't planned to stay long, just long enough to walk around a bit and make sure it was what they'd bargained for with the realtor before finalizing the sixty-million-dollar purchase of the twenty-five-hundred-acre island and its two smaller sister islands.

Under the shade of a big, broad acacia tree, Finn and Zimo talked about what to name the island and the resort, about how the ultimate plan would look, and what they were hoping the final total picture would include.

"Girls, lots of 'em," Zimo said, his dark eyes glittering.

"Don't let my wife hear you," Finn grinned.

"Oh come on, I won't say anything if you don't."

Finn shrugged. "Good restaurants, good bars, good swimming pools, and hot tubs, good golf courses and okay, yes, girls who are easy on the eyes, but I'll have to look not touch. What are we going to call it?"

"Call what? The island? The resort?"

"Okay, yes, both." Finn thought about it, gazing off at the white sand beach and the sun sparkling like diamonds across the perfect turquoise waters. It truly was a piece of paradise. And then it came to him as he thought about the Bible. "How about ... Eden?"

CHAPTER TWENTY-SEVEN

Finn and Lei visited Linda over the Christmas holidays, taking a few days off before it would be full swing ahead working with the investor, architects, and engineers to begin building the initial structures on Eden.

They arrived in the afternoon on Christmas Eve.

"Hello, Mom?" Finn called from the front foyer of his parent's home. Linda had given her new maid the day off to be with her family and had left the front door unlocked, knowing her son was arriving.

For a moment, he panicked. What if she were ill or had an accident of some sort? He couldn't bear the thought of losing his mother, although she was now seventy-two, and he knew it was inevitable at some point.

"I'm coming!" Finn sighed in relief, hearing her words ring out from upstairs. He and Lei dropped their suitcases in the foyer and removed their coats. He guessed his mother liked it warm in her house now that she was getting older. Ah well, she could afford the heating bills.

Linda Mitchell sauntered down the staircase of their Potomac mansion, which had been kept up by her staff of three—a maid, a cook, and a groundskeeper. She also was visited by a personal trainer to give her private workouts in her at-home gym.

Nothing to worry about with Mom. Finn whistled appreciatively. Linda looked more like she was sixty-one, fit and trim in her navy-blue jogging suit, her silver-dusted blonde hair cut in a stylish bob, her golden hazel eyes dancing. She wore light makeup over her still flawless skin, which showed no wrinkles. Linda was still a beauty, and time had been kind to her.

Finn's admiration drew a strained smile from his wife. He always sensed a bit of jealousy rise in Lei whenever they were around his mother. He couldn't fathom why but the one time they'd broached the subject when he questioned her about her feelings, she'd brushed it off, telling him he was imagining it. But she did let him know how she sometimes resented his mother doting on him like he was still a schoolboy. Finn couldn't argue with that, so he let it drop.

She warmly hugged them both. "It's so good to see you, it's been so long. Come on in, have a seat, I'm afraid I don't have any help, but Georgia made some fresh muffins, so let me go get them with some tea, or would you prefer coffee—"

"Mom, don't worry about all that. We just want to sit with you and catch up."

"Okay, dear, well come on into the living room and sit down and tell me about all of the exciting ... uh, ventures ... you've got going on." Linda Mitchell had expressed surprise and disappointment when Finn had told her over the phone he was giving up his seat on the bench to go on a book tour and then, especially, to become an online preacher. His mother was not fond of social media or virtual reality, believing it was mostly evil, and the devil was involved with it all somehow.

Finn darted a glance at Lei, wondering how much he should divulge. His wife nodded, and Linda smiled politely at Lei, then looked expectantly at him, a hint of worry on her face.

"Let's sit down," Finn said, and they all sat in the formal living room. "Mom, I wanted to wait to tell you in person that Lei's friend Zimo and I have become full-time business partners. That's why I vacated my Supreme Court seat and started preaching in the VR church, and—"

"I still don't understand that move, honey, I thought it was your dream to be a Supreme Court judge, and to give it all up for some ... online TV church thing. It just doesn't make any sense. But what do I know?"

Lei folded her arms, apparently biting her tongue to keep silent.

"Let me try to explain, Mom." Finn sat up straighter on the edge of the couch next to his wife, facing his mom in her leather easy chair. "You know, of course, that a lot of people left the church because they stopped going during the Covid pandemic and turned to, as you'd say, 'TV church.' Virtual reality gives them a much better church experience because they can actually participate with each other in the service. It's like being there, only online—not just passively watching on television or a computer screen. We now have over two million subscribers attending, which means my message goes out every Sunday to a whole lot of people. I was honored, I'm still honored, to be the lead pastor of the VR Church.

"But because there are many people like you who we will never reach because they can't, or won't, go online, we're going to build an actual church, the biggest, greatest church in the world, where people can go in person—that will be just like the virtual reality church we've built only 'live.' We will blend the two into a hybrid in hopes to bring the world together in prayer, worship, and song. We've already arranged to purchase a beautiful island off the coast of Queensland, Australia, to build the church and the Epitome VR experience adventure resort. I will fly you over there when it's all done so you can see it, Mom. It's breathtaking."

"Sounds expensive, who is funding this project?" Linda looked apprehensive.

"Well, Zimo and his staff are taking care of the investors for most of the development, operations and such, but we are always looking for contributions," he hinted. "I've invested some of my inheritance money—"

"Oh, Finn, you didn't." Linda's voice was filled with dismay. "How could you?"

"The investment is already turning a profit." Lei finally spoke up, her voice like dry ice.

"But it's about more than just money, of course." Finn tried not to sound defensive like his wife. He just wanted his mother to understand, and of course, to approve. Her opinion still mattered to him, more than he wanted it to, but some traits you grew up with—like codependency on your parents—became

278

ingrained and almost impossible to put aside. Or so he vaguely remembered he'd been told by a counselor he once saw when he was feeling stressed and overwhelmed in his early law days. "It's about God."

"So, Finley, you both ..." Linda cast a quick smile toward Lei and then turned back to him, her eyes dark and piercing. "You and Lei aren't moving to this island near Australia, right? You're going to stay here in Washington, DC, right?"

Finn exchanged a quick look with his wife. They'd talked about it and weren't planning to move to the island, at least not while she was still working here in the US. Lei had opened her own fashion house with a dress boutique on New York Avenue in DC, then had flown to New York City and opened another in Manhattan right on Madison Avenue where she featured her own designs. Her label, 'Lei Mitchell' had outfitted most of Washington's elite, including several senators and First Lady Joyce Newman herself, with gowns they'd worn to many balls and ceremonies.

Lei was enjoying her own success independent of her husband, and Finn was proud of her. But secretly, he hoped one day they would move to Eden and leave the trappings of fame and fortune aside to just enjoy life. Maybe raise a family and eventually retire there. "No, Mom, we're staying here, at least for now."

Linda narrowed her eyes skeptically. "All right, well, I'll trust you know what you're getting yourself into. Now, how about those muffins? It's so good to see you both, and I can't wait to give you your

Christmas presents! Speaking of that, you've got to come see my tree—it's out in the parlor. Georgia did such a great job of decorating it, and Lucy, my new cook, prepared a full-course turkey dinner for us since you couldn't be here for Thanksgiving. All I have to do is heat everything up. I'm sure she made way too much, though. One of these days, before I die, at least, I hope to see little ones running around ..."

Here it comes, Finn thought, a headache forming in his temples. Grandchildren. Another touchy subject with Lei who wasn't sure she even wanted to have children. They hadn't prevented it, or at least to his knowledge she hadn't. They should start soon, though, since his wife was thirty now. *Now is not the time, Finley*, he chided himself. *Just ignore Mother for now. Even though she's right. Again.*

Stone and marble were flown in from Greece and Italy to meet the architect's specifications. The church would be larger than St. Peter's Basilica in Rome, two-hundred-thousand square feet in size. The windows were elaborately filled with stained glass artistic renderings of the Book of Genesis— Adam alone in the Garden of Eden, Adam and Eve together, their private areas covered in fig leaves, Eve being tempted by the serpent, Eve reaching for the fig on the Tree of Good and Evil, Eve handing Adam the fig to take a bite and then Adam and Eve being banished from Eden.

Zimo had shipped in gold bullion, which was melted down and used to trim the interior marble archways and coat the altar as well as create two larger-than-life gold angels that stood on either side, their wings nearly touching.

Construction crews worked day and night and the church was finished that next year. Meanwhile Finn continued to preach on Epitome and talk up Eden and the church, which he named the Sanctuary.

Finn had remained Catholic like his mother, but since the VR church was open to all religious denominations, barring none, he had decided, along with Zimo's and The Investor's blessings, to keep it all-inclusive. All would be welcome at the Sanctuary.

There was a huge reflection pool off to the left of the church with fountains, and the architect built two towering white marble stallions to hold up the largest fountain in the center of the pool, which was filled with filtered crystal-clear aquamarine salt water that flowed directly from the Coral Sea.

While the church was being built, Finn took a sabbatical over the course of three months to write a book that God had put on his heart. He titled it "The Pursuit of Harmony." The book was filled with song lyrics, poetry, and prose Finn had started writing down in a journal dating back to when he was in high school.

The book was another instant New York Times bestseller and soon garnered tens of thousands of reviews on Amazon.

Finn held book signings across the US, Europe, China, and Australia, where folks lined up by the thousands to meet in person the judge turned pastor who had ruled in the famous US Supreme Court abortion case killing *Roe v. Wade*—and who was now the spiritual advisor to millions.

He loved meeting each of his adoring fans and loved the publicity as reporters covered each of the signings, shining their camera lights on him, thrusting their microphones at him to capture a soundbite or two.

Finn flowed all the millions of dollars he received from the proceeds of his book into hiring the same architect and construction crew working on the Sanctuary to build a house for himself and Lei and the staff they'd need.

It was constructed of the same marble and stone as the church and was nearly the same size in square footage but of a different layout. The house was more horizontal, sprawling, with various quarters including an in-law suite where Finn planned to move his mother. Linda Mitchell agreed to relocate, much to his wife's chagrin, to Eden, hoping to be with her future grandchildren, he was sure. Finn had argued the house was certainly big enough that three people could have their own living quarters and never even see each other if that's what they wanted.

When Finn had showed the architectural plans for the island house to Lei, she'd gasped. "Finn, it's as big ... or even bigger than the church! Isn't that too big ... too much for us, even if it is three of us?"

"Nothing's too much for us, or I should say you, my love." Finn did still love his wife, even though their marriage seemed strained lately with the constant physical distance since he traveled so much. Their emerging differences in opinion in religion and politics had unfortunately only grown over time.

He always wanted to please her, though. *Maybe I am codependent on women*, he thought one day as he got off a phone call with his mother, who'd lectured him on how the Pope should be the headline speaker at the church's Grand Opening. Finn had tried to argue with her, reminding her that the church was nondenominational, and if they brought the Pope in it might alienate those of other faiths, even other Christians—Protestants, Muslim Christians, and Jewish Christians—and how the Sanctuary was trying to be all-inclusive.

"I just don't understand," Linda had lamented. "How can you call this ... Sanctuary ... a church when it doesn't seem Christian much less Catholic?

"Times have changed, Mother," he tried to explain. "People, especially young people, don't want to label themselves a particular religion, they prefer to just consider themselves spiritual."

"Well, I was hoping you hadn't changed, but I guess you have. But I won't. I will always consider myself Catholic. Your poor father is probably rolling over in his grave ..."

Ouch. That one cut deep. Finn had nearly hung up on his mother for the first time out of hurt and anger. Instead, he'd said, "Okay, Mom, I'll invite the Pope."

CHAPTER TWENTY-EIGHT

The church's Grand Opening ceremony was scheduled for a gorgeous sunny day in September and covered by nearly every media station in the world.

The church could hold ninety-thousand people and was nearly packed to hear Finn preach that morning, the crowd overflowing onto the broad stairs leading up to the massive gold-plated doors that were opened to allow as many as possible a view into the phenomenal interior.

The Pope had declined to attend, thanking Finn for the invitation but saying he had a schedule conflict.

Finn was relieved. He didn't really want to share the stage with His Holiness anyway, who had a keen knack for stealing the show.

A grand stage it was, built up ten feet high at the front of the church facing the grassy mall that replicated the one in Washington, DC, covered with a pavilion in case of bad weather.

But the skies were gloriously blue and sunny that September morning.

God is with me, Finn thought as he prayed alone for a half hour in a small alcove in the Sanctuary, which had been closed to the public in preparation for the big event. He lit a votive candle and kneeled in a pew before a statue of the Blessed Mother holding the Baby Jesus.

Finn stared so long perhaps his vision fell askew but he could have sworn Mary's eyes had shifted to gaze right into his own and he could hear her speak to him. *"Don't forget from whence you came, my son,"* he heard a soft voice whisper that seemed to come directly from the statue. *"What you have built here, this church, will be blessed as long as you stay true to your faith."*

Finn raised his eyes to the Mother Mary's and saw they were no longer looking at him but were vacant again, merely made of stone.

He sighed. He was probably just tired. It was time to go address the crowds.

Lei and Linda Mitchell had flown to the island together for his address. Zimo brought them in a back door of the Sanctuary along with Mai-Yong to make their grand entrance through the front doors. Then they would step onto a red carpet that had been rolled out down the steps and onto the edge of the Mall, where tens of thousands of people thronged together to celebrate the Sanctuary's Grand Opening. It was bigger than the Academy Awards or any movie premier that had ever taken place, and Finn felt like a movie star as he paraded, smiling in his sunglasses, out into the sunlight, his wife's and mother's arms linked in each of his.

Finn wore a black tuxedo, and Lei wore one of her designer dresses, a modest champagne-colored, long lace-covered gown that showcased her black tresses and dark sultry eyes. His wife had also designed a gorgeous floor-length navy satin gown for his mother. Zimo and Mai-Yong flanked the couple, also sporting black tuxes. The Investor was a no-show, of course, as he apparently preferred to be.

A sound system had been set up for Finn's speech and afterward for the new Sanctuary Choir to sing several traditional hymn selections including "Amazing Grace" and Handel's "Halleluiah Chorus," and then a few contemporary songs, ending with a song Finn had written titled, "The Only One."

Finn approached the microphone, remembering his moment with Mary. He bowed his head and said a quick "Please Lord, give me the words," then spoke, his voice carrying out into the crowd. "Thank you all for gathering here on our beautiful island of Eden today on this special occasion of the Grand Opening of the Sanctuary. I know in my soul God is smiling upon us as we dedicate this church, his Church, our church ... for it is open to all people, of all ages, all nationalities, all colors, all creeds."

He could sense in his peripheral vision his mother staring at him in mild disapproval, but he carried on. "I am but a vessel for God to grace this holy church with his Word and deeds, a servant to gather you together in this House of Worship. No building can contain the Lord God, but we still ask him to bless this place that he called me ... called *us* to build." He did not look into Zimo's eyes but felt him glaring as well at his slip up.

Let him glare. Finn knew his wife and her family and friends did not believe in God, the Father, the Almighty, but rather a universal "spirit" in all humans, perhaps a "she" or "it" that manifested through nature, like the sun, moon, stars, and wind. He wasn't even sure if Lei's Chinese friends and family believed that much.

But right now, he was being moved by a power greater than himself and felt the Holy Spirit speaking through him. The crowd was silent. "God, know that I, your humble servant, am grateful, that we are all thankful you fulfill your promises in and through us. I have found life is beyond my wildest dreams when I stay humble and in your service.

"Grant safe passage to all who travel from afar, to those from all religions, nations, walks of life—whoever enters here and prays here, bless them with your Almighty hand and help us all to spread your Word from here because this is your chosen house in your chosen land.

"Finally, I ask, God, that you show special favor on all who enter these doors and this house because it truly is *your* house. Grant that your people, when gathered here to pray and worship in this sacred place, the Sanctuary, will find what they are searching for—will find forgiveness, healing, peace, joy, and love. That they will find you in their midst and find your favor. Lord, I ask your blessings on all those who enter here. Amen."

Finn reached down to a brass pitcher-like container at his feet that held an aspergillum, the tool that was used by priests to sprinkle holy water. He blessed the water by making the sign of the cross over it and then took the stick with the silver ball at the end and flung it out over the congregation, sending water spraying over their heads, walking right, then toward the middle, then left to try to bless as many as possible. Some made the sign of the cross while others bowed, prayed quietly, or just watched with fascination.

While Finn was blessing everyone, the chorus broke into singing the song he'd written.

THE WISE MAN

Toward the end, when he was finished with the blessing of Holy Water, Finn bent his head, feeling a swell of gratitude and joy, and he grasped his wife's and mom's hands tighter, wanting this moment to last forever as they sang the final verse—

> Like a reed in the river, I was bent but not broken,
> You helped me stand tall, feel the warmth of the
> sun,
> And though that river keeps raging around me,
> My roots are in you, I have nowhere to run.
> Nowhere to hide, nowhere to run,
> I turn to you Lord, you're the only one,
> The only one who can heal and forgive me,
> The only one who can make me my best,
> The only one who can shield and protect me,
> The only one who can help me find rest.
> The only one, the only one, the only one, the
> only one ...

As the choir's voices faded, the voices of those assembled rose to sing the chorus.

Finn blinked back tears as he heard their voices rise. Finally, they faded too, and Finn stretched out his arms and hands toward the people for a final benediction. "May the Lord our God be with us all as we go forth to spread the good news! Welcome to the Sanctuary!"

He cut the big red ribbon with the giant scissors, and the people cheered.

The doors opened and all filed in to see the magnificent interior, some to admire, some to kneel and pray.

Finn stood just within the front doors in the back of the Sanctuary in a shadowy corner quietly observing. His wife and mother had already gone in together to take a tour around the church's many alcoves. From there they would head over to the banquet tents to help oversee the feast prepared for the VIP guests who had been invited for a brunch service. He was just about to walk out to join them when he felt one of the security guards step up to him from behind and whisper in his ear. "We have a special guest, a dignitary, who has just flown in and requests your presence."

Princess Callista Alexandra, the daughter of King Omar Alexandra of Morocco, had flown to Eden that morning, arriving on the island just in time to watch the grand opening and dedication. She now viewed the affair privately from the balcony of her luxury condo unit in the Paradise Hotel, Eden's most opulent residence building overlooking the mall in front of the church.

She peered down at the crowd, all facing their newly crowned "king," or spiritual leader, former Chief Justice Finley Mitchell, although she knew he was no longer just a judge but apparently a priest turned prophet.

Callista had come to witness first-hand this American man's hold over so many people who had flocked to the island just to hear his supposed words of wisdom.

She was still wary, though, but curious enough to make the journey, enduring the long, bumpy flight through stormy skies that had lasted nearly twenty-four hours nonstop from Morocco to Sydney.

It was worth it, she thought now, as she basked in the island sun that shone onto the balcony, warming her face.

Her young attendant, an eighteen-year-old, dark-skinned African woman from Ghana named Sarah who had been hired to accompany her, softly spoke from the bed chamber adjacent to the balcony. "Excuse me, Your Highness, would you like a cup of tea?"

"Sarah, no need to use formal titles while we're here, you can call me Callista." One look into the young girl's bewildered big brown eyes, and the princess knew that would never happen. "Or we can continue with the formal address. I just want you to be comfortable."

A large white gleaming smile spread across the eager girl's face. "Thank you, ma'am, Your Highness Callista," she giggled.

"And no to the tea. Come here, Sarah, look at this crowd of people."

Sarah neared her side, although kept a foot's distance respectfully between them, and nervously peered over the marble ledge of their lofty perch from ten stories high.

A palm tree nearby waved in the breeze, its fronds partially obstructing their view for a moment, but they could still hear what the great Finley Mitchell was saying over the loudspeakers planted at the corners of the mall which lay about twenty yards away.

"He seems very ... sure of himself, doesn't he?" Callista glanced at Sarah who peered up at her quizzically. *She's probably wondering whether to agree with me or not, so I may as well give up on getting her true opinion. I will just have to find out for myself,* she decided. "We are invited to the banquet, so let's go freshen up."

The princess led the way back into the suite, stopping in front of the floor-length mirror against the wall of the bed chamber. She gazed at her reflection. Her headdress, which matched her azure floor-length silk day gown trimmed in small, white, and yellow flowers, was slightly askew. She pulled it off, letting her long, dark, chocolate-colored curly hair cascade down her back and shoulders. Almond-shaped topaz eyes, which she had been complimented on a thousand times over, stared back at her under arched eyebrows set in her smooth skin the color of creamy caramel. Her lipstick had faded but her full lips were still red, stained from the strawberries she'd quickly snacked on before stepping outside to hear Finn's address.

Finn. Finley Mitchell. She'd come all this way to meet the legendary man who she'd only met prior via her virtual reality headset. *We'll see soon enough what all the hype is about. Or whether the man is more of a myth than anything else.* She still had her doubts.

CHAPTER TWENTY-NINE

Their eyes locked together, sparking under the vast banquet tent—topaz and aquamarine, fire and ice. Finn knew who she was before meeting her—he had received the request for an invitation from one of Callista's public relations secretaries doing her bidding. His secretary had responded with a formal written invitation mailed to the Princess of Morocco, who'd passed along that she would like to see, and possibly invest, some of her country's money, into Eden and its future.

A business trip, the secretary explained.

A slight breeze from the fans gently whirring at the top of the tent caught the princess's long wavy tresses just as she'd turned and caught his eye. He gazed down her flowing white silk sundress which was accentuated with a coral belt, shoes, jewelry, and lipstick. He saw her smile, radiant, mesmerizing, her gorgeous face lighting up. Entranced, he walked toward her until he was standing in front of her, still holding his breath.

My wife is beautiful and a princess too, he reminded himself. *Still, there is something about this woman ...*

"Callista Alexandra, what a pleasure to make your acquaintance." Finn took her hand in his, expecting it to be petite, delicate. Instead, he got a firm handshake, and he looked her right in the eyes. Her lithe frame stood as tall as he.

The Moroccan princess proffered a gift. It was a gold box, about the size of a shoebox, wrapped in a royal blue velvet ribbon.

"Hmmm, what do we have here?" Finn smiled with delight. He loved gifts. As he took the box from her, their hands touched, and he felt his face flame.

He pulled the bow undone and opened the lid to reveal several jars of exotic spices.

Finn loved to cook and had revealed that little-known fact once in an interview he'd done on television. He especially enjoyed making dishes featuring lots of spices like Indian curries, Cajun jambalaya, and Mexican mole dishes.

Still, most people didn't know this about him. *Miss Callista must have done her homework*, he mused. He looked at the various jars of red, tan, orange, brown, gold, yellow and green. There were Moroccan spice blends like Kafta, Ras El Hanout, and Mrouzia and then expensive spices from around the world like chai, curry, saffron, Green Zahtar, White Cyprus Flake Salt, Shawarma Rub, Aleppo Pepper, Sumac, and Seven Spices as well as more common but wonderful single spices to experiment with and mix into blends—cardamom, paprika, turmeric, ginger, cinnamon, allspice, coriander, cayenne and cumin.

"Thank you, Your Highness. I couldn't think of a more perfect gift than this," Finn said, still feeling flushed with excitement. "How did you know I like to cook? Such rare spices as these will make me look forward to getting in the kitchen again. Just the other day I was telling my wife ..."

As if he'd magically summoned her, Lei appeared at his side, darting a sideways glance of warning. "Let me guess, my husband was saying how cooking was getting boring?"

"I guess I just needed to spice it up," Finn joked, and Callista emitted a laugh, a deep, throaty, yet melodic sound that he found enchanting. Lei didn't crack a smile but just rolled her eyes. "I'd like you to meet my wife, Wu Lei."

Callista handed Lei another smaller box, this one silver with a pink ribbon. Lei opened it, a little less dramatically, but was still impressed by its contents—an assortment of small bottles of rare perfumes.

"Why, thank you," Lei said, smiling, although remaining somewhat stoic.

"It's a pleasure to meet you both," Callista purred like a royal lioness.

Finn *felt* her power. "The pleasure is all mine ... ours."

"You must have had a very long flight. I'm surprised you made it here in time." Lei politely nodded. "And don't feel you have to stay, I'm sure you're exhausted. Once you get some rest, perhaps tomorrow, you can join me in touring the island. I'm sure Finn will have his hands full with this crowd." Finn thought Lei's tone sounded slightly sarcastic as she swept her arm out over the sea of people milling about under the tent.

They were all buzzing about Finn Mitchell's speech, his song, and about the promised tourism delights that lay ahead of them in their planned explorations of the island. Many had booked their stay as part of tour groups that had been arranged—most through a travel agency Zimo had Mai Yong set up through a friend who booked island getaways. Mai Yong had persuaded the friend to exclusively work for Epitome and already the man was making twice his income from the year prior.

The din of voices and glasses clinking, plates being filled, and easy listening music filled the tent and Finn started to get a headache from all the noise, and to feel claustrophobic.

He still had a lot of VIPs to greet and mingle amidst as he worked the vast crowd, but he desperately needed fresh air right now. "Excuse me, ladies," he bowed to the two regal women who were both turning heads from various directions—the Asian beauty and the African enchantress standing together like two models on a runway—creamy white skin next to burnished bronze.

Finn left them talking together and sidestepped through the melee. He'd nearly reached the tent's opening when he bumped into his mother, nearly knocking her drink out of her hand. "Mother, I'm sorry, I was just heading out for some fresh air."

"Finn, you look panic-stricken, what has come over you?" Linda looked at him with concern.

Finn glanced behind him, across the room at his wife and the Princess of Morocco. He didn't have to say anything, his mother knew him so well.

"Ah ... you felt overwhelmed, is that it?" His mother nodded knowingly. "Finn, let me remind you, now is not the time to flirt with disaster. In reality, there's never a good time. You have a lot of eyes on you now, watching your every move. Do you know how dangerous it would be for you to ... well, I don't know what you're thinking, but I know that look in your eyes. Mischievous. Scheming. It's the same look your father had when he met me. And while that turned out all right in the end, there was a big price to pay. Learn from your father's mistakes. Do not play with fire, Finley. You will get burned."

Finn was only half listening to his mom. His heartbeat throbbed in his ears, he was finding it hard to breathe, and he thought he might be sick. "You're right, Mother," he said to appease her and walked out into the bright sunny day, leaving the sweet heavy smells of breakfast foods behind and inhaling the clean, fresh saltwater air.

Just breathe, he told himself. But her face lingered temptingly in his memory. *Callista*. Even her name sounded bewitching.

Finn was feeling fine the next morning, but his wife was not. Apparently, something Lei had eaten had not agreed with her, so she said she needed to go back to bed and would regrettably have to miss their tour of the island.

Finn had planned to take Lei, Princess Alexandra and her assistant, Sarah, in his tour vehicle, a large four-wheel-drive Cadillac SUV driven by his personal chauffeur. They were planning to caravan with Zimo and Mai-Yong and their respective tour groups riding in similar transport.

The caravan of SUVs stopped at the hotel where the guests were all staying. The driver opened the right doors of the Cadillac for the ladies. Sarah sat in the front passenger seat while Callista sat in back with Finn.

Their first stop was the Sanctuary, where they all exited and toured the nave. The VIP guests snapped photos and gawked at the vaulted ceilings, stained glass windows, and massive marble columns. Then they gasped aloud when they saw the altar up close with its golden angels on either side, genuflecting toward one another on bended knee.

Finn glanced over at Callista to see her expression of awe as she stood gazing open-mouthed, her golden-brown eyes wide with wonder. He suppressed a smile of pride.

The next stop on the tour was his very own mansion, but since Lei was inside sleeping, even though she was sheltered by layers of soundproof doors and walls, Finn didn't want to invade her privacy. He promised the group that when his wife was feeling better they'd come back to see the home's interior.

The group was off next to go to the summit of the island, the tour's grand finale. There they'd climb Eden's pinnacle, "The Garden of Eden," and see where the virtual reality main attraction was housed within a grand, volcano-shaped structure that towered above the palm trees below it, dwarfing them. The structure was swathed in lush palm trees and colorful flowers and waterfalls cascaded down either side. Exotic animals roamed the tropical rain forest, and if you stood by quietly, you could hear a soft din of rare birds amid the rush of water. The architects had done an outstanding job, Finn knew, gazing with awe as he'd done hundreds of times already at "The Garden," marveling at how it looked like a scene straight out of Jurassic Park.

Finn led Callista and Sarah into the dark cave-like depths of the volcano, and it was so dark at one point, he took both of their hands to lead them. Electricity flowed from Callista's hand into his own, and he almost withdrew it out of shock and fear. *What was this hold she had on him?*

He led both ladies into the Secret Chamber, the large room where only two were allowed to put on headsets and summon their own virtual realities.

One could play alone, or two could play together, but there wasn't a third headset to be found.

There were many other chambers within the cavernous interior where very large groups of people could all don headsets and dive into their own virtual adventures together or smaller gatherings could have an Epitome party. But the Secret Chamber was different. It was dimmer, warmer, lit with a glowing candlelight effect, infused with aromatherapy scents of jasmine, musk, and vanilla, meant to enhance a couple's intimate experience if they chose one.

The selection of virtual reality programs was constantly being refined by the tech geniuses who now worked for Epitome. They already ranged from religious emersions or spiritual meditations called "heavenly realms" to geographic escapes like trips to Tahiti where you could relax totally in private on a white sand beach. Or you could dance along the streets of Rio de Janeiro where you could be immersed in a parade of thousands moving to thumping music in the heat of the night. Adventures were a big draw too—people wanted to not only see the world without having to travel but wanted to sky dive, go up in hot air balloons, climb Mount Everest, fly a jet, or scuba down into the depths of the ocean, all without risking their limbs or lives.

Finn had strongly stated to the manufacturers that no X-rated material would be allowed—no sexually explicit content, no foul language, no extreme violence would be permitted into the headsets despite their users' desires.

He gently picked up one of the two headsets which glowed softly in the dimly lit chamber and handed it to Callista. He glanced at Sarah and motioned for her to get the other headset on, but her eyes widened in fear, and she shook her head back and forth.

"Sarah, don't you want to try it?" Finn asked the girl, who was now trembling, backing away toward the corner of the room. He lowered the headset onto a nearby table and without getting any closer, softly said, "Hey, it's all right, there's nothing to be afraid of, you don't have to try it." He saw the girl's dark eyes grow even wider and he turned around to see the source of her fright.

Princess Callista had already donned the other headset and was widely smiling with joy, her hands raised up in a praise-like stance, her body swaying to some unknown sights and sounds.

She has no idea how provocative she is right now, he thought. He would give anything to know what she was seeing. *Why do I care?* He wondered. *Why am I so attracted to her when I am already happily married?* He cursed his father, blaming him. *I'm cut from the same cloth,* Finn ruminated.

Sarah was still staring, so he beckoned her with his finger, holding it up to his lips to indicate she should remain silent, then led her by the hand out the exit door of the Secret Chamber into the cool foyer outside. He told her to get a drink, pointing to a water cooler in the lobby. "Have a seat, Sarah, I'll go in to make sure Callista is okay, and then, we'll be out in a few minutes."

Sarah's eyes squinted at him, getting used to the light. *Or maybe she's wary of me,* he realized. *After all, her job is to protect her princess, the future queen.*

"Don't worry, I will make sure no harm comes to her," he added with a backwards glance before heading back into the softly lit, quiet chamber.

But the moment was over. Callista, flushed with exhilaration, was just taking off the headset, grinning. "Wow, that was ... breathtaking," she said, her cheeks blushing. "It really was heaven on earth."

Finn's own breath caught in his throat, and he couldn't speak.

She walked up to him, her body only inches away. "You've really got something here," she murmured, taking his hands in her own. "I thought this whole place was just a big tourist trap, that you were some egotistical American preacher like all the rest on TV, just trying to rake in big bucks and become rich and famous. But this ... this experience is phenomenal."

"I left Sarah out in the lobby, she was a bit shaken when she saw you, um, enjoying yourself," Finn said haltingly. "I don't think she knew what to make of it. Can I ask which experience you chose?"

"Heaven on earth," she said, releasing his hands and pointing her finger at his chest, then letting it trail down, sending a shiver through him.

Finn invited Callista as his guest out to dinner on the island that night since Lei was still sick and didn't want their island guest to catch her stomach bug by dining in their home.

Sarah stayed in the hotel condo that evening. The princess insisted she take the night off and have some alone time to herself, telling her it was an order.

They dined at La Casa Mer on raw oysters, lobster tails, Diver scallops and prawns, all cooked simply and served with drawn butter. For dessert, they split the house specialty, strawberry shortcake with fresh whipped cream.

The tiny restaurant was at the highest point on the island off a beaten path in The Garden of Eden, overlooking the sea for miles around. Finn was proud of Eden and wanted to show it off to his royal guest. Although most visitors to Eden preferred the French and Italian restaurants, Finn loved the quaint hilltop seafood restaurant with its thatched roof and open, airy feel. It wasn't fancy at all, just picnic tables on the sand under the hut and some palm trees, but you couldn't beat the view—the ocean stretched as far as one could see. A full moon that night lit up the sky and the water like a million diamonds sparkling. And it was very private, not too many tourists knew about it. Tonight, they were the only people in the secluded spot. Finn had requested they be the only guests, had paid to have the chef and his staff all to himself and his dining guest.

Callista dipped a claw full of lobster into the butter and then sucked the meat out, butter glistening on her lips. She gracefully dabbed her mouth with her napkin, then ate a bite of dessert, licking whipped cream from her spoon.

The waiter came to make sure they were satisfied. Finn let him know they were, and the chef and his crew and wait staff could be dismissed after cleaning up, that he and his guest would be okay to stay for a while on their own. The waiter nodded, clearing the dishes. Callista looked at Finn appreciatively. "You really do own this island, don't you?" she asked in awe, looking out over the amazing scenery before her, like a picture postcard, the full moon dancing on the wide sea, the surf lapping the shore. She had a dreamy faraway look on her face.

Finn switched the subject. "Penny for your thoughts?" he asked, sipping his coffee. He knew he was staring at her. She was so beautiful, sitting before him in a low-cut silver cocktail dress that shone in the moonlight.

"I was just thinking ... well, before today, I didn't really believe in God," she said, setting her spoon down and gazing at him, starry-eyed. "I'd sat in on your VR church and heard you preach a few times out of curiosity. But I didn't feel any connection. I didn't get why you were so popular. I didn't get the messages you were trying to convey about heaven, building the Kingdom, experiencing peace, forgiveness, joy, and love right here and now. I guess I just bought into Darwin's theory, that humans morphed from apes over time, and once we died, that was it, so we should live it up while we're here, do our own thing. And as long as we weren't harming anyone else, that was enough. You know, I was living the *I can do what I want* lifestyle, and of course, being a princess, I really could for the most part. But today, wow, I felt so close to God I couldn't deny the fact that he exists."

Her golden-brown eyes shimmered with the light of joy, hope, and faith.

"So, can I ask, what experience did you have?" Finn felt himself holding his breath in anticipation of her answer.

"Well, I truly did ask for the 'heaven on earth' experience, and then in a dream state, I found out I was pregnant and would give birth to a son. I was overwhelmed with a feeling of joy and gratitude."

"Oh." Finn of course would never know that feeling and was dumbstruck, not knowing what else to say. He wondered to himself who the father might be.

"I have to confess something," the princess said softly, leaning forward across the table so that their faces were closer. "I am a virgin, so I also experienced making love for the first time ... not in an X-rated or even R-rated way, but more of an intimate, truly loving way ... and it was with you."

Finn gulped, feeling heat rise within him and this time was truly speechless.

"I know you're married, and that this would be wrong, but it felt so right, so wonderful that I believed with all my heart it was a gift from God." Callista took his hand and he looked down at her slim brown manicured fingers and felt an ache rise within. He couldn't raise his eyes to hers until she squeezed his hand tight. "Finn, please show me this gift."

He drew her to him and whispered in her ear.

"Would you like to go swimming?"

She whispered back, "We don't have our bathing suits on, silly."

"Have you ever heard of skinny dipping?" he stood back and smiled, seeing her look of confusion. Apparently, she had not. "It's swimming without a bathing suit—without anything on."

The princess of Morocco blushed.

Finn had an idea. He told her to turn around, he'd go first, then he'd turn so he couldn't see her undress before she slipped into the water. No one was around.

But Callista was a step ahead and was already removing her dress. Finn rushed to join her, running after her, laughing all the way across the sand and into the sea. They made love there in the moonlit water under a canopy of stars.

CHAPTER THIRTY

In retrospect, Finn had felt like he had no choice. Callista had cast a spell on him that night under the full moon, the sea waves lightly rolling onto the beach in a rhythm like the one they found together as one.

But now this ... Finn felt an overwhelming guilt eat at him as he lay next to his wife.

How would he live with himself?

And yet, he felt closer to God, to heaven itself when he was with the Princess of Morocco, her warm brown skin the color and sweet taste of dark honey, her scent of cinnamon, cloves, and musk—earthy, spicy, intoxicating. Or so he'd reasoned earlier as he and Callista lay together blissfully under a blanket under the stars.

Only now, he knew for sure he definitely was as far from God as he'd ever been in his life.

Still, I want to be with her.

Finn slowly, silently slipped out of bed and into his robe and slippers and padded quietly down to the kitchen to fix himself a cup of coffee. He was transfixed as the coffee brewed, thinking about his day ahead.

He was already counting the hours until he'd see her again. They would be long, he knew, the day's plans stretching out before him, yawning, endless, wearying.

First, he was scheduled to have breakfast with the Board of Trustees of the island to discuss some of their concerns regarding a batch of VR headsets that were apparently malfunctioning. The box of one hundred Epitome sets had been damaged in transport from Bangkok and were causing a few issues with tourists such as headaches and vertigo after they were used.

A few board members wanted the headsets in question to be fixed since they were so expensive. Zimo had assured Finn he'd handle it but had stormed off in anger after one meeting, threatening to pull the plug on the entire virtual reality operation if they didn't back off.

They didn't need any bad press. His afternoon meeting was with one of the editors of the show *60 Minutes*. They wanted to do a documentary featuring Eden and the Epitome VR tourist attraction, but also focus on Finn and how he'd gone from being a Supreme Court justice to a virtual priest on an island in the Pacific. *It actually sounds kind of cultish*, he admitted to himself. Finn was worried about the interview, wary the producers could either cast everything in a good light—or a bad one. You never knew with that show until it was edited and televised.

And then he'd been informed that two of the guests flying in to stay on the island the following week were none other than Christine Walters and her eight-year-old son, Jesse. He'd added Christine on the VIP invitation list several months ago and hadn't heard anything ... until now.

The press were already starting to hound him on her impending arrival—"Was this a media stunt to draw attention to Eden? Or to promote the Epitome for Kids line of virtual reality games that had recently been manufactured? Would Jesse Walters be a poster child for the Pro-Life movement and the future of virtual reality?" Inquiring minds wanted to know.

Finn could answer *no* to all of their questions but knew they wouldn't believe him anyway, so he ignored the incoming press calls and was instantly regretting granting the *60 Minutes* interview.

Let me just get it all over with so I can go back to her.

"Finn!" His thoughts were interrupted by the distant shout coming from upstairs.

He filled his cup of coffee and made his wife one as well and hurried into the bedroom, a steaming mug in each hand.

"I have been calling you for twenty minutes." Lei lay on the king bed, covered with gold silk sheets and a red and gold threaded duvet that had cost over ten thousand dollars. Her tone was one of disgust.

"I'm sorry, my love, I was making you some coffee."

"What, to make me sick all over again?" Lei held up her hand as if to ward off the smell.

Finn sat both mugs on coasters atop a bureau and went to sit next to her, although he kept a distance, in case she was still contagious.

"Where were you last night?" she asked.

Finn snuck a glance at her sideways. Her face was pale, tired, and she frowned.

"I had dinner with Princess Alexandra at the Casa de Mer. Her assistant, Sarah, couldn't make it, so I dropped her back home to her condo."

"But I woke up around two in the morning, and you weren't here."

I can't do this to her. I can't tell her the entire truth.

"Well, then I took a late-night walk, came home and fixed a cup of warm milk because I couldn't sleep and stayed up and watched some comedy shows on television. I must have drifted off. When I woke up, I came back to bed with you."

Lei sat up in the bed, sitting back against her Asian silk-covered pillows against the headboard, also inlaid with real gold. It too had cost a fortune. She squinted at him, as if trying to discern whether he was telling the truth or not. She sighed tiredly. "I am feeling a little bit better. I guess I won't have to cancel my plans tomorrow with my women's group after all."

His wife had recently joined a small group on the island that practiced yoga, reiki, and crystal chakra healing. Finn was leery, but it seemed to keep her busy while he was otherwise occupied, so he didn't pay too much attention to it all.

He knew Lei was also still a professed atheist, although she'd agreed to keep it a secret so the press didn't uncover it. She often just fibbed if questioned in interviews saying her faith was nondenominational despite her family upbringing.

Finn suddenly felt an anger rise within, diminishing the guilt and remorse he'd been feeling—justifying it even. Lei had been so cold of late they hadn't been intimate in weeks. Along with her women's group, she'd also been focused on her design work and caught up in decorating their new mansion to the point where she'd practically ignored him lately.

In fact, Finn had begun to wonder what he ever saw in Lei to begin with. She'd vehemently disagreed with his stance as a judge on pro-life versus pro-abortion. She obviously didn't agree with his religious beliefs either, much less support him. Nor did she desire to have kids even though he'd wanted to start a family for years, pleading and prodding her to at least consider it, to no avail.

They'd drifted apart. *No wonder I sought the comfort of another woman.*

Finn quietly got up, showered, dressed, and headed out of the oversized mansion. There was nothing left to say.

The day was a blur, but he got through it all, including the interview with the *60 Minutes* reporter.

Afterward, Finn drove his private car, a black Ferrari Portofino, up to the Paradise hotel condos and parked in the back in a small VIP parking garage that had a private elevator to the penthouse suite so he wouldn't be noticed.

He got to the top floor and knocked on the door of Callista's condo unit, but no one answered. He put his ear up to the door and listened for voices. Nothing. Finn knocked again, louder, but again was met with silence. *Strange.* Maybe they were out shopping or getting their hair or nails done or something.

Finn had brought his master key just in case. He opened the door and walked in. "Hello, anyone home?" The interior was cool and dark. Finn flipped on a light switch and walked into the spacious penthouse. It was meticulously neat and clean. The cleaning crew must have just left. He felt like an intruder and turned to leave when he saw the note lying on the kitchen counter. It was a small white folded piece of personal stationery with a monogrammed "A" on the front along with his name, "Finley Mitchell."

Inside it read, "Dear Finn, I'm so grateful for our time together, but I felt it best if I left for home, my attention is needed in Morocco for an urgent matter. Please forgive our sudden departure. We really enjoyed our stay, thank you for everything— Callista and Sarah."

Finn's knees felt like they were buckling, and he grabbed the counter with both hands to steady himself, his heart racing and his head pounding. Maybe he was having a panic attack.

How could she leave him?

He wandered in a fog deeper into the condo and sat in the sunken living room on the leather sectional, staring at the blank flatscreen TV. He mindlessly grabbed the remote on the coffee table in front of him and flipped on the power, then ran through the cable stations until he found CNN. And there was a photo of her incredible, beautiful face staring back at him on the screen next to a photo of her father, King Ahu Alexander with a headline scrolling horizontally below it. "Moroccan King suffered stroke ..."

Finn curled up on the couch and wept.

He had no time to grieve. The next day, he met Christine Walters and her young boy, Jesse, in an official welcoming ceremony at the church to plan her son's baptism. She'd asked Finn if he would do the honors of officiating, so they met to discuss the details.

He walked the mother and eight-year-old boy down the main aisle of the massive church, smiling, watching their mouths open in amazement as they stared up at the towering golden arched ceilings held up by giant marble columns, and their eyes widen when they approached the golden altar and larger-than-life angels on each side.

"This is amazing," Christine said, awestruck.

"Here's the baptismal font," Finn motioned to the right of the altar, showing off a pool of water encased in a marble bath, a gentle waterfall cascading down its rock-hewn backdrop.

"Wow, this is so neat," Jesse exclaimed, approaching the pool, which was four times his size and could hold two adults at the same time if they chose to be submerged together. He reached his hand in to touch the warm clear water, but his mother scolded him. "Jesse, that's holy water."

"No, that's okay," Finn laughed. "He can touch it. Although you're right, it is holy water flown in from the Jordan River where Jesus was baptized. Just touch it ... reverently."

"Mom, what does rever ... what does that word mean?" Jesse looked at Finn and Christine with big blue eyes, his innocent young face framed by brown curls.

"It means you need to be serious, like you are in a church, Jesse, like we talked about at home, remember? Not play in the water but touch it like it is from God, because it is."

The boy backed away from the baptism font and clasped his hands in prayer in front of him, then shyly moved to his mom's side, peering up at Finn behind long eyelashes.

"It's okay, Jesse, you never have to be afraid in this church, here, take my hand." Finn extended his hand and took the boy's in his own, leading him back to the font. Then he cupped his hand, filling it with water and poured it into the boy's, letting it flow through his fingers. Jesse smiled up at Finn, dimples forming in his cherubic cheeks. "It's warm, it feels good."

"Good because we are going to be dunking you in it, but don't worry, we'll have a nice big towel nearby to dry you off. It will be like dipping into a warm pool. And like I just did in your hand, I'll do on your forehead as I say a prayer."

"Can I close my eyes, so I don't get water in them?"

"Of course, silly," Christine ruffled her son's hair in her hand, then shook Finn's hand with her own. "Thank you, this was the perfect practice."

Lei called Finn on his cell phone that afternoon to tell him she'd be delayed for dinner, she was meeting with her women's group for an extended yoga and meditation session. He'd had lunch with Christine and Jesse, then had gone back to the church sacristy alone to do some paperwork.

As he listened to his wife's voicemail message, Finn had an idea. He'd been feeling pent-up stress lately, not coincidentally since Callista had left the island, and his back and neck muscles were tense and sore. He didn't want to keep taking ibuprofen or muscle relaxers but also didn't want to go to the island spa since it was probably swarming with visitors.

He decided to join his wife in their small group yoga class and surprise her.

Finn had never tried yoga before, but knew it involved some stretching and strength exercises that he was pretty sure might help his aching body and maybe even relieve some of his anxieties, since he'd heard Lei also talk about meditation and mindfulness.

He tried to call Lei back, but she didn't pick up. She probably has no signal in the yoga studio, he realized. It was located out on the tip of the island, in a remote spot out by the volcano-like VR tourist attraction. You could only get to it by hiking a steep and winding trail. There were no roads, no parking lots, no cars even. Only palm trees and a stretch of grassland and beach where a large building with floor to ceiling windows perched on a cliff looking out over the sea. *Yoga might be just the thing I need*, he thought, hoping the women wouldn't mind his presence.

Finn climbed down the stairs from the back church sacristy to an underground entrance to his home. He'd made sure the two were connected for security, safety, and privacy reasons.

After a quick change into his gym shorts and a tee shirt, he was behind the wheel of his Ferrari and on his way down the coast of the island to the far tip they called "The Point."

Storm clouds were forming on the horizon, rolling in like bolls of cotton, turning the sea into a shadowy iron-gray dotted with whitecaps beneath, the wind whipping across its surface.

He hoped he'd get there before the rain started pelting down as he'd still have to hike the path out to the yoga building. He'd only been once before to check it out with Lei, who'd been proud to show it off. It had just been cleared out and a construction crew had laid drywall and soft plywood floors that would be comfortable under yoga mats and as a dance studio, so it was brand new when Finn had seen it. He'd been impressed and was looking forward to his first yoga class, which Lei had said started in about an hour.

Maybe I'll have a chance to meet the ladies and see my wife in her element. Maybe she will be happy for a change. Maybe.

He drove as far as he could to a parking lot on the Point. There were three other cars in the lot. *They must have carpooled.*

He donned a rain jacket he grabbed from the back seat of his sports car and pulled on the hood and zipped the front, as the wind was now picking up speed, flaying the palm tree fronds, although thankfully it still wasn't raining yet.

Finn marched along the wide dirt trail through the brush and bushes, not taking time to smell the flowers along the way.

The front door opened into a lobby where people could gather and wait for the next class inside to be over without disturbing those in meditative states. Finn took off his jacket and listened to what he thought at first was the wind howling around the building.

He stood still and listened again. It wasn't the wind he was hearing, he realized, but the soft incantation of women's voices, chanting. One voice rose above them all. It was Lei's. Finn could now make out her words. "We pray to the sun god for the rain to clear and the storm to do no harm. We pray to the moon goddess to calm the seas to do no harm. We pray to Mother Earth for a bountiful harvest this fall so that all the islanders will have plentiful food. We worship you, oh gods of all the animals, plants, air, fire, water, and land and pray for balance and prosperity. We pray to you, Hedone, and you, Aphrodite, that we may experience the pleasure you created us to feel ..."

He opened the door to the inner chamber where the yoga studio was and saw his wife seated facing five other women, all sitting cross-legged on various colored yoga mats. Finn couldn't believe his eyes. They were each wearing an Epitome headset, their palms raised within the corresponding hand controls. Their bodies were swaying rhythmically, and they were humming and chanting as Lei continued to pray loudly over a background boombox sound of waterfalls and the natural rush of the wind outside.

They didn't even see or hear him enter.

The smell of sage burning assaulted his nostrils and made him feel heady, almost high. He saw a low-lying wooden table toward the front of the room that held a clay ashtray with the smoking sage as well as several carved figurines of different sizes, including a Buddha, a lion, and a dragon. He also saw crystals displayed—quartz, amethyst, jade, red jasper, tiger's eye, hematite, serpentine, and lapis lazuli.

Finn looked around and saw various astrological symbols on the wall—the signs of the zodiac as well as a guide to the seven chakras of the body. He also saw a big poster advertising the benefits of CBD oil with a hemp leaf on it and could see from the ladies' glistening bodies that they had apparently rubbed the CBD oil or some type of essential oil over their skin.

He then watched, mesmerized for a moment, as the women laid back on their mats in a bridge pose and started moving their hips, humming then moaning.

He couldn't stand there any longer or listen to anymore and slipped quietly back out into the lobby, softly closing the door behind him.

CHAPTER THIRTY-ONE

My wife worships pagan gods.

Finn paced back and forth in his living room. Luckily, he had wood flooring, or he probably would have worn a rut in the carpet. He still could not believe what he'd just seen.

The trip back home was long. He'd had to drive slow as the wind buffeted his little Ferrari sports car on the island roads, and the rain cut down on his visibility. It gave him too much time to think, so he blared rock music on his Bose stereo, trying to blot out anything in his head but the raw sounds of Metallica, AC/DC, Led Zeppelin, and Pink Floyd.

But the images of his wife and the other women, gyrating to whatever images were appearing on their headsets filled his head. *No wonder Lei's never in the mood.*

He'd been waiting over an hour, pacing, stopping to down a shot of premium malt whiskey a few times, watching the sun set through the huge lanai that overlooked the sea.

Finally, Lei arrived home. Finn was sitting on the living room couch, sipping a glass of whiskey.

Lei glanced at her husband, then the half empty whiskey bottle on the counter and bustled off, claiming she'd pulled a muscle and needed to take some ibuprofen.

"Wait a minute ... please," Finn called out to her. "I need to talk to you."

"Can't it wait, honey, my shoulder is really aching," she said with a forced gaiety.

"No, it can't. Please sit for a minute. He patted the space on the sofa next to him, and Lei sat down on the edge, looking uncomfortable.

She looks guilty of something. "I saw you at yoga today."

"How did you possibly do that?" Lei's brows arched in surprise.

"I drove out to the Point and walked out. You ladies were ... um ... preoccupied, to say the least."

Lei nervously bit her lower lip. Then she became indignant, standing up and folding her arms in front of her. "What were you doing, spying on us? What is wrong with you?"

"What is wrong with *you*?" Finn stood up, his fists clenched. "It looked and sounded like some Wiccan tribe or satanic cult in there. I can only imagine what you were watching on those headsets. And by the way, how did you even get hold of them? They are only supposed to be for the island guests who visit the Epitome tourist attraction and use them under supervision ... and, might I add, pay to use them."

Lei practically sneered in triumph. "Did you forget that Zimo is *my* friend? And also that I can afford to buy them? I just had to ask him to get them for me. We are actually testing a new program for Zimo ..."

Finn could see in her eyes that Lei realized belatedly

she'd slipped out that last piece of information by mistake.

"What new program?" He was faced with her stubborn silence. "What were you listening to and watching?"

"That is my private business," she said, her voice shrill in defiance. "How dare you barge into our yoga practice? And not even let me know you were there! Is there nothing sacred?"

"Sacred?" Finn yelled the word. "How can you possibly call what you were doing in there *sacred*? It looked like the opposite of anything sacred or spiritual to me. I know you don't believe in the God I worship, the Father, Jesus, and the Holy Spirit. But to worship pagan gods of the sun, moon, and stars—I think that's worse than being an atheist."

Lei glared at him, her eyes becoming slits of anger. "You are the most hypocritical person I know. You say you believe in God—and then you go off and have an affair with that Moroccan princess."

She must have seen the shock on his face because her own registered a look of hurt, as if she'd been guessing at the truth but secretly hoping she'd guessed wrong ... and then finding out she was right. "How *could* you?" She turned away from him, wiping tears from her eyes so he wouldn't see her cry, see her in a weak moment. She started walking away from him.

"Wait, I'm sorry. Can we talk about it?"

"No. I'm going to my room. And since we have twenty-eight rooms in this house, I'd suggest you go to the farthest one away from me if you still want to live here." Her back was turned as she uttered the words, but she suddenly stopped and turned around to face him again. "And you better leave us alone out there on the Point. No more spying."

He saw the tears in her eyes, and his former righteousness dissolved into guilt, regret, and remorse. "I promise, I won't come out there again."

Finn immediately confronted his business partner the next morning. He waited for Zimo in his office at church trying to prepare his sermon for the coming Sunday morning when his cell phone buzzed. It was a text from Zimo. He was here.

Zimo entered Finn's office breathless. "Hey, I just wanted to let you know that we need to order another shipment of headsets from the manufacturer."

"Sit down, Zimo." Finn pointed to one of two leather chairs in front of his desk.

Zimo's smile was not reflected in his black eyes, which glittered and darted around the room.

"Are you okay, you seem to be nervous?" Finn himself was trying not to sound too anxious. *Be cool,* he told himself. *Don't let him see you're angry.*

"Sure, I'm great, business is hopping." Zimo was wearing a light jacket and removed it, sweat showing through the armpits of his lavender polo shirt. He had lost weight and his arms were bony and wan, the color of oatmeal. *He looks unhealthy,* Finn thought, feeling a measure of concern for him despite his latest deception.

It was a cool seventy degrees in Finn's office.

"That's what I wanted to talk to you about. Business. I am still part of the business, right?" Finn felt jealous that he'd been relegated to the church front of the business and had not been privy to the inner workings of Epitome or even Eden lately.

"Of course." Zimo shifted his bony body in his chair, crossing his white chino-clad legs.

"Because that's not how it feels."

"What do you mean?" Zimo asked, feigning innocence.

That did it. Finn felt his rage boil up inside him and erupt in a seething sarcasm. "I think you've been keeping me out of the business. In fact, I know it. And *friends* don't treat each other that way. It's dishonest and disrespectful. So how much have you been hiding from me?"

Zimo sat upright in his chair, his Adam's apple bobbing in his throat. "I have no idea what you're talking about."

Finn barked a short laugh. "Lei happened to tell me you gave her some headsets with a new program on them." *There it is, I dare you to deny it.*

Zimo took a deep breath in, then exhaled slowly. "She paid for them. Besides, it was Mai Yong's idea."

He's probably passing the buck. "Why don't we get Mai on the phone then and ask him about it?" Finn reached for his cell phone, but Zimo held out his hand to stop him.

"Wait. Okay, it was partly my idea too. But mostly, it was The Investor's creation."

"What is *it*?" Finn heard the frustration in his own voice but couldn't help himself.

Zimo proceeded to unveil the new program, the "Seven Deadly Sins." It was a virtual reality game where users could enter one of seven portals where they would literally experience, in a 4-D realistic way, what it would be like to give in to their temptations—whether they be pride, lust, greed, gluttony, envy, sloth, or wrath.

"Why didn't you include me in the development stage?" Finn stood and leaned across the desk, his own wrath rising within. He wanted to wrap his hands around his partner's skinny throat and choke him, but instead he leaned on his balled-up fists and glared into Zimo's dark fearful eyes, waiting for an answer. Finn could feel all the muscles in his arms and chest tighten, harden like steel, and he knew he could pulverize Zimo if he so chose. He'd been working out every day, getting stronger, his muscles bulking up to the point where he'd had to buy all new suits to fit. Even the white polo shirt he wore now stretched across his bulky frame. He pounded his fist angrily on his desk right in front of Zimo's face. "How dare you do this without me?" he bellowed.

"I'm sorry, Finn, we wanted to make sure it was ready before we unveiled it—we were under pressure from the Investor, who threatened to pull the financing if we didn't get it out quickly enough. And we wanted to protect you." Zimo was now visibly trembling and stuffed his shaking hands into his pants pockets. He saw Finn notice. "Too much caffeine lately, I guess."

"What was the rush?" Finn stood up and crossed his arms, skeptical.

"I guess it was all about the money, like everything is these days. We are planning to charge four times the amount for island tourists to use this program versus the others ... if it's okay with you, of course."

Finn shrugged that aside, knowing Zimo was simply placating him. Something Zimo said earlier had caught his attention, though. "What do you mean by making sure it was *ready* and wanting to *protect* me?"

Zimo sucked in his breath and suddenly started coughing until he was gasping for air. "Can I get some water?"

Finn wanted to make him suffer, but getting answers was more important. "Here." He filled a cup from his nearby filtered water cooler and handed it to Zimo, who gulped the contents down before continuing. "There are controls in place to block users from going too "dark"—too violent or gory, too promiscuous or lascivious, et cetera. It doesn't allow any explicit language to be used. And there is an adult-only age limit on it. But there's also an additional feature in the program, called the "Hell on Earth" experience, which is similar to "Heaven on Earth", only ... well ... you know, the opposite."

"Why would anyone on earth want to experience hell?" Finn rubbed his chin with his hand, baffled.

"The thought behind it is the daredevils who want a thrill will enter the virtual hell reality and be scared off from it enough to want to come back and try the heaven experience. Or vice versa. Extreme adventurers, curiosity seekers, risk takers, fate tempters all would want to pay to try it ... but would only be allowed to try it once. It'll come at a premium price, just like the heaven experience, compared to all the VR travel, adventure and gaming programs. Only hell will be twice as expensive as the heaven option. The Investor thinks it will sell itself. And the 'Seven Deadly Sins' portals each lead into the 'Hell' portal if users want to go one step further in exploring the experience. They just push a button making an additional payment right there on the spot. If people want an ultimate scary thrill, this will definitely give it to them."

"Wow, this does not sound good at all." Finn's anger and jealousy in not being on the ground level fizzled into worrying about the people who would be coming to the island, probably in droves, only to be scared out of their wits. *This was not our original intention behind Eden at all.* "So, you were basically hiding this whole thing from me since you knew I probably wouldn't approve?"

"You need to understand the Investor swore us, Mai Yong and I, to secrecy. He was the one who had a creative team develop the product, then had to get patents and didn't want it to leak out and be stolen. That was the main reason behind the rush. There are others out there—Japanese anime developers, the big metaverse outfits, Microsoft, Google, you name it, developing new VR experiences daily. It's exploding. The Investor wanted to be first."

"Don't you think it's about time I know the real identity of the Investor?"

"He's promised to reveal himself after this program is launched. I think he wants the credit. I swear you'll be the first to know, after me of course. I still don't know his name."

Finn sat back down, his adrenaline cooling down as he reflected on all he'd just heard, worried now about his wife. "So why did you let Lei and her yoga women try out the program? Aren't you afraid they'll let the secret slip out?"

"I trust Lei." Zimo had regained his composure, realizing Finn had decided not to do him bodily harm. "We needed a test group. They have all signed non-disclosure papers, and all agreed to have a chip put in them to monitor their reactions to the program as well as any, uh, indiscretions."

"Need I remind you my *wife* has one of these chips in her?" Finn was incredulous, his voice rising again.

"Yes, but they assure us they're not harmful at all."

"They being the Investor? And you don't even know his real name?!" Finn thundered, walking around his desk to stand towering over Zimo now. *I want so badly to hit him. But it's not worth it.* Finn stormed out of his office, leaving Zimo still sitting in his chair.

Finn went right to the Point. He was going to get to the bottom of all this, with or without Zimo, the Investor, or even Lei, before any of them tried to hide anything else from him.

He jumped in his Ferrari and took off, speeding down the road. Fortunately, he knew all of the police on the island, and they knew him and his little black sportscar. They wouldn't dare stop him, much less give him a ticket.

He zipped into the parking lot and stomped on the brake. There was one other car, a light blue Volkswagen, parked in one of the other spaces. He'd seen it the other day as well. Lei drove a silver Jaguar, so he knew it wasn't her car. *Great, now I have to deal with one of these other women,* he thought angrily.

He would just have to ask her to leave, tell her there was an emergency he had to handle in the building, a malfunction that he needed to investigate. It wasn't a total lie.

He jogged down the trail, anxious to get to his destination. Unlike the last time he had ventured out here, the skies were clear and blue, and it was unusually warm. Even though it was late afternoon, by the time he got to the yoga building the sun had burned hot all day, and Finn was perspiring as he went to open the front door. He didn't have to use his master key since it was unlocked.

He rushed through the lobby and flung open the door to the yoga room. There, in the front, sitting cross-legged on the floor in shorts and a sports bra was a young, athletically built blonde, barely in her twenties he guessed. Her eyes were closed, her hands resting on her knees in a meditative position. She looked peaceful, blissful with a slight smile on her face for a second, then flung open her eyes at his intrusion, and jumped to her feet startled. "What are you doing here?"

Finn was equally nonplussed. *I must look like a sweaty, deranged mess.*

"I'm sorry ... I, I ..."

"You were probably looking for Wu-Lei, your wife, right?"

"Um, well, not exactly. I came out here to ... uh, do some yoga," he lied.

"Well, I'm the yoga instructor on the island, so you have good timing. I can give you a private lesson if you like. I'm Claire." She clearly knew who he was and held out her hand, flashing him a beautiful bright smile, her baby-blue eyes sparkling eagerly. Finn noticed that although she was young, she was very shapely, with a toned yet curvy figure that was slightly tanned. Her cheeks were flushed by the surprise fluster he'd caused and her skinned glistened all over and smelled of vanilla and tangerine, probably from oils she'd rubbed over her body. *Stay focused on why you're here*, Finn reminded himself.

"Actually, I'm also going to try using one of the VR headsets, my wife told me about them, and I wanted to experience the new program."

Claire's eyes widened and she looked worried. "I don't know—"

"Claire, I'm the founder of Eden, I started this whole island, it's okay, I just met with one of the program's developers, he told me to come out to try it."

"Do you have the chip ...?"

"Yes," he lied. "I got it installed this morning. No worries."

"They're over there." Claire pointed to a door in the far corner of the room. Finn walked past the table with its idol trinkets and crystals, past the astrological and chakra posters, past the stale burned out sage bowl to the unmarked door and opened it. Inside was another small anteroom with shelves holding ten Epitome headsets with matching hand controls.

He randomly selected one, picked it up, and brought it out into the yoga room, closing the door behind him. He was going to ask the young girl to leave but decided perhaps it might be best if she stay, to spot him like a gymnastic instructor. Just in case.

"Would you mind staying while I try this?"

"No, not at all. I'll just go over there on my yoga mat. Let me know if you need me."

MICHELE CHYNOWETH

Finn pulled a folding chair from a rack on the side of the room, sat down in it in the center of the room, and put on the hand controls then the headset, adjusting it all until it was comfortable.

The instructions came on and he saw he had a selection of programs from which to choose—Heaven on Earth, The Seven Deadly Sins, Hell on Earth, The Bucket List, Adventure Destinations, Love, and Games. He assumed each would offer various selections, but he didn't want to waste time shopping around. He knew he was after Hell on Earth to see what it was all about. When he clicked on it, a red sign with black lettering appeared that read, 'you must choose one of the Seven Deadly Sins and enter the portal there to get to Hell on Earth.' There were seven buttons below that listed each of the deadly sins in glowing capital letters.

Finn forgot Zimo had said this was the only way to go straight to the hell experience. He didn't know which to choose so he selected lust. *How bad could it be?* Zimo had said there wouldn't be excessive violence. The key word, Finn came to realize, was excessive.

He was suddenly in a dark, eerily glowing room with a strobe light amidst a dance party. Men and women of varying ages were dancing to the blaring beat of some wild hip hop music. Finn couldn't understand most of the lyrics, although he caught a few which sounded sensual in nature. Suddenly a woman took his hand and started dancing, her body touching his. She teased him, moving away then drawing near to him again, then she kissed him hungrily. Finn felt a fire building, burning inside.

330

He tried to escape and suddenly saw the Hell on Earth button. He hit it, and he was instantly transported into an empty, pitch black, hot and humid room where he was still left in the state of impossible yearning he'd last been in, only there was no relief. The girl had disappeared, and he felt trapped in a suspended state of desperate wanting, needing to be fulfilled. He searched in a panic for some exit button. He could feel his pulse and temperature rapidly rise and a pressure start to build in his chest and thought for a minute that he might have a heart attack. And then she appeared. Claire was in front of him, stretched prone on her back on her yoga mat, eyes closed lying in Savasana, or the corpse pose, a posture of total relaxation and submission.

Finn ripped off the hand controls and headset, but he was still in a trance-like state. He was so hot he took off his shirt and could see himself in the mirrors that circled the room, his bare chest heaving above his jogging shorts. He stood over her and she looked up at him with her big blue eyes. He recklessly ignored the warning signals going off in his head. Nothing else mattered but quenching this burning desire. *No one would see or hear ...*

CHAPTER THIRTY-TWO

When he arrived home, he was relieved his wife was out. Finn almost felt like he'd been drugged—as if he'd ingested some powerful potion or poison that was controlling his body and mind, keeping him in an addicted state. Already he wanted another woman despite the fact he'd just been intimate with one an hour ago. The worst part was he had been in such a comatose state he couldn't remember whether Claire had wanted to engage with him, had willingly participated in the act or not. He had left her there, still in his fog. At least he didn't recall her crying or being upset. He didn't remember much of anything, though. It was almost as if he'd been in a blackout.

"Hello? Mister Mitchell? Hola?" He heard the young girl's voice and realized it was Lizzy, one of the teenage Latina cleaning girls who worked for him. She must have just been finishing her shift. She came into the living room where he sat holding his head in his hands. "Are you okay?"

Lizzy bent down on one knee in front of him until he looked up and saw her big, brown doe eyes staring into his. *I think she's coming on to me.* Her lips were pouty, her black curls falling onto her shoulders. He

wanted to hold her, kiss her, feel her body ... *Stop!*
He stood up almost knocking her sprawling across
the floor.

"Hey, I was only trying to help," she said, her
voice belying her hurt, cutting through the shroud
of his desire.

"I'm sorry, Lizzy, I don't know what got into
me." He didn't turn to face her but headed toward
the stairs. "I'm not feeling well. I'm going to go up
and lie down. Please leave a note from me for Mrs.
Mitchell letting her know I went to bed early." Finn
really did think he was going to be sick and bounded
up the staircase for his bedroom.

Hell on Earth.

Finn rarely saw Lei anymore since they lived on
opposite ends of the giant mansion. He even had his
own food pantry, but mostly he ate out.

Eden now boasted two dozen restaurants and eating
establishments. From coffee and donuts to a full-course
prime rib or lobster dinner, one could get anything they
wanted to eat on the island, cooked to order, or even
brought to them via a meal delivery service.

The next morning after the yoga studio incident,
Finn called Zimo as soon as he'd had his morning
coffee to tell him about his experience. He'd gone
straight into the office to take care of church and
business matters, then planned to go straight home
so he wouldn't face any undue temptations.

"We can't put these things on the market, they're
dangerous," Finn said emphatically.

"How so? I tried it myself and it seemed harmless enough."

"What sin did you pick?"

"Greed. And it's all working out fine—money is pouring in." Zimo gave a short laugh, but Finn was not amused. "Why, what sin did you choose?"

Finn was ashamed to answer but felt he had no choice except to be honest. "Lust. And now it's ... well, I don't know if this is happening for you, but it seems to be planted in my brain, wired in my system. I don't know how to shake it."

"Hey, bro, maybe you need some counseling. Or maybe you just need to focus on your wife. You didn't have the chip implanted, did you? That's the failsafe, the magnetic block that grounds the neurotransmitters in your brain from continuing to fire the messages you received. Finn ... Finn?"

Oh, my Lord, help me. Finn cried a silent foxhole prayer just then that he wasn't damaged forever, beyond saving. His fear clutched him. Maybe he couldn't be saved, but he sure could try to save others.

"Don't worry, they're not ready to go to market yet," Zimo seemed to read his mind. "The program is still being refined, so I'll give the developers your feedback. We don't need any more sex addicts out there running around." Zimo stifled a laugh.

"Very funny. You also don't need to be any greedier than you already are."

"Look who's talking. You are one of the wealthiest men, if not *the* wealthiest man on earth. Look at yourself, man."

Touché, Finn thought. No arguing there. But he'd worked hard for his money, right? God had blessed him, to be sure, but he'd earned it, built it up, invested wisely, right? *Who am I arguing with?* He scolded himself. Zimo just had the ability to push his buttons sometimes.

He could blame Zimo all he wanted, but in the end, he'd made the choice to tempt fate and play a dangerous game.

Finn went home that evening with flowers he'd bought at a local florist, a mix of native, exotic, and fragrant flora—eucalyptus, hibiscus, and orchids arranged in a gorgeous bouquet. He had already called and sent Lizzy and their chef, Marie, home for the evening and arrived to set the dining room table with the flowers and some candles along with place settings for two.

Then he boiled some slipper lobsters he'd bought at the local fish market, one of Lei's favorite dishes, made some asparagus and white truffle risotto, and paired it with a bottle of Sauvignon Blanc. Finally, he'd bought some of Lei's favorite rum raisin ice cream and some whipped cream for dessert ... although he hoped they wouldn't need the ice cream.

When Lei walked in the front door, the shopping bags she was carrying fell from her hands onto the floor and her mouth dropped open in surprise.

Finn had dimmed the lights and lit dozens of candles that surrounded the foyer, living room, kitchen, and dining room, which were now romantically aglow.

He saw her dark brown eyes widen in amazement and then fill with tears that glimmered in the candlelight, and his heart filled with love. He didn't say a word but gave her a big hug and then lifted her shopping bags off the floor and carried them into the adjoining parlor closet.

The Swarovski crystals in the chandelier above the long mahogany table glittered like diamonds, and the flowers and candles combined to make the house smell heavenly.

After they dined, Finn cleared the dishes and suggested they sit out back on their lanai and gaze at the full moon and stars. He'd lit a few tiki torches which lit up the palm trees surrounding the infinity pool they'd had built in their huge backyard along the beachfront.

He held out his hand, and Lei smiled for the first time in a long time putting her hand in his. But when he drew her to him, thinking he'd whisper in her ear that they could go for a moonlight swim, images of Callista's eyes, lips, and body appeared, and he withdrew, intaking a sharp breath.

"Finn, what's the matter, honey?"

He looked at his wife's pale face, pinched with concern, and the images vanished. "Nothing. I just had a little shortness of breath is all. I'm fine."

"Are you having a panic attack?"

More like an attack of conscience. Please God, let me only have thoughts of my wife now, he prayed. He studied Lei, her eyes, her hair, her body, sheathed in the short black cocktail dress. *Come on man, she is beautiful,* he told himself. *You can do this.*

He reached out his arms, enfolding her in them, kissed her slowly, passionately, then whispered in her ear, "Let's go to my bedroom."

"Okay," she said simply, and they headed to Finn's master bedroom, where they made love and then fell asleep in each other's arms.

Lei sprang the news on Finn she was expecting after taking a home pregnancy test about two months after their romantic evening together.

But they didn't have a chance to celebrate. She had found out from Alana that their mother was dying of cancer. She'd also confided Finn's infidelity to her family. Wu Kai had begged her husband to allow Lei to travel home to see her one last time. Zimo accompanied her to go back home to China at her mother's insistence. Finn had warned his wife not to go, having misgivings about her traveling, but she'd insisted, indignant that her husband thought she was in a fragile state.

They'd been there for about a month when Finn called via FaceTime for Lei—and Zimo appeared on his screen.

"How's her mom?" Finn asked, trying to mask his impatience. A tension had developed again between him and his wife's friend ever since they'd both confessed to their VR experiences and realized, albeit indirectly, that their prideful egos clashed with one another. Neither trusted the other after all this time, and yet they were locked together through marriage and business—and a kindred desire to acquire more of everything—more wealth, more power, more prestige. It was like they brought out the worst in each other.

"Wu Kai is doing much better, thank you." Finn noticed a catch, a hesitation in Zimo's voice.

338

"And how is my wife? Where is she, how come she didn't answer?"

"Lei is ... well, she's not doing well. I guess you will learn this sooner or later, so I may as well tell you. She had a miscarriage."

Finn sat stunned, holding the cell phone in his hand like it was a scorpion. "What do you mean, she had a miscarriage?"

"Oh ... I'm sorry to be the one to tell you, but I guess you need to know—"

Finn felt a painful stab in his chest. His relationship with Lei was still strained, plus he'd been super busy the past two weeks and had missed a few of her calls. She'd become suspicious and then refused to talk to him the past week. "When? How ... how far along was she?"

"It happened just two days ago. I think she was about fifteen or sixteen weeks along. I'm sorry."

"How did this happen? How is she? Where is she? Can I talk to her?" Thoughts, emotions, fears raced through Finn as he shot out rapid-fire questions as fast as he could think of them.

"Finn, you need to calm down ..."

"Calm down? After the news you just told me?"

"Lei is sleeping right now, she's doing okay, just resting." Zimo spoke calmly, evenly through the screen. "I think it just happened is all." Finn could hear background voices arguing. Lei's parents.

Suddenly Zimo disappeared, and Lei's father appeared on his phone. "My daughter is okay, she is in our care," he said gruffly, matter-of-factly.

"But I think I should come over to be with her."

"There is nothing you can do, and that will only upset her. She told us about your infidelity and that she specifically did not want you to come here. You are absolutely not welcome again ever in our home. I believe she is going to stay here in China with us for an indeterminant amount of time." His face had aged a bit but was still as hard and stern as ever. "You just stay on that island of yours. We will make sure Zimo stays here with her." And with that, the screen went blank.

Finn knew that Wu Shin Hai had never approved of his daughter's marriage to an American and a Christian, no less. On top of that, he had difficulty with his daughter getting involved with a place called Eden, even if she was cut off from the family. The Chinese president and patriarch did not believe in God or the Bible story of Genesis and thought the whole concept of the tourist island and virtual reality attraction was hedonistic. He would not give credit to their venture, much less its name by saying it aloud.

Finn felt the rush of emotions ebb listening to his father-in-law, whose stoicism ran through the veins of his wife. Although in Lei's case, her steadiness usually had a calming effect on him.

He felt anything but calm now. Finn still felt guilty he wasn't there with Lei and defensive they would shun him at a time like this. *How dare they keep this news, this information about my wife from me, even for a couple days.*

After the call ended, Finn sat on his expensive living room sofa watching the flames dance in the mammoth fireplace. While the island temperatures were in the low seventies, Finn couldn't get warm.

He pondered what to do now. Should he just fire the three extra au pairs he'd hired to help with the baby? He knew he'd gone overboard hiring three of them, but it had been hard to decide between them who to weed out, so he'd kept them all. He reasoned to himself he and Lei had hectic schedules, and they'd need the help.

All three of them were young, highly qualified ... and very pretty.

One was an Irish lass who had long, curly red hair the color of copper, another was a honey-blonde Scandinavian, and the third a brunette from Australia's mainland.

Finn had interviewed about fifty girls from all over the world and had narrowed it down to these three.

They would each work various shifts, so one of them was always there while he was away at work, which was nearly all his waking hours lately.

He was so bereft at the news he'd just received that he was too emotionally drained to even think about the matter of the au pairs, and he got up and poured some Remi Martin brandy into a Waterford glass snifter and stoked the fire before sitting back down again. It was midnight, but there was no way he'd sleep now.

God was so unfair lately.

He wasn't sure from where the thought crept, but as it lodged within, he ruminated on it. *Yes, very unfair indeed.*

Finn couldn't understand how the omniscient, all-powerful, almighty *God*—and he said this with sarcasm to himself—could allow a tiny baby, his little baby, to die in his mother's womb when he so badly wanted a child.

He'd been obedient as a good son, a good judge, a good pastor, a good steward. Okay, not the best husband. But it was all the fault of Epitome, wasn't it? *That Zimo.* He'd started it all. He was partially to blame as well. And of course, Finn reasoned that his wife wasn't blame-free either. She'd been cold, distant—and come to think of it, she had never believed in him, or in God for that matter—so maybe this was *her* punishment, not his.

The liquor went down smoothly, warming his insides, and he poured another, filling the glass to the brim with the rich amber liquid.

He'd wished he'd never even gone to Hamilton Island, never met his wife or any of the Chinese Wu family, stayed single and on the Supreme Court in the good ol' United States of America ... or maybe just remained an attorney, working like most people, nine to five in a cushy job with not a care in the world.

Why did he always want *more?*

Finn ended up having seven snifters of brandy before passing out on the couch, his last drink spilling out of the wine glass and onto the white carpeting, staining it brown.

CHAPTER THIRTY-THREE

Waking up with a terrible hangover the next morning, Finn showered, shaved, popped two Tylenol, and went through his private passageway into the bowels of the church, climbed the stairwell to the main vestibule, and found a pew in the Sanctuary. There were a few people, heads bent in prayer, dotting the vast interior.

Finn quickly knelt, eyes closed, mustering all the sincerity and humility he could summon, and silently prayed. *Dear God, please have mercy on me, I know I've done some pretty horrible things ... I know I've hurt my wife by my betrayals. Is this my punishment, God? I thought you weren't a punishing God ... but I guess you are. Well, please don't punish my wife anymore. She didn't deserve this. Please, allow us to have another child. Please, keep my wife and my mother safe and healthy. And thank you for all the blessings you have given us—my family, the gift of my ministry, this church, my house, and most of all my beautiful island, Eden. Please, continue to bless me and help me to do your will. Amen.*

Finn slowly opened his eyes. He wasn't sure what he was expecting, but he saw no magic rays of light shining down from the rafters, heard no voices or singing of angels, felt no answer from the Almighty. He felt his faith weaken then, like trying to hold water in his hands.

Water. The baptism! It was in three weeks. He needed to make sure everything was ready. He was hoping to preach to a full crowd that day and hadn't even prepared his sermon, he'd been so preoccupied.

Finn got up, bowed to the cross hanging over the altar, and headed to his office. *I have a lot of work to do. I can't waste any more time on my knees.*

"I would like to call the whole baptism thing off." Christine Walters' voice mail greeted him as soon as he sat down at his desk and took his phone out of his pocket to check his messages. "I'll explain when you call me. Thanks."

Finn looked around his large, contemporary office with its expensive art hanging on the walls— paintings of the Blessed Mother, the infant child, a few of the saints. He'd purchased them for millions of dollars at various auctions, but they all seemed to be mocking him now.

He pressed the call button on his phone, and Christine answered on the first ring.

"Hi, Finn. About my message, I'm sorry to have to do this but—"

"Christine, you can't do this," Finn spat out, barely controlling his anger. "It's taken a lot of effort to arrange everything, we are going to make a big statement with Jesse's baptism, so it's not just about you and your son but about sending a message—"

"I'm afraid."

"Afraid of what?" Finn realized most people weren't as comfortable as he was in the limelight of success, fame, and fortune—maybe she just needed some coaching. "There's nothing to worry about, I'll guide you every step of the way, you'll just follow my lead up there, don't even look out into the audience ..."

"No, I'm not afraid of the baptism itself. I'm afraid of *them*."

"Who ... what are you talking about? What *them*?"

Christine proceeded to tell him about the scare she'd had the night before—how she'd woken to see a fire on her front lawn, a cross burning like one of the old KKK crosses. Only she and her son weren't Black, and the KKK didn't commit those acts anymore, at least to her knowledge. Still, it was a warning. Then the rock had smashed through her window with a note attached that simply read in a handwritten scrawl, "Don't go through with the baptism. Or else. That child doesn't belong to you."

She told him how Jesse had been sleeping but woke up when he heard the crash of broken glass, running from his bedroom in their condo unit at the Paradise Hotel, shaking and crying with fright.

They were staying in the same luxury VIP suite that Princess Callista had stayed in up on the tenth floor, but somehow someone had managed to catapult the fist-sized rock with the note rubber-banded on, hard enough to smash the picture window.

"It's not worth going through with it," Christine said now in a voice that belied her own fear. "I've got to protect my son. In fact, I think we should just leave the island today and fly back to the US. I'll just get the earliest flight out. You don't need to say goodbye. I'm sure you're busy, and we don't need all the extra attention anyway. I'm not going to tell Jesse, though. He will be heartbroken because he was so looking forward to it all. If it was up to him, he'd want to stay. But ..."

"Wait, Christine." Finn thought frantically about what to do. He felt like he desperately wanted the baptism to take place, that he needed to focus his attention on something other than his wretched state of affairs. Besides their romantic evening together, Lei remained cold and distant. She had still not forgiven him for his affair with Callista. And now he had the one with Claire hanging over his head.

Finn also believed the baptism event would cast him into the spotlight he craved. He needed this baptism to take place. Finn suddenly had an idea. "You and Jesse can stay here at my house. Lei is away, and I have au pairs working for me anyway who can help tutor your son and care for him should you need to go out for anything. You can have a whole private suite here with privacy and round-the-clock security. Although, I think the whole rock thing was an empty threat, probably by some fanatic pro-abortionists. But regardless, my house is physically connected to the church with a private underground entrance where we can all go without anyone even seeing us, much less getting close to us, to get to the church vestibule and right to the baptism font. No one is going to bother you in the church itself. Once it's over, I'll arrange a charter plane and will drive you to the airport myself. We'll come right back to the house after the service, a limo will pick us up and take us to the airstrip, and then you and your son can safely board the private plane and fly home. It will be much safer than if you and he try to arrange and board a commercial flight, and no one will know the plan. What do you say?"

"Okay ..." Her voice was halting, hesitant.

"You can trust me, I promise." Finn said, delighted his plan would go forward.

Finn felt his neck, shoulder, and back muscles tense up during the call with Christine, and after he hung up, he was so stressed and anxious, he knew he needed relief. He called Claire and asked her to meet him for a private yoga session at the Point.

He drove his Ferrari out to the lot, parked, hiked out to the yoga studio, let himself in to the lobby and then met her there promptly at two o'clock in the afternoon for their arranged session.

Claire had already gotten their mats out. His was in front of hers, lined up vertically in the middle of the wooden floor. The smell of sage filled the warm, dimly lit room, and the sound of waterfalls cascading hummed in the background.

She was sitting on her mat, eyes closed, in a lotus pose when he entered.

Her eyes fluttered open, and she smiled, gently hopping up onto her hands and feet into a downward dog. She stretched and stood up, wearing the typical yoga outfit of an athletic tank top and leggings, her blonde hair pulled back in a ponytail. She motioned for him to join her on his own mat.

"Before we get started, um ... I'd like to say I'm sorry and ..."

"No need." Claire seemed to be shockingly all business-like.

"Well, I wanted to clear the air and ..."

"It's okay, Finn, what happened will stay between us."

"No, it's not okay. I blame the Epitome headset, I unfortunately chose the deadly sin of lust and ..."

"I know. And you didn't do anything I didn't want you to do. But it was a one-time thing and ..."

"It won't happen again." Finn breathed a huge sigh of relief.

Claire gave him a professional smile. "Okay, then, let's get started on our yoga session, shall we?" She began guiding him through an hour of poses and deep breathing exercises. An hour later, Finn was warmed throughout his body, feeling more at peace and, in the moment, his body more limber, his jaw and stomach less clenched, his achy back muscles relaxed.

After lying for a few minutes in Savasana, Claire had Finn sit up and bow as they both finished with the traditional *namaste*.

"Thank you." Finn sat contentedly for a moment and was ready to stand up and head back home when Claire's question stopped him.

"How is Lei?" she asked, her concern sounding genuine.

"She's okay as far as I know," he said. "I talked with her family yesterday."

Claire looked solemn, casting her eyes down, and sighed.

Finn started to fidget, feeling awkward and uncomfortable now. "Is there something else, or am I free to go?"

The yoga instructor looked up, her clear blue eyes piercing his. "I want you to know I'm really sorry."

"Oh ... well, thanks." Finn assumed she was talking about the miscarriage but wondered how she'd found out. "Did you know ...?"

"Yes, I gave her the herbal medicine that caused the abortion."

Suddenly the background sound of the ocean sounded deafeningly loud, and Finn couldn't breathe, feeling like the waves were crashing on him, drowning him.

"What?" His vision blurred, he blinked, and took a deep stuttering breath. *Claire just made a mistake*, he thought. "Lei had a miscarriage," he corrected her, frozen on his yoga mat.

She stood and walked over to him and sat down in front of him cross-legged on the floor in front of his mat, grasping his hands in hers. "Finn, I'm so sorry. I just couldn't live with the lie any longer. I'm glad you came today so I could tell you the truth. Lei came to me and asked me if I had anything that would cause a voluntary miscarriage. She didn't use the word abortion, but I knew that was what she meant. Since she couldn't risk you finding out, she didn't want to go to a doctor, although, now with your ... the Supreme Court's mandate, I'm not sure a doctor on the island would have seen her anyway, knowing she is your wife. She was already nine weeks along when she came to me.

"I took her back to my cottage and gave her the abortion pill to take with her on her trip. It usually takes about a week to work. Actually, I gave her two treatments to make sure they worked. Lei called me from Beijing to tell me she'd arrived at her parents' house, unsure whether she wanted to carry through with it. Then, two weeks later, she called again to tell me she was having cramping and some bleeding, which I told her was normal. Then she lost it ... um ... the baby."

Finn drew his hands from hers and pushed himself up onto his feet, standing on his mat, hands on hips, towering over her. He felt outraged. "Are you crazy?" he screamed. "That was *my* baby! You killed my baby!"

Claire lithely jumped to her feet too. "I did no such thing, your wife decided that was what she wanted." She spoke in a calm, icy tone. "Now, Finn, you both will get through this. Lei told me she just wasn't ready to have a child now, not yet with her design career blossoming and you always gone with your ministry work and the VR tourism exploding ..."

"I don't care about any of that." Finn lowered his voice, filled with a dull sadness now. What good was yelling and screaming when he couldn't change what had happened?

"If it helps, here." Claire approached him slowly and warily, as a cat might a fox, and handed him two crystals she'd apparently grabbed from the nearby table when he wasn't looking. One was a smooth, multi-faceted, clear white stone with a point at the top and the other was a jagged, shiny small black rock. She told him they were clear quartz and black tourmaline, both crystals that were used in healing, both by removing negative energies and bringing peace and comfort to those who were feeling distress. Finn looked at the crystals in his hand in bewilderment. "Just try to believe," she said, her voice soft, soothing.

He didn't know what to believe anymore.

She walked over to the table and picked up one of several other larger, oval-shaped smooth gemstones with a striped pattern in reddish-brown and grayish-tan or taupe colors that were surrounding a statue of a bull carved of wood, about six inches high and nine inches long. "This is the God of Fertility. These stones are called *shiva lingam* stones, which represent fertility. Shiva is the god of destruction. If you pray to both of them ..."

Finn stared at all of the items on the table, all foreign to him, and cut her off. "I get the first one, but why would I pray to a god of destruction?"

"The Hindus believe that Shiva, the most powerful god, also represents new life. That you must tear down to build up. Like your Bible Scriptures also say."

Claire placed a shiva lingam stone in his hand, and Finn fingered the smoothness of its long round shape. She kept her hand for a moment over Finn's palm with the stones and closed her eyes. "I see you are going to have a child soon," she said, as if seeing the future.

"Well, of course we were supposed to until—" He wanted to say, *until you helped my wife get an abortion,* but she silenced him.

"Shh, do not argue with the gods. This child ... will not come from your wife."

Finn's heart started to beat rapidly, and he glanced down at Claire's abdomen, clad in tight leggings. She didn't look pregnant, but still ...

"And it is not mine." Claire sighed but kept her eyes closed, her hand cupped over the stones in Finn's, their fingers gently touching. "I am not sure whose it is, but it is coming. You will know great fulfillment—and great longing. Great joy—and great pain. But again, you must believe for the gods to carry out all they have planned for you."

Perhaps if he believed the crystals were a key to healing, they would be, Finn thought. Maybe if he had faith that these gods could bring him children, they would.

What could it hurt? Finn felt his anger dissolve. Claire had merely carried out his wife's wishes. She opened her eyes and looked at him, a joyful innocence in those pools of blue, and he was too choked up to say anything, not wanting her to see him cry. So he simply nodded and walked out of the yoga studio, gulping in the fresh air and sun.

He could use a swim. That always helped.

CHAPTER THIRTY-FOUR

Within an hour, Finn had donned his bathing suit and was swimming laps in the clear blue Coral Sea just beyond his house. It was his happy place.

He always felt joy surge in his heart as he did the backstroke, sending sprays of water into the air, feeling his strong legs kick and the cool water exhilarate his soul as the sun beat warm on his face. Out here, despite everything he was going through, he didn't seem to have a care in the world.

After he toweled dry on his back patio then went inside his kitchen for an iced tea, he heard his cell phone ring.

It was an unfamiliar number, but he decided to answer it.

"Hi, Finn, please don't hang up. It's me, Callista, and I have some news for you."

Finn could barely breathe. "Um ... wow, this is a surprise."

"I know. I have to be brief. I just wanted you to know ... you're going to be a dad."

Finn's knees felt weak, and he had to grab the nearest chair to sit down before his legs gave out.

"Are you still there ... Finn?"

Deep breaths. "You're ... we're going to have a baby? When ... how ...?"

"Well, silly, I think you know how. And he's due in three months."

Finn did the math. Callista had said she was a virgin. And they'd been intimate exactly six months ago before she'd left. "I don't know what to say. You're sure ..."

"Yes, I'm sure the baby is yours, if that's what you were going to ask. You are the only one I've been with. But I have to tell you I had to get engaged and married. I can't have a baby out of wedlock. I'm sorry ..."

Finn thought she'd broken his heart when she left. But now he felt it shatter, painful shards ripping it open, making it bleed. His chest hurt, and he thought maybe he was having a heart attack.

Great joy and great pain. Claire's words came back to him, and he saw the three precious gemstones on the kitchen table. He reached out and took the shiva lingam, grasping it tightly in his fist. The gods were kind and cruel at the same time.

"Callista, can I come over there to see you? My wife is in China visiting her family. Please ... I want to be there. I need to see you—and our son. I don't care if you're married to another man. Although, it breaks my heart ..."

"Finn, no, please. My dad must never find out who the real father is. My father is dying ... he has so little time left I don't want the truth to mar it for him. He needs to die in peace."

"Would it have been so awful if you and I ..."

"Finn, you're still married! In Morocco, I would be considered a harlot, a homewrecker, a prostitute. I would literally be outcast or maybe even worse, hung for my crimes. And I don't care about all of that, but it would bring such shame on my family ... and, of course, on my unborn child. Please, Finn, promise me you won't come over here?"

"Why did you even bother telling me, Callista?" Finn was so hurt he didn't have the capacity to be angry, but it felt better to try to be mad at her.

"Because I wanted you to know the truth. I wanted you to know ..." Finn could hear her voice break, and she started to cry. "I have to go now. I'm sorry, I made a mistake ..."

"No ... Callista ... you didn't. I'm sorry, please keep in touch.

And with that the phone call went dead.

Something in him snapped that night.

He'd been adding CBD oil, which he'd purchased at the island's local cannabis store, into his tea and coffee, then when he occasionally cooked, into eggs, stews, and other dishes, just like the spices he got from Callista.

Since marijuana was legal on an individually owned island, the little store sold everything from oils and edibles to vaporizers, papers, pipes, and many kinds of herbal drugs.

The devastating news of Callista's marriage to another man coupled with his wife's abortion lit a fire inside him. He hadn't seen Christine and Jesse, who were staying in the far end of the house, since they moved in a few days ago. No one would know.

He rolled and smoked a huge joint that night sitting out on his lanai, then emptied the brandy bottle's contents and started drinking tequila straight up until he'd emptied another liquor bottle.

He'd forgotten he'd scheduled one of the au pairs, Rhonda the redhead, to show up for work that evening to help with the laundry, along with Lizzy, the Latina cleaning girl.

The drugs and alcohol had fueled the part of his brain still wired to the Epitome Hell on Earth experience he'd been stuck in when he'd gone through the "Lust" portal, and now he felt a need to quench the smoldering desire that burned like hot lava inside.

He had to have them both. And he did, taking them one by one back to his master suite on the right end of the house. Fortunately, Christine and Jesse stayed up in their rooms on the left end that evening, and there was enough distance in between that they didn't see or hear a thing.

Finn was on a collision course, and he knew it.

Lei, fully recuperated now, unexpectedly arrived home a few days later, so Finn instructed the entire household staff, now numbering five, to report for work and clean the mansion from top to bottom, erasing any shreds of evidence of what he'd done while she was gone. Lei was barely speaking to him, only enough to inform him her mother had passed away and that she had decided to come back to their island home.

Zimo was staying in China to conduct some business affairs that involved Epitome. He'd informed Finn all the programs had been approved and that tens of thousands of headsets geared up with them were on course to be shipped out to the US and Europe that week, with South America, Africa, and the rest of Asia to follow. The Investor was backing all the initial expenses, but the return on his investment would be huge, and Zimo and Finn would, of course, get a huge cut of the profits as well.

Finn didn't care about making money anymore. He had enough to worry about—namely, how to overcome his guilt and fears that mounted on a daily basis. He turned to yoga, meditation, crystals, praying to the gods ... but his depression and anxiety only grew deeper with each passing day.

Then the Sunday of the baptism ceremony arrived.

Christine Walters wore a knee-length burgundy short-sleeved dress with a black belt at the waist and matching pumps, a silver beret in her shoulder-length, wavy brown hair. She'd dressed her son, Jesse, in slacks, a white button-down shirt, a tie, and a sportscoat and combed his unruly curls.

Arriving early, they sat in the front pew, listening to the gospel choir practice their hymns. Today the choir was singing contemporary songs and was accompanied by a drummer, acoustic and bass guitarists and a keyboard player, so Jesse watched, fascinated.

Although there were still twenty minutes to go until the service started at eleven o'clock, the church pews were starting to fill up.

Finn had been informed by his wife that she had no desire to attend. He was secretly relieved—a break from her was a welcome departure from the constant guilt he felt being in her presence, and he could better focus on his ministry.

She stayed away from their houseguests, who would only be staying two more nights before flying back to the states and their lives back home.

Christine and Jesse had walked with Finn through the underground stairs and hallway connecting his mansion and the church, so none of them had seen the protestors collecting out front of the Sanctuary on the front parking lot.

Even here in Eden, a tropical paradise where people went to escape, the controversy over the Supreme Court ruling still raged strong.

And little did anyone know it had been fueled much further by the Epitome virtual reality Seven Deadly Sins program. Those who chose the "Wrath" portal were able to fully experience revenge, vigilante justice, getting even, or just letting off some steam.

For a few women who were still frustrated by the Supreme Court's ruling on *Walters v. Gold*, the target was Christine Walters and her eight-year-old son, who was considered by some to be collateral damage. The women, still angry over the court's decision, got mad every time they saw the young boy's face. To some, he represented the child they'd chosen not to have through abortion and was a reminder of guilt they felt deep down, although they'd never admit it. To some, he was the poster child of the decision they'd lost that to them represented the chains that barred their future choice in whether to get an abortion.

The beautiful fountains gracefully adorned the front lawn of the church, glistening in the abundant sunshine that glorious spring morning. This was the day God had made.

But the dozen or so women marching in front of the Sanctuary carried dark signs, some had pictures of baby Jesse, others had his eight-year-old face caught in a sad look with sayings like "I miss my REAL mom," "Stolen," "US Women Are Slaves," and of course, "Pro-Women, Pro-Choice."

Finn was back in the anteroom behind the front nave of the church, where he still often came to pray, meditate on the Word, and talk to God. Today, he was focused on asking for forgiveness. He knew he needed to formally repent through the sacrament of Reconciliation again soon, that he'd need to see a priest to confess his sins. But there wasn't time for that—he had a church service to conduct and an important baptism to perform.

The rock band played loudly beyond the wall that separated him from the bustling, growing congregation out front. It was noisy, and the sounds reverberated even here in his tiny private chapel.

He looked up at the cross on the wall bearing the crucified Jesus. *Lord, help me, I am not worthy to go out there and preach to these people after all I've done*, he prayed silently.

But people are counting on you, he heard. Was that God or just his own ego talking back? He didn't know anymore.

Suddenly, he heard an unexpected rap on his door. Who could possibly know he was back here or have the gall to bother him?

He opened the heavy wooden door to his private grotto and peered out, seeing a stranger's face. He blinked, adjusting his eyes to the light, and saw it was one of his parishioners, one of the men who served as an usher. "You need to come quick, they're gathering in front of the church and some are coming in."

"Who are 'they'? What are you talking about?" Finn tried hard to hold his temper in check. *How dare he barge into his private prayer chambers?* Maybe this man had just lost it.

"Protestors. Pro-abortion activists are marching on the church's front lawn, and some are storming inside now or worse yet, taking seats in the pews. Who knows what they plan to do once you start the service? But they're against Christine Walters and Jesse being baptized, so I'm sure it won't be pretty."

"All right, I'm coming, I'll meet you on the front lawn."

Finn thought quickly. There was another underground tunnel leading from the front of the church all the way to the back, built for times when he might need to go unnoticed to another part of the church or for times of an emergency exit. Times like this.

He hastened through the concrete tunnel, and as soon as he emerged upstairs and had cell phone service again, called the chief security guard telling him to meet him at the big fountain at the main entrance—and to bring backup.

Finn was nearly blinded by the sun, and his hangover kicked in. He tried to ignore the pain searing his left temple, stabbing his nerves like an ice pick.

He was nearly trampled by a group of women who stormed past him yelling, "Pro-Women, Pro-Choice!" marching in a circle around the fountain. When one

360

spotted him, she screamed, "He's the one. That's Judge Finley Mitchell—he took away our rights!"

Finn saw the glaring faces of women, all ages, all sizes, all colors, headed his way, and was seized by terror. They looked like they wanted to kill him, and maybe would have, but the chief security officer and two of his men blocked their path, stepping out in front of Finn with batons, barring their way, threatening to use force if the women advanced. He recognized a few of the faces ... women he'd seen at the yoga studio, in shops in town, waitressing at restaurants on the island.

"Back away and disperse or you will be arrested!" one of the guards yelled through his megaphone.

Finn ran back toward the underground entrance of the Sanctuary, shut the door behind him, locked it, and tried to catch his breath and still his racing heart.

How had this lynch mob manage to form? he wondered.

And then it dawned on him. *Wrath.* Their anger was manifesting itself through the portal of the deadly sin, just like his had with lust. He would have to call Zimo and somehow stop the shipments.

More security guards had gathered, and the crowd outside had finally been disbursed, and the front doors of the church locked so no one else could enter.

The choir had stopped singing, and the congregation inside were on their knees quietly praying, although a murmur started up when Finn walked down the aisle, up to the altar, and turned around. He looked over at Christine and Jesse, who knelt praying, although they'd opened their eyes and were gazing at him now in confusion and fear.

Finn spoke into the wireless microphone he had attached to his jacket collar. "Everyone gathered here, thank you for coming today and staying the past hour to wait for the service. I will perform a shortened version of the baptism because that is the real reason we are here. Today is not about me, and you don't need to hear another one of my sermons." A few nervous laughs erupted. "As many of you have heard, there was a protest on the front lawn, but the police have now removed the perpetrators. Still, we want to perform the ceremony which we came for and then get back to the safety of our homes, so we will have a very brief service." Finn glanced over at the choir director, singers, and musicians who were up on a platform to the left of the altar, waiting for a signal to begin performing. "I'm sorry to our choir and band. I know they would have sounded wonderful, but we will have to wait to hear them, hopefully next Sunday.

"Now I'd like to have Christine Walters and her son, Jesse Walters, come up to the baptismal font, and I ask that the rest of you stand and extend your right hand in blessing and a sign of welcome to our newest member of the Sanctuary about to be baptized."

The mother and her young son climbed the few steps up the altar to the right and over to the baptismal font. Jesse removed his jacket and tie, handing them to his mom, and Finn performed the ritual, submersing the boy backward into the pool, baptizing him in the name of the Father, the Son, and the Holy Spirit. A wet but smiling Jesse beamed, and the congregation clapped loudly.

Christine lovingly wrapped her son in a large white cotton towel and hugged him, tears falling down her face.

Tears fell down Finn's cheeks too, and he brushed them away. *One day I'll have a son,* he realized, feeling profoundly happy and sad in the same moment that he might never get to know his boy.

Finn concluded the ceremony with a prayer and then dismissed the congregation, blessing them and thanking them again, then gently warning them to find their way home quickly and safely.

The security guards stood in force inside and outside, at each corner of the church building and a few around the fountain, looking menacing in their sunglasses and black uniforms, their batons still drawn and guns at the ready.

He and Christine and Jesse all snuck down the back stairwell into the underground passage and then up into the house.

A worried Lei greeted them as they walked into the kitchen. She shook Christine's hand, congratulating her and her son. "Finn, I saw what happened on the news, the protests ... I'm sorry I wasn't there at the ceremony, but I just felt it would have been hypocritical of me since ..." she glanced at Christine, "well, you know how my beliefs are different. But I would never condone what those women were doing. I think they've gone off the deep end. I think it's all because of that VR stuff. Finn, it's evil, I've tried to talk to Zimo about it, but he shuts me out. You need to get to him before it's too late and something bad happens."

Finn saw the fear and confusion mount in the boy's eyes and took his wife by the elbow to steer her away to a place where they could talk privately. "Jesse, would you like some cookies and milk?" He watched the boy's face light up and then look to his mom for approval. Christine smiled and tousled his curls. "That would be great, I think I'll join him if that's okay?"

"Of course," Lei smiled back and went to the refrigerator to get the milk while Finn grabbed the tin of Oreos he always kept handy ever since his fondness for them as a child.

"You two have a seat there at the kitchen table, and we'll just go freshen up and then come back and join you for some lunch," Finn said, giving Lei a knowing look. *We don't want to scare the boy or his mom.*

CHAPTER THIRTY-FIVE

When he and his wife were out of earshot in the living room, Finn questioned her. "I think I recognized some of those women at the rally in front of the church—a few from your yoga studio," he said, trying to banish images of Claire from his head as he said it. "Have they been using those headsets?"

"I don't know. I've been away in China, remember?" Lei's pretense of civility she'd shown with Christine and Jesse had already worn off with her husband. She was still perturbed with him. "I think you need to call Zimo and warn him."

Finn called the house and office numbers of his wife's friend in Beijing, but Zimo didn't answer. "I've got to find out what they're putting into those VR programs that are inciting people." Memories of Claire in the yoga studio, of the two au pairs the other night, came back to him. He'd been aggressive, nearly violent in his need to give in to his base desires, and he knew the seed had been planted when he'd gone through the Epitome portal.

"It's got to be stopped. They've got to stop the shipments to other countries. We need to pull the plug on the whole Epitome enterprise. It's dangerous, and it could be lethal. I've got to get to the kingpin behind it all, the Investor. I'm sure Zimo knows who he is but has been sworn to secrecy on his identity. I don't want to put your friend in danger, but I'm not sure how else to stop this. I think Zimo is just a pawn in his evil game and under his spell somehow. I've got to get to the top."

He picked up his cell phone and hit the speed dial number for Zimo. He was lucky this time. Zimo picked up on the first ring.

"Hey, I don't know if you're aware of the protests going on here in Eden ..."

"Yep, I saw it on the news here on the internet, but no problem man, it looks like just a few angry women ..."

"No, Zimo, I think we have a huge problem on our hands. Have you explored any other Seven Deadly Sins portals?"

"Why?"

"Just answer my question."

"Well, yeah, a few."

"And are you experiencing any problems? Because I know I sure am. And Lei and I think these women are too."

Zimo was silent for a minute before answering. "So, what are you getting at? Because I'm sitting here looking at massive shipments ready to go out all over the world. I think you've waited a little too late to stop them."

"If they haven't gone out the door yet, it's not too late. Can you stall them, just for a few days?"

"I can try. But what are you going to do? You can't fix them all. That would cost millions, if not billions, of dollars. The Investor would have my head. Literally."

"Who is he, Zimo? I'm willing to take responsibility for pulling the plug. I'll face up to this guy, I just need to know who he is."

Zimo hesitated. "I'm afraid I can't tell you. I wish I could. I'm in my own private hell right now, Finn. I want nothing more than to get out myself. But it's too late ..." Finn thought he heard Zimo sniff as if he was crying. This was bad.

"Well, at least tell me where he is. I'll come find him."

"That's ironic, because I believe he's on his way to your little island."

"Zimo, please tell me his name. For my sake, for your sister's sake, for your sake ... or I swear I'll go on the internet, and every TV station across the world will be looking for him publicly until I find him ..."

"Lucifer. It's his code name. You know him. He was behind the whole JAB scheme with Ralston."

"Lucifer is still in operation? He's in China?" Finn could hear the desperate shrillness in his own voice.

"He was. Right now, I believe he's on a plane headed to Eden to see you."

No sooner had Finn hung up from his call with Zimo than Christine came running wildly into the living room. "He's gone!" she shrieked, her face red, puffy, and tear-streaked.

Lei had been sitting on the living room couch and jumped to her feet. "Who is gone?"

"My son! Jesse. He was playing in the back yard. I told him after he changed his clothes he could go outside for a little while. And now I can't find him anywhere!"

"All right, calm down, maybe he's still out back or out on the beach. Can he swim?"

"Y-yes, he's a pretty good s-swimmer," Christine said in between sobs.

"Okay, you need to calm down and breathe," Finn said. "I'm sure he's out there somewhere. You being upset won't help. Don't forget I own this island, so I'll make a phone call and get the sheriff's deputies down here looking for him, along with some of my church staff, and the house staff for that matter. Why don't you stay here with Lei at home base by your phones and I'll head up a search party?"

"Th-thank you." Christine wiped fresh tears with tissues from a box Lei had fetched.

His wife put her arm around Christine's shoulders to comfort her, and they sat down together on the sofa. "We'll stay here, call us when you find him," Lei said.

"Thanks, honey. Will do."

Finn gathered a search party of a dozen men, and within an hour, they were combing the mansion, the church grounds, the underground tunnels, the shoreline, and the water itself. They looked for the boy for hours until it got dark and then even longer with searchlights. Finn called in a helicopter to search as well.

Finally, around seven o'clock in the evening, Finn got a call on his cell from the helicopter rescue team.

"No sign of the boy, but we do see an abnormally big bonfire on the other end of the island, out by the volcano on the Point," the copilot said. "There's no place for us to land at that end, but we'll try to get closer to see what's up. You may want to send a few four-wheelers down there to check it out."

"Roger that," Finn said, scratching his chin. A big bonfire out on the Point. That was unusual, although not unheard of. The yoga crowd, recovery meetings, church groups, and other private parties occasionally had a bonfire party down there. *Maybe they're just having one of their get-togethers*, he hoped.

He called Lei to tell her he was headed out to that end of the island to investigate the fire.

"Huh, I didn't know of any parties," Lei said. "I know I just returned from China, but usually I get a text about upcoming events at the studio. Maybe it is a private affair."

"Okay, I'll keep you posted."

Finn rode with Sheriff John Dunne in his big black four-wheel pickup with the siren on top blaring the entire way.

Enroute, he got a call from Lei, who sounded panic-stricken. "Finn, it's Christine—now *she's* gone."

"What do you mean gone?"

"I went to the bathroom, and when I came out she was gone. She's probably headed down to the Point. Your car's missing too."

"Okay, thanks. You stay put—we need someone to stay at the house."

"I'm sorry, Finn ..."

"It's not your fault. You couldn't hold her against her will. She's a mom. I just hope she's all right and doesn't get in an accident."

The roads were dark on the island once you headed out of the main street in the center onto either end. People liked it that way—they wanted their privacy.

Much of the island was still undeveloped, although it was constantly changing as new tourists continued to flock there on vacation or for the unique VR experience. Many never wanted to leave and stayed to live and work on Eden, becoming residents, merchants, or employees.

John's truck almost hit a wallaby that wandered onto the road out of the brush, and he veered off to avoid hitting it. He braked but not soon enough to avoid crashing into a big palm tree.

The burly sheriff cursed, then apologized, realizing Finn was a church pastor. He got out of the truck to survey the wreckage, then climbed back in. "Not too much damage, should be okay to drive," he said, putting a wad of chewing tobacco in his mouth. He started the engine, but it clicked then stalled. The gray-haired sheriff nearly cursed again, then tried to start the truck but had no luck.

Finn got another phone call from the helicopter copilot. "Hey, you might want to call a fire engine or two out there just in case," he said. "I see some people down there, but I'm not sure if they're dancing around the fire or running to and from it to try to put it out. It's windy, so we can only get so close without sending up a sandstorm on the beach."

"Thanks, I'll call a few in now." Finn called the nearest of two fire stations on Eden and asked them if one of the trucks could pick him and the Sheriff up on the way.

They arrived in another twenty minutes. The fire trucks were so large that, unlike the pickup, they couldn't get down the dirt roads at all, so everyone had to run on foot, the firefighters lugging extended hoses in their heavy coats and helmets.

By the time they ran, sweating and panting, past the yoga studio out onto the beach, the fire was ablaze, shooting flames out ten yards wide and another fifteen yards high. It was an eerie almost surreal tribal-like sight—the fire's light glowing in front of the backdrop of the volcano.

Finn could feel the heat singe his skin as he walked onto the beach. He was only wearing shorts and a tee shirt, so he couldn't even imagine how hot the firefighters were since he was already sweating in the furnace blast the fire threw off.

He took off his shirt and covered his face so he could breathe and tried to get closer but was stopped by Sheriff Dunne. "You need to stay put. You don't have the training we do. Just stay here and I'll be back in a few minutes to let you know what we find."

Finn felt helpless and stood by watching the firefighters shoot water from the hoses onto the mountainous flames which seemed to lick the sky with their hot orange tongues.

He pulled out his cell phone and called Lei. No answer.

Sheriff Dunne was back in five minutes, shaking his head.

371

"They found a small body. Eight-year-old male, charred beyond recognition. His remains were in the fire." The sheriff's radio crackled, and he answered it. "Ten-four," he said into it and then shook his head again. "And a woman in her forties or fifties, also dead in the fire."

Finn crumpled to his knees sobbing. It had to be Christine and Jesse.

"I'm sorry, there was nothing they could do to save them. But they'll get this fire under control so no one else gets hurt. It looks like it was set by arsonists."

Suddenly Finn had a horrific thought strike him. *Lei.* What if his wife were in danger? He called her again, but she didn't pick up. He stood, put his shirt on, and grabbed the sheriff by the arm. "John, we need to get back to the house. I think the same people who set this fire might be after Lei."

Finn felt his cell phone buzz. Thank God, he thought and looked down to answer it, and then he felt his heart lurch. It wasn't Lei but the helicopter copilot again.

"Mister Mitchell, I'm afraid we have bad news. There were reports of another fire breaking out on the other end of the island, so we headed back up there to check it out. I'm sorry but your house and the church are now on fire. Unfortunately, most of the fire trucks went out here to the north end but some are headed back now and there was a truck still left at the station to man the south end and it's arriving shortly."

"I'm on my way." He turned to John who was already radioing for a police jeep to come get them.

Finn prayed the entire forty-five-minute ride to his house while Sheriff Dunne drove in silence—broken only by the wailing siren.

A scene similar to the fire at Eden's other end awaited them, although the blaze was even bigger since there were more buildings in proximity to catch fire along with more trees and brush. It appeared two fires were set, one at the house and one at the church.

As he approached the Sanctuary, Finn saw Lei standing in the street out front of the parking lot of the church along with a small crowd of onlookers.

She was covered in soot and coughing, but she was alive, and Finn had never been happier to see her in his entire life.

He broke down weeping with relief as he folded her into his arms. "I ... I thought you were ... I'm so glad you're ..." Finn couldn't get an entire sentence out. He pulled away to look into her tear-filled eyes. "What happened?"

"I had just hung up from being on the phone with you when the next thing I knew, the house was on fire. Luckily all the staff had gone with you on the search for Jesse—wait, where are Christine and Jesse—?"

Finn started sobbing again, shaking his head, unable to speak.

"Oh no ... don't tell me ... no!"

There was a whirlwind of police and firefighters suddenly on the scene and they told everyone to go back to their homes. Sheriff Dunne had called an ambulance and guided Finn and Lei to the EMT unit, where their vital signs were checked, and they were wrapped in light blankets. Finn had signs of mild heat stroke, and Lei had a sprained ankle from running out of the house. Other than that, they were suffering signs of shock more than anything else.

Both refused to go to the island's hospital, but they couldn't go home either.

Home. There was no more home here, Finn realized.

It was all gone. *And it's all my fault.*

A man stood laughing in the distance, although no one could hear him.

He went by several names—Lucky Lou to his friends, The investor to his business associates, Lucifer to those who got tangled in his web of political dealings and power plays. By Lu-Chin Xang to his mother. And he went by Satan to his enemies.

Lucifer was the one man richer than Finn or any of the top ten wealthiest men in the world put together. Although he was of Chinese and Russian descent and quite proud of it, he ran syndicates and cartels not only in his homeland but in Asia, Africa, South America, Haiti, Mexico, and the US and was involved in human trafficking, sex trafficking, drug trafficking, money laundering, and many other illegal and illicit schemes.

He'd invested heavily in Eden and Epitome, so he was not happy about it being set ablaze. But one had to take a loss occasionally in order to exact justice ... and burn the evidence.

Besides, it had been worth it to him to see poor Finley Mitchell suffer and finally pay the price for all his father, President Leif Mitchell, had done to him many years ago.

Leif Mitchell had been the only president brave enough to send the FBI after him. They'd investigated Lu-Chin Xang and his Chinese underground mafia many times. And while they'd managed to weaken the monster by nailing some of the hired hands, they'd failed to cut off its head. Lucifer always managed to escape, and each time vowed to one day make Leif Mitchell—or his offspring—pay dearly.

He hoped they both rotted in hell—right beside him when he got there.

EPILOGUE

At least I wasn't disbarred. Finn knelt in the small side chapel in the Basilica in Washington, DC, after lighting a candle, ruminating over the mess he'd made the past few years, wishing he would have just stayed an attorney and kept life simple. Now his license to practice law was suspended by the Illinois Bar Association, and he had tainted his legacy as a former Chief Justice of the US Supreme Court.

He'd also had to declare bankruptcy after selling Eden at a huge loss to a real estate firm and to move in with his mother back in Washington along with Lei until they could find an apartment to rent once he got a job.

All because of the seven deadly sins. Not just the VR experience but literally—he looked back and realized he had delved into them all. Pride, of course, believing he was entitled to a life that was better than most because he was so wise—so smart, so well off, so favored. Greed, constantly wanting to accumulate more wealth, power, status, and attention—and never being truly content with what he already had. Lust for all those women. Sloth ... so many days he'd indulged in pampering himself on his paradise island instead of asking himself how he could give to those less fortunate. Envy for his dead half-brother who, he saw in retrospect, never had even a sliver of the doting attention and love Leif Mitchell displayed for him—a misplaced, petty jealousy that fueled his wrath against Tony. And although he hadn't directly caused his death in prison, Finn had complained enough about Tony to fellow prosecutors who knew inmates who would kill for an extra pack of cigarettes. Even gluttony by indulging in too much partying, drinking, and drugs, not to mention giving into his desire to try the Seven Deadly Sins 'game'—despite his conscience telling him it would lead to disaster.

And so it had. But Finn couldn't blame everything on Epitome or Zimo or even Lucifer.

God had a plan, and he had followed it. Until he hadn't. Looking back, Finn wasn't sure exactly when he'd turned away from God and started worshipping false idols ... crystals, animals, sun gods, money, fame, power, even women like Callista. He'd worshipped her too, forsaking his wife whom he'd vowed to love until death did they part.

Lei could have died in the fire he ultimately caused.

He stood in line, waiting his turn to go into the confessional. It was one of those modern ones where you sat in a chair facing the priest. He'd wished he'd gone to one of the old-fashioned ones where you still knelt before a mesh grate, and at least, there was some measure of separation.

There was only one person who went in before he did, and she was quick. So, before he felt ready, the door stood open, the priest waiting inside. It was now or never.

This is a man of God, Finn reminded himself, taking a deep breath and blessing himself, making the sign of the cross from forehead to heart and shoulder to shoulder with his right hand. *Here goes.* "Bless me father for I have sinned ... it's been, well, I forget how long, years ... no decades, since I went to my last confession ..."

He hoped the priest had enough time to hear his many sins.

Instead of the five Hail Marys or Act of Contrition or rote prayers he'd been expecting to have to recite as part of his penance after confessing his sins, Finn was surprised the priest told him a different course of action he'd need to take to repent.

First, the priest told him, he'd need to practice humility.

He knelt back in the pew and looked up at Jesus hanging on the wooden crucifix. *Haven't I been humbled enough?* Finn asked. He was still living with his mother. He was driving a used gray Pontiac, forty minutes to and from work as an assistant legal aid for the National Right to Life Committee at its headquarters in Alexandria, Virginia. Once the suspension on his license was lifted, he hoped to become an attorney for the NRLC. Finn knew that even though the Supreme Court had, in effect, completely overturned *Roe v. Wade*, there would always be protestors wanting to reverse it back, presidents who sat liberal justices on the court with new opinions, legislators lobbying for bills to change the laws. *But right now, I feel like a school kid—living with my mommy, driving a beat-up old car, working as an assistant to an assistant. What a sad little life.*

And there it is, he thought. *Humility isn't humiliation but acceptance and contentment that I will go back to being just another attorney, just another guy, just another bozo on the bus.* Finn bowed his head, ashamed of himself. *How lucky am I, Lord?*

Suddenly, his heart was filled with gratitude, the second penitence the priest told him he'd need to practice.

Finn was extremely grateful his wife had not been hurt in the fire. He realized he could have lost her too. He said a prayer of thanks for Lei, his mother, and his son born by Callista. And then he felt a deep aching hurt inside.

Still kneeling before the cross, Finn recalled the last penitential act the priest had also told him to do—make amends to all the people he had harmed, unless it would cause more harm than good.

He knew he'd need to make amends to Lei by being a good and faithful husband the rest of his days and to forgive her for deciding not to have their child—to let it go.

He also needed to let go of Callista. That would be his amends to her, to allow her to live in peace with her new family. It would be hard, but he vowed to himself and to God he would do it.

Finally, he would make amends to his mother, whom he knew he'd blamed over the years for his own greed, envy, entitlement, pride. *I'll have to work on my codependence on her*, he thought, smiling to himself.

He'd been at the basilica for over two hours. He finally stood, genuflected, and then walked out into the winter sunshine breaking through gray clouds. It was a beautiful January day the Lord had made, and Finn felt a heartbeat of joy.

After a few months of living with Linda, Finn and Lei were finally able to find an apartment just outside downtown DC closer to Alexandria at a rent they could afford on both of their incomes, Finn's from the NRLC and Lei's from her online designer boutique.

Finn whistled as he walked from the metro station to his car on the city commuter lot with flowers in his hands he'd bought at the local market, one bunch for his mom and one for his wife. He noticed crocuses and daffodils bursting through the hard earth, signaling spring was on its way.

He parked his Pontiac sedan on the street, walked up the front drive, looking up at the large, two-story, stone mansion he'd called home most of his life, and marveled at how lucky he'd been to grow up here.

The "For Sale" sign stood, small for such a big lawn but still noticeable in the center of the sprawling front yard.

Finn was determined not to let anything, including the sign, dampen his grateful spirit. *This is for the best*, he sighed, recalling his conversation with his eighty-one-year-old mother, who'd told him she just couldn't maintain the enormous house and lawn any longer, even if she got new hired help, and didn't want to live there alone anymore.

He'd wanted to argue, "then give the house to Lei and me," but knew he had no right. Just like the Prodigal Son, he'd already spent his inheritance and then some, squandering it on a private island, private jet rides, private parties, and a virtual reality tourist empire that had fallen down around him like a gigantic house of cards.

Tears still sprang to his eyes when he thought of the cruelty that had erupted out of people due to the evil Epitome seeds implanted in them, the unnecessary deaths of Christine and Jesse, who'd both been burned alive as a human sacrifice to the gods like in some old witch's tale—the son tied to a stake and the mother sacrificing her own life trying to save him.

God was ironic, he thought. *I worked through my Supreme Court decision to save the mother and son, then had a hand in destroying them.* But then Finn realized, these were not the acts of God but of man. *Perhaps life itself was just ironic.*

Finn shuddered at the memory. He'd read the police report after the investigation was over while standing in the sheriff's office. *Suspects have admitted to taking the boy, who had been given a sedative so he would be compliant, out onto the Point beachfront on the island of Eden, where they had built a large, wooden pyre or teepee-like structure filled with dry wood to build a bonfire. They report they tied the boy with silk scarves to the pyre frame, doused the wood with lighter fluid, and then lit it on fire, chanting and dancing to loud tribal music that blared on a boombox. They were wearing Epitome Virtual Reality headsets they had purchased through Lei Mitchell, wife of Finn Mitchell, the owner of said island and part owner and partner of the VR program and Epitome company. They reported they were under a spell cast by the "Seven Deadly Sins Wrath Portal" which encouraged them to seek justice for all women wronged by the ruling in the case of* Walters v. Gold *and to take out their anger through this act of vigilante justice—that they were also offering the boy as a sacrifice to the fertility gods so they wouldn't be angry when they were ready to have babies. Christine Walters appeared at the scene as her son was being burned alive. She ran up to free him, but a gust of wind swept the pyre, her hair and clothing caught fire, and she burned to death along with the boy.*

Finn had broken down weeping right there in the police station.

He read the rest of the report through the blur of his tears. *The suspects had already left the scene as the fire burned to drive up the island coast to the south end. There they met with another suspect who had already set up a similar pyre in the back lawn of the Mitchell residence and who had placed a series of firebombs around the perimeter of the Sanctuary and church grounds. The suspects collectively started lighting the fires at both the house and church. Before firefighters could respond, both buildings were engulfed in flames. There were no casualties as the owner of the house, Lei Mitchell, was the only person home and managed to escape in time. Luckily, no one was at the church.*

The five women who were the "suspects" in the report, all islanders who had been part of a new Wiccan cult, were arrested and charged with first-degree murder and arson. They were currently locked up in the holding cell at the police station on Eden until they could be extradited to their native countries of Australia, Europe, and the US.

The lone suspect on the south end of the island known as the Investor was never found, although there was a report he was believed to be an older Asian man wearing a black, hooded cape.

The Mitchells spent the rest of their fortune they hadn't already invested in restoring the island on the best criminal attorney in the US and his team of crackerjack lawyers. Finn and Lei's legal team fought their case and won, getting the couple off on brilliant oral arguments that convinced the jury they were not guilty because they were unaware of what the women had planned to do and thus were not complicit in the crime.

Even though he was found not guilty and there were no civil charges brought against him, Finn decided the right thing to do was to give one million dollars each to the families of Christine Walters and Marianne Birch for their losses, which wiped out the rest of his bank account.

Meanwhile, Finn's license to practice law was suspended in the interim while he awaited trial. He and Lei had had to go into hiding in Linda Mitchell's basement. Once the media found out their location, though, the former First Lady's home was under assault by the press, and she was a prisoner in her own home, along with her son and daughter-in-law. Fortunately, the house was big enough and well-stocked with everything they needed thanks to in-home deliveries by various stores, but they had to let the staff go for their own safety and well-being.

Still, the past year had taken its toll financially, mentally, and emotionally on all three of them.

Linda had blamed Lei for all of it of course, and the two were locked in a cold war with Finn stuck uncomfortably and awkwardly in the middle. He and his wife had slept in separate bedrooms for most of that year, except for a time or two when they turned to each other for comfort.

Finn had sunk into a deep depression, made worse by his wife's grief when her father died. She went to China for the funeral without him because they were afraid he would attract too much negative attention—and there was too much bad blood between him and her family now.

Zimo and his friend Mai-Yong were allowed to plead guilty to lesser misdemeanor charges of complicity for their roles in the Epitome venture. They were allowed, without repercussions, to actually help prove the mind-altering effects of the electronic program that fed into the arson and murder—in return for giving information to the FBI to help them locate Lu-Chin Xang—who still had not been found.

Zimo and Mai-Yong knew they were risking their lives in giving the FBI that information, so they were put in a witness protection program, which meant Zimo had to miss the funeral of his own father. He was angry that Finn had fared better, at least in his eyes.

But Finn felt just as much a captive as he was sure Zimo did. The only thing that saved him from complete despair and committing suicide was his songwriting. He remembered how his father would often find comfort in strumming his guitar and singing songs he'd written.

Ready to lose his mind with boredom while holed up in his mother's basement, Finn started to escape by writing songs down in a notebook. Songs that were light and dark, about lost love, doubts and fear, guilt and worry, man's sinful nature and the folly of life itself. He spewed his anger at God and then prayed to be forgiven in beautiful sonnets he figured would never see the light of day. But the writing was healing, cleansing, and kept him sane, giving him a reason to live.

The Mitchell family was finally given relief when a major news story about underground terrorists in Las Vegas broke, and they were no longer people of interest to the media.

Now, his mom just wanted to move out of her 'jail cell' and into a community of seniors where she would have socialization and freedom in her final years.

They were all ready for a new beginning.

As he crossed the threshold of the foyer of the Mitchell home, Finn thanked God for the gift of freedom and finally being able to come and go at will. The media, as they always did, found a new story to follow that was more exciting than camping out to cover the same old, forlorn saga of the ex-Supreme Court justice who had fallen into destitution, shame, and remorse. He was now a has-been, a regular Joe, just a "normal" guy, whatever that was. *Thank God.*

He heard voices excitedly chattering beyond in the kitchen.

Linda and Lei were talking! Now that was a pleasant surprise.

He walked in to present the two women in his life with the bouquets he'd bought and noticed they were both ... *happy.*

Lei looked radiant in a silk kimono she'd borrowed from Linda's closet. It was pink with white flowers daintily dotting the fabric. Her beautiful wavy black hair fell to her shoulders. She wore no makeup, but her skin was flawless. Finn also noticed her wife's big dark brown eyes were shining as if she held a secret.

He looked at his mother, who had the same gleam in her hazel eyes, and her smile sent crinkles fanning out from them.

They were both *smiling.* Finn felt as if he had woken up into some dream state or fantasy world. He literally could not remember the last time he'd seen his mother *and* his wife together in a happy state.

"Okay, what's going on?" Finn cautiously approached his wife then his mother, hugging them both and handing them the flowers.

"Oh, Finn. How thoughtful, thank you!" Linda Mitchell took the flowers, a fragrant spring mix of primroses, lilies of the valley, and hyacinths, and started opening cabinets in search of two vases.

He warily held out the other bouquet to Lei.

"Thank you, honey, these are gorgeous." She buried her nose in them, inhaling their scent, and then handed them to her mother-in-law to put in one of the Waterford glass vases she'd retrieved.

"Okay, what's up you two? Don't get me wrong, I love seeing you this way, but I know it's not the flowers."

"You might want to sit down for this." Lei motioned him to be seated at the big farmhouse kitchen table. The two women sat down in chairs on either side.

Finn held his breath.

"I'm pregnant!" Lei exclaimed, grinning.

Finn felt his head reel as if he'd suddenly lost his balance or been attacked with vertigo. Did he hear her correctly? "Pregnant? You're ... we're ...?"

"Yes, my love. We are going to have a baby!"

"Isn't it the best news ever?" Linda gushed. She clasped his hand in her right hand, then reached out her left to take Lei's. "Honey ... did you hear us? You're going to have a baby! I'm going to have a grandson!"

Finn felt like he was in shock, but then the last word finally sifted through the fog in his brain. "A grandson ... a son? A boy?"

"Yes, I found out I was pregnant and went in for an ultrasound while you were at work.

"I'm sorry, I was experiencing some mild cramping, and your mom thought I should go in and get checked out ... and they discovered I'm sixteen weeks along, and it's a boy!"

He wanted badly to ask, "so we're going to keep it?" But his wife's elation seemed to be so obvious he knew it would have been in bad form. *Trust God,* he told himself. *I'm going to have a baby, a son!* Finn stood and went around the table, kissing his beaming wife, then giving his mom a bear hug.

"Well, this calls for a celebration!" Finn went to the refrigerator and pulled out a full gallon of milk. "Mom, you do have Oreos on hand, right?"

By now the two women were standing and embracing each other, crying with joy.

"Of course, silly," Linda told her son.

"Thanks, Mom." He hugged her again and turned to his wife. "Lei, I am the happiest man alive right now. I love you, Wu Lei Mitchell, with all my heart and soul."

"I love you too, Finley Daniel Mitchell."

"What are we going to call our little guy?" Finn mused aloud.

"How about Phillip?" Lei suggested, which caused Linda to cry happy tears all over again.

Finn received another piece of good news a few weeks later when he opened the mail. There was a plain envelope from a company Finn had never heard of before called "Blue Sky LLC."

He almost threw it in the trash, but something made him rip it open out of curiosity.

Inside was a letter from Blue Sky, a division of Sony Music, offering him a check for fifty thousand dollars to purchase ten songs he'd written.

Finn stood incredulous at the kitchen table. *How did they get hold of my songs?*

Lei walked in just then, a tiny bump already started to grow under her T-shirt. It was warm for springtime in Maryland, so she wore her hair up in a ponytail and looked like an excited teenager as she saw the letter in his hand. "Is that what I think it is?"

"It's from Sony Records—they want to buy some of my songs." He eyed her skeptically. "You sent them my songs?"

She whooped with delight. "I knew you wouldn't do it, so I made copies and sent them for you. Finn, they're so good, they need to be produced into records. This could open up a whole new career as a songwriter for you, if you wanted. But it's up to you—I just thought I'd explore the possibility."

"Heck, yeah!" Finn circled his arms around his wife's waist and kissed her on the cheek. "This is a miracle. Thank you." He picked up the check and stared at it. "Wow, we're richer than we've been in a long time. What are we going to do with all of this money?"

Lei nabbed the check from out of his hands and playfully held it up. "I think it's going to go into Phillip's college fund. And Finn ..."

"Yes, my love?"

"We were already rich."

"Yes, we were."

THE END

ABOUT THE AUTHOR

Michele Chynoweth's novels bring stories in the Bible to life for today's readers with contemporary characters and plots so they can better understand and relate to God's messages of faith and hope. Michele's universally appealing inspirational novels are filled with suspense, drama, and romance, including *The Faithful One* based on the Book of Job, *The Peace Maker* based on the story of David and Abigail in the first Book of Samuel, *The Runaway Prophet* based on the Book of Jonah, and *The Jealous Son* based on the story of Cain and Abel.

Michele believes while the Old Testament stories in the Bible are compelling, they are often difficult to read and comprehend, so she hopes reimagining them in contemporary times with fiction that's fast paced and entertaining will help readers appreciate God's messages and hopefully bring people back to the Bible itself. Her stories will not only grip you, taking you for a wild ride and leaving you hanging on until the end, they will also inspire you to search your own heart for God's will in your life and to find a deeper faith in God's plan.

In addition to being an author, Michele is an inspirational speaker, book coach, editor, and college instructor of writing, publishing, and marketing fiction. A graduate of the University of Notre Dame, Michele and her husband have a blended family of five children and several grandchildren and live in Northeast Maryland. For more information, visit Michele's website, www.michelechynoweth.com

ALSO BY
MICHELE CHYNOWETH:

THE FAITHFUL ONE

THE PEACE MAKER

THE RUNAWAY PROPHET

THE JEALOUS SON

Made in the USA
Middletown, DE
26 July 2022

70045281R00230